T0366248

URBAN GNOME

BY TOM R. LUPARA

 **PUBLISHING®** **www.trafford.com**

North America & international
toll-free: 1 888 232 4444 (USA & Canada)
phone: 250 383 6864 ♦ fax: 812 355 4082

INTRODUCTION

Once upon a time, in a world that had become a strange and scary place, where hobbits no longer tilled the land, where elves didn't sing their songs nor cast their spells, and dragons had long been extinct, there lived a small and isolated community of gnomes in a remote forest stretched along an outlying mountain range.

Before I take you to this corner of the world to begin with my tale though, let me first describe this long forgotten and overlooked race of magical tiny beings in what detail I can hope to manage, for little is known about their kind today, and what is is often portrayed in an oddly meretricious fashion.

Gnomes are a mysterious little people of the forest that are one of the last few remaining relics from the time long ago when magic and wonder were still the prevailing forces in nature. They are seldom heard and almost never seen other than in the occasional flicker of movement glimpsed from the corner of a traveler's eye. Or, more often, their presence is felt in the slightly unnerving sensation that comes with being quietly watched.

Indeed, one should consider themself fortunate to receive even that from a gnome, for they are sly and stealthy and their numbers are dwindling and almost gone now. But on the chance that you were to ever meet a gnome while out in the deep forest, which is far more than unlikely, this is what you could expect to perceive of their physical qualities:

They are extremely short in stature, rarely growing over a
foot in height and getting smaller as the generations pass.
They are also delicately petite in build, although round
potbellies are common to be seen among them.

Their ears are the second most notable of their features,
which tend to be much too large for their heads and sharply
pointed at the tips with fleshy ridges ringing the insides.
They are exceptionally sensitive to noise and vibration as
most ears in the wild are, and capable of cocking back and
forth like a dog's or a deer's to better alert them of any
dangers in the forest, which are inherently common and fre-
quent when being bite-sized such as they are.

Their faces, both the males' and the females', are well
defined with large, intelligently bright eyes, long narrow
noses, and sharp chins. The males' beards grow slow and
sparsely, and are usually dark brown or a slightly lighter
color, as is most gnome hair.

Their hands are delicate and clever, with long slender
fingers that serve as excellent tools for their insatiable
curiosity, for they can be poked or wiggled with ease into
even the slightest crevice of wood or stone in search of
food or things unknown.

Their feet are normal in length compared to their small
bodies, but are so exceptionally wide and thick-soled with
leathery calluses that they must waddle slightly when they

walk lest they step on their own feet. They do serve a practical purpose though, as they can tread so lightly over even the most impressionable of surfaces that no one in history has ever claimed to have found a gnome's track, nor to have heard one fall.

Their clothes, which are the same now as they have always been, are simple browns and greens that blend in well with the forest and do not stand out in the least. The males wear robes that are knee length and tie snugly around their waists with a sash, and on their heads they wear tall pointed caps. These caps are the only thing that varies in style for the males once they get old enough to wear them, because some prefer no brim at all while others like them to be quite wide. The reason for this, of course, is their large ears that stick far up on either side of their head. With no brim there is nothing to get in their way, while a wide brim will simply have holes cut in it so their ears can poke up through.

The females wear no such caps, only modest dresses that fall to just below their knees. They are drab and simple and plain, but on special occasions the females have been known to become creative and decorate them with grass skirts, pretty weaves of pedals, or bright wild flowers braided into their hair.

Thick forests in large mountain ranges is where their kind most prefer to reside and can most often be found, but they have been known to also inhabit swamps, alongside remote lakes, and even rivers that don't have much traffic along them. Because of their cautious nature, gnomes do not feel comfortable in places that offer little or no vegetation to hide among. They do not appreciate in any way low cut grass, or roads, or trails, or any cleared area of any kind; they believe it to be quite unnatural for such places to even exist. Rumors and stories of barren deserts and salt flats appall them.

Living in lavish homes like the elves and hobbits once did with their chimneys and doorknobs, windows and roofs, walkways and gardens, had never attracted their kind, for gnomes have no want of such prominent dwellings. Indeed, their humble unobtrusiveness is one of the biggest reasons their race has continued to survive far past the time most others from long ago have perished. They are instead a quite earthly bunch that make their homes by burrowing into cleverly hidden nooks and crannies throughout the forest and then digging out a simple den to live in. Seldom do their burrows have more than one or two connecting rooms, if any.

As I have said earlier, gnomes are a magical folk that have long mastered and employed the use of spells and incantations into their daily lives. But this magic is neither outlandish nor astounding in its workings, and cannot make things suddenly appear, or fly away, or change into something that it wasn't to begin with. Their magic is instead

an elemental one, if it could even be called magic at all,
for it only manipulates natural energies and forces and di-
rects them in concentrated points to achieve various effects. It is common, mundane knowledge to their kind, as are
appliances and engines to ours, but if exchanged they would
each appear sorceris to the other.

They are known to have a habit of greatly embellishing
anything that comes from their minds and out across their
tongues, for they enjoy telling a good tale or length of
gossip almost as much as they enjoy hearing it. For that
reason, and also because they have never been fond of keeping written records of any kind, attaining a clear history
of their background, such as that of their origins and an-
cestry, is nearly impossible. Simply too many dramatic battles and amazing miracles have been attached to the stories
of long ago over the generations to discern any actual facts
of their lineage. It has been whispered though, that gnomes
are a vague, distantly removed relative of the elves. But
this has never been agreed upon by either side, for the two
have never fancied the notion of being kin.

They are notoriously greedy, and are known to be fond of
food and treasure, in much the same way we are; the food
consisting mostly of nuts and berries, tasty roots and certain types of mushrooms. Plump insects are also eaten with
delight and little discrimination when they can be caught.
Their valuables are usually simple items, but nonetheless

frantically hoarded and jealously protected. Pretty stones, sparkling crystals, odd shaped sticks, and colorful bird feathers are the kinds of treasures you might expect to find hidden and hoarded away in a gnome's burrow, but usually nothing that holds any kind of real value. At least not to our kind anyway.

Since the time of our early explorations, mapping, and conquering of new lands, gnomes have gradually and steadily   in fear to the furthest, most desolate corners of the world to avoid us; for they have watched from the cover of foliage and shadows the many wars and battles we have waged against one another in the quest for land. Their once large colonies that had found safety against the trolls and goblins of the past were forced to break apart and branch off into smaller, less conspicuous groups while our population expanded across the frontiers and grew in size, as did their terror for us. You see, gnomes are a peaceful and gentle sort that avoid conflict at all costs, and will only resort to violence in self-defense or in protection of a loved one. They understand courage, but not gratuitous rage nor the impulse to hurt others without cause, which is sadly all they have ever seen from us in the past. Therefor, they believe our kind to be bloodthirsty monsters that are to be feared more than even the worst of their forest tormentors.

Perhaps it's the mystery of never having the privilege to see one of these delightfully peculiar little people of the forest that makes them so fascinating to our kind, or maybe it's their strange qualities and simple magic they possess that we have foolishly lost long ago. Either way, they are indeed a wonderful bunch to know, but there's one in particular that I would like for you to become acquainted with.

His name is Ono, and he has quite a story to tell, one that needs not the aid of gnomish exaggeration. So if you will follow me down this path of written words, I would be delighted to take you to meet him. He certainly is an interesting fellow.

PART ONE

THE LITTLE WORLD

CHAPTER ONE

The Trinity Mountains are located in the north-western re-
gion of California, and are a beautiful sight to behold in
the spring time. The mountains themselves are tall and steep
and green and too numerous to be counted, filled with soaring pines and oaks that grow so densely that sometimes it is
nearly impossible to see more than fifty yards in any direction due to the seemingly endless throng of trees that crowd
one another.

The forest floor is just as thick, and on practically every square foot of it there is some kind of plant life
squeezing up from the ground to bloom as they greet the new
warming sun of spring time. Ferns are common here, growing
big, lush green leaves that sprout up from the forest floor
and alongside the many springs that trickle down the mountains and flow between the moss covered rocks. Wild flowers,
of many shapes and colors, grow wherever it is convenient,
making small patches of red, blue, pink, yellow and orange
that sway and dance in the gentle mountain breeze as if to
allude the plump bumblebees that tirelessly pursue them.

The forest creatures, both large and small, are outgoing
and rambunctious because they rarely encounter a human being, and are not overly paranoid or suspicious like animals
living closer to civilization are. A pair of squirrels leap
and bound through the branches high up in the trees above
with their fluffy tails in tow, while the birds chirp and
sing and occasionally squawk at them for running through

their nests; a herd of deer lays on the mountain side lazily chewing grass and nuzzling one another, while the restless chipmunks scamper around, bothering over acorns and pine nuts as they work to restock their supply of food; a black bear lumbering between the trees stops to shake its head and a large cloud of dust, accumulated from its long hibernation, is cast off into the air before it moves on in search of a long-awaited meal; a banded king snake slips out from beneath a rock and tests the air with its forked tongue, then slithers off into the underbrush.

After a long and drizzly winter, the forest is once again waking up and stirring about.

It is here, in this secluded part of the world, where our friend Ono resides. He lives in a burrow near the bottom of a mountain side, cleverly hidden between two green bushes at the foot of an old gnarled pine tree. If you were to crouch down and spread those bushes apart and lift up the small slab of bark covering its entrance, you would find a hole between two thick roots that disappears down into the earth.

Down this tunnel we go, twisting and turning through the darkness until the walls of the tunnel fall away and we come out into a cozy little den. It's dark and quiet until a small, high-pitched voice chants in the shadows, "She'ora, therry simosealep." And with that, a dazzling thread of orange light flows through the air and touches to the wick of a candle resting on an exposed root in the wall not far away. Magically ignited, the candle's flame grows and the burrow is illuminated with its warm yellow glow, and in it we first meet Ono getting ready for the day.

He has just awaken. With a big yawn and a stretch of his arms, Ono blows on the end of his wand, which is little more than a reed tip, and the orange light sputters off like glitter and disappears. Then he folds back a blanket made of woven leaves and gets out of a bed fashioned from a nest of moss clumps and grass.

Ono, even by gnome standards, is short for a male. Barely over eight inches tall with a modest potbelly, he could be considered average in both height and weight for a female. But what he lacks in stature he certainly makes up for in good character, for he is a rather joyful and altogether agreeable sort that all the other gnomes in the small community had grown to appreciate very much indeed.

His ears are large, like all gnomes are, but his have a tendency to flop over and sag, giving his already small frame a meek, droopy appearance. He is fairly young in age, considered by others to be just out of his mid-years, and the brown hairs of his beard are few and sparse.

Dressing in a light brown robe, Ono tied his sash, tucked his wand in at his waist, and carefully fixed his cap on his head. Males are usually finicky when concerning their caps, and Ono was certainly no exception. Being the only article of clothing that made him appear taller than what he really was, he kept it meticulously creased so it stood up straight

and tall. It is also light brown, with no brim to speak of.

Once he was done positioning his cap just so, Ono picked

up his gathering pouch off the floor beside his bed, which

resembled a large burlap purse, and slid the strap on his

shoulder. The floor of his burrow was cluttered and scatter-

ed with various odd little treasures that he had acquired o-

ver the years, and after blowing out the candle he had to

carefully tiptoe around his things to make his way out.

Lifting up the slab of bark and popping his head up from

his burrow like a prairie dog, Ono peered cautiously into

the surrounding forest with a pair of large gray eyes that

missed not a thing. His floppy ears perked up and swiveled

from side to side like tiny pointed satellites listening for

any threatening or unusual noises.

Detecting no danger, he hopped out of the hole, closed the

bark behind him, and pushed through the two bushes and began

waddling down the mountain side. He is going off to gather

in the forest today, just like he does nearly every day.

He will not venture far though, at least by our standards.

Like most forest creatures, Ono's world is limited to a

small range of land consisting of three mountains and their

surrounding perimeters; Boulder Mountain, which he lives on;

Mud Hill, to the north; and Pine Ridge, to the south. Any

land beyond makes him uncomfortable, as it does with nearly

all the gnomes, and he will turn back as soon as the forest

floor begins to slope upward towards an unknown mountain.

No sound is made as he navigates the many obstacles on the forest floor but his whistling. It is a cheery, delightful sound that carries along nicely in its high, wavering tune. The melody doesn't even break when he climbs over fallen logs or rustles through the underbrush as he neared the creek that flowed alongside the three mountains.

The early morning chill was giving way to the gentle spring warmth, and the occasional breeze brought with it the scent of pine and earth and the sweet potpourri of plants in bloom. In the canopy above, a pair of small brown birds fluttered around and fussed over one another.

Pushing through a wall of ferns, Ono climbed up a moss covered rock and arrived at the creek. It was small, approximately ten inches deep at its middle and two feet across, but to a body as small as Ono's it certainly seemed like a fair sized river. The water was crystal clear, babbling to itself as if flowed over the rocky bottom. A small trout darted off like a flash of silver when Ono got on his hands and knees and lowered his face down to drink from the cold water.

Slurping up his fill, he smacked his lips, stood up, and let out a surprisingly loud belch before hopping down off the rock and moving off in the direction of Pine Ridge.

Like I mentioned before, gnomes are a curious bunch, sometimes to a fault, and it wasn't long at all before Ono found something that piqued his interest as he was waddling through the underbrush. It was a small, perfectly round hole bored through the side of a rotting overgrown log on the ground, and something about it seemed almost mysterious and alluring to Ono, who never failed to be intrigued by little nooks and crannies.

"Hmm.." he wondered and frowned at it. After a moment of pondering on what it could be he shuffled forward and bent down to squint inside. But the depths of the hole, and whatever was at its bottom, was too dark to be glimpsed. Frustrated, Ono huffed and pursed his lips with a curious glare, even more intent on finding out what was in there.

The hole was just wide enough for his arm to fit in, so he eagerly wiggled his fingers and begun to slide his hand into it with his tongue clamped between his teeth in concentration. But just as his fingertips were sliding in the shadows of the mysterious little hole, a familiar voice cried out from behind him. Startled, Ono pulled out his hand and spun around.

"I would not do that! Not now, not ever!" Ezquit called out as he limped down the mountain side with the assistance of a walking stick.

"Oh, hello there!" Ono smiled, then lifted his would-be probe in a wave.

Ezquit was the oldest gnome within the small community, and was well respected for his knowledge of spells and his

eloquent tales of old. He had been slight when he was younger, but with his age had come an ample belly and a wrinkled
face. His beard was completely gray and hung neatly combed
down to his waist, and was the envy of every young male who
had ever laid their eyes upon it. His eyebrows were bushy
and beetled, and wiggled beneath the large brim of his cap
when he spoke as if to accentuate his words. His robe was a
dark green that matched his mate's dress, Nez, who waddled
along beside him.

"Ono! How lovely to see you dear! And just in time as
well!" she said as they waddled past a bush and arrived at
the log.

Nez, even at her old age, was still a beautiful gnome. Her
kind gentle face had wrinkles, but they were not deep or
numerous like her mate's, and they gave her an air of dis-
tinction that was nicely complimented by the single streak
of gray that ran down her long dark hair.

Ono was happy to see them both, but was slightly annoyed
that the hole had already been discovered by someone else
before him.

Ezquit pointed at the log with a leathery, crooked finger
and regarded the hole in its side with a look of contempt.
"A wasp's nest," he said, his scraggly eyebrows wiggling
vigorously. "And they must have just moved in as well, because I made the same mistake you did, having never seen
that odd hole before. Except I reached all the way to the

bottom and stirred up quite a mess of angry wasps. Good thing I had my walking stick handy, because I used it as a club to strike them down as they buzzed around me in an infuriated swarm! Saved my life again it did," Ezquit said and tapped the end of his walking stick to the ground with a proud smile beneath his beard.

Standing beside him, Nez rolled her eyes dramatically for Ono to see, then slyly wiggled two slender fingers on her hand like a pair of legs running. Ono smiled at her and listened to Ezquit as he continued talking.

"Anyway, there is a nice patch of mushrooms near the top of Pine Ridge growing in a gully just left of the big rock, and we found a rather full bush of blueberries in the meadow early this morning, just a short distance beyond the mossy log there, in case you're interested," Ezquit said, then leaned forward to whisper discretely, "But don't tell anyone else, let them find out on their own!" he said, then straightened back up and looked around the forest suspiciously, as if for eavesdroppers.

It is not often that gnomes reveal their good gathering spots to one another, at least to anyone that falls short of family anyway. Such is their greed that especially profitable areas, such as places with good berry bushes or rotten stumps filled with plump grubs, are often times gossiped about as being prowled by vicious animals in an attempt to keep others away from it.

Ono thanked him for the information and said he would go there directly. Then Nez, who is normally quiet compared to her boisterous mate, cocked an eyebrow at him and smiled.

"That reminds me Ono. I've heard that blueberries are Bej's favorite. I'm sure she would enjoy it very much if you invited her over and shared them with her some time," she said with a knowing wink.

Ono blushed and dropped his gaze to his stubby little toes that scrunched in the dirt. "Oh... well, yes, I suppose," he he mumbled and scratched behind his ear as he tried to hold back an embarrassed smile.

Ono was in love with Bej, and Bej was in love with Ono. They flirted when they happened to run into one another while out gathering, which by no mistake of either one of them happened much too frequently to be by sheer coincidence alone. Each thought they were being discreet in their court-ing, as was proper, but it was blaringly obvious to every other gnome in the forest, and the two were currently the hot topic for gossip and giggles.

"Bah! Don't let her embarrass you my friend! Why, in my younger days I too was hounded by hoards of relentless beauties. Being a handsome devil is nothing at all to be ashamed of, I should certainly know," Ezquit said and stroked his beard.

Nez snorted and rolled her eyes much less discretely this time, then turned back to Ono. "Dear, we must be on our way now, for I have much to gather for supper tonight, and he many ears to fill with his nonsense, I'm sure, so you do be careful today," she said and gave him a quick hug. "And don't forget the blueberries! Trush me, she would love them! Take my word for it," she whispered in his ear, then took Ezquit's hand and began leading him away after he tipped his cap farewell.

"Thank you! And good-day!" Ono called to them and waved as he watched them waddle through the underbrush. Once they were gone from view he thoughtfully put a hand on his chin and tugged at his starting of a beard.

Hugh... blueberries, I will have to remember that, he thought to himself and smiled his big crooked smile.

CHAPTER TWO

Ono left from the log and waddled through the underbrush
with the tip of his cap occasionally poking up through the
green tangles as he made his way up the rather steep slope
of Pine Ridge. After some time he arrived at the big rock,
which was a large jagged boulder that appeared to be crumbling with a scrawny sapling growing awkwardly out from a
crack in its side.

Per Ezquit's directions, Ono turned left at it and hiked
across the mountain side until he came to the small gully.
It would be more of a ditch to one of our kind seeing it,
but to him it looked like it was cut deep in the hillside
and filled with big ferns and rocks and frilly shrubs whose
tops were level to the ground around it.

Carefully, Ono sat down on his rump at the edge of the
gully and slid down, disappearing through the ferns and coming to a stop at the bottom. There he stood up, brushed himself off, and saw the mushrooms that could not be seen from
above growing up through the moss and around the stalks of
the ferns. They were pale and plump with green spots on
their broad caps, Ono's favorite for making mushworm stew,
which was a tasty concoction of earthworms and mushrooms
that he enjoyed slurping down after a long day of gathering.

Ono rubbed his hands together happily, then slid his pouch
off his shoulder and began picking and whistling. It took
much longer than you might imagine to fill the little pouch,

for while he worked he frequently stopped to test each mushroom by taking a nibble out of them, sometimes several, before deciding on whether or not to keep them. The older the
mushroom the more flimsy and soft they tend to be, while
the younger firmer and dense, and he wanted only the ones
that were pleasantly in between.

After he had picked all that he could, Ono heaved the
bulging pouch to his shoulder, climbed out of the gully with
much effort, and began waddling down the mountain in the direction he had come to unload the mushrooms back at his burrow. If what Nez had said was true, then he certainly wanted
as much room in his pouch as he could get for all the blueberries he could manage to carry back with him.

But as so often happens with gnomes, Ono became distracted
on his way back. Nearing the bottom of the mountain he
stopped to wipe the beads of sweat from his face and to lean
against an old oak to rest for a moment. The morning was beginning to warm into the afternoon, and the bright sun was
blazing in the blue, cloudless sky above.

Ono smiled and took a deep breath, then set his pouch down
on the ground and went behind the tree to relieve himself of
the creek water he had drank earlier. "Aahhh.." he sighed
and tilted his head back in relief.

When he did so, he noticed a large heehive hanging in the
limbs high up in the tree above, looking like a big brown
drop about to fall away. Intrigued, Ono squinted at it and

perked up his ears while he stood there.

Hearing the steady hum of busy bees, Ono quickly finished
with his business, smoothed out his robe, and began searching for materials to build a bucket with. He found a green
twig on the ground not far away, and bent it into a circle
and tied the ends together with a pine needle, making a
loop. Then he pulled a big round leaf from a shrub nearby
and pushed the middle of it through the loop so it made a
deep bowl. Finally he tucked the edges of the leaf under itself so it stayed in place, and the bucket, although flimsy,
was completed in no time at all.

Using his sash he tied the crude bucket to his waist, and
after a few moments of trepidation and stretching his legs
he began climbing determinedly up the side of the oak, using
the cracks in the bark as handholds on his way up.

It is not common or even usual that gnomes will climb
trees, but for a chance at a rare and sweet treat such as
honey they are willing to do much worse to get it.

Ono continued to climb until he came to the base of the
limb that was just beneath the hive. Slowly so as not to
bring attention to himself, he stepped out on the branch and
began inching down its length, holding out his arms for balance and hoping dearly that a strong wind wouldn't come and
blow him off.

Midway down the branch a dark swirling cloud of honey bees
buzzed around the hive as they came and went from the open-

ing at the bottom to drop off their loads of pollen and leave to get some more.

When he was close enough, Ono ever so carefully reached to his sash and gently pulled out his wand. Then he pointed its tip at the hive, closed his eyes and began to chant, "Nac'i reven, givoref fle'smy," over and over as he drew a circle in the air with his wand as if to outline the hive's perimeter.

At the end of the wand the air began to flow and dance towards the hive like a snaking heat wave from a hot surface, and as it stretched further it expanded until the whole colony of bees were engulfed in its shimmering, transparent cloud.

Ono's chanting grew quieter with each recital and the circles he drew in the air became smaller with every pass, until finally both trailed off. Lowering his wand and opening his eyes, Ono was quite pleased to see that the entire hive was still. Bees that had only moments before been buzzing around through the air were now clinging to the branches and leaves, having fallen fast asleep. Bees that hadn't found a place to land before the spell ended had simply seized up and dropped from the air, spinning lazily down through the branches to the forest floor far below.

This was only a temporary spell though, and Ono knew that he had to work quickly. Tucking his wand back in his sash, he begun walking down the length of the tree limb as quickly

as he dared, kicking sleeping bees out of his way and off
the branch as he did so. Positioning himself beneath the
hive's opening at the bottom, he stretched his arm up and in
and began feeling around inside.

"Aha! Jackpot!" Ono cried happily when his fingers touched
the sticky honeycomb within. He began scooping large chunks
of it away and plopping them down in the bucket on his
waist. It was quickly filled, so he began slurping up handful after handful of the sweet honey as if it were water and
he was horribly parched. This is my last! Just this one
more, then I must go! But it is so good! he thought many
times while he licked the gooey sweetness from his greedy
fingers. But it never was the last, and he soon lost all
track of time.

In the branches around him, the lethargic bees slowly begun to stir as the spell wore off. Their antennas wobbled
quizzically, their pincers opened and closed, and they began
to shift readily on their legs. It wasn't until one tried
its wings that Ono suddenly realized what a grave mistake he
had made.

Bzzz.

Ono flinched and spun around to see the surrounding
branches rippling with awakening bees. His eyes were as
round as saucers, and stuck in his beard were guilty globs
of golden honey.

Another bee, this one just a few feet down the branch from

him, lifted off an inch into the air before setting unsteadily back down again.

Bzzzzz.

They were just groggy enough to not be able to fly, but
that wasn't going to last much longer. Terrified of being
stung to death by the soon to be angry mob of bees, Ono
slowly backed away from the hive with his sticky hands held
high. Then he bumped against the tree, and he spun around
and scaled back down as fast as he could.

By the time he reached the safety of the ground the bees
were once again humming like usual, and Ono was more than
relieved to still be alive and without a single stinger
stuck into his back side. Picking up his pouch and dipping a
finger down in the bucket of honey, he smiled triumphantly
to himself and began waddling back down the mountain, whistling merrily between licks and smacks.

Twenty feet up in the branches of the oak, the angry honey
bees were swarming around their damaged hive and eagerly
looking for something to sting.

CHAPTER THREE

Ono continued walking down the mountain, whistling like a sparrow on his way back to his burrow. He was certainly having an extraordinarily good day today, what with gathering the mushrooms and honey like he had, so he couldn't believe his luck when he waddled around a rock just in time to discover a big black beetle scampering beneath a dried leaf on the forest floor. If he had been just a moment later in coming he would have missed the rather appetizing meal altogether.

"Ha ha! Lunch it is then," Ono laughed and rubbed his hands together. He had only eaten bits of mushrooms and honey so far in the day, so a late snack would suit him just fine.

Setting his pouch and bucket down beside the rock, Ono silently crept forward, bent down, and jerked the leave away like a magician with a table cloth. The beetle, quite startled at being found out, clicked in surprise and tried to scamper off. But his hands darted out and snatched the big bug up off the ground before it could get far.

"Got you!" Ono said and smacked his lips. The beetle's legs kicked in the air and its pincers searched in vain for its tormentor as it clicked its protest.

Carrying the beetle back to the rock, Ono sat down beside his things to enjoy his lunch. He wiggled his toes happily, then leaned over and dunked the beetle's head into the honey bucket. Then he pulled it back out, held it before his face like we would a hamburger, and decapitated the insect with a loud crunch!

The beetle's legs went rigid at its sides, twitched, and then slowly went limp.

Content with the world, Ono leaned back into the soft moss on the rock, simultaneously chewing and smiling while he looked out at the forest. The sun was passing into the west, though still high and bright in the sky, and it sent golden columns of sunlight shining down through the tree branches above like dazzling spotlights. A young deer trotted through the brush near the bottom of the mountain, making nary a noise as it went, then was gone as quickly at it had ap-peared.

Ono's thoughts wandered to many gnomish things while he sat there chewing on the crunchy beetle shells. He thought of tiny places and tunnels, food and recipes and spells, cubbyholes and shiny things, and also what exactly it was that left the occasional white streak spreading through the sky above, for that was a thing that he often puzzled over. But those thoughts and all the others were like planets a-round the sun, steadily coming and going while the biggest, brightest one of all stayed stubbornly in the middle and eclipsed all the others.

It was Bej, of course, that filled his mind, and after he swallowed the last bite he licked his fingers clean, folded his hands behind his head and crossed his feet. His belly

was round and bulging with beetle meat, and he sighed and

closed his eyes for a moment to picture her face, which hav-

ing been memorized long ago, materialized instantly and

clearly.

Bej's features were delicate and feminine, so much so that

she appeared almost fragile. Her large eyes were a bright

green that shined like polished jade, and her long hair fell

down the sides of her beautiful face like dark waves of

brown parted by sharply pointed ears. A single dimple pitted

each cheek when she smiled, revealing neat rows of teeth

that glimmered like pearls.

Ono's stomach tingled as he thought of her, and his crook-

ed smile spread over his face. I must say, it certainly has

been a wonderful day so far, he thought to himself and snug-

gled against the moss.

But just as he was getting comfortable enough for a nap,

Ono heard something off in the forest that greatly alarmed

him and made Bej's smiling face disappear from his mind like

a puff of smoke.

Fwump.

Surprised, Ono's eyes snapped open and he sprang up to

his feet with his hand already resting on the wand in his

sash. His ears perked up and swiveled from side to side, the

tips twitching nervously. He squinted between the trees, but

could see nothing. Then he heard the sound again, much closer this time and seeming to come from his left.

Fwump.

Ono turned around, looking up through the branches and to the sky, but saw nothing but thick green forest all around him. "Ohhh!" he worried and wrung his hands together, not knowing in what direction to run or even from where it was coming.

Fwump!

Then suddenly he knew. The hairs on the back of his neck stood up on end and tingled as the presence behind him grew, and he spun around just in time to see the owl's hooked talons coming straight at his face.

CHAPTER FOUR

Ono had just enough time to gasp and dive to the ground when the gray owl swept down through the air and ripped a chunk of moss away from the side of the rock where his head had been just a moment before. He felt the whoosh of air pass over him as the owl sailed by only inches above. Terrified, he got back to his feet and began running down the mountain so quickly that the tip of his cap flapped in the wind behind him.

"Eek!" the owl cried as it banked in the air and prepared for another pass. Its furious yellow eyes locked onto the fleeing gnome like a pair of crosshairs as it beat its wings and began to gain on its intended victim.

Ono hurtled over rocks and fallen pine cones as he ran, desperately searching for a crevice or rotted stump to hide in. But the forest floor provided only ferns and small shrubs, certainly not enough cover to save him from the owl.

"Eh! Ehhhh!" he shrilled as he ran, seeing the owl's shadow sliding across the ground from behind him as he zigzagged between the trees in an attempt to outmaneuver the bird.

In the air not far behind him, the owl banked from side to side through the trees, losing a few feathers when its wings scraped against the bark but gaining nonetheless. As it neared, its pupils shrank down to tiny dark dots as it closed in on him.

Rounding a corner and nearly losing his balance, Ono saw a

big green bush further down the mountain side and decided it
would have to work. He sprinted as fast as his feet would
carry him across the open ground, praying that the owl
wouldn't catch up to him. He leaped over a small rock and
was almost to the protection of the tangle of branches when
he felt the crushing force of the owl's talons close over
his head and squeeze mercilessly.

"No! Please, please no! Noo!" he cried out as the ground
fell away from his feet. "Eek! Eek!" the owl screeched at
him in victory and began to fly up into the branches above
with its prize.

Ono struggled to wrench the talons away with one hand and
was fumbling for his wand with the other as he was hauled
higher into the air. Horrible images of stringy entrails
being tugged from his belly like worms by a nest full of
pecking baby owls flashed through his mind, and the grim and
gruesome reality of it happening only made him scream and
fight and thrash about all the harder.

But as quickly as the terror had been set upon him, it was
replaced by confusion when he suddenly felt weightless and
the talons weren't squeezing his head any longer. Wind was
hissing by his ears, and the tree tops all around him seemed
to be stretching up towards the sky. Panicked, Ono looked
down between his kicking legs and saw the forest floor rushing up at him. "Ugh!" he grunted when he hit the ground with
a thud, sending up a cloud of dust that puffed up around

him.

The owl had dropped him, and still clenched in its talons was his cap that had slipped off, saving him for the moment from whatever horrible fate the owl had sure planned. "Eek! Eek!" it cried out and dropped the cap, then banked in the air to retrieve its meal.

On the ground, Ono groaned and coughed up a mouthful of dirt before rolling over and getting to his hands and knees. His ears were ringing like bells and he felt dizzy, but he was still aware of the owl swooping back down towards him. As quickly as he could manage, Ono crawled across the ground and into the safety of the bush just as the owl landed behind him and snapped its beak at his feet.

"Eek! Eek!" the owl screeched as it beat its wings against the bush and looked in at Ono with its angry yellow eyes blazing.

Ono, quite angry himself, backed up further into the tangle of branches and pulled out his wand from his sash, intent on showing the owl a thing or two about magic. But as he pointed the wand at the owl, he noticed that it had been snapped in half from his fall, the tip hanging uselessly from the end.

"Snakes! Oh, snakes to it!" he cursed and threw the broken pieces at the bird.

And so for the next hour and sometime past that, Ono was confined to the safety of the bush because the owl, knowing

that he was cornered, waited patiently for him to try and
escape. Under siege and not willing to give in, Ono could
only cross his arms and glare up at the hateful bird through
the long period of silence with his talon-messed hair shooting out in all directions.

On several occasions the owl had ruffled up its feathers
and squawked impatiently, then flown off. But Ono was wise
to the old trick and watched as the owl had doubled back and
peered over the branches from a tree further away around the
mountain.

When the owl finally did leave to find less stubborn prey,
Ono didn't move for quite some time. But after watching the
forest around him carefully and not seeing the gray of the
owl nor the yellow of its eyes, he scooted carefully from
the bush, for he was sore from the fall and stiff from sitting, and ventured back out into the forest.

After dusting himself off and walking back up the mountain side he found his cap dangling from a low sapling
branch. Reaching up, he pulled it off and saw the large ragged holes the owl's talons had punched through it. He grumbled to himself, then slid it back on his head where it sat
bent and awkward.

Limping slowly back up to the mossy rock where he had
left his things, Ono was quite relieved to see that his
bucket of honey, shining like a pot of gold in the sun's
rays, wasn't lost or damaged. Wincing, he bent over and

picked up his pouch of mushrooms and tied the bucket back to his hip before limping off.

He was still angry and sore and disheveled from the attack, but as he made his way down through the woods the thought of Bej's sweet smile still managed to give him one of his own.

CHAPTER FIVE

Ono was left parched from the owl's attack and was also
covered in dust from his fall, so he stopped along the creek
on the way back to his burrow to wash up and get a drink of
water. He was still dreadfully sore, as if the ends of all
his bones were feuding with one another, but the walk down
the mountain had eased him and his limp had waned.

Pushing through the ferns and coming to a bend in the
stream, Ono carefully sat his things among the rocks and
bent down. Cupping his hands, he splashed the cold water on
his face and arms and scrubbed the dirt away. Then he drank
several generous handfuls, feeling better again about the
day with each swallow he took. While drinking, he caught his
blurry reflection on the stream's surface, so he lowered his
hands away to smile at himself with a mouthful of square,
blocky teeth. Feeling a bit foolish, he then crossed his
eyes and wiggled the tips of his ears back and forth. Looking absurd, Ono snickered at his reflection, then made a
serious face and raised up a single eyebrow into a rather
sly-looking expression.

"Hello Bej, I've got blueberries and honey if you're interested in having supper with me," he asked in a husky
voice the question he had been rehearsing for so long.

He managed to keep a straight face for only a moment longer before shaking his head and laughing again at his ridiculous self. Clearing his throat, Ono tried another face, this

time with a suave smile.

"Why hello there Bej, would you care to join me for a pleasant supper of blueberries and honey on this fine evening?" he asked smoothly with a jump of his eyebrows.

Suddenly, and without any warning whatsoever, something splashed into the center of the creek not far away, sending droplets of water misting over him. Frightened, and already put on edge by the owl, Ono snapped up to his feet to see what had made such a splash. When the perpetrator came to the surface amid a mass of bubbles, Ono blushed like a red berry and stomped his feet angrily on the creek bank.

"Snakes! Sced, what are you doing here? you should give a warning before doing such foolish and frightening things!" he shouted, hoping dearly that he hadn't been overheard practicing his lines by the puckish youngster.

"We was here first Ono! So what is it you're doing here, hmm? Jabbering with yourself?" Sced asked in a shrill voice and playfully splashed a handful of water in his direction.

Annoyed and embarrassed, Ono hopped out of the way of the splash and glanced across the stream to see Kei standing on a rock laughing and pointing at him also.

Sced and Kei were twins that shared dark shaggy hair, and were horrendously unruly. They were little more than children, but both shared such a perpetual look of sinister mischief and craftiness on their sharp little faces that they unnerved many of the older, less capable gnomes. If they had

heard what Ono had said, then it would surely be known by
every ear in the forest before nightfall.

"No!" Ono shouted back at them, a little too defensively.
"I was... just ugh, clearing my throat, that's all. Yes,
I've had a beetle leg lodged in there all afternoon, and
it's been quite a bother," he explained, then made a few un-
convincing coughs and grunts into his fist.

Sced and Kei didn't seem to believe him with their suspicious glares and slight smirks, but didn't appear to care
either, so Ono was rather relieved when the two shrugged to
each other and went back about their playing. Thank goodness
they didn't hear that! I would have just as soon been eaten
alive by that retched owl, he thought with a sigh, then
hurriedly began gathering up his things to leave. While he
did, he watched the two youngsters from the corner of his
eye as they took turns to climb up on a rock, take hold of a
rope dangling down from a low branch, and then swing out o-
ver the water and splash into the creek with a variety of
spins, flips, and twirls.

"Did you see that? I just did a double!" Kei shouted and
laughed as he swam back to the stream bank.

"No you did not! This is a double, so you just watch and
learn how it's really done!" Sced called down, then proceeded to swing through the air with his scrawny limbs flailing
wildly and belly flop with a great splash.

"Bwaaaa! Ha ha ha! A double indeed!" Kei laughed and

pointed and clapped as his twin came up from the water sputtering and red-bellied.

Having just gathered up his things to leave, Ono stopped
to squint at the rope the two were using to swing into the
creek with. It was light brown with green bands at each end,
and was, for some add reason, vaguely familiar to him.
"Where did you two get that from?" he asked and pointed to
it as Sced climbed back out of the creek and stood up shaking the water from his ears.

The twins exchanged a queer look that almost seemed to
send a silent message between them before looking back at
him from across the stream. "We found it," they said, sounding like one voice.

Ono narrowed his eyes at them suspiciously, and they, simultaneously of course, smiled slyly back at him. After a
moment Ono decided he wanted nothing more to do with the
mischievous little youngsters, and pointed a warning finger
at them both before turning around and waddling off through
the ferns.

As soon as he left the two burst out with shrill laughter
and gave each other a high five.

Ono walked north along the creek, and as he did so the
racket of the two youngsters faded away and disappeared behind him. The afternoon was getting late, and the sun was
several hours away from touching the mountain tops in the
west. The day was still warm, but the shadows in the forest

were beginning to stretch and lean, and Ono knew he would
have to hurry back to his burrow to unload if he was to
gather any of the blueberries today.

Picking up his pace, he waddled along through the woods
and was making good time until he heard something crashing
through the underbrush ahead. Quickly, Ono ducked into a
hollow at the base of an old tree stump and vanished from
view like he had never even been there. Whatever was coming
was panting and heaving along, and as he hid in the shadows
he hoped that it was nothing vicious, for he had no wand or
even his dagger that he had left at home for protection.

The panting and crashing grew louder and closer, and Ono
watched nervously from his hiding spot the wall of weeds
where the strange noises were coming with his ears tall and
cocked forward. After a tense moment the weeds burst aside,
and a plump round creature came barreling through. Ono
flinched at what he saw, then scooted further back into the
shadows as old Brufit stopped to catch his breath.

Brufit was an especially fat, angry old gnome that was
generally avoided by others who wanted to enjoy their day.
His face was pockmarked and wrinkled, and his beard was long
and scraggly and disheveled. He had a bad reputation for
throwing stones at others who came too close to his burrow,
which was as unkempt as he, and Ono had suffered more than a
few lumps and bruises on account of his wickedly good aim.

Ono wanted no part of whatever it was he was up to, and

stayed completely still and silent.

After catching his breath in ragged wheezes, Brufit straightened back up and cupped his hands around his mouth. "Sced! Kei!" he yelled, "I have many rocks in my pockets, so you had better bring me back my sash this very instant! Or else!"

Crouched inside the dark hollow, Ono smiled when he remembered what it was the youngsters were using to swing into the creek with. He had always thought of the two as tiresome with all their antics, but he took a cruel delight in seeing old Brufit so flustered and hoped he wouldn't find them any time soon.

Brufit scanned the forest with a menacing gaze and his ears high alongside his cap, then grumbled and cursed under his breath before continuing on. He passed right by the hollow on his way down towards the creek, and Ono had to bite his tongue not to cry out with laughter at what he saw.

Without his sash, Brufit's robe was flapping loosely all around him as he hurried along, and although he tried his best to hide it, his massive dimpled backside was being exposed, and it jiggled and bounced as he ran off through the underbrush.

Ono waited a moment until he was gone, then squeezed back out of the hollow and continued waddling back to his burrow, snorting with laughter as he went.

CHAPTER SIX

Ono soon arrived back at his burrow at the base of the old pine tree and went inside to unload his things. It was pitch black inside, for gnomes would scoff at windows or leaving a candle burning longer than necessary, and he had to feel his way around in the darkness until he found the recessed shelf dug in the wall beside his bed. There his hand brushed over his father's old wand, which was a well-used shaft of dark, polished oak with grooves worn smooth at one end for grip, and he used it to light the candle.

Once the den was lit, Ono tossed the wand on his bed and went about unloading his things. He upended the pouch of mushrooms in the far corner and stacked them in a neat pile so they would dry for later use, then took the bucket of honey off his hip and sat it gently on the shelf like a prized possession.

Eager and ready to be on his way again, Ono picked up his empty pouch and slid its strap back on his shoulder. Then he grabbed his father's wand and stuffed it between his sash before turning around to blow out the candle. But before he exhaled, he was reminded by the wand's heft that he hadn't stopped by to see his father in quite some time. Letting out his breath in a sigh, Ono frowned at himself for being so thoughtless, then decided to bring his dad some of the honey to make up for it.

He hurried up the tunnel and outside, then came back a

moment later with a round green leaf held in his hands. He
flattened it out on the dirt floor, then grabbed the bucket
off the shelf and poured a generous amount of honey on its
center. Before the pool could spread over the sides of the
leaf, Ono quickly folded up its edges and twisted them together at the top to make a handle. Then he put the bucket
away, picked up his things, and blew out the candle.

He left from his burrow whistling happily and swinging the
package of honey at his side while he waddled up the mountain. Just on the other side was the meadow where the blueberries were supposed to be, and also where his father resided. It wasn't a long trip, which was well because the sun
would be setting within a few hours and he wanted to get
back home and mend the holes in his cap. He pushed through a
tangle of shrubs on his way, hopped over a fallen branch,
then came around a pile of rocks only to come to a sudden
halt. His floppy ears shot up and his heart began to thump
against his ribs as he gaped at what he saw in front of him.

Bej, who was only a short distance away, was bent over at
the waist picking wild flowers on the mountain side. She
hummed quietly to herself as she worked at pulling and
stacking the flowers like a bouquet in her arms, and her
bottom swayed from side to side with the soft, pleasant
tune.

Ono swallowed and opened his mouth to say something, but
no words came to mind, so he just stood there and watched

her pick flowers with big round eyes.

After a moment Bej seemed to sense a presence behind her, and she glanced back over her shoulder to see Ono standing there with his ears tall, his shoulders slumped, and his jaw hanging down nearly to his knees.

"Ono!" she laughed, setting down her flowers and turning around with her dimples deep. "What are you doing? And how long have you been spying?" she asked as she pranced down to greet him.

Ono seemed to suddenly wake up, and after blinking several times he shook his head and smiled. "What? Oh! Yes, well... I just arrived, and wasn't spying at all. Hello," he said, and then, not knowing what else to do, waved.

Bej was just as tall as him, wearing a bright green dress with her dark hair pulled back in a tail and tied with a flower stem. She regarded him with a playful look of suspicion for a moment, then giggled behind a delicate little hand when she noticed how disheveled Ono appeared today. His cheeks were covered in a bright red blush, his cap was bent and crooked, his robe dirty and wrinkled, and, like usual, spread across his face was a toothy lopsided grin.

"Ono," she said, "**what** happened to you today? You look a mess!"

Ono's smile faded when he remembered how he must look, and he somberly glanced down at his robe and dusted himself off with a few flicks of his hand. "Yes, I'm sorry, I sup-

pose I do look a little untidy," he said and sighed heavily.
"If it wasn't for that cursed owl..." he trailed off and
winced dramatically like an old injury had suddenly flared
up again.

Alarmed, Bej gasped and perked up her ears. "An owl?! What
do you mean an owl? You weren't attacked by one were you? Oh
dear!" she cried and covered her mouth.

Ono nodded grimly like he was recalling a rather painful
memory, then took a deep, brave breath. "Yes Bej, I was. It
came out of nowhere and just snatched me up and tried viciously to kill me," he said and took off his cap to show
her the ragged holes its talons had made.

Bej whined when she saw the rips in the fabric, then threw
her arms around him and wrapped him in a tight hug. "Ono!
I'm so glad you're okay! You poor thing! How ever did you
survive?" she asked and pawed comfortingly at the back of
his head.

Ono smiled slyly over her shoulder as she squeezed and
fussed over him, but as soon as she stepped back to look at
him the smile was replaced by a deep look of discomfort.

"Oh, well you see, once it had me in its death grip there
was only one thing I could possibly do," he said, then began
his own version of the story. In it, instead of squealing in
terror and luckily being dropped, he had anchored his feet
beneath a rock, pulled the owl from the air, and pummeled
the squawking bird into submission with his wand, which was
broken over its beak during the intense assault.

To demonstrate the harrowing battle, he acted out each scene with pummels and jabs of his fists, then curled his fingers and swiped them through the air like talons tearing at flesh. He bent down, then leapt into the air and kicked his legs out at his sides, swinging and twirling an invisible wand like a warrior's staff. He made a grabbing gesture and lifted his hands high in the air, then brought them down again like he was smashing something violently to the ground.

Bej soaked up the story, gasping and sighing with relief in all the right spots, and by the time Ono finished he nearly believed it himself. "And that's how it all happened, just like that," he finally said and proudly put his cap back on. Bej was amazed with his story, and he thought he could almost feel his cap getting increasingly tighter while she praised him for his bravery.

The conversation moved on, and the two chatted and flirted for quite a while. Bej told him all about her day, of the gathering and gossiping that had gone on, and Ono listened well to every bit of it. "-And after that Notzil decided that she wasn't going to stand for it any longer," she said, her eyes alight with gossip, "So she tossed all of Hupet's things out on the mountain side in heaps and piles and wouldn't let him in no matter how much he knocked and squawked. Can you believe it? He had to sleep under the ferns for two nights in a row! Isn't that just terrible?"

she giggled and glanced around.

Notzil and Hupet were a turbulent couple that lived further down the creek who never failed to ignite wagging tongues into action. They were always bickering and fussing with each other, and on any given night, if one were to stand near enough to their burrow with their hand cupped patiently around an ear, there would more than likely be heard a heated argument as the two shrilled back and forth at one another and stomped around inside their burrow. Every community has at least one couple just like them I suppose, who on a weekly basis provide their neighbors with something new to whisper and point about.

Ono laughed and shook his head, then announced, quite regretfully, that it was getting late and he had to be off to visit his father. He didn't tell her that he was going to pick blueberries as well because he wanted it to be a surprise when he asked her over for supper. That is, if he ever managed to work up the nerve to do such a thing.

Bej nodded her head sadly and slowly, for she knew that Ono and his father shared an unfortunate relationship with one another, but also because she had something else on her mind and didn't want him to leave quite yet. The two stood there for an awkward moment, each pondering what to say until she finally broke the silence.

"Soo.. I'll see you later then?" she asked hopefully and batted her green eyes at him.

Ono smiled and his face lit up. "Of course! Yes, I'll be around tomorrow, here and there, you know, like always," he fumbled along, feeling like a moron.

"Well okay then. But you just be careful to watch out for those owls Ono!" she warned playfully.

"Bah! I'll be fine. It's the owls that should be scared of me!" Ono bragged and cocked an eyebrow up at the branches a-bove.

Then the two hugged, for just a moment longer and tighter than was necessary, and said their good-nights for the evening. When they parted ways, Ono waddled up the mountain and Bej waddled down. As they went, each was silently cursing themselves for not saying what they had practiced earlier.

CHAPTER SEVEN

At the top of the mountain the forest floor gradually leveled, and it wasn't long before Ono could see the meadow past the tree trunks and over the tree tops that grew further down the opposite slope. It was a gorgeous sight, one that had never grown old for him to see, so he stopped walking for a moment and leaned against a rock to admire its beauty.

The meadow was, from a gnome's eye, massive. Approximately a half mile in length and almost as wide, it sat on a plateau surrounded by a barrier of steep, imposing mountains that seemed to isolate the meadow from the rest of the world, and its tall grass rippled and swayed like an ocean of green in the gusts of wind that swept down off their peaks.

The meadow was not perfectly flat or symmetrical like its name implies, but instead had many dips and knolls and bushes, and even the occasional brown oak tree rising up from the grass and stretching its branches. The edge of the meadow was well defined where it met against the tree line, but was never regular in its border, for it snaked along the bottoms of the mountains, disappearing around their bends and then reappearing further off in the distance.

At the moment, the sun was blazing red behind a smear of clouds in the west, and its dazzling rays were shooting over the mountain tops as it prepared to sink in the sky.

Ono could have watched the beautiful scene and basked in the sense of peace it instilled in him for hours on end, but he still had work to do and wanted to get done with it. So with one final elevated look at the meadow, he sighed and began waddling down the slope. His travel didn't take long because of the steep hillside and also because the meadow was considerably higher than the land surrounding the mountains bordering it, and he soon arrived at its edge.

The tall blades of grass rose up far over his head and made an almost solid wall where they met the forest. There, Ono took one last look behind him and up to the sky for danger, then pulled the shoots of grass apart and stepped in to the meadow. Once he was through, the grass closed behind like a green curtain, and he vanished from view.

From Ono's perspective, traveling through the meadow resembled a hike through an alien jungle. The tall grass made a thick canopy high above him that sent down thin shadows that danced and shifted all around him whenever a breeze hissed over the meadow, and the ground beneath his feet was damp and soft and laced with a network of pale, scraggly roots.

It was not uncomfortable in the least for Ono to be here, but rather the opposite; he was well concealed among the thick grass, and had not the worries of being followed by any larger animals without hearing their travel far in advance first. He would have dug his burrow here ages ago if not for the damp ground that accumulated water so easily.

The smaller creatures of the wilderness also seemed to appreciate this grass forest as much as he, and while Ono waddled silently through the shoots he saw many of them going about their last chores of the day without a care in the world. There was a quail pecking and scratching the ground for worms; a brown mouse nibbling on a morsel held between its little paws; a black salamander with white speckles lounging beneath the canopy of a large mushroom; a dark spider in the center of its intricate web stretched between the blades of grass wrapping a fly into a neat little package; and a fat green toad that almost resembled a lumpy mud puddle with eyes that followed him as he went by.

Ono soon came to the log Ezquit had described, which was a long, moss covered lump that was half consumed by the earth and dotted with leaning mushrooms whose caps were tall and steepled. He climbed over the log and continued on, humming to himself as he went. Not many yards beyond he came to the berry bush, which grew in a small clearing in the grass just large enough to accommodate its size. Along its branches and between its leaves thick clusters of blueberries burst through in such a quantity that the bush seemed to sag and droop beneath their weight.

Ono smiled and rubbed his hands together, knowing that if what Nez had told him about Bej liking blueberries was correct, then he would certainly have enough to entice her.

He sat the package of honey on the ground and quickly began his meticulous picking of only the plumpest, prettiest, bluest berries that the bush had to offer. Each one pulled off the branch was scrutinized for flaws, no matter how slight, and if they passed the inspection Ono fogged them with his breath and polished them to a shine on his robe before setting them gently in his pouch. This choosy picking did not take long though, for the bush was full and the berries almost always perfect, and Ono soon had more than two gnomes could possibly hope to eat in one sitting.

So with a grunt of effort he picked up his things and began traveling north through the field to visit his father, Proi, who resided at the base of the nearest oak tree that grew among the grass. It wasn't far away, and Ono arrived there just as the sun sank behind the mountains, turning the sky a deep purple. The brightest stars had begun to twinkle, and the evening cool was chilled by a light steady breeze that hissed over the meadow.

When he pushed through the grass and came to the base of the oak, he slid his pouch off his shoulder and sat down with his back against the tree. He took a deep breath of the fragrant air and was quiet for a spell.

Two birds, indiscernible in the dim light, flew overhead chirping back and forth as they headed to wherever it was they called home for the night before fading away into the shadows. The meadow slowly began to come to life with an or-

chestra of nighttime creatures and insects, and they played
all around him in a symphony of clicks, croaks, whistles,
and hums. After a time of listening to the relaxing sounds
with a slight smile on his face, Ono announced his arrival.

"Hello father, I'm here. I know it's late and all, but
I've been quite busy today," he said quietly, then began to
recall the day's events. "You wouldn't believe it, but an
owl almost got me this morning! I was lucky though, because
it dropped me before it had a chance to peck my belly out.
It put holes in my cap and broke my wand, but I'm fine
otherwise, besides being scared nearly to death that is. I'm
going to have to borrow your wand until I replace mine, so I
hope you don't mind."

He went on to tell his father the tale about old Brufit's
sash being stolen by Sced and Kei, and how the two youngsters were using it to swing into the creek with. He laughed
and giggled as he told it, but his story was met only with
silence.

Ono went on nonetheless, rambling on and on about his
feelings for Bej and the insecurities he felt when being a-
round her and the trepidation he had about asking her over
for supper. He spoke about it often, and it certainly was
not the first time Proi had listened to the exact same words
before.

You see, although easily frightened and often jumpy for
little reason, Ono was not unduly nervous in his dilemma,

for the first date between two courting gnomes carries with
it a special significance, one that we humans have callously
begun to regard as a forgettable anniversary. Since their
kind do not have weddings or rituals or ceremonies of any
kind, nor exchange vows or rings to signify their devotion,
they believe the first date to be a serious affair, one worthy of much consideration by the one being invited. The older gnome-folk call this date the first joining, for it sig-
nifies the ending of courtship and the beginning of a relationship. A gnome will have only one first joining it its
life, because they are completely and naturally monogamous
in their relationships with one another. Even in the most
unfortunate circumstance that one's companion should die before their time, the other will not seek to replace them.

By our standards, a first joining is akin to a marriage
proposal, for it binds but does not formalize the two as a
couple. Only once they have become mates does that happen,
but I will not attempt to describe that process in anymore
detail than I already have, for it is self-explanatory and a
matter of privacy.

Sometime later Ono began telling the story about the near
miss with the bees, and his eyes lit up. "Oh! I nearly forgot! I brought you a little honey," he said, leaning over
and picking up the leaf package. He sat it in his lap, then
scooped a small hole in the dirt beside him with his hands.
"Here you are father, I hope you enjoy it," he whispered,

then poured the honey in the ground.

Proi had been dead for many years now. Although Ono was hardly a child when his dad had died, he could still see his face in his memories, one so much like his own, smiling down at him and playfully ruffling his hair.

Proi was something of a legend among the gnomes that had had the privilege to know him, for he was unusually brave. Like Ono, he was rather short and bashful, but he had on several occasions saved the lives of others by risking his own. The most notable, and still talked about incident, was when a large black bear had been digging into a burrow filled with a family of frightened, screaming gnomes, and Proi had ran out in front of the beast and cast every spell he knew to drive it away. The bear had roared and stood up on its hind legs, furiously swiping its paws through the air. But the sparks and flames and bolts shooting from Proi's wand had finally driven it away, saving the entire family from its hungry jaws.

He was also a kind soul though, and Ono still remembered playing the many games of hide and seek with him in the grass of that very same meadow when he was but a wee-gnome. Ono had never known his mother as she had passed away soon after giving birth to him, so he had been abandoned, heart-broken, and confused when Proi had suddenly died from a disease that had withered him up like a dried berry and left him on his own.

Ever since then Ono had stopped by his grave at the foot
of the old oak at least once every week to talk with him,
and still took the childish comfort in knowing that somewhere, however far away, his father was looking down on him
and smiling the same crooked smile that he had passed on to
him.

After a while Ono smoothed the dirt back over the pool of
honey and packed it down again. Then he stood up, brushed
himself off and picked up his gathering pouch. "Well, I've
made up my mind dad, I'm going to ask her tomorrow. It's going to be a big day for me, so be sure to wish me luck! I
love you," he said, then turned around and waddled back
through the dark meadow towards his burrow in the mountains.

CHAPTER EIGHT

Ono giggled in his sleep and rolled over in bed. In his dreams he was running and leaping through the forest in pursuit of a giant cloud of colorful butterflies that flew along just above his head like teasing hors d'oeuvres. They twirled and fluttered away from his grasping fingers, their bright wings all flapping together in unison as their many colors, almost fluidly, shined and sparkled in the sunlight. The cloud of butterflies would drop and raise, turn and spin away from him in a rainbow of colors so close that Ono dreamed he could feel the gentle puffs of air coming off of their graceful wings.

He smacked his lips together and smiled as he chased after them hungrily, but was pulled back to reality when a long, low gurgle rumbled from his stomach.

"Oooohh.." Ono moaned as he awoke, realizing that he'd been dreaming. Grumbling, he folded back the leaf blanket and sat up in bed. He wiped the drool from his cheek and yawned, then felt around in the darkness for his father's wand. He found it, then lit the bedside candle and began to dress in its pale glow.

The previous night he had patched the holes the owl's talons had made in his cap, and the intricate stitching was so precise that there could be no doubt that it was done by the nimble hands of a gnome; for the damage was not only mended, but had disappeared altogether as if the incident had never even occurred. His robe was also cleaned and creased and hung neatly from a root in the wall.

After he was done dressing, Ono slid the wand between his sash, picked up his gathering pouch, and blew out the candle. Still groggy, he wiped a hand down his face and waddled up the tunnel yawning. Pushing the slab of bark aside, he squinted out into the forest and greeted the morning with puffy eyes.

The sun was just beginning to rise over the mountains like a halo, and the sky was filled with fluffy white clouds, although still far from being overcast. There was a morning chill, but the wind, occasional and gentle, did nothing to worsen it and the day promised to be a warm one later in the afternoon.

Ono's stomach gurgled emptily while he stood there, so he left from his burrow quite hungry and in search of breakfast. His pleasant dream of butterflies had whetted his appetite for something a little more lively than berries or nuts, and he passed up several bushes filled with them on his silent prowl of the mountain side. Occasionally, when he found one small enough to tip on its side, Ono would check under rocks for insects, but all he discovered was a dried spider's skin and a pink earthworm that slipped back in the ground before he could get a grip on the slimy thing. A little frustrated and a bit hungrier, Ono kept looking.

He checked under dead leaves on the forest floor, careful-

ly combed through a clump of weeds, and poked a pine needle
down into an anthill only to find that it had been abandoned
when the needle came out clean of any angry ants. It wasn't
until he came waddling around a small hummock that he spied
a big green grasshopper clinging to a thistle stalk, and he
quickly ducked down behind a fern. He waited a moment, then
stealthily crawled diagonally across the ground on his hands
and knees to take cover behind a rock closer to the thistle.
Once there, he leaned out from the rock just enough to peek
an eye around its side.

The grasshopper, unaware that it was being stalked, casually chewed the new leaves sprouting from the thistle and
occasionally twitched its antennas.

Ono's mouth watered just at the sight of the juicy insect,
and he was preparing to lunge out from behind the rock and
snatch it up when a dark shadow suddenly swept over him.
Startled, he ducked down and pulled his wand with his face
hidden in the crook of his arm. When he wasn't attacked
though, he looked up cautiously and saw a crow land beside
the thistle bush and pick the grasshopper off with a quick
snip of its beak.

Angry, he narrowed his eyes and shook his little fist at
the bird. "Hey you! Go away! That's mine, I saw it first!"
he stood up and protested.

The crow, almost seeming to consider his words, or perhaps
just wanting to tease him, held the kicking grasshopper be-

tween its beak for a moment before finally tossing back its head and swallowing it whole. Then it cocked its head sideways to look at him and arrogantly puffed out its feathered chest. "Kaw! Kaw!" it screeched at him before taking to the air and landing in the branches above.

Ono put his hands on his hips and glared up at the bird for a moment as it gloated from its perch. But when his empty stomach reminded him with a cramp that there were more important things to tend to, he left and began scouring the forest floor once again in search of breakfast.

Crows and gnomes are not friendly with one another in the least bit of way. Although crows do not eat gnomes or attack them in any way, they do have a sneaky tendency to follow them around to find out where their good gathering spots are located. Many unattended baskets and pouches have been lost in this fashion and never seen again.

Likewise, gnomes have been known to throw rocks at them and cast rude spells in their direction when they see them. But if asked, they would insist it is only in retaliation that they do such things, which is partly true because the crow is a rather sneaky, opportunistic bird that enjoys stealing things.

Still angry at losing such a tasty meal, Ono continued walking along the mountain side, grumbling to himself about how ugly crows' black feathers were and wishing horrid things on all of them.

Beside a boulder further down the hill he discovered a thick, swirling mass of flies buzzing over the ground. He considered snatching a few from the air to serve as appetizers until he was that what they were fussing over was a pile of fresh, steaming deer dung. "Blah!" he spat and pinched his nose shut before moving off in search of a more appetizing prospect.

After a time he arrived at an old log on the ground that was laying horizontally on the mountain side. The log was mostly deteriorated with a cluster of red wild flowers growing on top and its bark laying on the ground around it.

Soft, rotten logs are an excellent place to find bugs, and Ono was soon eagerly digging through its debris while his stomach gurgled in anticipation. Once he was driven off when he uncovered a crotchety scorpion that snapped its pincers and jabbed its tail at him. Undeterred, he had only moved further down the log and continued with his search, which soon paid off when he found a large black millipede curled up within a niche in the wood.

"Aha! Breakfast!" he said and smiled. Millipedes, once you get through the thick shell, are quite a tasty meal for a gnome. He reached in the log and pulled the placid bug out and sat it on the ground where it curled into a tight ball spiraling around itself. He rubbed his hands together and smacked his lips, and was preparing to have a morning feast when he heard the soft beat of wings and the rustle of leaves behind him.

Ono's face grew red as he turned around, not at all surprised to see the same crow only a short distance away standing beside a shrub. The greedy bird shifted from foot to foot and craned its neck one way to the other, trying to see what it was he had found.

Ono narrowed his eyes and moved his body from side to side to block the crow's curious rubbernecking, hoping that the bothersome bird would get frustrated and fly off to find its own food. But his shifty behavior only intrigued the bird further.

The little gnome's hiding something! And it must be good, whatever it is! the crow thought as it craned its neck and took another step towards him.

Ono swallowed nervously and reached into his robe so his hand was resting on his wand. "Not.. another.. step," he said and gave the bird his meanest look, which only amounted to wrinkling up his nose and raising his eyebrows.

The crow, seeming to weigh its options, ruffled its feathers and turned its head to eye him suspiciously. The two stared at one another for a long moment, each unblinking, before the crow slowly lifted its foot and stretched its leg forward.

"Don't..." Ono warned and pulled his robe aside to reveal hilt of his wand.

The crow's foot hovered just over the ground, and a tense

moment of silence hung in the air as the two tried to guage what the other was willing to do to get the meal.

It's not getting this one! It cannot, I'm starving! Ono thought to himself and squinted an eye menacingly at the bird.

I want whatever the gnome has! I must have it, and will! the crow thought and slowly lowered its foot. When it touch- ed the ground a brittle pine needle snapped under its weight.

In the blink of an eye, Ono's hand slapped cloth, pulled the wand from his sash, and had it aimed at the bird's chest. "Dekif pehl miks ci!" he shrilled and flicked the wand.

The crow squawked with surprise and lifted its wings to fly away, but was much too late. A bright pink flash of light shot from Ono's wand and struck the bird with a loud BLAP! sending sparks flying into the air in an explosion of colors.

"Kawkawkaw!" the crow shrieked as it flew off through the forest, leaving behind a raining trail of smoking black feathers in its wake.

Ono stood there for a moment to watch the crow flee, then blew the thread of smoke away from the wand's tip, twirled it around in his hand, and slid it back between his sash, all in one fluid motion. Then, with a smug grin on his face, he turned around and enjoyed his breakfast.

CHAPTER NINE

After finishing with his breakfast, Ono licked his fingers clean and sighed. He was sitting on top of the log amid the patch of wild flowers with his legs dangling over the side. On the ground beneath his feet was a large pile of millipede shells, licked clean and shiny black.

He hiccuped and rubbed his belly, then decided that he was much too full to do anything but rest for a spell. So he laid back on the log and folded his hands behind his head and looked up into the sky.

Past the flower tops that grew up all around him and through the tree branches far overhead, Ono watched the scattered clouds drift by on the breeze, as if being carried along by a lazy tide in a blue sea. The white puffs were becoming thin as the sun rose higher, and the gentle warmth that spilled through was relaxing.

As so often happens when one is full and content, Ono's eyelids slowly began to droop and sag and pull apart only reluctantly when he blinked. A short nap would do me well I suppose, to get me ready for today, Ono thought sleepily and yawned. But only for a... a.. He never finished the thought, for his mind drifted off to soft pleasant things as he fell asleep. His chest began to rise and fall steadily, and his mouth dropped open as he began to snore.

Meanwhile, deeper in the forest, a lone doe walked along through the trees. She would stop occasionally to nibble the

leaves growing from the various shrubs and bushes, and also
to scratch at the ground with her hooves, searching for tender new sprouts. Every so often she would raise up her head
and listen to the forest, but it was a quiet day and she
went about her business with little worry. The doe proceeded
with her leisurely stroll along the mountain side, sampling
the plants and leaping gracefully over fallen logs when they
crossed her path. On her way she stopped at a small spring
that bubbled up between a cluster of mossy stones for a
drink of its sweet water.

When she had had her fill, she raised her head back up and
was preparing to continue on when she noticed a small patch
of red wild flowers growing on a rotten log a short distance
away. Not willing to pass up the tasty flowers, she trotted
quietly down the mountain. Coming to the log, the doe lowered her head down to crop the red tops, but suddenly froze
with a puzzled look on her furry face. Oddly enough, splayed
out among the flowers was a limp, snoring gnome. Caught off
guard at finding such a strange little creature, the doe
cautiously dipped her face down and sniffed at it. The gnome
smelled of musky grass and pine.

Oblivious to her presence, Ono continued to snore.

Without knowing quite what to do, the doe simply stood
there for a time and studied him with a curious look. Beneath her gaze the gnome would occasionally mumble to itself, or wiggle its toes, or twitch its ears as it slept.

The doe soon grew bored and impatient with him though, for he was in the way of the flowers and she was hungry, so she leaned down and gave him a gentle nudge with her nose to wake him up. She certainly didn't expect what happened next.

When Ono woke up and saw the big blurry brown face looming just inches above him, he sat up and squealed with absolute terror and grabbed desperately for his wand.

The doe, shocked that such a loud noise could come from su   tiny body, snorted with surprise and sprang into the   before bounding off through the brush.

Th king that some horrible predator had sneaked up on him while he was sleeping, Ono scrambled backwards through the flowers and tumbled down the side of the log. He hit the ground running in the opposite direction the deer had gone, darting through the underbrush and squealing like an injured piglet until he squeezed through a split in the side of a boulder some distance down the hill and vanished from view.

There in the dark, tiny space, huddled and shaking, Ono fought to catch his breath while he looked out into the forest, hoping that he had outran the beast stalking him. He was awake now, with eyes wide and scared and ears tall and twitching nervously. A clammy hand was resting on his wand, and he vowed to zap anything that moved too quickly or suspiciously in his direction.

After what seemed like a long period of silence and waiting, Ono's ears alerted him to something traveling quietly

through the underbrush off to the right of the boulder.
Squeezed in the tight crack, he had only a narrow line of
sight to the forest, and had no way of knowing what was coming. Trembling, he pulled out his wand and held it at the
ready.

The sounds, indistinct at first, gradually became clear as
the light rustling of leaves, and whatever traveled through
them, came closer. They stopped for a moment, as if to listen, then started up again.

The noises steadily neared, and Ono watched as a shadow,
distorted by the dead leaves and sticks on the forest floor,
slid around the side of the boulder. Shaking horribly, he
squeezed one eye shut and aimed his wand at the sliver of
daylight.

Out on the ground the shadow suddenly stopped, then shifted, before a silhouette leaned over to peer into the crack
where he was hiding. "Egh! Ono! Be careful with that thing!
You'll damage someone's eye pointing it like that!" Ezquit
cried and ducked away.

Ono, more relieved than I could hope to explain, lowered
his wand and sighed so heavily that he seemed to almost de-
flate. "Oh Ezquit, thank goodness!" he said and began working and squirming his way back out of the tight crevasse.

Ezquit and Nez, both wearing brown today and the same
concerned expressions on their wrinkled faces, watched as he
pulled himself from the boulder and dusted off his robe.

"Ono, sweetheart, we heard a ruckus. Are you alright?" Nez asked once Ono had situated himself.

He tucked his wand back in his sash and fixed his cap back on his head, then looked warily around the forest. "Yes, I suppose. But did you see it? It was huge! Giant! Or perhaps I frightened it off before you two arrived. Oh, I hope so! That horrible thing!" he babbled in a quiver with his eyes darting back and forth between the trees around him.

The two old gnomes exchanged a queer glance to one another, then looked back at Ono, whose strange behavior was more than peculiar. After pondering on him for a moment, Ezquit shuffled forward and checked him for a fever.

"Have you eaten any odd mushrooms today?" he asked as he slid his hand over Ono's sweaty brow. "With pink spots or yellow speckles maybe? I've said it before and I shall say it again: they should never be so much as touched! Why, when I was your age I ran across a whole patch of the hideous things and foolishly stuffed my belly full with them. By the time I came to my senses, some few days later as I recall, I found myself sitting at the top of the tallest tree around, covered in mud and as bare as-"

Ono, who was frowning and watching Ezquit's hand on his forehead with crossed eyes, stamped his foot impatiently and cut him off. "No! I have not eaten any mushrooms today, nor any other thing with speckles or spots for that matter," he said, then pointed over his shoulder with his thumb in the

general direction of the log without taking his eyes away
from them. "I was taking a nap earlier among a patch of wild
flowers over ther," he explained, "when I was suddenly awak-
en by a ravenous..." He frowned as if trying to recall what
exactly he had seen. After thinking a moment he snapped his
fingers and continued on with convincing sincerity. "By a
mountain lion! Yes, that's what it must have been, although
I only caught a passing glance of it as it ran from me," he
said, folding his arms and nodding confidently. He seemed to
have forgotten that he had been found huddling in a crevasse
shaking and sweating.

This time the queer glance between Ezquit and Nez shared
with it a hint of a smile, for they both had figured out
what had happened to poor Ono. It wasn't hard to realize
really, because while he was speaking, the doe, cautious and
quiet, had returned to nibble the flowers on the hillside
behind him.

Not wanting to embarrass him for the mistaken identity,
the two quickly changed the subject and invited him further
down the mountain for lunch, for it was nearly noon. When
Ono agreed, they were careful that he didn't look over his
shoulder and spot the shy culprit going about her harmless
business.

Around the bend and out of sight of the grazing doe, the
three came to the large green bush where Nez and Ezquit had
been picking when they heard Ono's desperate cries. A basket

made of woven grass blades sat on the ground beside it, and Ezquit reached down in it and came out with a handful of shiny red berries that he passed around. And so the three gnomes ate a light lunch together there on the forest floor, talking and laughing like a family would for quite sometime. The berries were sweet and ripe, and the day had warmed nicely. The breeze smelled just as good as the berries tasted, and all the clouds had gone.

Ono feeling much better now that he had company, told them about the incident with the crow earlier in the morning, adding just a few inches to the bird's gleaming, razor sharp beak. This in turn led to Ezquit's lengthy and rambling tale of being swallowed whole by a bobcat when he was younger, only to be regurgitated several hours later in a puddle of feathers and bile. "Just like a furball! I say, I must be a rather bitter morsel for a bobcat to reject me in such a rude fashion!" he said and laughed hysterically at his own story, making his eyebrows bounce and squirm like caterpillars.

After a while, their merry lunch was interrupted when a shrill voice called out to them from further down the mountain side, "Hi! Hello? Hi! You over there, hello!" the voice called out.

When they heard Igit's greetings all three of them groaned and rolled their eyes, but smiled politely and exchanged pleasantries when she came waddling up the mountain and gave them all an elegant curtsy.

Igit was a rather high-strung, stingy sort that most everyone had hard time appreciating. She wasn't overly rude, or
spiteful, or unusually nasty in any way, but her constant
barrage of fast spoken words and stinginess could wither a
tree if left unprotected by its bark. Today she wore a woven
grass skirt over a green dress, and had a delicate yellow
flower braided into her light brown hair. She refused to
leave her burrow in anything less.

"So how is it we can help you today dear?" Nez asked once
the greetings had passed and Igit had finished showing off
her new clothes, to politely push the conversation to a
close.

Igit smiled at her in her almost exaggerated way, then
turned her attention to Ono. "Have you seen Corq today? He
was supposed to be back at the burrow helping me clean and
rearrange all of our things for the spring time, but we just
have so much stuff, and all if it's valuable and quite heavy
and I cannot manage it by myself. I just hate it when he
runs off like this, and I suspect that he may do it on purpose. I can't turn my back on him for even a second! You
have seen him, haven't you?" she asked all in one breath,
then somehow managed to pout instead of gasp for air.

Corq was Igit's mate of course, but was also one of Ono's
dearest and closest friends, for they had grown up with one
another and nearly thought of each other as brothers. He

often visited Ono's burrow unexpectedly, sweaty and panting
and nervous, only to leave again once Igit's shrill calls
had passed by outside and disappeared in the distance.

Ono was about to say that he had not seen Corq at all that
day, but she regarded him with such an unnerving look of
suspicion that he decided it best to think back for a moment, just to be sure. "Ugh, no, not today I haven't," he
finally answered with a shake of his head.

She eyed him for a moment with a dubious look, as if wondering if he was harboring Corq at that very moment so his
friend could escape his cleaning duties, but soon relented.
"Well alright. If any of you see him will you please tell
him to come home directly? Thank you. I must be going now,
for I'm sure he's hiding around here someplace. But I will
find him! He must eat sometime! Good day to you!" she said,
then left as fast as she had arrived, shrilling out Corq's
name as she went.

After she disappeared into the underbrush and was out of
hearing range, Ezquit leaned forward and and smiled. "Where
is he hiding Ono?" he asked quietly.

Ono took a bite from his berry and shrugged. "Don't know,"
he said around the mouthful, wondering the same. Corq was
usually scarce when his mate wanted him to work, so he was-
n't entirely worried over not seeing him around.

Ezquit straightened back up and smiled slyly. "Oh, sure,
of course you don't," he said, sounding amused.

CHAPTER TEN

The three continued to bandy around the basket while they finished the berries, and it wasn't long before Nez, quite abruptly, inquired about Bej.

"So when **are** you going to ask that beauty out on a date Ono?" she asked directly. "It's not polite to keep her waiting like you are, you know. And what about the blueberries? Did you pick any for her? Remember, everything must be perfect!"

Ono blushed and twirled his toes in the dirt. "Yes, I picked the berries yesterday, like you said, and I was actually planning on asking her today. I already told my father I would," he said with a bashful smile and wilted ears.

"Oh, finally! Your first joining! How wonderful Ono!" Nez cheered and clapped and hopped up and down, for she had been watching the two and hoping for this news for quite some time. Once she learned the two had taken a liking for one another she had done her fair share of meddling to bring them together, and she felt as though she could take at least part of the credit for the joyous affair.

A jolly Ezquit took off his cap and bowed low to him, then took hold of Ono's hand and vigorously shook it like he was pumping water from a well. "Congratulations my friend! Haha! And the children? How soon, how many, and what will their names be?" he asked with a bearded smile, drawing a look of shocked disbelief from Ono and a playful slap on the hand from Nez.

"You hush about all that you dirty old gnome!" she chastised him, then turned to Ono with an excited glint in her eyes. "Are you going to ask her right now? Of course you are! What are you doing standing here jabbering with old folks like up? You're wasting time, leave and be gone! Love cannot wait!" she cried, grabbing his shoulders and turning him around with surprising strength. "And on your way stop at the creek and wash up, and for goodness sakes, bring flowers!" she instructed and gave him a healthy push down the mountain side.

Ono, feeling whirled and stunned as if he had suddenly gone through a lot in a very short period of time, walked several feet and looked back to see Ezquit and Nez standing abreast on the hillside, smiling proudly down at him and shooing him along. "Good luck!" they called out to him.

Ono managed a nervous smile and a weak flick of a wave before turning around and heading off with what felt like a crazed mob of butterflies in his stomach. Oh! Why did I tell them? I should have waited, but now I have to ask her. And what if she sais no? Then everyone will know and think I'm a fool, and that's just great! he thought and worriedly wrung his hands together as he waddled off, nearly dragging his feet.

The reality of finally popping the big question was terrifying for Ono, to say but the very least, for he had been rehearsing his lines and building up his courage for quite a while, and had never seemed to get either of them just right. Being put on the spot certainly didn't help his nerves much either, of course.

Apprehensive but also very hopeful, he made his way towards the creek, whistling a nervous tune as he went. He ducked through the underbrush and climbed over a boulder, then came to a steep drop off where a section of the hillside had recently slid away. At its edge a tree had toppled as a result from the split in the earth, and it laid across the gap like a bridge. Ono hopped up on the log, waddled across, then hopped back down once on the other side.

He was nearing the bottom of the mountain and mumbling over his lines once again when he smelled an almost rotten, musky scent that was carried to him on the breeze. Alarmed, Ono quickly dove into the nearest bush, hiding himself in its tangle of green branches and peering through a gap in the leaves.

After a minute he spotted several fluffy gray tails poking up over the underbrush as they came around a bend just down the slope from him. The tails bobbed and wiggled as they came near, zigzagging through the brush until their owners came into view in a small clearing not far from Ono's hiding spot. The pack of coyotes stepped out of the brush, each one after the other, following the biggest and meanest looking one of them all. The leader was taller than the rest with a long muzzle covered in a cobweb of scars and filled with sharp, yellow teeth. Its flanks were missing patches of hair, and dark crusted scabs were covering the skin beneath, either from a recent battle or from a nasty case of mange.

When the leader stopped to scent the air, all the others obediently sat on their haunches behind him and panted with their long pink tongues lolling from their mouths and dripping sticky drops of drool in the dirt.

Ono was so close that he could hear well the air snuffling through the leader's questioning nostrils, so he slowly put a hand on his wand and stayed completely still.

Soon the leader, having apparently gleaned what information he needed from the smells in the air, looked back at his resting gang and barked. Then he trotted off into the forest, followed closely by the rest of the pack.

Relieved, Ono watched them trot through the woods until they disappeared around the mountain, then climbed from the bush and made his way down the slope towards the creek. When he arrived, he pushed through a wall of ferns and knelt down at the water's edge and took off his cap. He hung it on a branch beside him, then cupped his hands in the water and began scrubbing his face to get cleaned up for the big question.

Okay! Be calm. Don't let your ears sag, and don't slouch. And remember, stick to the lines, and don't stutter or mumble them! Ono thought as he washed up.

He bent down and slurped up a mouthful of water, gurgled
and swished it around in his mouth, then leaned back down to
spit. He had so many thoughts flying around and overlapping
in his mind about Bej and his supper proposal that he was
taken completely by surprise when he felt a warm splat! on
the back of his head, the force of which dunked his face in
to the stream.

"Plugh! Ack!" Ono choked as he pulled his dripping head
from the creek and coughed out the cold water. Whatever had
struck him was oozing down the back of his neck, and his
first thought was that one of the youngsters had thrown a
mud ball at him, which they have been known to do from time
to time.

"Snakes! Sced! Kei! That was not funny at all!" he yelled
as he stood up and looked around for the rowdy little
gnomes. But oddly enough, Ono could neither see them nor
hear their mischievous giggling. Usually they would make it
a point to laugh and make faces before running off.

Puzzled, he stood there for a moment and scanned the woods
with a menacing scowl, then reached behind his head and
touched the goo running down the back of his neck. It was
warm and runny, and when he pulled his hand away it made a
wet sucking noise. "What in the...?" Ono wondered out loud
as he stared at his fingers, which were covered in a glistening white substance. He was bewildered about what the
strange goo was, or where it came from, until he looked up.

"Kaw! Kaw!" the crow with singed feathers squawked triumphantly from the branches above before taking to the air.

Ono's face became as red as a strawberry, and he threw
back his head and shook his white-knuckled fists in the air.
"Aaaeeeeh!" he yelled as the crow disappeared around the
mountain side, screeching hysterically as it went.

And so for the next couple of minutes, angry and defiled,
Ono threw quite the tantrum beside the creek. He stomped and
spat, pummeled ferns with his fists and threw stones in the
water. Then he bent, but was unable to break, a number of
reeds and tore chunks of moss away from the rocks, all the
while cursing bitterly the crow's impeccable aim. But the
fit quickly drained him of energy, and at last he sat down
on the creek bank with one last huff, exhausted and perturbed.

Snakes to those thieving, profane, ugly birds! he thought,
then bitterly took off his robe and thoroughly cleaned himself in the creek of the bird poop, which had congealed to a
thick, tacky texture on the back of his neck. He scrubbed
himself with a clump of moss, like we would with a sponge,
and he soon felt cleansed of the crow's disgrace, physically
anyway.

Stepping back out of the creek, Ono dried himself with a
fern leaf and shook the water from his hair, making the tips
of his ears slap against the sides of his head. Then he got
dressed, snugged his cap on, and took a long, deep breath.

"If she sais no, then I'm sure it can only be as bad as that was," he sighed, then puffed out his chest and began walking determinedly down the creek towards Bej's burrow.

CHAPTER ELEVEN

"Hello? Bej? Are you here?" Ono called out as he neared her burrow at the bottom of Mud Hill. Clutched in his hands was a colorful bouquet of wild flowers he had picked on his way, and he fidgeted with them as he waddled along. His voice was steady and even, but his flaccid ears showed his fear clearly.

Bej's burrow was unlike that of most gnomes', for hers was not dug beneath ground in the normal fashion. Being u-nique like she was, she had instead made her home inside a fallen, hollow log. It laid on level ground, covered in a thick blanket of moss and surrounded by a bed of ferns and other wide-leafed undergrowth that cast a maze of shadows to the ground. It was difficult to notice in the thick tangles of green, but Ono had walked her home on many occasions and had no trouble finding the neat path that wound through the brush.

"Bej? It's me Ono! Hello?" he asked as he came down the path towards the entranceway.

The entrance to her home was located at the end of the log, and an eave of splintered bark hung over the doorway, which was carved into the bottom center of the wood. Its o-pening was covered with strands of dried grass that hung down from above, so one had only to pull the curtain of blades apart and step inside. A large acorn cap filled with soil sprouted a single pink wild flower beside the doorway, and a woven mat of leaves laid on the ground before it.

Ono gulped nervously, then knocked timidly on the wood beside the entrance. "Bej? Are you home? I.. I've got something to ask you! If you're here, please answer!" he called
out, his high voice beginning to waver.

Poor Ono's hands were clammy and his legs weak as he stood
there with a hopeful smile on his face. But no answer or
acknowledgment came despite his repeated attempts, and it
soon became apparent that she wasn't home. So with a long
disappointed sigh, he turned around and slumped away.

On the walk back to his burrow he tossed the bouquet of
flowers over his shoulder and practiced his invitation for
the next time he saw her.

CHAPTER TWELVE

"Hi? Ono, it's me! Are you home?" Bej called out as she backed up through the brush before his burrow. When she was through the tangle of branches she turned around, and held tightly in her hands was a big brown June bug that clicked and wildly thrashed its legs in the air. With a grunt of effort she hoisted the heavy beetle up to get a better grip on its shell, then stuck out her leg and tapped her foot against the slab of bark covering his tunnel. "Ono! Surprise! I brought you supper! A big juicy beetle, it's your favorite!" she called down with a lovely smile.

She was wearing the best dress she owned, which was light brown with intricate green embroidery of flowers and pedals flowing along the hem. Her hair was beautifully braided in two tails that hung down behind her ears, and she smelled like lilacs, for she had just bathed in the creek and dried herself on the soft pedals.

The petulant June bug she held captive had taken her all morning to find, and she hoped dearly that Ono was home because it had been quite a grapple trying to wrestle it into submission and then carry the struggling beetle all this way.

After knocking with her foot several times more though, she finally gave up on him being home and sat the June bug down. The beetle, quite relieved at being set free, clicked happily and scampered off through the underbrush.

Bej sighed and rubbed her sore hands as she watched the hard earned meal go. "Oh Ono, why won't you ask me? Or at least be home when I ask you?" she wondered quietly before turning around with a pout and heading back to her burrow. As she waddled down the mountain side she loosened her braids and tried to think of reasons why Ono didn't seem to like her enough to ask her out.

Unbeknownst to either of them, the two gnomes were so busy worrying over one another that they passed within fifteen yards of each other while walking through a thicket of brush in opposite directions.

CHAPTER THIRTEEN

Early the following morning, when the golden glow of dawn
was just falling on the forest and the dew still clung to
the leaves in sparkling beads, Ono was suddenly awoken in
the darkness of his burrow. His eyes popped open and he sat
up in bed with a jerk, alerted but not aware of what had
disturbed him from his slumber. He sat there listening for a
moment with a sleepy frown on his face, but after hearing
only unbroken silence he mumbled indiscernibly and fluffed
up his moss pillow. Figuring it had been a nightmare or some
other unpleasant thought, he laid back down, pulled the
blanket over him, and settled in for another hour or so of
sleep.

But then the noise that had awoken him sounded again,
clear and loud and crisp in the early morning air, and Ono
sprang out of bed with surprise.

"Heeelp! Heeelp! Somebody please! Help!" a panicked gnome
screamed and pleaded somewhere out in the forest.

Recognizing the distressed voice and moving quickly, Ono
didn't bother to light a candle as he pulled his clothes
off the root and grabbed his wand and dagger from the sunken
shelf.

His dagger was made from a stubby shard of obsidian with a
crude, uneven blade and a handle made of green cloth wrapped
around one end. It was mostly used for chopping food and
digging our splinters from between his toes. Seldon was it

cleaned between the two uses, for gnomes know little of

germs or their workings.

Stumbling over the clutter in his burrow, Ono struggled to

get dressed and run at the same time with his wand and dag-

ger held clamped in his teeth. The panicked ruckus continued

as he hurried up the tunnel and pushed aside the bark.

"It's getting my berries! Heeelp! Shoo, be gone you fil-

thy, dirty beast! Someone help me!" Koilli's voice squealed

from down the hill.

Ono hopped out of the tunnel, then pushed through the

bushes and began hurrying down the slope as fast as he could

manage. As he neared the cluster of bushes where Koilli was

shouting, he could make out the distinct sounds of a scuf-

fle. Twigs were snapping and branches were shaking, and

there was a strange wet smacking noise, as if something was

eating with a full mouth.

Worried that something horrible was happening to poor old

Koilli, Ono held his dagger in one hand and his wand in the

other.

"My berries! Get away you ugly thing!" she cried from be-

hind the trembling bushes as he neared.

Expecting the worst, Ono lowered a shoulder and charged

through the green shrubs. When he came plowing through to

the other side he was quite shocked by what he saw.

In the small clearing surrounded by bushes before him,

Koilli was trying her best to fight off a gray squirrel that

had its head buried up to its ears in her gathering basket,
slurping and chomping on the berries she had picked. Koilli,
an old heavyset gray-haired gnome in a faded green dress,
was valiantly swinging a stick like a club and shouting curses at the glutton squirrel. In what could only be described
as an oddly improvised sword fight, the squirrel in turn
kept her at bay with parries and sweeps of its fluffy tail
while it gorged on her berries.

"Oh stop it! Stop it this very instant you abhorrent rat!"
Koilli shouted and continued to swing her stick to no avail.

Knowing that such drastic measures would not be needed to
be rid of the squirrel, Ono tucked his wand and dagger between his sash, then bent down and picked up a stone. Then
he squeezed one eye shut, bit his tongue in concentration,
and stretched back his arm. Ono didn't have the impeccable
placement of old Brufit, but he was confident with rocks and
his aim was true. When he threw it, the stone connected with
the squirrel's bulging stomach with a dull thump! that sent
it reeling into the dirt with the basket still fastened over
its head.

"Hurray! Ono! You've come to save me!" Koilli cried and
clapped when she saw him scooping up more rocks. But she
quickly backed out of the way when the squirrel reached up
with its paws and pulled the basket of its head, revealing
its red, berry stained face.

"Chitchitchitchit!" it chittered angrily at him, spitting

berry juice from between its large buckteeth and slapping at the ground with its front paws.

Ono narrowed his eyes at the irate animal, then deliberately tossed a stone up in the air and caught it, tossed it up and caught it.

As if understanding the implied threat, the squirrel narrowed its eyes back at him, flattened its red ears against its head and let out a shrill growl. It seemed to be daring him to throw another.

Ono shrugged and pulled his arm back, but before he could throw it the squirrel spun around with a flick of its tail and scampered off through the underbrush with one last angry chitter.

"Ono! Thank you dear!" Koilli cried, then opened up her arms wide and ran to him with a big toothy grin stretched across her wrinkled face.

"You're quite welcome, but you don't have..!" Ono stammered and held up his hands with an alarmed look on his face as she charged at him.

Too overjoyed to hear his protests, Koilli grabbed a hold of little Ono and squeezed him tightly against her ample bosom. "Thank you, thank you! You saved my life dear! Oh, you're so brave Ono! Just like your father was!" she said as she hugged him.

Ono's face was buried to the ears and his response was muffled, his arms flailing at his sides.

"Proi would be proud of you Ono! He surely would, for rescuing an old gnome like you did," she said and gave him one last bone-bending squeeze before setting him down.

Ono wheezed and coughed and wobbled dizzily on his feet. "You're.. welcome," he said between breaths and straightened his cap back on his head.

Koilli turned around with her hands on her hips and surveyed the damage done by the squirrel and frowned with a huff. Her basket was on its side dripping red juice from its lip, and shredded berry scraps littered the ground around it. It didn't appear that a single berry had escaped the squirrel's binge unscathed.

The sound of running feet pitter-pattering over the forest floor alerted the two gnomes of a new arrival a moment later, and Ono had just managed to catch his breath when his friend Corq came barreling through the bushes. When he came into the clearing and saw the red stains splashed over the ground, he stopped and gasped with fright.

"What has happened here? Are you two alright? What was that sound?" he asked, looking from Koilli to Ono with big, round eyes. His ears were erect, and the tips twitched nervously back and forth.

Corq was not much older than Ono, with a light beard of about the same length and a big sharp nose that seemed to point to wherever he happened to be looking. He was a kindly fellow, but was unusually tall for a gnome. At just over a

foot by our measure in height, he was considered awkward and
lanky among the residents of the community. Or bumbling, as
they so affectionately like to say it.

Furthermore, his manner of dress did nothing to dissuade
that opinion of himself. His cap, which lacked a brim, was
crooked and bent at the top as if it had been knocked askew,
and his brown robe was faded and patched in several areas
with fabrics of different shades. His sash was worn and
threadbare, and tied to one side in a lumped, clumsy knot.
He seemed to be the complete opposite of Igit, but Ono had
always had a sneaking suspicion that he only chose to look
the way he did in passive retaliation of his dapper mate.

"Hello! Yes, everything is fine Corq. I just had to scare
away a bothersome squir-" Ono begun to explain, but was cut
off when Koilli suddenly became animated and hopped out in
front of him.

"Hogwash! Corq, Ono is being modest! If you could have only seen the amazing feat of bravery! Oh! I was screaming and
hollering for help when suddenly **he**," she cried out, then
turned and pointed at Ono with a great thrust of her finger,
"-saved me from being eaten alive by a rabid squirrel with
blazing red eyes! He came charging in, pummeling the furry
beast with stones until it ran squealing for safety. Thank
goodness it only got my berries, because I'm positive it was
preparing to pounce on me next, their insatiable hunger being what it is, you know," she said, then had to stop and
sit down on the ground, for the morning's excitement was

quickly catching up to her.

Corq aimed his nose at Ono and regarded him with a look of astonishment, then tucked his wand back into his sash with a nod of his head. "Well, whoever said that short stature e- quals short courage was either a fool or no friend of yours Ono," he said then took off his cap and gave him a bow. Then he straightened back up and flipped his cap carelessly back on his head, where it sat leaning in the opposite direction than when he had come.

"And whoever said that being tall was an advantage must have never met you nor the branches your head has crippled," Ono replied with a big smile and returned his bow with an extravagantly low one of his own, causing Koilli to giggle and bounce and Corq to laugh in his infectious braying man- ner.

The tittering was heartier and lasted longer than neces- sary, for all three gnomes were relieved and the laughter felt good after such a scare. When the chuckles finally did die out and the tears wiped away, Koilli announced that she was in dire need of a bush, so Corq and Ono each grabbed a hand and pulled her to her feet.

"Thank you Ono, and you as well Corq, for coming to the rescue of an old gnome like me. Bless you both," she said and patted their cheeks. "I'll have to make you each a pot of my special honey water some time to thank you."

She picked up her empty basket and blew them each a kiss,

then waddled off into the underbrush. They waved her good-bye, then as soon as she was gone Corq turned and looked angrily at Ono.

"Why on earth didn't you tell me that you finally asked Bej out on a first joining? After all the rehearsing I've done with you? Let me tell you my friend, having you repeatedly asking me out to supper is not something I prefer to do in my spare time!" he squawked incredulously.

Ono gave him a blank stare for a moment, then frowned curiously. "What exactly is it you're ranting about? I haven't asked her yet you fool. How did you hear that?" he asked with an askant look on his face.

Puzzled, Corq took off his cap and scratched behind an ear. "Hugh. Well, that's what Ezquit and Nez told me when I met them at the creek earlier. They said you had finally asked her yesterday and that they were spreading the good news to everyone. They were awfully proud, and could hardly stop talking about it," he said with a frown, then put his cap back on. "Now why would they tell me such a thing like that I wonder?"

When it dawned on Ono a moment later he groaned and smacked his palm against his forehead. "Snakes! Snakes snakes! Oh! I told them yesterday that I was going to ask her, but she wasn't home! Those loose-lips! Now she's going to hear about it before I even get a chance to ask her. She'll think I'm a fool!" he said and stomped his foot to the ground and blushed like an ember.

Ono was devastated and humiliated, for word of such matters spread like wildfire among the community, and he was
already picturing the vacant look on Bej's face when the
first tongue wagging meddler questioned her about his invitation, which they were surely on their way to do. Suddenly,
the urge to run back to his burrow, clog up the entranceway
with dirt and stones, and hide forever from the embarrassment seemed appealing. Feeling doomed, he slumped over with
his ears wilted and sighed.

But then Corq grasped him by the shoulders and gave him a
jolting shake that brought the world around him back into
focus. "Then we must find Bej at this very instant so you
can ask her! It's still early in the morning, perhaps no one
has thought to go over to her burrow yet to ask her about
it!" he said and watched Ono's face fade from bright red to
ghost white.

Ono whined and looked around the forest for a moment, then
rubbed his hands together and straightened up his ears. "Yes
you're right, I should go directly," he said, then began to
hurry off towards Mud Hill. Before he could get far though,
Corq's voice called after him and he turned around impatiently. "What?! I'm in a hurry you know!" he squawked nervously.

Corq, with a sheepish grin, nodded his head and tugged on
his beard. "I know, but.. can I come with you? Please?" he

asked hopefully and raised his eyebrows.

"Why in the world would you want to do that?" Ono asked
with a confused look on his face, for his friend had never
been one to appreciate tender moments.

"Because I'm avoiding Igit and her dreadful chores and I
need something to do," he mumbled.

Ono considered it for a moment, then snapped his fingers.
"Fine! But only to help me find her, then you must leave and
fend for yourself! Now let's go, there isn't much time to
waste!" he said and sprinted off.

"Haha! Thank you Ono! And we shall find your love! A first
joining it is!" Corq cried as he chased through the brush
after him.

CHAPTER FOURTEEN

Hoping to head off any meddlesome gossipers, the two scurried through the underbrush as quickly as their cumbersome feet would carry them. Desperate to get there in time, Ono scrambled over logs and rocks, while Corq, almost without effort, simply bounded over the obstacles.

"Ono! There is no time to dally! Unless you want the invitation to be ruined I suggest you hurry over and come along!" he called over his shoulder on more than one occasion to his lagging friend.

"Once my legs grow as long and thin as willow branches like yours have, then I can be expected to keep up with you. ButuntilthenIcannot!" a petulant Ono squawked back at him as he struggled to keep up.

On their way they passed several other gnomes gathering along the mountain side, and to Ono's horror each put aside their baskets and pouches to call out his name and wave with smiles.

Snakes! Everyone already knows! he thought as he ran along behind Corq, who served well as a battering ram through the thick underbrush. The two slid down a gully, raced up the other side, slipped and tumbled down a drop off, zigzagged through the ferns, then hurried along the twisting creek bank towards Bej's burrow.

Gnomes do not often run further or faster than is necessary to get from one place to another, for exercise is unknown to them and would be scoffed at as a ridiculous waste of effort if it were, so by the time the two arrived at the brush surrounding her log they were both gasping for air and unsteady on their feet. They stood there for a while with their hands on their knees catching their breath and coughing, until Corq reached out and pushed Ono forward. "Go. If she's home then you better hurry before anyone else comes," he panted.

"Yes, I suppose you're right," Ono said, straightening back up and taking a deep breath. "Wish me luck."

"Good luck my friend, although I'm sure you won't be in much need of it," he said kindly and clapped him on the back, then turned around and began walking off. "Now if I can only find another excuse to avoid my chores. Oh! You have so much to look forward to Ono. Mates are great, I'm sure," he trailed off as he went, leaving Ono stranded and nervous.

When Corq was gone from view, Ono smoothed out his robe and tightened his sash, then fixed his cap just so on his head. Bej's burrow, which he had always found welcoming in its quaint fashion, was suddenly a looming, intimidating place to be. Just looking at it made his stomach queasy.

Okay! This is it, it's now or never. I can do this! Ono thought to himself and willed his legs to move forward. Nervously, he waddled to the end of the log and stopped at the screen of grass at the doorway. Many deep breaths and several wipes of his perspiring brow followed before he gently knocked on the wood.

"Bej? Are you home? It's me, Ono!" he called out and waited. After a moment of not hearing any response he felt his stomach slowly begin to sink with grief. Oooh, goodness, she's already left, he thought and looked down at the ground where he saw the ears on his shadow wilt. Devastated, he slowly turned around and stepped away with his head bowed.

But just as he got to the foot of the path to leave, he heard a stirring within the log behind him, and his ears perked up again.

"Ono? Is that you I hear out there?" Bej called from inside, sounding neither embarrassed nor disgusted, but rather hopeful that it was him who had been knocking.

Relieved at hearing her voice, Ono hurried back and danced a quick jig on the mat before the doorway, for he was sure she had not yet heard about his plans. "Yes! It's me! I was just, ugh, stopping by. I'm sorry if I woke you, but I was out and about and I thought it would be a nice morning for a... a walk! Yes, a walk. You're not busy today, are you?" he asked, then squeezed his eyes shut and grimaced, as if preparing for a painful blow.

More sounds of movement came from within, then her voice, sounding much shriller than normal and closer to the doorway, called out to him, "No! I'm not busy at all today. But give me a minute could you? I just awoke and I'm all in a mess. A walk would be lovely though, yes!"

Inside the hollow log, Bej began scrambling back and forth across her burrow, frantically looking for her things. "Oh! Where is my brown dress? Snakes! I know I put it here somewhere, now where is it?" she mumbled to herself as she flung items of clothing over her shoulder and on to the floor behind her. After she found the dress she quickly slipped and wiggled it on, then rummaged through a basket filled with flower pedals, making quite a mess of her little home as she did so.

Never has he just come over so unexpectedly to invite me for a walk. I wonder what it is he's up to? Maybe to ask me out to supper? Oh, I do hope so! she thought anxiously as she pulled a wild rose pedal from the basket and vigorously rubbed it on her neck and underneath her arms. "I'll be right there! I'm almost ready!" she called out and began brushing her sleep-tangled hair with a brush fashioned from a lump of hardened clay with pine needle tips stuck in it as bristles.

While she was scrambling to get ready, Ono was standing out in front of her log, whistling nervously and rocking back and forth on his feet. He was going over in his mind his lines when he suddenly remembered that in his haste to get there he had forgotten to bring flowers like Nez had advised him to.

"Oh curses!" Ono mumbled and looked around for something that would work. The only one nearby was the single pink flower growing from the acorn cap beside the doorway.

"Almost ready Ono! Just another moment!" Bej called from inside.

"Take as much time as you need, I'll wait!" he replied, then pulled his dagger from his sash and bent down.

When Bej parted the blades of grass and emerged from the log a few minutes later with a smile of pure beauty on her delicate face, Ono's stomach nearly cramped. Her long hair was worn down today, parted on either side by her ears and falling to her shoulders in dark curls. Since he had not yet seen it, she wore the same dress she had worn over to his burrow the day before.

Ono, momentarily overwhelmed by her beauty and the faint, alluring scent of roses that came with her, could only smile nervously and thrust out his fist, which was wrapped tightly around the flower's stem.

"Oh, Pink's my favorite color! How did you know? Thank you Ono!" Bej said and greeted him with a lingering hug. When they separated, Ono took her hand and began tying the stem around her wrist.

"I don't want you to carry it while we walk," he explained with a smile as he gently snugged the knot, making a cor-sage.

"Ono, it's lovely! Just the best!" Bej said and admired the pink flower blooming from her wrist, one that for some strange reason looked awfylly familiar to her. "But why don't you want me to carry it?" she wondered, for it struck her odd that he should say such a thing.

Ono smiled his big lopsided smile and did his best not to lose his nerve. "Because now," he explained as he reached out his arm and wove his fingers through hers, "-I can do that," he said with a wink.

Both surprised and flattered by Ono's sudden brazenness, Bej's eyes lit up and her smile turned half agape. "Ah! A wonderful trade off!" she giggled and blushed.

And so, laughing and smiling without a care in all the world, the two gnomes left from her burrow and waddled off into the forest hand in hand.

Beside the doorway a green stem, hacked clean off at the top, poked up from the soil in the acorn cap.

CHAPTER FIFTEEN

As Bej and Ono waddled along hand in hand through the ferns and shrubs, the morning gradually began to warm all a-round them. The sun rose over the mountains and floated into the cloudless blue above the tree tops, and the occasional breeze swayed the branches and whispered through the leaves.

The sparrows were busy that day with their fluttering and chirping, as were the coveys of quail with their scratching and pecking and ah-hooing. Off in the distance a woodpeck-er's insistent tap-tap-tapping knocked against a tree, and the fidgety chipmunks popped up from their crannies and darted across the logs to begin with their mischief.

It was turning into a beautiful spring afternoon, and the two gnomes could not have asked for, nor imagined, anything or anywhere better in the entire world.

While they waddled along they spoke of many casual, light-hearted things with the enthusiasm and playful banter that only flirting couples do: not really caring about the topic or the issues of the discussion just so long as they could continue hearing the other's voice. Completely engrossed with the other's company, they laughed easily and often and exchanged more than a few eye-batting looks of affection that were received with bashful smiles and gentle hand squeezes.

The words came effortlessly for Ono while they talked, and flowed confidently without the stutters or stammers that had always plagued him as he told her about his morning ad-venture with the squirrel. He spoke in great length and dramatic detail about what had happened, adopting Koilli's version of events of course. To prove his marksmanship, he finished the tale by scooping up a stone and throwing it side armed at a daisy growing atop a stump as they passed it. The stone hit dead center on the flower, causing it to wobble back and forth and drop several of its pedals.

"Ha! Just like that! Except much harder and with a much larger stone," he said and smiled with a proud nod.

Bej laughed in her sweet giggly way, for she always enjoyed his stories, and his crooked smile, which was much bigger and brighter today, was horribly contagious. "Well, I must say, Koilli is certainly fortunate that she had such a brave gnome like **you** to save her Ono," she said and tapped her finger on the tip of his nose.

Ono blushed, as he always did when she gave him such compliments, but rather than becoming shy or bashful or nervous he managed to puff out his chest and even waddle with a hint of a swagger in his step.

They walked south along the creek bank towards Pine Ridge, occasionally spotting other gnomes on their way. When they did, they were met with smiles and waves and encouraging hand gestures from the older folk and muffled giggles and pointed fingers from the youngsters. No one stopped to talk to them or question their joined hands or interrupt their passage though, for the majority of them had already heard the whispered rumors of Ono's coming proposal and gave the two their respectful distance and privacy. As I have said earlier, a first joining is a rare, joyful affair for gnomes and as soon as Bej and Ono walked past those that saw them together turned and eagerly scurried off to confirm the good news to all the others.

Red-faced and smiling from the attention they were receiving from the passersby, the two continued on with their stroll along the creek bank. They waddled along between the mossy rocks and through the dangling vines of willow branches towards the outskirts of their little world where the chances of having some privacy were a little better.

In no hurry whatsoever, they followed the twists and curves of the babbling stream and took turns talking about the inconsequential quirks and details of themselves that only those in love seem to truly listen to and cherish. Of them, Bej spoke about her fear of rabbits and how she despised their nose wiggling and hopping gait, and blamed the phobia on an encounter she had when she was little.

"I was giggling and fiddling with this big fuzzy caterpillar I had found, and was poking at it to watch it wiggle across the ground. I was having so much fun that I didn't pay any attention at all to where I was following it or even how long. After I got bored with it though, I stood up and looked around and realized I didn't know where I was anymore! Oh Ono, I was so terribly frightened that I just plopped down right there on my bottom and began to cry and wail for my family to come rescue me. But I had wondered so far off that no one could hear me! So guess what I did? Try and guess!" she said and smiled at him as he put a hand on his chin and bent his eyebrows together in thought. After a moment of tugging his beard he snapped his gingers.

"Aha. Well, judging on what I would have done, I would have to guess that you chased down a rabbit, wrestled it to the ground, climbed on its back, and then pulled on its ears until it carried you home," he said with a self-assured nod, as if he had done it several times before.

Bej giggled and tickled his ear. "Oh would you have?" she asked sarcastically. "Well no, I did no such ridiculous and reckless thing as ride a rabbit. Besides, I was small you must remember, and practically trembling in my dress. Anyway, not knowing what else to do, I began searching for a neighbor's burrow for some help, and I found a tunnel beneath a big old stump. Not knowing any better, I hurried inside crying out for directions, and out pops a big crazed-eyed rabbit from the shadows with giant teeth snapping! The wild beast trampled me over and sent me flying out of its burrow. I'm surprised I'm still here today, I really am. So I have never trusted them since, or liked their company anywhere near me," she explained as they walked. "They're simply awful, vicious creatures, and I do not like them in the least bit of way."

Ono laughed and squeezed her hand reassuringly, for he

certainly had many tales of awkward encounters with animals, but decided it wise to hold his tongue and save them for later. He still had yet to ask her out for supper and he didn't want her to have second thoughts about him because, among many other things, a green bullfrog had once startled him so badly when it had hopped out of the reeds and arched over his head that he had cried out in terror and fainted.

So instead he told her all about the spells Ezquit had taught him over the years and all the bad incidents he had had with trying to learn them. Bej listened intently with her ears cocked towards him and laughed along with him when he explained how badly it had hurt accidentally zapping himself in the foot.

"And that's how I learned the rule: never put a wand back in your sash with half a chant spoken to it. It can go off at any moment!" he laughed. Then he showed her his father's old wand and turned it in the air for her to see, then used it to send a yellow, crackling ball of flame into the side of a moss covered stone.

Startled, Bej recoiled with a gasp when it struck the rock and sizzled out in a flash of sparks and smoke.

Ono smiled and nodded his head like a show-off.

"Ono! Yes, I believe you! Now put that thing away before you start a forest fire!" Bej laughed as she pulled him away by his hand before he could shoot off another.

The two continued on down the stream, and not long after

they came to a bend where the water branched off and flowed

around the side of an unknown mountain and disappeared

through a green tangle of bramblets. The two were in the

middle of gossiping and snickering about several of the old-

er folk when Bej suddenly stopped and looked around.

"Oh my. We've already walked quite a ways, haven't we

Ono?" Bej asked. "Perhaps we should sit down and rest for a

spell?"

The color of Ono's face turned a light shade of red, and

his ears twitched once, twice. "Um... yeah, yes. Good idea,

let's do," he said, his voice becoming high and pinched.

The time had finally come to ask her the big question,

Ono knew, and his heart began to thump against his ribs

like it was angry and wanted out of its cage. The confidence

he had had only a moment before drained out of him like wa-

ter from a leaky basin, and he struggled to keep his ears

ears from wilting, for he was suddenly nervous about asking

her those few, simple words.

They waddled over and sat down on a flat, moss cushioned

stone that hung out over the stream and dangled their legs

over the edge. The water flowed between their toes and gent-

ly tickled their feet, and Bej sighed and laid her head down

on his shoulder.

"I've certainly had a lovely time with you today Ono," she

said and sniffed her corsage. "We should do this more often.

What do you think?"

Ono's forehead had begun to glisten, so he wiped his face and looked around. "Yes, I... I think we should. Go on walks I mean," he said and cringed.

Bej giggled and turned her head to look curiously up at him with an eyebrow cocked quizzically. "Of course walks silly. What on earth did you think I was talking about?" she asked with a mischievous smile that put a dimple on each one of her cheeks.

Ono swallowed and managed a nervous grin. "Oh, I didn't mean... I meant we should, ugh," he stammered and fumbled a-long. Just ask her you coward! **Do it!** Now! She's waiting! he thought. Then from the corner of his eye he saw a brown beetle scamper across a fern leaf nearby, and he thrust a finger at it. "Lunch. I'm awfully hungry, aren't you?" he asked.

A look of disappointment washed over her face, but she quickly smiled and sat up. "Oh, yes! That would be nice Ono, thank you," she said and nodded.

He stood up and hurried over to the ferns and snatched the bug off, then waddled back and sat down again. Grasping the clicking beetle sideways in his hands, he lifted it over his head and brought it down over his knee with a wet crack! that split it clean in half. "Here you are," he said and handed her the better of the two halves.

With the big moment delayed, Ono relaxed a little and planned for how he was going to bring it up to her, for his

head felt like there was a swarm of flies buzzing around
where his brain was supposed to be and it was quite difficult to concentrate. He nibbled slowly and chewed thoughtfully as the water flowed and babbled by, and after a while
he heard a soft squeak of a belch beside him. Looking over,
he saw Bej smiling bashfully behind a delicate hand and the
beetle shells clean in her lap.

"Excuse me! I was nearly ravenous, and that hit just the
right spot!" she laughed, then tucked a strand of hair behind her ear and looked out over the creek.

She looked as beautiful as ever, just then, and Ono could-
n't help but stare at her as the sunlight reflecting off the
stream's surface danced and swam across her face. She had a
small smile pulling at the corners of her lips, and her
bright green eyes sparkled and shimmered like precious gems.

Ono felt his heart warm in his chest and melt down into
his belly, and he sighed a great sigh and firmly sat the
rest of his beetle half aside.

Bej looked over and saw him getting to his feet. Suddenly
he had a very odd look on his face. "Ono, what are you..?"
she wondered as he stood up tall and held down a hand to
her. She took it, and he pulled her to her feet and cleared
his throat into his fist.

"Bej," he said simply and smiled nervously for a long moment. She was bewildered, and was about to ask what odd an-
tic he was up to until he took off his cap and knelt down

before her. "Will you do me the honor of joining me for a supper of blueberries and honey?" he asked and hopefully scrunched up his eyebrows.

Bej gasped, then began hopping up and down and flapping her hands and squealing with delight. "Yes! Yes I will! Of course I will Ono!" she cried and laughed.

Ono was just as surprised, and he jumped to his feet waving his cap and wrapped her in a hug and spun her around laughing. When he set her down both their ears were twitching with sheer happiness, and they looked at one another with beatific smiles.

"When? When should I come over?" she asked and squirmed excitedly under her dress.

Ono's brain was spinning and reeling madly, and he thought quickly of all the things he needed to have done before he would be ready. "How.. how about tomorrow evening?" he asked a moment later, making Bej clap and her eyes light up.

"Perfect! Oh, I've been waiting so long for you to ask! It'll be wonderful!" she cried out, then kissed his cheek and clung to him like bark around a tree.

Ono hugged her back, for it was certainly the very best day he had ever had in his entire life and he couldn't quite bring himself to believe that something so good was happening to him. It made him smile bigger and bigger as he squeezed her, showing pure happiness on his face and brown bits of beetle shells stuck in his teeth.

CHAPTER SIXTEEN

After walking Bej back to her burrow and parting ways with yet another quick peck on the cheek, Ono hurried home, whistling and clapping more joyously than ever he had done. On his way, he couldn't help but stop several times to dance and jig among the wild flowers, or simply throw his head back to shout and laugh up at the branches. Having never been so ebullient in all his life, Ono couldn't contain the happiness that burst and bubbled out of him even if he had wanted to. He even waved and smiled at a pair of chipmunks sitting abreast on a log as he walked past them.

Puzzled by the gnome's queer behavior, the two chipmunks only glared suspiciously back at him as he went by.

He finally arrived back at his burrow sometime in the mid afternoon and went inside to tidy up. But when he came skipping down the tunnel and into the den, he suddenly stopped in his tracks and groaned, for the burrow before him was messier than he remembered it being.

It was exactly what you might expect a bachelor's burrow to look like. Bug legs, beetle shells, and other half-eaten late night snacks laid scattered along the floor around his bed, hardening and stiffening, and several dirty robes were heaped and wrinkled in the corner. Melted bee's wax from the candle had dripped down the wall and puddled on the floor and hardened, and his accumulation of treasures was a disorganized pile of crystals, iron pyrite, jade, and bird feathers. Having not been swept in ages, the dirt floor was scuffled and clumped, and for the first time he noticed a curious sour smell that hung in the air.

"Oh! This will not do!" Ono said and thought of the embarrassment he would feel if he was to subject Bej's pretty eyes to such an ugly sight.

So he began cleaning and organizing his burrow with a determined vigor that he had never before harbored for such a bothersome task. For the next couple of hours he went about picking up and throwing out, moving and stacking, wiping down and rearranging. During this time he ran across several items he had long ago deemed lost, and also the source of the disagreeable odor filling his burrow.

"Ugh! Uuuuughh!" Ono turned and gagged when he moved away a dried leaf in the corner and uncovered the bucket of rotten worms beneath it.

Several weeks before he had spent a whole day catching the worms from under rocks and forest debris to make a feast for himself, but then Corq had offered to split a praying mantis with him, and Ono had set the worms in the corner and forgotten all about them. Since then the pink, writhering worms had decomposed and liquefied into a gelatinous, puss-yellow puddle of slime, and a gray layer of fuzz had begun to grow on the surface like hair on an old man's head. Left uncovered, the smell was so pungent that Ono's eyes watered.

"Goodness is that horrible! How awful!" he cried, muffled

by his hand that he held clamped over his nose.

Only once he had a pebble plugging up each nostril did he find the courage to go near the worms again. When he did, he picked up the bucket and ran from his burrow with it held as far away from his body as possible. He threw it down a gully further down the mountain side, and the bucket hit the ground with a thick sounding Blump! spewing out its glistening yellow contents that splattered against the rocks like infected mucus from a violent sneeze.

"Ugh!" Ono gagged again just at the sight of it, then ran back home and finished cleaning.

Once he was done, with the worms removed and his belongings organized and neat, his burrow was more presentable and proper than he had ever had it. His bed was made with the moss pillows fluffed and the leaf blanket smoothed and tucked, his treasures dusted off and neatly arranged, and the floor swept clean and even.

Carefully surveying his home, Ono gave it an approving nod and rubbed his hands together with a big smile on his face, for he was sure Bej would be impressed when she came over the following evening.

After making a few more minor adjustments here and there, he decided he should go share with his father the good news, for Proi had been hearing all about her for quite some time. And so Ono soon left from his burrow and began the hike over the mountain towards the meadow, whistling so joyously and beautifully that any songbird with any sense would have gladly traded its feathers for his lips.

The afternoon had passed into evening while he was cleaning his burrow, and the sun rested just above the mountain tops. The forest was cool and quiet, mellow in the way only an evening after a full and busy day can be.

Ono went over the mountain top and started down the other side towards the meadow below, skipping merrily along. He didn't run into or see any other gnomes to brag to about his big date as he went, but met instead a scraggly old opossum crossing his path on the hillside. Ono stayed a respectable distance up the slope from the animal, for opossums like their privacy and guard it fiercely, but he was simply too happy to let a pair of ears go by, no matter how ragged and ugly, without first hearing the good news.

"Hello my friend! A good day it was! She said yes, can you believe it? She said yes! Haha!" he called out to the lumbering animal and wiggled his toes in the dirt with a smile.

The opossum stopped in its tracks as if it had been disturbed, then slowly turned its head to scowl at Ono with a pair of grumpy, red-rimmed eyes.

Ono gave it a quick jump of his eyebrows and a thumbs-up. "She said yes!" he said again and pumped his fist in triumph.

As if understanding the little gnome's words and jealous of its good fortune, the opossum bared its jagged stumps of yellow teeth and hissed bitterly before lumbering away.

Undaunted by the opossum's scorn, Ono waited until its fleshy tail slid off through the underbrush before continuing on down the mountain with a smile. He came to the meadow's edge and began skipping and whistling through the grass stalks towards his dad's oak tree, scaring the occasional quail and grouse up from the meadow as he went.

"Father! You won't believe it!" he called out when he saw the oak's twisted branches through the canopy of grass above him. He hurried to the base of the tree and drummed his hands excitedly on its trunk. "I asked her, and she said yes! Oh! And she even kissed me! Twice!" Ono laughed, then sat down in his normal spot with his back against the tree beside Proi's grave.

For the next twenty minutes he sat there babbling on and on like a brook after a good rain, pausing only for breath and to laugh with joy. He told his father all about their walk and of the hand holding and the corsage he had made her, and how he had finally found the courage to ask her out. "Bej didn't even think about it! She just said yes like she had been expecting me to ask, then kissed me right on the cheek!" he bragged, then went on to explain how well he had cleaned his burrow for the big date the following evening.

It was some time later when he was in the middle of talking about which robe to wear, either the green one or brown

one and contrasting which looked better in the candle light,
when he suddenly heard a deep, unsettling murmur from somewhere far out in the meadow. It was brief and low, like a
garbled, sinister whisper followed a moment later by a faint
click... click... click.

Although there are many, it was not a sound he had ever
heard made in the forest.

Alarmed, Ono became silent and quickly got to his feet,
waiting for the sound to come again. His tall ears twitched
and cocked back and forth, and he squinted curiously into
the wall of grass around, for he was almost certain that he
had been hearing things. While he had been talking with his
father the sun had gradually sank behind the mountains and
darkened the meadow. The grass that rose up all around him
was too tall for him to see over, and the shadows between
the shoots were too thick to see any distance between.

Wary and uneasy, he listened for a time to the sound of
the wind hissing over the grass. Then he heard the same
noises again, this time closer. "...Stakes over here," a
deep baritone voice grumbled, followed again by the strange
tapping.

Ono gasped with fright when he heard the bizarre, disturbing sounds, then scurried into the grass for cover. There,
shaking and nervous with his wide eyes darting about, he
crouched between the shoots and pulled his wand and held it
at the ready in his fist. Ono didn't know and could not i-

magine what was out there making such sounds, but he knew he
should want nothing to do with it.

Run you fool! There's **something** big out there! Run and run
now! his common sense shouted at him. But before he could,
his curiosity made him hesitate, as it sometimes did in such
awkward and inconvenient moments.

Click... click... click... the sound came again, like two
stones being tapped together. Then the murmurs, faint and
low and indiscernible, drifted to him on a gust of wind that
swayed and hissed over the meadow.

Ono wrung his hands together and worried over what he
should do as he crouched in the dense grass.

I wonder what is out there? It's surely nothing I've ever
seen before! he thought, to the severe annoyance of his
common sense. No! It's probably nothing that you need to see
anyway, if you enjoy living! it shouted back.

Ono sat undecided for a long moment while the two argued
back and forth, chewing on his bottom lip with his ear tips
twitching nervously and listening to the strange noises.
Then, suddenly giving in to his inherent and overwhelming
curiosity, Ono stood up and tiptoed off into the meadow to
investigate.

CHAPTER SEVENTEEN

Ono snuck carefully through the shoots of grass as he made his way closer to the frightening sounds, making not a rustle of noise as he went. He held his wand readily out in front of him, and beads of sweat had begun to dot his brow. The deep murmurs became louder and less obscure as he neared, but the tone of the voices was so much lower and guttural than that of a gnome's that he could not make out what was being said.

Surely it must be trolls! Oh no! Why have they come here? I thought they were all dead and gone! he thought as he crept closer through the blades of grass.

Ono had never even seen or encountered a troll, but Ezquit had told him many tales of when they had once roamed the land, terrorizing the gnomes and hanging those captured up by their ears in neat rows to dry in the sun for jerky.

Horrid things! But I must see them so I can warn the others! he thought to himself.

Creeping through the meadow, he began to hear the rustle and crunch of grass being crushed beneath heavy feet, and the faint clicks gradually turned into harsh CLACKS! as he neared the origins of the sounds. Very carefully and gently so as not to make a sway in the meadow, he pulled two shoots of grass apart, then stepped through them and tiptoed even closer to catch a glimpse of what was making such frightening noises.

It did not take him long.

Looking up through the screen of grass above him, Ono suddenly made out two figures, little more than shadows in the twilight, walking back and forth through the meadow in the distance. As he watched with terror stricken eyes, the figure on the right bent down in the grass with a huge, vicious looking stake and stabbed it into the earth with a grunt. Then the other, this one wielding a brutal club, stepped forward and raised the bludgeon high over its head before hammering it down on the stake's end with a grunt of its own.

CLACK! the noise came again as the stake was driven deeper into the ground with each powerful strike of the club. CLACK! CLACK!

Ono's breath had caught in his throat and his mouth hung down in disbelief. His eyes were wide and scared, and his hands trembled horribly, as did the tips of his ears. The rest of his body was simply too frightened to move though, so he just stood there in the grass and watched the two dark figures stab and pound at the earth, grunting and grumbling as they worked.

They were not trolls at all, but something far worse of a threat: they were humans.

Ono had heard many tales about them also, but the stories were always hushed and discreet, for their kind was not the tale to be told over supper or right before dusk unless one

wished a poor appetite and a restless night's sleep on another. They made up the characters in stories that older
gnomes only reluctantly spoke about in short lengths, because they were tales of death and destruction, anguish and
woe that would wilt even the bravest of ears.

Ono had always disregarded these stories and the abysmal
humans in them as a vague, distant threat because he could
never imagine such monstrosities invading his quiet little
world. But suddenly they were there, as wretched and as ugly
as even the most outlandish tale made them out to be.

They were both little more than silhouettes in the fading
light, but Ono could make out more than he wanted or needed
to of them in the waning dusk.

The mammoth humans were so tall that the blades of grass
that grew high over his head hardly came up to their waists,
and the features of their hideous faces were soft and round
and beady-eyed. They wore strange caps as well, with long
narrow bills that stuck out from their brows. There was no
brim around them, and instead of tapering off to a point at
the tops they cupped the humans' heads. Their small ears
were not pointed or angular as was normal in nature, but instead matched their faces in their thick, stubby fleshiness.
Almost like mushroom caps stuck on the sides of their heads,
Ono imagined with disgust.

The clothes they wore were almost as alien as they were,
for both had on plain white garments that covered everything

from the base of their necks to mid-arm, and down to their midsections. There, the white garments were tucked beneath a puzzling blue material that encircled their waists and clung snugly down the length of their towering legs. This fabric ended abruptly at their feet, which were both clad in dull black encasings with twine zigzagging up from the toes and tied at the top in big loopy knots.

Ono had never seen such things more heinous in all of his life, and he was forced to stand there quivering with fright while the two grunting monsters stabbed and bludgeoned the earth until at last his paralysis broke. When it did, he opened his mouth wide and let out a shrill scream of terror as he turned and bolted for the mountains.

CHAPTER EIGHTEEN

"Whoa! What the heck?!" Tom shouted and flinched in surprise when he heard the shrill squeal from behind him. Turning around, he saw a trail of quivering grass blades cut across the meadow as something scurried off towards the dark woods at the edge of the field. "Did you see that Jay? Holy Moley was it close! Just about scared my lunch clean out of me!" he said and squinted out into the shadows.

Jay thoroughly scratched himself over his jeans and grunted disinterestedly. "Hmph. Probly' just a piglet or somethin' that saw your big ol' bee-hind and turned tail and ran off. Can't blame it none, poor thang," he said, then spit a brown stream of tobacco juice in to the grass beside him with a smile that revealed several crooked and missing teeth.

Tom, who was evidently not as comfortable being out in the wilderness with wild animals so late like his friend seemed to be, shifted nervously on his feet and adjusted his grip on the bundle of survey stakes he had beneath his arm. He continued looking for some movement, but the animal's squeals gradually faded off into the shadowy distance.

After a moment Jay reached out and poked him in the ribs with his hammer. "It's called wildlife genius. Sometimes it bites, and sometimes it don't. Now common, boss said he wants these stakes done by tommorra' mornin', and it's already gettin' dark," Jay said and began walking off across the meadow with the hammer swinging at his side.

Tom clucked his tongue in his mouth and gave the dark mountain side one last suspicious look. "Yeah, I guess you're right. It is getting late..." he said, but lingered for a moment longer before turning around and following Jay through the grass.

CHAPTER NINETEEN

"Hiiiiide! Hiiiiide yourselves! Humans are here! They're in the meadow! Hiide!" Ono squawked at the top of his lungs as he ran through the dark forest. He darted through ferns and underbrush, screaming like a banshee to warn all the others of the coming monsters.

Trees and bushes blurred past him in a smear of shadows as he ran, and Ono thought he could feel the savage, beady eyes of the humans watching him hungrily from the darkness all a- round him. He imagined their giant clubs swinging and smash- ing, their stakes stabbing and impaling, and the frightening images flashing through his mind made him run faster and yell louder.

Cresting the top of Boulder Mountain, he began running down the other side as fast as his short legs would take him. So fast, in fact, that he did not have time to stop himself or move out of the way when a gnarled root appeared directly in front of him from around a corner. "Aaiiee!" he cried out when his foot snagged the root and sent him tum- bling through the air in a ball of flailing limbs and flap- ping robe. Luckily, his fall was broken when he crashed cap first into a shrub further down the slope, tangling him up in its branches like a fly in a spider's web. "Help me! Oh please, help me! They're coming!" he squawked and struggled to get away.

He managed to squirm and kick and thrash his way free of

the bush, then turned and continued running as fast as he
could from the humans, who Ono thought were surely coming
down the mountain after him, dragging their knuckles across
the forest floor and foaming wickedly from their giant
mouths. He darted past a pile of rocks and plowed through a
wall of weeds towards the safety of his burrow, desperate to
get as far away as possible.

A fat raccoon accompanied by her two babies was casually
picking through a log when Ono zipped past them in a flash
of movement and an earsplitting squeal, shaking the underbrush and sending leaves flying up in his wake as he sped
by. Alarmed by the sudden commotion, the two babies jumped
up and clung to their mother while she chittered defensively
and scurried away through the forest with the two on her
back.

"Save yourselves and hide! Humans are coming!" Ono continued to scream as he ran recklessly towards his burrow. He
came barreling around a boulder and suddenly came face to
face with a dark shadow standing before him. "Aaaah!" he
squawked and fell back on his rump.

He was scrambling backwards to get away from the shadowy
figure when he heard Ezquit's voice, sounding rather alarmed
and unsettled, come from it.

"Ono, **what** are you doing? And what's the matter with you?
Is everything alright?" he asked, looking down at his small
shaky friend with a worried gaze and scrunched eyebrows.

Scared that Ezquit might fall prey to the humans' clubs and spears, Ono sprang to his feet and grabbed him by the front of his robe. "Run Ezquit! Run and hide! They're coming! I saw them in the meadow!" he shrilled.

Rattled by Ono's vehement rantings, Ezquit tried his best to calm him and get him under control. "Ono! Calm yourself! You must-" he began.

But Ono was not hearing or having any of it. He shook Ezquit by his robe and continued screeching like he was possessed. "No! You must find Nez and hide at this very instant! They're coming I said!" he screamed up into his face.

Ezquit sighed and shook his head as Ono went on, for he did not wish to take such measures to steady him, but saw no other alternative to put an end to his panicked delirium.

"They have giant clubs! And huge spears! They'll kill us all!" Ono continued to yell as Ezquit reached into his robe and pulled out his bent, worn old wand.

"Alapos efid olri," he said and smartly tapped the end of his wand on Ono's forehead.

Cut off instantly in the middle of his shouted warnings, Ono went simultaneously silent, rigid, and still. He wobbled on his feet for a moment, then crossed his eyes and fell back on the ground like a toppled tree.

With the aid of his walking stick, Ezquit crouched down beside him and lightly patted his cheeks to revive him from the spell. Ono blinked and shook his head in response, feeling both dizzy and dazed, as if from a powerful strike to the head.

"You're alright Ono, you're alright. Just sit up and tell me, calmly and slowly this time, what's the matter with you and what these things are you've been ranting about," Ezquit said quietly.

Feeling like he had just been awoken from a dream, Ono frowned up at Ezquit, who was crouched and leaning over him. "What? Hugh?" he asked and shook his head, knowing he had something extremely important to say but unable to grasp the thought from the fog in his brain.

Ezquit snapped his fingers in front of his disoriented face and pulled him to his feet. "You were shouting all a-bout clubs and spears and vicious things coming. Now what of it?" he asked wiggling his eyebrows quizzically, hoping for Ono's sake that he had not been frightened yet again by a grazing doe.

"Oh! ... Yes, well," Ono said, suddenly remembering the cause of his fear again. He looked warily around him at the dark forest, then leaned towards Ezquit and whispered ur-gently, "I saw humans, two of them! With clubs and stakes!" He begun to tremble.

Ezquit, who had seen many things in his long life and did-n't frighten neither easily or often, gasped in shock and covered Ono's mouth with his hand. "Hush Ono!" he said forcefully. "Such things are not to be spoken where they

can be heard by others. Not so much as a whisper! But I
hope, and am also sure, that you are mistaken with what you
saw, for the day is gone and the grass can play tricks on
the eyes. Nonetheless, we must discuss this matter immediately and far away from any innocent ears. Come," he said,
then took hold of Ono's hand and jerked him through the
forest with a speed that defied both his limp and walking
stick.

CHAPTER TWENTY

Although gnomes are not normally nocturnal, their large keen eyes can see remarkably well in the darkness, and Ezquit and Ono hurried through the deep nighttime shadows with no trouble at all.

Leading the way, Ezquit hurried down the mountain side, followed closely by Ono, who wanted nothing less than to be once again alone in the forest with the humans out and about. The two scurried through a bed of ferns, along a steep embankment, then down into a dried, empty ravine of some long ago exhausted spring. They traveled over and around the stones at the bottom as they followed the snaking turns of the ravine, and they soon came to a tall wall of moss covered boulders where a waterfall had once poured over. The two hurried to the base of this overgrown ledge, where upon further inspection there could be seen a small arched crevice separating two of the boulders at the bottom.

One after the other they squeezed between the tight crevice, then waddled briskly through the darkness of a long, gradually upward sloping tunnel that went far into the nearby mountain. After a time of walking in silence, a faint golden glow gradually appeared at the end of the tunnel, and the two came waddling out into the large, brightly lit burrow that was Nez and Ezquit's home.

The burrow was certainly an elegant one, judging by a gnome's eye for decoration that is. The den was wide and

deep and round in circumference, illuminated by many burning
candles placed evenly along the earthen walls in small cub-
bies. In the gaps between were recessed shelves, lined and
filled with many quaint treasures the two gnomes had collected over their lives; some of which even we would find
valuable, for there were more than a few sparkling gold nug-
gets and lumps of sapphire among the ample collection.

The dirt floor was swept smooth and level, and on either
side of the den were two dark hallways leading to adjoining
rooms. In the center of the den was a long, wide table fashioned from a slab of bark turned smooth side up and placed
on legs of stacked pebbles. On the floor around it were
thick white mushroom caps that served as sitting cushions.

"Nez! I am back and have dragged Ono with me! Come quickly! We all must have a discussion immediately!" Ezquit called out as he led Ono to the table where they both sat down
on the mushroom cushions.

"Hold your cap on, I'm coming directly! Ono, dear, would
you like some hot pine water? I've just made up a batch!"
Nez's voice drifted in from the next room.

"Yes please!" Ono answered, for now that he was in the
safety of a burrow he had calmed enough to feel just how
dreadfully parched his frantic run from the meadow had left
him.

After a moment Nez emerged from the dark hallway with a
steaming mug of pine water. The mug was fashioned from a

tiny speckled quail's egg with the top broken clean off at the mouth, with a clay handle and base mounted on it.

Nez enjoyed company and entertaining her guests, and on her face was a welcoming smile as she waddled across the den, for she thought that Ono's presence had to do with the news of his first joining. She had been telling everyone she saw that day of the good news, and was excited to hear the details of just how it had happened.

But when she saw the apprehensive looks on both of their faces, the warm smile vanished and she quickly hurried over to the table and sat the mug down before Ono. "What's the matter dear? Why do you look so worried? She didn't say no, did she?" Nez asked and sat down beside Ezquit.

Across the table, Ono took a sip of his pine water and cleared his throat. "It's not that, I... I saw two humans, just a short time ago. In the meadow," he said and flinched when Nez gasped in fright.

Alarmed, she looked to Ezquit for some explanation to Ono's claims. He simply held up a hand, as if to calm the matter, then lowered it back down again. "We must not jump to conclusions and frighten ourselves into a panick. Ono, my friend, you have had the supremely good fortune of never having encountered such monstrosities in the past, so your identification of them may not be sound," he said with an almost hopeful tinge in his voice. His normally vigorous eyebrows had stopped their wiggling and dancing when he spoke, and instead were knit tightly together in a scared way that Ono had never seen before.

Then Ezquit pointed to himself and Nez. "We, on the other hand, have had such rotten luck. We know exactly what their kind looks like, and have seen them clearly in the daylight more times than we like to admit. So what we will do is this: Nez and I will ask you questions about them, and then determine by your answers if what you saw this evening was indeed a pair of humans. This is the first: how big were they, exactly?" he asked, then leaned forward and folded his hands on the tabletop. Nez's forehead wrinkled in concern and her ears cocked forward, listening intently.

"Okay.. " Ono sighed, feeling as if he were the unwilling messenger of horrible news. He squeezed his eyes shut and reluctantly brought the frightening scenes back into his mind. After a brief moment of silence, he began telling them exactly what he saw. "They were both huge. I was looking up at them through the grass, and the meadow didn't even touch their bellies," he recalled, seeming to be unsettled by what he saw behind his eyelids, for his ears twitched uncomfortably.

Nez asked the next question. "What did their ears look like? Were they pointed like ours, or.. " she trailed off with her eyebrows raised, hoping for the wrong answer.

But without hesitation Ono shook his head. "No, they were small and round and ugly. Not at all like ours," he answered with his eyes still closed and a distasteful look on his face.

The questions kept coming for sometime; what their faces looked like; what they wore; how they sounded; how they behaved; and about the strange things covering their feet. They became increasingly intricate as they went along, not because they doubted Ono's sincerity, but because they were desperately hoping for a harmless explanation for what he saw that would show it all to be just a simple mistake. But as the questioning continued, Ono's answers only proved that there could be no doubt about what he had seen.

Defeated, Ezquit put his elbow on the tabletop and rested his cheek in his palm. "What were they doing?" he asked in a sigh.

Ono stirred in his seat and frowned. "They were pounding big wooden stakes, or spears, or something of that sort into the ground with a giant club. It was horrible," he said and waited for the next question.

A long period of silence followed, and after a moment Ono sensed that the inquiry had finished. He opened his eyes and saw Ezquit and Nez still sitting across the table, both slumped and somber. Each had a detached, melancholic look in their eyes as if they were watching something sad take place in the far distance, and the wrinkles on their old faces, usually accompanied by laughs and cheer, were etched deep with worry.

"They weren't really humans, were they? It was, after all, getting dark when I saw them, so it could have been something else altogether, right? Trolls perhaps?" he asked hopefully.

Ezquit, whose ears had become so flaccid by the horrible news that the tips now laid flopped over on the brim of his cap, managed a weak smile and shook his head. "No Ono, from what you explained and from our recollection, they were undoubtedly humans. But try not to fret over them, because from time to time their kind will wonder aimlessly through the land only to leave again as quickly as they had come, as I hope they will now. I'm sure there is little here that would interest their sick appetites." He straightened up and cleared his throat. "Either way, I want you to stay on this side of the mountains and far away from the meadow for a while, just as a precaution. Nez and I will warn the others of the danger there and deal with the situation from here. In the meantime, there is no cause for spreading gossip and needless panic, if you do understand my meaning," he said and stood up from the table. "Come Ono, I will walk you back to your burrow. Nez and I have much to discuss this night."

Ono, not sure whether to feel frightened or relieved by Ezquit's vague explanation, graciously declined the offer of company back home and quickly finished his pine water, which had cooled during their discussion. Then he sat the mug back on the table and whispered his appreciation for the drink to

a rather forlorn looking Nez, then tipped his cap good
night. Feeling horrible for unleashing such news on the two
old gnomes, Ono then turned and waddled across the den with
wilted ears and out through the tunnel.

When he was gone, Ezquit closed his eyes and sighed heavily. "Those stakes Ono said the humans were pounding into the
meadow... I've seen them before," he said quietly, going
back many decades in his memory to his far away homeland
when the humans had come and destroyed it all. He shivered
at the thought, remembering the devastation that had soon
followed those strange harbingers.

Sitting at the table with her head in her hands and dark
hair falling around her face, Nez began to cry. "So have I,"
she sobbed, for she too knew all too well, just as so many
other gnomes did, of the destruction that was surely to
come.

The humans had marked the meadow as their territory, and
it was only a matter of time before they came to claim it.

CHAPTER TWENTY ONE

Over the following few days there was a tense, lingering apprehension that fell over the small community, for Ezquit had made it a point the very next morning to visit each burrow and warn everyone with an ominous urgency in his voice that the meadow was not a safe place to travel, nor anywhere around it. He also said, quite somberly, that there would be no need of foolish curiosity or investigation, because he would be checking into the matter himself and would keep them all abreast on any new developments, whether it be good or bad.

Not surprisingly, this vague, frightening warning, coming from such a well-respected elder such as Ezquit, sparked a frenzied wave of gossip throughout the community.

The rumors and stories of what could possibly be prowling the meadow flowed quickly and contagiously from listening ears to jabbering mouths, being passed along with suspicious glances and hushed whispers. The monsters and serpents and unutterable terrors grew bigger in size and longer in claw and fang as the villains in stories told by gnomes tend to do, and within just a few days the whole community had spoken themselves into a silent tizzy.

Youngsters, such as Sced and Kei and a handful of other whining, protesting others, were forbidden to leave the safety of their burrows with no explanation for the sudden strictness other than: "It is for your own good! You should be grateful!" from their worried parents before being shoved down inside and locked away behind slabs of bark and rocks to block their escape.

Those that had a stock of food stored away in their burrows opted to stay inside, while those that had to venture out to gather went about their business quickly and quietly and returned back home soon after with a wipe of their brow and a relieved sigh.

Frightened and wary, everyone waited with bated apprehension for news from Ezquit, who spent his days walking the borders of the community and patiently watching the meadow from the cover of the surrounding mountains for any sign of the humans.

Ono's date with Bej went on as it had been planned the following evening. Although the two had a pleasant time at his burrow, with much flirting and laughter over the scrumptious dinner of blueberries and honey, the experience was robbed of its charm for Ono. Throughout the date, he couldn't help but see the humans in the back of his mind pounding their stakes into the earth and hearing their low grunts. He also saw the worried looks on Nez and Ezquit's faces and heard the frightened tremors in their voices. To make matters even worse for him, Bej, like everyone else, was eager to speak about the strange happenings in the meadow.

"What do you think is out there? I've heard that it's a pack of rabid bobcats from Igit, but Pefil swears it to be a

huge black snake with wicked yellow eyes. She claims she's
even seen it too, but you know how she jabbers," Bej had
said over dinner, her big green eyes shining with the thrill
of all the new gossip going about.

"Oh, I'm sure it's nothing," Ono had replied and fought to
keep his ears from wilting. He felt horrible for hiding
something from her, but Ezquit had cautioned him not to talk
about it and he didn't want to frighten her with such news.
"And whater it is, it will probably move on... I hope," he
had said, then gave her his best smile and squeezed her
hand. "But why should we be discussing such scary things at
a time like this? This is our first joining! Let's make
plans for many more of them!"

"Oh! You're right Ono, let's do that!" Bej had giggled
and clapped her hands happily.

Ono had laughed and smiled along with her, but his laugh
was forced and awkward, and his smile strained and unsteady.
Later that night when he walked her back to her burrow she
had kissed him again, but even that too was denied its
charm, and Ono had waddled home feeling nervous, frightened,
and horribly guilty.

CHAPTER TWENTY TWO

On this morning, some three days after his date with Bej had come and gone, Ono awoke just as the sun rose over the mountains with a protestingly empty stomach. Yawning and stretching his arms, he sat up in bed and lit the candle beside him. Still groggy, he stood up out of bed and shuffled across the den to the far corner where he kept his supply of food to grab a bite of breakfast, not bothering to put on a robe.

But when he managed to open his sleepy eyes enough to see by the candle's dim, flickering light, all he saw was a bare fern leaf spread out on the floor before him with a few scattered crumbs left on top of it.

As if annoyed at him for having eaten all the food he had tucked away, Ono's stomach gurgled and bubbled and cramped, and he grumbled right back down at it, for he did not care to go gathering until Ezquit declared the forest once again safe to travel through. "Snakes.." Ono mumbled, for a gnome's stomach is not a thing to be ignored, and he knew that he would have to find something to eat to quiet its rumblings.

So, quite grumpily, Ono dressed and picked up his gathering pouch off the floor, then tucked his wand into his sash and blew out the candle. When he pushed the bark aside and popped his head up from the ground, he waited much longer than he normally did before leaving. Wary of the forest and reluctant to leave the safety of his burrow, he listened to the woods around him with tall ears and scanned along the trees and brush with squinted, suspicious eyes.

It was a typical spring time morning, with the dew still light and fresh on the crisp green leaves, and the sky above clear and alight with the sun's early rays. The usual forest noises could be heard as the morning breeze swayed the tree limbs and waking birds began their whistling and chirping.

After a time of watching and listening, Ono hopped out of his tunnel and waddled quietly through the bushes and out in to the forest. Too wary to whistle, he hummed a light tune as he made his way down the mountain side to check on a new blackberry vine that had sprouted up the year before along the creek. Seeing no other gnomes as he went, Ono climbed down a mossy scarp and ducked through a grove of thistles, then walked the rest of the way down the mountain through the underbrush. By the time he arrived at the creek some time later, his stomach was more than ready for breakfast, and he hoped that the berries were beginning to ripen.

When he pushed through the ferns and began tiptoeing care-fully around the prickly vines that snaked and looped across the ground to check beneath their rough leaves though, all he found were hard, tight little green balls. Disappointed and hungry, Ono huffed and snapped his fingers, then walked off again in search of breakfast.

He was nearing a bend in the creek where he knew there to

be a reliably stocked redberry bush when he heard a faint,
guttural rumble far in the distance behind him.

Rummmbabababum.

It picked up and died out almost as quickly as it started,
but it was enough to give Ono goose bumps along his arms and
set his heart thudding against his ribs. Wordlessly cursing
his insistent stomach for making him venture outside his
burrow, he quickly scurried into the shadow of an overhang-
ing slab of stone and listened for the sound to come again
with twitching, alert ears.

As he stood there crouched and nervous, he had a dreadful
recollection that this was the same fashion in which he had
encountered the humans only several days before. It's them
again! Oh snakes! They're back, I know it! he thought and
began to tremble with fright.

Rummmbabababum, the throaty sound came and went again.

Ono's ears cocked up and forward towards the top of Boulder Mountain where the noise seemed to be traveling over
from the meadow. He listened to the disturbing sound repeat
itself several more times, all in short bursts, until suddenly the noise erupted into a continuous gurgling roar as
ugly and alien as any sound could ever be.

Rumrumrumrumrumrumrum.

The sound was not anything like the ones Ono had heard the
two humans in the meadow make, but was instead a deep, pene-
trating rumble that almost seemed to vibrate the very air

that it flowed through. Looking out from the shadows at the forest around around him, Ono saw several other gnomes poke their heads up from the ground and out of knotholes to see what was making such a ruckus. Even the birds in the branches and the chipmunks on the logs stopped their whistling and chittering to turn their heads to the side and listen.

Rumrumrumrumrumrumrum, the sound continued to come over the mountain.

Ono wrung his hands together and worried over being away from his burrow when something that could make such a noise was within hearing distance. Ohh! This hiding place will not do! Not at all! he thought as he pulled out his wand and prepared to make a run for it back to his burrow.

But before he could force himself to flee, he looked down at the wand in his hand and had a thought slip through his mind about his father's grave that worried him horribly. I wonder what's going on over there, and what could they be doing? Oh! I hope they're not disturbing him! They better not be! he thought, then pictured an ugly human bending down and pounding a wooden stake into Proi's grave with its huge bludgeon, making its sharp Clack! Clack! Clack!

The thought of such an awful thing made Ono's stomach cramp as if it was Proi himself being impaled by the stake, for ever since Ono was a wee youngster all he had ever known of him was his grave.

No, surely they couldn't do such a thing! But perhaps I

should go and check to make sure? Oh! Ono wondered and
whined as the steady rumrumrumrum continued to rumble and
gurgle from the direction of the meadow. His gnomish nature
told him to scurry off and hide, but the urge to run to the
top of the mountain and make sure his father's grave wasn't
being desecrated by whatever was over there left him worried
and undecided.

A few moments later, several of the gnomes who had popped
their heads up to listen to the strange noises were even
further bewildered about what was going on when they suddenly saw Ono go running up the hillside towards the bizarre
sounds.

Well, since he's going to go see what that horrid racket
is, I suppose I don't need to go as well. Two eyes are as
good as four on any day! most of them thought before quickly
ducking back down into their burrows.

CHAPTER TWENTY THREE

Two brown birds launched themselves from the underbrush in an explosion of flapping wings and startled squawks as Ono came running between them up the mountain side. On his sweaty face was an alarmed, distressed look with wide worried eyes, for whatever it was that was on the other side of the mountain did not sound amiable in the least bit of way.

The throaty rumrumrumrum noise was loud and potent in the crisp morning air, and as he ran further up the slope several other sounds began to mix with it, creating a grotesquely cacophonous racket. There was a shrill and insistent Reeneeneeeeen! and a splitting, monotonous beep-beep-beep that pierced through the air like arrows. Beneath it all was a dull but rapid clunkclunkclunk that could hardly be discerned through the rest of the ruckus.

To Ono's ears, the sounds were huge and monstrous, like things heard in a nightmare on the deepest, darkest of nights.

There was also a faint, pungent odor that drifted into his nostrils as he ran, one that smelled both sour and musky. Like the noises that accompanied it, the rank stench was completely unnatural and horrid, growing worse as he neared them.

Almost panicked with worry, Ono continued running, nearly to the top of the mountain now. There was an outcropping of mossy granite that he had to hurry around as the ground began to level, and as he passed by it he heard Ezquit's voice yelling out to him over the loud noise, "Ono! Where do you thing you're going? Go back to your burrow! Now! And at this very moment!" he screamed.

Ono stopped in his tracks, surprised by the angry tone of his voice, then looked back over his shoulder at him. Ezquit had been sitting among the clumps of stone, looking old and exhausted and horribly ashen-faced. He wore his usual green robe and brimmed cap, and was leaning forward on his walking stick. Ono couldn't see it from where he stood, but on the ground at Ezquit's feet was a splash of watery vomit.

"Turn around Ono! Now I say!" Ezquit yelled again, looking at him with a troubled, red-rimmed pair of eyes and frowned brows.

Ono's ears wilted just at the sight of him, for he knew that whatever was happening in the meadow must be hideously awful to make him look such a way. "I want to make sure they're not disturbing him first! That's all!" Ono yelled back at him in a high tremoring voice and pointed towards the meadow.

Ezquit shook his head angrily, making his long beard sway from side to side, then stood up suddenly. "No Ono! You do not need to see this! We are leaving! Proi is passed away and gone, and it does not matter what they do to his grave!" he shouted back and pointed his walking stick down the mountain with an angry thrust of his arm.

Stunned by Ezquit's words and manner, Ono just stood there agape for a moment, not sure of what to do. The sounds and smells around them were loud and thick, drowning out everything else in the forest.

Ezquit thrust his walking stick down the mountain once more. "Come Ono! You and I are leaving!" he yelled, then began to hurry towards him, intent on dragging him away if that was what it took to keep him from seeing such a thing. But before he could reach him, Ono quickly turned and darted off into the underbrush. "Ono! No! Come back here!" Ezquit yelled as he hobbled after him.

Ono didn't hear his cries, for as he ran through the undergrowth he was almost deafened by the harsh sounds that reverberated up the slope and filled his ears.

Rumrumrumrumrumrumrumrumrumrum

Beep!-Beep!-Beep!-Beep!-Beep!

Reeeneeeneeneeeen-Eeeeeeeen!

Clunkclunkclunkclunkclunk

The dense gaseous stench was sickening, and it seemed to hang in the air like a flatulent cloud, saturating and polluting.

Ono crested the mountain's ridge, running through ferns, brush, branches, leaves, grass, and shrubs that all rushed past him, slapping his face and arms as he hurried through them. Then he burst through a wall of weeds and suddenly the forest opened up, giving him a clear view of the meadow below. When he saw what was happening, Ono gasped in terror and froze, too shocked to move.

The construction crew and their giant pieces of orange e-quipment looked like a pack of alien monsters, ones far worse than he could have ever imagined.

He saw several bulldozers pushing across the meadow, the tall grass toppling over and then disappearing into the churning mass of earth they pushed along with their giant blades. The tracks on the bulldozers ripped into the ground, running over everything in the way and trailing bare, ragged earth in their wake.

Clunkclunkclunkclunk

Their exhaust pipes, looking like giant horns to Ono, spewed out black clouds that puffed and mushroomed high up into the air in hellish bellows.

Rumrumrumrumrumrumrum

There were also several backhoes working among them, their booms extending out like giant scorpion tails with the claws of their buckets sinking into the earth and tearing away massive chunks of ground that left yawning craters where lush grass once grew.

Beep!-Beep!-Beep!-Beep!

A scattered crowd of humans walked busily among the equip-ment swinging pickaxes and thrusting shovels and yelling to one another. Several of them wielded chainsaws at the small-er trees that grew in the meadow, and Ono let out a low,

pitiful groan as he watched them reduce a beautiful willow
to a gnarled stump with only a few swipes of their blades.

Reeeneeeeneen-Eeeeeen!

The brutal sight of the meadow being massacred by such
monsters made Ono sway on his feet, dizzy with shock. An
eternity seemed to pass for him within those next few moments as he watched them destroy everything within reach in
a sort of dreamy, detached sort of way. He heard the sounds
of the machinery and the humans calling to one another, but
they sounded more like echoes, far and distant. He didn't
smell the pungent odor of diesel exhaust, because he didn't
breathe.

There is no telling how long he would have stood there at
the top of the mountain petrified and numb with fear, because some time later he was snapped from his trance when
he saw a bulldozer suddenly spin in its tracks and head a-
cross the meadow towards the oak tree marking his father's
grave. The colossal machine, which Ono thought was a live,
nightmarish creature, circled once around the old oak and
stopped before it. Then its front blade lowered and tilted
downward, the sun winking off its sharp edges.

"...No! Please, no!" Ono screamed when he saw the bulldozer's tracks dig into the earth and begin to push forward.
Not thinking about what he was going to do once he got down
there, he pulled out his wand and made to run down the hillside. But before he could get more than two steps, there was

a strong pair of arms locked around him like steel cords
holding him back.

"Ono! Listen to me! We must leave!" Ezquit shouted in his
ear as he struggled to keep his grip around Ono, who thrashed and kicked and squirmed violently.

"Snakes to you! Now let me go! Now!" Ono screamed back at
him. Although he had always loved Ezquit dearly for practically raising him since Proi had died, Ono couldn't have
hated him more at that very moment. He snapped his head back
to try and headbutt him in the face, kicked his legs behind
him to buckle his knees, and bit at his arms that pinned his
own to his sides, all in trying to get loose so he could
somehow stop the horrid beast from desecrating his father's
grave.

Down in the noisy meadow, the bulldozer charged the oak
tree and rammed its blade against its trunk. Its limbs shook
and shuddered, dropping leaves to the ground like green con-
fetti. For a brief moment the bulldozer and the tree seemed
to come to a standstill, and Ono had a flicker of hope that
the oak was the stronger of the two.

But then the bulldozer let out a guttural roar and sent a
soot-black cloud of smoke shooting from its horn. Then its
tracks spun and caught in the dirt, and it slowly began to
push forward.

"No! Go away! Please don't! Please, no!" Ono screamed at
the orange monster, still fighting to get away from Ezquit's

grip.

The oak continued to lean away from the bulldozer as the muffled ssssnap! of roots breaking beneath the earth began to sound. Then, with one final push, the oak tree toppled o-ver and hit the ground with a crunching of broken limbs and a pluming cloud of dust.

Tears poured from Ono's eyes and his screams faded off in to long, agonized sobs as two humans with chainsaws casually walked over and began to sink their blades into the oak's side, sending up chips of sawdust as they lopped off branch-es. Having done its job, the bulldozer spun in its tracks and began searching for another victim.

"Nooo... please.. " Ono whimpered one last time and slowly went limp in Ezquit's arms, all the fight having been drained out of him.

"Come Ono, there is nothing we can do here," Ezquit said gently and then began dragging him away through the under-brush as the massacre continued.

CHAPTER TWENTY FOUR

A community meeting was called later in the afternoon by way of several shouters who hurried along through the forest. "Everyone! Come along! Come along! Ezquit said to meet around the big stump by the creek! It is urgent!" they yelled out through their cupped hands.

The faint gurgling rumbles were still sounding from over the mountains, and those that heart the shouters were quite reluctant to leave the safety of their burrows. But they all hurried towards the big stump as quickly as they could anyway, each hoping for some kind of relieving news but certainly not expecting any.

As the anxious crowd grew around the ragged, overgrown stump, Ono sat slumped and crumpled at the foot of a tree a short distance away. He watched the gathering crowd through dull watery eyes, for he was still too shocked at what he had seen to react in any reasonable way. His cap sat askew on his head, and his father's wand was still clutched in his hand. He said nothing and wasn't noticed, because the crowd of gnomes were busy whispering and murmuring among themselves as they waited for word from Ezquit. Many fingers were pointed at the top of the mountain where the ghastly sounds were coming, as were many pairs of suspiciously wary eyes.

Within the assembly there were quite a few familiar faces, and some others that were less so. Igit stood nervously clutching Corq's hand and whispering discretely to Pefil, while Corq, looking his normally disheveled self, peered over the heads of everyone else as if he were searching for someone. Old Koilli seemed to be eavesdropping as she sat on an overturned basket near the center of the crowd, her wrinkled ears flicking this way and that towards all the different conversations. Even Brufit who lived far down the creek had hiked up to hear what was to be said about the strange ruckus. He stood beside the stump with his arms folded over his belly and an angry frown on his face.

Others pushed through the surrounding brush and trickled into the clearing from all directions for the next several minutes, and one of the last to arrive was Bej, looking both frightened and confused. She wore a faded brown dress and her dark hair had been pulled hastily back into a tail.

She stopped and scanned the crowd several times before spotting Ono sitting at the base of the tree on the outskirts of the assembly. "Oh, thank goodness! Ono!" she cried out, then hurriedly waddled over to him. "I've been so worried about you dear! I rushed over to your burrow this morning when these scary sounds started, but you were gone. I was frightened!" she said as she neared. Then Bej saw how horribly dreary he looked sitting there all alone, and she gasped behind her little hand. "Ono? Are you alright?" she asked and sat down beside him, taking his hand in hers. It was clammy and weak and cold.

Before Ono could answer her though, if indeed he had been able to at the time, Ezquit was standing atop the stump above the crowd, smacking his walking stick between his feet to get everyone's attention. "Hear me! Hear me I say!" he cried and held his arms up as the whispers and murmured chatter quickly died out. In the brief moment of silence that followed, the alien noises pouring over from the meadow were eerily vivid and near, causing several gnomes to shiver and shift uncomfortably on their feet.

Ezquit lowered his arms and looked solemnly down at the crowd below, his grimace showing even behind his thick beard and his ears flaccid and wilted on the brim of his cap. "My good friends! I have gathered you here today to bring you dire and horrid news. I have always hoped this day would not come again for me in all my life, but it has, and there is nothing any of us could do to change it. But we all must remember-"

He was cut off suddenly by Brufit, who stomped his foot impatiently and wrinkled his ugly face. "Oh get on with it already! Enough with the jabbering, tell us what's making that hideous noise! I cannot take a peaceful nap because of it!" he squawked belligerently, causing a noisy ripple of agreements to spread throughout the crowd.

While Ezquit was once again raising his arms and smacking his walking stick against the stump for silence, Bej and Ono still sat side by side, hand in hand.

"You didn't go over the mountains did you? Was that where you were this morning?" she asked in a whisper, for she had never seen him look so troubled.

Ono's large gray eyes were misty and red, and he glanced over at her for only a moment before looking away towards the crowd again. Saying nothing, he nodded his head somberly and squeezed her hand with a tremulous grip.

In his mind Ono kept hearing the sickening sssnap! playing over and over again as the old oak fell to the ground, being pushed down by the giant orange monster. Then he saw the humans working their screaming blades into the tree, their booted feet stomping and trampling all over his father's grave. He was so angry and hurt that all he could do was grit his teeth and squeeze his eyes shut, for he did not want Bej to see him cry.

Noticing his pain, she politely looked away towards the crowd. She had many questions about what was happening in the meadow, but thought it better to wait for Ezquit to explain.

"Quiet! I will tell you what I have seen with my very eyes if you will just silence yourselves!" Ezquit shouted. The restless crowd quieted once more, and their tall twitching ears perked up and cocked towards him as if in salute, waiting expectantly.

He sighed heavily and dropped his gaze to his feet, all but his beard hidden behind the brim of his cap. "The noises are being made by a pack of humans and their horrid beasts. They have come here and they're destroying the meadow as we speak," he said with little strength in his voice. As if to put a frightening emphasis on his words, a rather long and powerful Rummmm! came over the mountain as a bulldozer's throaty engine was revved.

The crowd recoiled and gasped in unison like they had suddenly been splashed in the face with cold water. Several shrill screams were cried out in terror. Panic seized the assembly, and the frightened gnomes began to jostle and squawk at one another as they started to hurry off towards their burrows to hide, bumping and pushing.

"Wait! Do not leave! There is still more to be said! Calm yourselves and be still!" Ezquit was shouting over the noise and waving his arms, fighting to get control of the crowd once again.

The only one who seemed not to be affected by the sudden uproar was Ono, who hadn't yet spoken so much as a single word, nor reacted in any way to the commotion before him. He just sat, steadily blinking his watery eyes like he was having a troubling daydream.

Beside him, Bej's pretty face was pale and taut, and her ears sagged and trembled in terror. She turned her head and looked at him. "Is it true Ono? Are there really humans over there?" she asked in a high quivering voice, sounding as if she were close to panic herself.

After a long moment filled with Ezquit's cries for order and nervous chatter of shaken gnomes, Ono said, "It is. I saw them and their beasts destroying everything. They even pushed over the tree at my father's grave... " he trailed off. Although he kept his gaze forward towards the calming assembly, Bej still saw the tear slide down along his nostril and run into the light hairs of his beard.

"Oh goodness," she whimpered, remembering all the horrid tales she had heard about the humans. Like everyone else, she had the sudden urge to run into the underbrush and hide. But Ezquit had just managed to calm the crowd once more and she thought it best to listen to what he had to say. She squeezed Ono's hand again, this time with a clammy grip of her own.

"It is important that we stay calm! We must! If we just run about in a panic, then we are sure to be found out by the humans and killed!" he shouted from the stump's platform.

The crowd finally got a hold on themselves somewhat, although nervous weeping could be heard among them as they looked desperately up at Ezquit for some kind of guidance. Even Brufit, as stubborn as he was known to be, stared up at him with an anxious look on his red face.

"As some of you may know, I have been placed in this predicament before," he began, holding up an authoritative finger in front of his pained face. Now that the news had been broken his voice had found some if its old strength. "And I, as well as a few others of you, know what **their** kind is capable of." He pointed the finger at the top of the mountain, and every wide, nervous eye followed its guide to where the ugly sounds were coming from. He let them listen to the throaty rumrumrums and piercing beep-beep-beeps for a moment before pulling their attention back to himself. "As sad as it makes me to say this, we must flee this land immediately, to somewhere far away. Preferably by tomorrow morning and none the later... They're just too close," he said solemnly.

Many heads and caps were bowed in fear and defeat throughout the crowd when this was said, for most had spent their entire lives there and were loathe to abandon such a beautiful land. Some even cried, scared both of the humans and the idea of venturing out into an unknown world. For a gnome, each prospect was a dire one.

But their fear of the humans was terrible, and they could think of no other alternative.

Ezquit continued talking for some time, giving various instructions and explaining that only the most cherished of possessions should be taken along so their passage wouldn't be slowed by heavy baskets and pouches being dragged across the ground. Everyone listened intently, earnestly planning on following his advice, for he was the wisest and eldest, as his flowing beard declared.

Everyone, that is, except for Ono. He was angry beyond anything he had ever experienced and hardly heard Ezquit's words at all. His face had turned as red as a ripe berry, and his little fists were squeezed into tight, trembling white-knuckled balls. All he could think about were the humans and their giant beasts desecrating his father's grave and then running him out of his own land, the only place he had ever known, to someplace unfamiliar and far away. He heard the snap of the roots, the beast's roar as it pushed, then the shrill saws as the humans began cutting.

And all of a sudden, he couldn't take it anymore.

Ezquit was in the middle of giving the vague, uncertain instructions of what direction he thought it best for them to leave in when Ono suddenly stood up and yelled out in his shrill voice, "No! I will not!"

Already put on edge by the day's events, the crowd flinched when they heard this and turned to stare at him with looks of utter bewilderment. Bej was especially confounded by Ono's odd outburst because he had never been one to lose his temper, and she sat looking up at him with her mouth hung open in surprise.

It was silent for a long moment while everyone stared at him, for they had never before seen Ono red-faced and enraged like he was just then. Up on the stump, Ezquit's scraggly eyebrows bent together. "You.. ? Wait, what?" he puzzled and cocked his ears towards him.

Ono huffed and angrily stomped his foot. "You heard me! I am staying right here!" he shouted and pointed his finger at the ground with a jab, as if to declare the exact spot that he would be staying.

There were several surprised gasps, and a ripple of murmurs went through the crowd. Even though terribly horrid things were happening just over the mountains as they stood there helplessly, the small assembly couldn't help but lean forward, gnomishly intrigued by the disruption. Looking like a group of spectators, their attention then shifted to Ezquit.

He shook his head and leaned forward on his walking stick. "That is more than ridiculous Ono. You can't, the humans are taking over the land! You saw what they were doing! No, you must flee if you value your life at all, as the rest of us here do."

For some reason, Ezquit's words of sense only enraged Ono further, like a gust of wind blowing on hot embers. "I will not! The humans are in the meadow, not in the mountains where we live. And until they have come and torn those away as well I will stay here!" he shouted, then turned to the crowd. "Who else does not want to leave our land? We don't have to give it away so easily to these monsters! We can stay here like we always have! We'll just have to be more careful! Snakes to those humans, we were here first! Let's keep it that way!" he said and looked at the many familiar faces that he had grown up around with watery, pleading eyes.

Not one of them would meet his gaze, but only shifted uncomfortably and looked at their feet as if they couldn't hear his rantings nor see him standing before them. Corq's head stuck up above the rest of the gnomes, so Ono pointed to him out of desperation.

"Corq! My best of friends! I know you wouldn't give up so easily on your home! Let's at least give it a try! It couldn't hurt to at least give our land that! Please! Let's stay here!"

Corq's ears trembled and he shook his head sadly from side to side, unable to look at him. "I'm sorry Ono, I would, you know I would, but the humans are-"

Ono cut him off. "No! We cannot let them take everything from us! We cannot!" he cried and stomped the ground, close to tears and shaking with emotion.

Many in the crowd cringed and shook their heads miserably, for it pained them to see Ono act in such a way. Several others simply turned their backs on him, too ashamed to face him or no longer willing to listen.

The afternoon was beginning to pass into evening, and the shadows in the forest were becoming soft and long. There was no breeze to rattle the leaves, and no birds chirped or sang. The only sound was the steady rumble from over the mountain, and the noise seemed to fill the woods with an ominous tension.

After a time, Ono sighed heavily and slumped his shoulders. "Okay then, alright," he said around the growing lump in his throat. Then he turned to Bej and held his hand down to her. "Looks like it'll just be you and me," he said with a painfully sad smile on his face.

She was sitting down with her knees pulled up to her chest, and she looked up at him with glistening tears running from her brilliant green eyes. "I'm scared Ono... I can't," she said quietly, then lowered her face and began to sob.

Ono curled his fingers on his outstretched hand and brought it back to his side. He felt stunned, and even with the assembly standing just feet away, he also felt isolated and alone. "Oh... " he said as the sting of tears came to his eyes. Dazed, he turned and began waddling away as the silent crowd looked on.

But then he suddenly turned around and pointed his finger at them, his emotions clear from the look on his face. "I hate you all! You're cowards, every single one! Snakes to each of you! You're... " he trailed off as tears slid down his face. Ashamed and humiliated, he then turned and ran away sobbing through the underbrush.

CHAPTER TWENTY FIVE

That night the forest was as still as a painting. The half
moon hung in the smooth black sky above, its pale glow turning the flowing stream silver and the leaves on the bushes
gray. Under any other circumstances it could have been considered a peacefully calm and placid night, one worthy of a
late stroll through the woods to enjoy its tranquillity.

That was where the serenity expired though, for within the
many nooks and crannies of the forest, tucked away in their
burrows, the gnomes of the small community were restless and
jittery and hurrying about. They were up and busy packing
the things they wanted to take with them in the morning and
worrying over what to leave behind, which is quite a difficult predicament for any gnome to be in without the threat
of humans taking over the land hanging over them. More than
a few belongings were hastily put into baskets only to be
taken out again and replaced by another item a moment later.

Frustrated and frightened, there were squabbles and bickering between couples as nerves frayed; tantrums and wailing
from confused youngsters; and slow, steady tears from those
old and alone as they all packed their possessions for the
long journey into a new land. No one slept so much as a
wink, and the night seemed both long in its misery and short
in its lasting, for nobody looked forward to the morning
time.

Ono didn't sleep either. He laid in his bed all night with

his arms folded behind his head and his glistening eyes
staring up into the darkness of his burrow. He still wore
his robe, but his cap was on the bed beside him and his wispy brown hair was disheveled and messed. Occasionally a tear
would pool at the corner of his eye, then slip down his
cheek and run along the folds of his ear before dropping to
the moss mattress.

Far too many thoughts and memories played through his mind
that night for me to describe them all in the painful detail
in which they came to him, but there was much heartbreaking
nostalgia of days long passed. He thought of his father,
whom he knew now in fond memories and stories, but loved the
same in death. Many others had told him over the years that
he reminded them much of Proi, and Ono wondered what he
would do if he were still alive. Would he give in and leave?
Or would he stay?

Pictures of Bej leaning forward and kissing his cheek when
he had popped the big question flashed by in his mind, as
did that of Corq stumbling and falling head first into the
mud and coming up muck-faced and sputtering; Ezquit teaching
him spells, then frantically slapping his robe and squawking
when Ono had caught its him on fire with his poor aim; Nez
leaning down with her soft motherly smile and holding out to
him a steaming mug of her pine water when he was still
little; and Sced and Kei laughing and scrambling away from
old Quibel as he hurried after them with a switch in his

hand and a large mud ball splattered on the side of his angry red face.

The memories brought with them not a single smile as they once had, but only a deep anguish, for Ono knew that in the morning all of his friends in them would be leaving to a land far away from him.

At other times thoughts of the humans would come, and his anger would flare up through his melancholy like a tongue of flame. When it did, Ono would lay there grinding his teeth bitterly and mumbling curses, wondering why they had chosen his land to destroy.

Tears flowed steadily from his eyes that entire night, those seemingly endless hours of miserable darkness.

When the morning finally did come around, it was as equally deceptive as the night was, for it was golden and clear and crisp, the kind that promises a beautiful day and colorful butterflies. The ugly humans' noise hadn't started yet, and the early breeze rattled the leaves in a gentle whisper.

Haggard looking and apprehensive, the gnomes of the forest gradually began to emerge from their various burrows, dragging out behind them baskets and pouches stuffed and bulging awkwardly with belongings. A hapless Corq had an especially heavy load of two full pouches hung on each shoulder and a large basket held in his arms as he stepped out from his burrow in the mountain side and pushed past the ferns concealing it.

"Be careful with those I said!" Igit's shrill voice
squawked irritably after him from inside.

Corq stopped and sighed, for he had been bombarded with
his mate's fussiness all throughout the night and was more
than tired of it. Like everyone else, he had dark circles
beneath his eyes and his ears drooped. The luggage he carried was mostly Igit's clothes and valuables with a few of
his robes thrown in where there had luckily been room.
Everything else had to be left behind, and she was not happy
about it in the least.

Suddenly, he let the pouch straps slip off his shoulders
and dropped the basket to the ground. "I'll be right back!"
he turned and shouted behind him.

"Where do you think you're going?! We must leave soon!
Get back in here and help me!" she snapped at him from inside. She was awfully scared to come out of the burrow and
was still trying to work up the courage to leave.

"I'm going to say good-bye to Ono first! Now get off of
it!" he shouted back grumpily and kept walking down the
hillside.

She protested shrilly, but he didn't catch the words and
didn't care to. Besides, they lived at the bottom of Pine
Ridge, so it wouldn't take long to hike to Ono's home and
come back for her.

Corq did not want to leave his best friend behind to fend
for himself against the humans, but he saw no other way to

go about it. He was almost angry at Ono for his nonsensical stubbornness to stay, for he worried about him much like a brother would. Still, he could not leave him behind without saying something that might change his mind, or at the very least smooth out what had been said the previous night.

He hurried down the mountain side and through the under-brush. On his way he passed several others already leaving and headed east, directly away from the meadow as Ezquit had instructed.

It was a very sad sight for him to see.

Ono of those leaving was old Koilli, who waddled silently along the creek bank, her meager possessions stacked in a basket and clutched tightly to her bosom. Her mate had died many years before, and she traveled alone, her laugh-wrin-kled face slack and downcast. She walked slowly by, her glazed eyes not noticing him in the least. Then she pushed through a clump of weeds further down the creek bank and was gone.

Corq knew that he would catch up to her later on down the trail, but the sight of her lonely departure was dishearten-ing, and he drug his feet the rest of the way to Ono's bur-row, slumped and wilted. When he arrived at the old pine tree he stopped for a moment to take a deep breath, then pushed between the brush and looked down at the slab of bark. He bent over and rapped his knuckles against it.

"Ono? Are you here? I... I'm leaving in a moment and I

just wanted to speak with you before I left, to say good-bye
I suppose. And that I'm sorry about all of this," he called
out and waited, hoping for at least a few words from his
friend. He received no response.

Inside, Ono was still lying on his bed and listening to
Corq with an angry frown on his face and tears running from
his eyes. He was mad at everyone who was leaving the land,
and he didn't want to speak to any of them. Nonetheless, his
friend's words sent knives into his heart, and he squeezed
his eyes shut each time he heard them.

Corq sighed and wiped a hand down his face. "Alright Ono.
I wish you only the very best of luck. But if you ever decide to join the rest of us, I'm going to leave markers behind as we go. All you'll have to do is follow them and
you'll find us. Maybe I'll even come back to visit you if
things here haven't gotten any worse."

Then he stood up and tipped his cap farewell. "Good-bye
Ono, take care my dear friend," he said softly, then pushed
through the brush, wiping his nose on his sleeve and snif-
fling as he waddled away.

CHAPTER TWENTY SIX

Ezquit was the next to stop by Ono's burrow before leaving, but he was nowhere near as subdued as Corq had been,
and he hobbled up the mountain side grim-faced and alone.
Nez was waiting at the creek and was plagued with tears and
couldn't bear to say good-bye to him. She thought his decision to stay was a death wish surely to be granted, and
she had been inconsolable at the notion all night long. She
was waiting with their things for Ezquit to return so they
could begin leading the way into the new land.

Ezquit shuffled through the brush, then began pounding
the end of his walking stick down on the slab of bark, making a rudely loud Crack! Crack! Crack! that was sure to wake
anyone inside from even the most sound of sleeps. After a
moment he relented and crouched down, cupping his hands a-
round his mouth.

"Ono! You may be angry at us all, but you're going to have
to come out and speak with me before I leave whether you
like it or not! I have your wand that you dropped last night
in the heat of your fit, and I will not return it until you
come out. That is, unless of course you feel comfortable e-
nough to share land with the humans without it," he called
down and stood back up, waiting patiently.

After a minute of silence, sounds of rustling activity
began to come from inside as if Ono were moving things a-
round and searching for his wand, which he was sure to be

doing. A short time and a few muffled curses later, the bark was pulled aside and Ono reluctantly climbed out, for in his anger and stomping off he had indeed dropped his wand somewhere along the way. He stood up and looked at Ezquit with his eyes slightly narrowed, as if he were too weary to fully glare at him, then held out his hand.

Ezquit reached into his robe and pulled out the wand, then held it up before his face, turning it from side to side to admire the dark, worn oak. "I believe this was your father's wand, was it not?" he asked with a cock of his eyebrow.

Ono's glare faltered and softened, for he realized that he was going to miss those bushy, wiggly things horribly. He lowered his hand and nodded his head. "It was," he said quietly.

"And do you remember all the good things he did with it? The brave things that no one else probably would have done?"

Ono nodded again, but said nothing.

Ezquit shuffled forward and reached out to put his hand on his shoulder. "I helped look after you when Proi died, because I gave him my good word that I would, but you are old enough now to know better and not my kin Ono. No offspring of mine would ever do such a foolhardy thing as you're doing right now, and if one had, then I would have cast a wretched spell on them and drug them through the thistles to teach them better," he said, his voice an angry quiver.

Ono's ears wilted further and he dropped his gaze to his

feet, for he had never seen Ezquit so mad at him.

Ezquit gave his shoulder a jolting shake. "Look at me Ono! And listen carefully, for I'm leaving now and will no longer be here to help you," he said and held the wand before Ono's nose. "I think this whole mess you're putting yourself in is absurd, but Proi was your father, not I. I could have never found it in myself to do half the things he did, because I thought he was a fool for doing them at the time. Just like I think of you now." He lowered the wand and pressed it into Ono's palm. "But I suppose he would be proud of you for holding your ground like you are. I didn't know it until now, but you're just like him; as stubborn as a gopher when the time arrives."

Ono took the wand and turned it carefully over in his hands, wondering what it was going to be like without Ezquit around any longer. "I.. I didn't really mean what I said last night," he began to say, but Ezquit released his shoulder and stepped away.

"I know you didn't young Ono, and I do not hold it against you in the least. But I must be leaving now, and you must be on your own to fulfill whatever it is you think is in need of fulfilling. If you change your mind about this shenanigan like I dearly hope you will, simply head east. You'll find us there somewhere." he said, then tipped his cap and gave Ono one last jump of his eyebrows and a wink, trying his best to make their parting a little less miserable.

Ono felt none better, but gave him a weak smile and a flick of a wave as he turned around and limped away.

"As stubborn as a gopher I say! It must run in the family! Nonetheless, I will be expecting you shortly Ono!" he called out, then disappeared through the brush and was gone.

Ono tucked the wand in his robe and sighed. Ezquit's words had waned his anger towards those leaving, but they had done nothing to diminish the dark cloud of gloom that hung over his thoughts. Indeed, they seemed to nourish it, for they made their parting only that much harder to accept. In its various ways, the community was the only family he had, and he didn't want them to leave him behind with the humans just over the mountains from him. But he couldn't find it in himself to leave his homeland so easily either, and he felt hopelessly caught in the middle, like a rope being tugged at both ends.

He stood there before his burrow for a time, turning things over in his mind and fighting back tears. Then he wiped his damp eyes on the back of his hand and lifted up the bark to go back inside. He was horribly drained by what was happening, and he suddenly wanted nothing more than to curl up in the darkness and sleep for a very, very long time. He stepped down into the tunnel and was pulling the bark down behind him when he heard Bej's voice, usually soft and sweet, calling out his name in the distance. She sounded choked and ragged.

Ono's first thought was that he didn't want to speak with her, or even to see her for that matter, for he knew that if he had to say good-bye to her it would be the hardest thing ever for him to do. Her voice alone made his stomach hurt something fierce, where it had once only bubbled with excitement. He cringed and swallowed the lump in his throat, but stepped back out just as she came rustling through the tangle of brush. When she pushed through, she stopped suddenly before him and put a hand over her heart, as if it hurt just at the sight of him.

She did not look at all well. Her eyes were red and swollen from the passage of many tears, and her face was pale and taut. She wore the same dress she had worn prior, which was dusty and dirty and ripped at a stitch. It somehow seemed much too large on her, for she appeared feeble and frail beneath it.

She waddled over to him and wrapped her arms tightly around him. "Ono! Please come with us! **Please!**" she cried out as she squeezed him.

Ono squeezed her back, for he knew he was going to miss the feel of her more than anything in the world. He didn't reply, because his chest hitched with sobs and he fought to keep them back.

The two stood there for a time, each in the other's embrace and reluctant to let go, until she finally stepped back from him with a painfully confused look on her face.

"Why are you being such a fool Ono? Just come with us! Why do you wish to stay here when you'll be living next to a pack of humans that will more than likely find you out and then kill you? What sense does that make? To die over land?" she asked, sounding desperate for a reasonable answer.

Ono shook his head sadly and shrugged. "Because Bej, I can't let those monsters take everything away from me. You should have seen what they were doing to the meadow! No, this is my home, all of our homes, and I'm not about to a-bandon it at the first sight of danger. I won't let them have it so easily, what will I ever have if I let them take all of this from me?" he asked, sweeping a hand towards the surrounding forest. He hoped she would understand why he felt so strongly that he needed to stay, but from the pained look on her face he knew she didn't.

"You would have me," she said, then leaned forward and kissed him on the mouth. Then the kiss ended abruptly, and she stepped away. "But I suppose that no longer matters much to you. I love you Ono, good-bye," she said, her voice cracking. Then she turned and waddled off, sobbing into her hands as she hurried away.

Ono could only stand there, numb and disconnected as she disappeared into the underbrush and out of his life. "I love you too," he said quietly and hung his head as he watched her go.

Not long after, the rumbling humans' noise started up again as the construction crew began their day.

CHAPTER TWENTY SEVEN

The depression that fell over Ono was as confining and un-wielding as a stone tomb. He laid in the darkness of his burrow, his mind drifting in and out of consciousness like a steady tide on the shores of thoughts and dreams, occasion-ally letting out a sleepy whimper or wet snivel when painful thoughts flickered across his brain. He tossed and turned in bed, kicked the blanket off of himself when he began to sweat, then pulled it back on when he began to tremble, nev-er once finding comfort.

He saw faces he loved in his dreams; heard voiced he cher-ished echoing in his ears; and felt the happiness of times passed, only to have them fade away and disappear like puffs of smoke when he awoke.

Ono had no way of knowing how long he was stuck in this dismal, forlorn state, but through the thick melancholic haze and darkness he thought he sensed the passage of whole days flowing by as he fought the pain of reality with the sanctuary of sleep.

Indeed, it was several days later that he finally sat up in bed with a long groan, feeling nauseated and downcast and in dire need of fresh air, for his burrow suddenly felt stuffy and humid. He was achy and stiff, but he managed to swing his legs over the side of the bed and stand up. Get-ting dressed in the darkness, Ono picked up his wand and drug his feet all the way out of his burrow, not caring in

the least that the knot on his sash was sloppy and loose,
nor that his cap was bent at the top and sitting crookedly
on his head.

When he emerged from the tunnel he winced and shaded his
eyes with a hand, for he had been in the darkness much too
long and the sudden light stung his eyes. He stood there
for a moment, blinking away the bright flashes that dazzled
beneath his eyelids before the forest around him came into
focus.

It had changed significantly while he was hidden away in
his burrow.

The surrounding woods were not at all like the ones he had
always known, for they seemed empty and lifeless. No birds
chirped or whistled in the branches above; no chipmunks darted over the logs; no deer grazed the shrubs; and of course,
no other gnomes went about their gathering and gossiping.
Not even so much as a breeze rattled through the leaves. The
only sounds were the continuous gurgles and belches from o-
ver the mountains, and they seemed to fill every corner of
the forest with their moroseness.

Although it was warm and bright with not a single cloud
in the blue sky, Ono had never seen his homeland appear so
ugly and empty. So with a sigh and a feeling that matched
that of the woods around him, Ono climbed out from the tunnel and pushed through the bushes, then began waddling down
the mountain side.

Not knowing where to go or what else to do, he simply wondered aimlessly through the underbrush, peering around him carefully as he went for any other forms of life. Once, he thought he heard the faint call of a quail somewhere off in the distance, but it quickly died out beneath the humans' noise and wasn't answered.

Walking down the mountain he passed by several full berry bushes and even a plump cricket sitting on a rock with little more than a fleeting glance, for he was not at all feeling up to a meal of any kind. He stopped at the creek bank where the water still babbled and flowed like not a thing was wrong in the world and stood in the shade of a fallen log, watching the steady ripples and swirls of the eddies. The horrid noise was fainter there, and the damp aroma of moss and ferns smelled good in his nostrils.

His thoughts wondered while he stood there watching the movement of the stream, but when tears began to well up in his eyes he shook his head to clear his mind and wiped his eyes on his sleeve. Then he turned around and climbed the side of the log, grabbing handfuls of moss to pull himself up. When he got on top he stood up and looked around over the underbrush in every direction. Still seeing no other life, he cupped his hands around his mouth and called out in sad desperation, "Hello?! Is anyone out there? Anyone at all?! Can you hear me?!" His shrill voice echoed along down the stream and trailed off.

Ono waited with his hands on his hips and a hopeful look on his face for a time, but no one answered him. He knew he should have expected such a response, but he hadn't been a-ware of just how completely abandoned he really was until at that very moment. Everyone else was gone and not returning, and he was there all alone.

"Ohhh..." he whined dishearteningly and wrung his hands together. He suddenly missed everyone, even old Brufit and his stinging stones, with a terrible longing.

Climbing down off the log, Ono began to wander through the forest again, his feet dragging and his flaccid ears bobbing with each step. He waddled along this way for some time, his attention lost in the gloomy cloud of thoughts that hung in his mind. The usual worries of owls and hawks, bobcats and coyotes didn't come to him, and he wandered through open areas without a thought of caution as he went.

It was sometime much later in the afternoon judging by the position of the sun, that Ono suddenly snapped out of his gloomy stupor to find himself standing before the tangle of shrubs at Bej's burrow. He had no recollection of where he had traveled, or in what direction, or even how long he had been standing there in that very spot.

Feeling his heart sink further down in his chest at the thought of her being gone, he pushed through the brush and walked to the end of the log. He stopped at the screen of grass on weak legs and wiped the beads of sweat from his brow. The acorn flowerpot was turned on its side with the soil spilled over the woven mat, and it crunched beneath his feet as he parted the blades of grass and stepped inside.

Ono had never been inside her burrow, and although he knew seeing it would only make things harder on him, he had a queer urge to do so that nudged him forward. It wasn't gnomish curiosity that drove this urge, as you might have been guessing, but rather a longing to again be close to her in any way, even if it was as futile as seeing her home. Our kind has photographs and letters to satisfy this reminiscent feeling.

It was cool inside, and it took a moment for his eyes to adjust to the darkness. It smelled just like her in there; a pleasantly faint aroma of flowers and earth that had always intrigued him, but now only made his heart hurt. Ono inhaled deeply until his lungs could hold no more air, savoring her scent for as long as he could, for he knew he would not smell it again for a long while, if ever again. Then he released it in a long sigh and opened his eyes.

Bej's burrow was surprisingly bigger than the outward view suggested. The inside of the log had been hollowed out to many feet back, and the den was a long open space with an arched ceiling curving down to meet a smooth, level floor. Several baskets littered the ground, some spilling flower pedals and others various kinds of nuts and berries. A neat bed fashioned from a pile of fern leaves and moss sat in the back, and a bark table resting on four stones stood by the corner. There was a large white feather propped up beside it, and a row of sparkling crystals lined the opposite wall, carefully arranged from smallest to largest.

From the looks of her burrow, she had left in a hurry and taken little but her clothes and a few valuables along with her.

Ono's chin trembled beneath his beard as he tried to picture her there eating supper or going about her daily chores and his knees began to feel weak and unsteady. He faltered, then reached out his hand and pressed his palm against the wall beside him to steady himself, feeling nearly overcome with sorrow.

That was when he noticed the irregular feel of grooves beneath his palm, so he glanced over to see what he was touching on the wall. When he saw the carving he slowly slid his hand away and let his arm drop limply to his side as he stared at it, his face suddenly going slack.

On the wall before him, there was the shape of a heart beautifully carved into the wood, its detailing neither sharp nor fresh, suggesting that it had been there for quite sometome. And carved within the heart, in gracefully flowing feminine letters, was his name. Ono.

After a long while, and with the same blank expression on his face, Ono turned and slowly waddled from Bej's burrow and back out into the lonely forest.

He would never return there again.

CHAPTER TWENTY EIGHT

Not knowing what else to do or where else to go, and figuring that his day could not possibly get any worse than
what it already was, Ono began walking up Mud Hill to see
what the humans had done to the meadow since he had last
seen it. The monstrous noises grew strong as he waddled sul-
lenly through the underbrush, as did the sour, pungent odor
of diesel emissions.

Oddly enough though, he felt not a touch of fear nor apprehension as he went, but rather an unspeakably dreadful
sense of helplessness. Having always been the shortest of
the bunch, feelings of inadequacy were not new to him, for
he had grown up with them and long ago accepted them as a
part of everyday life. But what he felt as he waddled up the
mountain side was far worse than that. His whole world was
being changed all around him by a gang of barbarically savage humans and their giant beasts, and there was not a thing
he could do to stop it but hope to keep but a fraction of
his life intact. Never once had he felt so small and weak in
all of his life.

He crested the top of the mountain, then had to duck and
twist and bend himself through a snarl of blackberry vines
before coming to a tall narrow boulder protruding up at an
angle from the forest floor. It appeared high enough to give
him a clear view over the underbrush and down into the meadow without getting too close, so he began to climb gingerly

up its side.

The humans and their giant beasts had only just invaded the meadow the last time Ono had seen it, and although they had been doing devastating harm, there was still plenty of tall flowing grass left. But that had been several days ago, and little did Ono know that we humans and our bulldozers work quickly and efficiently.

When he came to the top of the boulder and stood up, he gasped in shock, for he was not at all prepared for what he saw below him.

The meadow, and everything in it, was simply gone as completely as if the hand of god himself had reached down from the heavens and wiped it away into a smudge of dirt. Bare, churned earth was all that was left. Several orange bulldozers rumbled back and forth, smoothing out the ground with their giant blades and spewing billowing black clouds from their tall horns. Among them, several dozen humans with measuring scopes and clipboards and tools walked around pointing and shouting indiscernibly to one another.

Beneath their feet and tracks, his father's grave was but a bare patch of dirt that they walked and rolled over.

Ono whimpered pitifully and flopped down on his rump, for it was all too much for him to take in. The day had worn him down and drained him completely, and he was far too exhausted to even cry anymore. So, with his brain feeling like a burned out cinder, Ono just sat there and watched the hu-

mans and their beasts work while their harsh melody of destruction played all around him.

CHAPTER TWENTY NINE

The days slowly drizzled away and stretched into weeks.

To explain what this length of time was like for poor Ono is a difficult task, for it was doleful and bleak. There were no laughs, or pranks, or gossip, or adventures whatsoever to tell about, but only depression and hatred and loneliness and tears. There is little that can be said about this period other than that it seemed to go on and on forever for Ono, as times of misery tend to do, with each and every day seeming to be the same.

Anger came easily and frequently for him during this dark time, and is probably the only thing that broke up the monotony, for such is an emotion not often harbored by gnomes. When it came upon him, he would make it a point to stomp to the top of the nearest mountain red-faced and bitter where he would scream curses down at the humans to die while shaking his little fists in rage and vowing to cast each and every last wicked spell he knew at them before he would abandon his homeland.

But his tiny high-pitched squeals and screams were drowned out by the indifferent rumblings and beepings of the construction crew's equipment, and they continued digging into and leveling the ground unfazed and unaware of his protests.

As time went on though, this seemingly infinite well of anger became fatiguing and wearisome on him, and soon he didn't find it the least bit satisfying to even kick dirt and spit in their direction anymore.

His loathing for the humans and their beasts gradually lost its potency, and it soon subsided to something akin to the pain of a sore tooth; it was always there, pulsing and hurting, but also having to be ignored the best it could, which was not a thing easily done, for Ono was saturated with grief.

As does happen when one becomes depressed for a long period of time, his physical appearance began to reflect how he felt on the inside. Without even realizing it, he went days without eating or drinking a thing, and his face became pallid and sickly. His eyes, usually clear and gray, seemed to cloud over and dull as they sank into their sockets. His modest potbelly sucked in until his ribs were visible beneath his skin. His ears went completely flaccid, and his clothes became filthy with grime.

To the casual observer seeing him for the first time, Ono would have appeared very near death at the end of that period of affliction. And, indeed, this story came precariously close to never being told any further, for he was.

PART TWO

SEASONS OF CHANGE

CHAPTER THIRTY

Perhaps it was a basic instinct of survival being summoned by his ailing health that gave Ono his first moment of clarity early on that morning weeks later, or perhaps just merely a shift in attitude. Either way, when he awoke in his bed and opened his eyes in the darkness of his burrow, he was suddenly and completely aware that he could no longer go on living in the fashion he was any longer.

He felt as if he had been mercifully drawn away from a long and miserable dream and awaken to himself once more, although left feeling shaken and feeble by the grueling experience. He laid there thinking for a time about what he had and was still going through, and almost not believing any of it since the time that everyone had left, for it all seemed too muddled and vague to be real.

After a while Ono managed to sit up in bed and wipe his clammy hands down his face. "Wooo.. " he groaned, feeling a bit dizzy. Then a burp puffed out his cheeks, and the foul taste of it made him shiver. He blew it out and waved it away, then leaned over and felt around for his wand.

"She'ora, therry simosealep," he chanted in a yawn and flicked his wrist. The dazzling orange light flared and flowed from the wand's tip and shimmered through the darkness to the candle. When the wick came alight, Ono shook out the wand and scooted to the edge of his bed as the candle's glow filled the burrow. He put his feet on the floor and rubbed the thick crust from the corners of his eyes while grumbling to himself, for he did not feel at all well. Then he blinked away the blur that clouded his vision, and his burrow came into focus around him.

It was an utter mess.

During those long weeks of deep depression, Ono had neglected his home to the extent of which he had done to himself. There were rotting leftovers of food dotting the floor that he had taken a single bite from only to have disardently tossed aside, not caring for their taste or where they landed. Scattered among them there were more than a few berries, all of them dark and wrinkled and deflated; a whole mushroom cap, shriveled and pale, sat on the floor beside his bed; a dead moth, now only brittle wings and frilly antennas, laid crumpled in the corner; and a light colored beetle was on its back across the den, its legs folded over its middle where less than two bites had been chewed away. There were also several other curious lumps on the floor, but what exactly they were was no longer clear, for most were covered in a layer of fungus.

The smell was an unpleasantly peculiar one, to say the least.

Ono sighed and rested his head in his hands, unable to believe that his life had gone so awry that he would keep such a home. He had never been especially tidy, but what he sat amongst was not the way any self-respecting gnome would live.

Deciding that he was going to have to start anew in his

deplorable situation, and at that very moment, Ono stood up

and searched for his robe and cap. He found them both not

hanging neatly from the exposed root in the wall where he

usually put them, but rather tossed into a pile, crumpled

and wrinkled, beside an overturned basket on the floor.

Bending down with a grimace, Ono picked up his robe and

dusted it off, noting with a shameful eye that there were

blotches and ugly stains all over it. He put it on and tied

his sash, then picked up his cap and pulled it bitterly down

on his head.

At that moment he felt his hatred for the humans and all

their beasts flare up inside of him again in all its malig-

nant glory, for it was them who had reduced him to such an

embarrassment after taking away everything else he once had.

Oh do I hate them! Snakes! I would kill them all with pleas-

ure if only I could! he thought as he squeezed his hands in

to fists.

But instead of throwing the petulant fit that felt proper

to do, he took a long deep breath and let his fingers unroll

from his fists. Then he closed his eyes shut and thought of

the things that were in need of doing both for himself and

for his burrow, which were each in dire need of mending.

And remarkably, after a time the glowing ember of hatred

and loathing he had within him gradually dimmed, as did the

crimson hue of his face.

Feeling somewhat better, Ono opened his eyes and looked a-
round his burrow. Then he glanced down at himself, noticing
that his feet were almost black with dirt. His toenails were
long and jagged, each with its own border of grime curving
beneath them.

Yes, there certainly is much to do, so let's get on with
it already, he thought to himself, then turned and left from
his burrow, being careful of where he stepped on the floor.

Outside early summer was creeping up, and the morning was
clear and bright and comfortably cool. The sun had not yet
risen over the mountains in the east, but its blazing halo
was lighting the new sky with its golden rays. The forest
still appeared silent of life, and an early breeze hissed
through the branches.

Ono came out from his burrow and pushed through the bushes, then stopped to look around the woods, for it felt to
him that he had not seen them through his own eyes for quite
a time. Although the fresh colors of spring had begun to
fade, the trees and brush and ferns all still looked the
same to him. This relieved him, for at least they hadn't
changed while everything else seemed to have.

Ono began waddling down the mountain on shaky legs, grip-
ing and grunting when he had to climb over logs and rocks
in his way, for he felt much too exhausted for such activity. He didn't whistle his normal melodies nor hum his nor-

mal tunes as he traveled down through the underbrush, and
the desire to do so never once crossed his mind.

A short time later Ono arrived at the stream's edge, and
although he knew that there was no one left to spy on him,
he still peered modestly around before slipping off his
clothes and setting them on a stone. "Oooh! Aaah! Eee!" he
shivered as he lowered himself down into the cold water.

With teeth chattering and ears trembling, he quickly
dunked himself under the surface and began to vigorously
scrub his body. He cleaned between his toes and behind his
ears, then gurgled and spat like a fountain while the stream
carried away his brown cloud of dirt in its current. The water was indeed cold, for it was fed by several springs and
the melted snow from taller mountains, but as his skin began
to tingle and go numb, Ono felt his thoughts clear and his
heart quicken in a way that was pleasantly refreshing.

He shook the drops of water from his hair and scrubbed his
beard with his fingers, then pulled each foot up to his
mouth and snipped his toenails down with his teeth. Then he
reached to the creek bank and pulled his robe in with him.
When he pushed it under the water and began to work the
cloth between his hands, thick plumes of dirt came from it
and swirled away down the stream. It took a great deal of
time, but the stains were finally cleaned from his robe so
he wrung it out and hung it on a bush.

It was when he turned and reached for his cap that he

caught his reflection in a tiny pool between the stones on the creek bank. When he saw it he froze suddenly with shock, for the face looking back at him was a dreadfully familiar one.

But it was not his own. The watery face before him had sunken eyes and pallid skin, narrow cheeks and dangling ears. The very sight of it invoked an old and painful memory from when he was a youngster.

There had been quite a crowd of whispering, melancholic gnomes gathered around the burrow that day when a much smaller and beardless Ono had come hurrying through the underbrush with Corq at his side, who had always been lanky and long of nose. The two had been laughing and giggling as young friends will until they spotted all the pained faces turning to look back at them.

They both went quiet and stopped to look at one another, for they could sense that something was the matter and were hoping dearly that they had not caused such concern.

Nez pushed through the crowd, her long dark hair not yet showing a streak of gray, and hurried over to them with a grim expression on her face. "My dear Ono!" she said in a whisper as she came and took hold of his little hand. "I need you to come with me directly, it's importand." She began leading him away, and Ono looked back at Corq, who only shrugged his shoulders and waved good-bye.

The two passed quickly through the crowd, and Ono could

hear bits and pieces of the words being whispered from above
as he waddled by all the grown gnomes.

"Poor child, I wonder what... "

"My nephew once came down with it, and what a... "

"I can hardly bear to think... "

"Make it through? I wouldn't suppose such... "

The whispered words were certainly not cheerful, and Ono's
ears wilted further with each one that he heard, for he was
becoming frightened and confused.

They came through the crowd and to the entrance of the
burrow, which was where Ono lived then. It was dug at the
base of an overgrown pile of boulders located high on Pine
Ridge. The tunnel was hidden by a tall clump of bright green
grass, and Nez parted the blades for him and followed him
inside.

The passage was long and winding and dark, with low, indiscernible murmurs heard echoing from inside. At its end,
Ono waddled out into the modest den that he and his father
shared and saw two shadowy figures standing around Proi's
bed in the far corner. The room was dim, because the two
were huddled around the only lit candle, speaking softly and
quietly.

"Go on Ono, your dad wants to speak with you," Nez had
crouched down and whispered in his ear, giving him a gentle
nudge forward.

Ono could not understand what was going on, for when he

had gone out to play that morning Proi had been blowing his nose on a leaf and waving for him to go on without him from bed. "You go and have fun Ono! I'm feeling a bit tired and in need of a little more rest. But be back before sundown because I'll have supper ready!" he had called after him, sounding his usual cheerful self.

What on earth could have happened since then?

Timidly, Ono waddled across the room with his hands clasped nervously before him and his large innocent eyes glimmering in the candle light. The two limp-eared figures turned to look down at him, and Ono saw the pained expressions on both Ezquit and Mikret's faces. They both shook their heads solemnly, then slowly shuffled past him to leave him be with Proi. As they went by, Ezquit gave his shoulder a gently and reassuring pat.

"Ono.. come.. come," Proi had said in a weak voice. He was sitting up in bed with his head hung down, his face hidden in the shadows.

Ono hurried to the bedside and began to climb up to sit beside his father, but Proi reached out and softly pushed pushed him away. "No Ono.. you mustn't get too.. close to me," he wheezed.

"But why? What's happening father?" Ono had pouted shrilly then pointed to the tunnel. "You should tell everyone out there to go home and be gone! They're whispering frightful things!"

Proi's face was still too dark to be seen, but Ono could sense him smile sadly. "I'm sure they are, but.. don't you worry a.. thing about them.. Ono," he said, his voice sounding hollow and laced with tremors.

Ono's eyes had filled with tears and the tips of his ears had began to tremble, for even at his young age he knew without question that something was very wrong with his father. Frightened, he stood up on his toes and leaned over the bed and grabbed his dad's hand. "Stop talking like that please! And why are you still in bed? Come outside and teach Corq and I more spells! It'll be fun!" he had cried in a tiny pleading voice and tugged at his father's hand, which was dreadfully cold and sweaty.

"Calm yourself son!... And listen.. well," Proi said with as much power as he could muster, then hacked forth a series of harsh, phlegmy coughs.

Ono had stopped pulling his father's hand and wiped his eyes on his sleeve, his ears cocking forward intently.

"I have fallen ill Ono... and will not be here much longer. But I want you to know that I love... you son, and always will." Another fit of coughing ensued, and it took Proi considerably more time and effort to get over it. Once it had, he sounded even more frail and weary than before. He was fading quickly.

"I have arranged for you... to be taken care of, and I... want you to be on your best... behavior, just like it's your own... home." he slumped down in the bed and pulled the blanket up to his chest before going on. Most of his face was still turned away from the candle's glow, but the side of his head could just be made out in the dim threshold of shadows. His temple glistened and ran with beads of sweat, and his cheeks puffed in and out with each labored breath. His ear was completely limp and hung flaccidly down to his jaw line.

Ono whimpered and began to snivel pitifully, for he had never been so frightened, and his sharp little chin wrinkled and quivered as the tears began to flow.

Proi's hand reached out and patted the side of the bed, searching for his son's hand. When he found it he gave it a weak squeeze and didn't let go. "There is no need of tears.. everything will be just... fine, as long as you always stay good... and strong Ono. Love you... my son... " his voice trailed off. As it did, his grip on Ono's hand slowly loosened until it was just a cold weight.

Confused, Ono pulled his hand away and reached over the side of the bed. "Father! Wake up please! I don't understand, what's going on?! What do you mean?!" he squawked in his little voice and pulled desperately at Proi's robe. Not understanding quite what death was yet at his age, he had jerked and strained and pleaded for his father to stop ignoring him and answer his questions, for he had many. As he pulled, Proi's head slid off the moss clumps and lolled lifelessly onto his shoulder and into the candle light.

Ono had cried out in terror and jumped back when he saw his father's face. His eyes were dull and half open and sunken in their sockets, and his skin was sickly pale and almost green. His mouth was hung slightly open, and his cheeks were hollow and sucked in.

It was the same deceased, blank face that was starring back at Ono now as he stood there belly deep in the stream.

He stood there for a time, shocked and unbelieving, not even noticing the cold water flowing around him until the faint rumrumrum! of a bulldozer being started up in the meadow brought him back.

Ono looked up at the mountain where the sounds of the construction crew starting their day flowed over, and he narrowed his eyes angrily, for he realized then that like his father he too was battling a wicked disease. The only difference was that his was a lot of big, smelly, barbarous beast and human diseases that were stealing his life away.

Ono huffed bitterly and perked up his ears, then looked back down at that pained, watery face starring up at him from the creek's surface. He frowned at it, then pulled his hand back and slapped it away with a great splash. Then he reached to the shore and pulled his cap off the stone and began zealously scrubbing it in the water.

As he worked, he promised himself that unlike his beloved father, he was not going to die from his misfortune laying down.

CHAPTER THIRTY ONE

After Ono finished up at the creek, he waddled back to his burrow and made an honest attempt at getting his home back into order. But before he could get much done by way of cleaning, he stumbled over to his bed and fell limply into it, snoring soundly even before his face hit the pillow. Even though he had not done anything especially strenuous so far in the day, the simple act of once again going about his normal business was dreadfully taxing on a body so long in depression, and he slept deep and uninterrupted without so much as a dream to disturb him.

When he finally did awake from his lengthy nap the day had passed nearly into evening, and he grumbled and moaned and rubbed his eyes, reluctant to get up. He could have easily continued on sleeping for much longer, but he knew it wouldn't do him well to keep such a schedule anymore, and he forced himself to get out of bed.

His robe and cap were once again hanging in their proper places neatly creased, cleaned, and dried, and Ono dressed himself carefully in them, for he was stiff and weak. He tied his sash in a neat knot and slid both his dagger and wand in his robe, then picked up his gathering pouch off the floor, which had not been of much use to him in quite a while. When he slid its strap on his shoulder his stomach let out a long empty gurgle, and with it came the first pang of hunger to hit him in weeks. And hit him it did, for his mouth watered at the thought of a long needed hearty meal.

Ono patted his flat belly, not at all liking the firm feel of it, for a gnome without a bulge beneath his robe is considered an unfortunate or lazy one who is either not clever or motivated enough to gather profitably. Oh! This will not do! I will have to find something to eat immediately or I will waste away and be blown off on the wind like a withered leaf! he thought to himself.

And so Ono waddled across his den and up the tunnel and out into the gentle cool of an evening following a warm day. The sun was still above the mountains in the west, but was not far from sinking behind them. The humans had evidently called it a day, for they nor the rumble of their beasts could be heard anymore. The forest, for the time being, was completely calm and quiet.

He pushed through the brush, then headed south across the mountain in the direction of Pine Ridge. His travel was slow as he rustled quietly through the underbrush, for his legs did not yet feel entirely strong or sure, and he feared that if he were to fall it would be quite a pain to get back up again.

After a time he arrived at his destination, and he stopped to wipe the sweat from his brow and to catch his breath. On the steep slope before him was a large round boulder with two halves of a rotting log laying on the ground on either side of it, for long ago the tree had fallen and was broken in two by the rock. A thick green layer of moss had since blanketed the logs, and was also creeping up and around the boulder so that it looked almost like a giant balding head.

Ono reached into his robe and pulled out his dagger, then waddled up the slope to the top half of the log. When he came to it he peeled a large patch of the moss away, then began to stab his blade in the soft wood beneath and pry chunks of it loose. Within only a few minutes of working, he nimbly reached his hand into the hole he had made and pulled out a plump white grub that wriggled and squirmed in his grip.

"Aha! A juicy one!" he said, then smacked his lips hungrily and sat down with his back to the log. Holding the insect like our kind would a foot-long hot dog, Ono bit into its soft writhering body with a wet pffft. Sticky green ichor oozed down into the hairs on his chin, so he wiped it away with a finger and licked it clean. He chewed slowly and contently, savoring the taste of food again and not thinking of any other thing but finishing the entire grub. It took him a while to do so, and while he ate the sun slowly sank behind the mountains and the shadows in the forest began to darken.

By the time he finished his meal, dusk had settled well on the land. He stood up with a full belly and headed off to a nearby spring to wash his supper down, which was just around the mountain, gurgling up from the damp ground amidst a grove of ferns and tall grass.

Ono knelt down beside it and lowered his face to the crisp water and slurped up his fill. Then he stood up and hiccuped into his hand, and was turning to go back to his burrow for the night when the memory of his father from the creek earlier flickered by in his thoughts again. It was not one he often brought purposely to his mind, for it was in no way a pleasant memory, but this time it reminded him in its quick passing that he hadn't visited Proi's grave in a dreadfully long time. Much longer than he had ever gone before.

"Ohh, snakes!" Ono groaned and slapped his forehead, suddenly feeling horrible for being so inconsiderate.

But the thought of the humans and their giant orange beasts prowling what remained of the meadow made him think twice about going. He stood there undecided for a time with his fingers wiggling thoughtfully at his sides, for he wanted to tell his father he was still there and hadn't left him alone, but was also deathly afraid of being on cleared, level ground with such monsters afoot.

Normally, any logical and sensible gnome that valued his skin would have opted to live with the feelings of guilt rather than venture to a place filled with such horrors just to visit a loved one's grave. As of lately though, Ono hadn't been behaving in such a predictable manner.

How awfully lonely he must be! Oh! I have to at least give it a try! he thought to himself, then began waddling nervously off through the underbrush.

CHAPTER THIRTY TWO

For me to say that Ono was scared at the idea of venturing down to the meadow would be quite an understatement, for each step he took was nearly a feat of bravery. As he traveled through the dark forest his mouth seemed to dry further until it felt as if he had sand for a tongue, as did his heart beat faster until it was a steady flutter in his chest. He had only spied on the monstrous intruders from the safety of distance and cover, so to get so close to where they labored each day was a terrifying notion for Ono. But he was determined to speak with his father, even if it was for just a brief moment, and he kept walking undeterred around the mountain.

By the time the meadow, or what it once was, came into view, the sun's last dying rays had disappeared from the horizon altogether, and the stars were twinkling brightly in the dark sky with the moon nowhere to be seen.

Ono stopped walking and peered cautiously out from between the split in two pine saplings conjoined at the base before traveling the rest of the way down the hillside. His gray eyes were wide and alert for the first time in weeks as he carefully surveyed the vast, barren destruction that was just below the slope from him.

The entire place looked like death incarnate.

The nighttime breeze that had once swayed the tall grass like rolling waves on an ocean now only blew dirt across the bare ground and dust into small twisting columns that picked up and died out as soon as they were formed. The earth had been ripped open in giant yawning trenches that stretched off into the darkness, and mountains of loose soil were piled beside them.

The orange beasts were many that night, and they were scattered throughout the length of the clearing, sitting quietly and still. There was a grater parked off to the left, its glinting headlights peering out from the shadows like watchful eyes; several bulldozers were parked in a row directly ahead, their massive blades looking like long, viciously sinister smiles stretched beneath their blocky snouts; a backhoe sat just to the right of them with its boom curled behind it at one end, and at the other was a wide bucket that was tilted up with its teeth in the air as if waiting hungrily for a morsel to be dropped down from above; sprinkled among these beasts were a number of smaller bobcats, and to Ono's discouragement one sat far apart from the rest of the crowd like an awaiting sentry to guard his passage to his father's grave.

Ever so carefully and as silently as his feet would carry him, Ono snuck down through the thick underbrush with his wand held at the ready in a trembling hand. Without so much as a rustle of noise he came to the abrupt border where the clearing met the forest, and he pulled aside a fern leaf to peer out at the lone beast blocking his way.

The bobcat simply sat there with its bucket resting on the ground, its dull headlights peering vacuously off into the darkness.

Ono narrowed his eyes suspiciously at the beast, for he was not at all buying its unaware ruse. Yes! I'm sure that's just what it wants me to believe! Ha! Well, I am not quite as foolish as it thinks! he thought to himself as the tips of his ears flexed nervously back and forth.

He planted his feet beneath him, then clasped his free hand around the wrist of the other to steady his shakes, much like a shooter holding a pistol would. Biting his tongue in concentration, he then squinted one eye shut and lowered his face slightly to peer down the length of the wand. The beast sat a good twenty yards away from him, so he aimed carefully at what he guessed most likely to be its head, which was in actuality the operator's cage. Then, very quietly, he whispered, "Volethir cobaey eni!" and flicked his wrist.

From the end of the wand the air bulged into an elongated oval that slid transparently through the darkness without making a sound. It shot across the clearing, and when it struck the bobcat the shadows around the machine rippled and shimmered for a moment as if it were trapped in a bubble. When the ripples faded, the bobcat still sat there, seeming- ly unfazed by the spell which had been cast upon it.

Ono lowered his wand and frowned at it, for that spell was

indeed a powerful and overwhelming one. When done properly
it caused a body to become dreadfully confused and disoriented for a period of time. He had used it on several occasions in the past; once against a rather mangy-looking old
fox that had cornered him beneath a log, and the animal had
only been able to sway its head from side to side for nearly
ten minutes while slinging sticky roped of drool from its
mouth.

Concerned that perhaps he had recited it wrong, Ono repeated the same spell several times more, always with the
same result.

"Hmm," he puzzled, wondering with a dubious look on his
face if the beast was indeed asleep and therefor unable to
be affected by the spell. After a moment of pondering, he
slid his wand between his sash and picked up a small stone
off the ground beside him. He hefted the rock in his hand
for a moment to get a feel for it while carefully judging
the distance to the beast. Then he pulled his arm back and
threw it with all the strength his weakened body could muster and dove for cover in the shadows. He hit the ground and
rolled onto his side and looked up just in time to see the
pebble arch down through the air and click off the bobcat's
headlight.

Nothing happened, not even a blink.

Perplexed, Ono got up, hesitated for a second, then hopped
out from the cover of the underbrush and into the clearing.

"Hey! Hey!" he called out and clapped his hands before darting back into the shadows.

Still nothing.

Ono took a deep breath and fixed his cap on his head, then
pulled out his dagger and wand, not quite believing what he
was preparing to do. I will just hurry out there, say hello,
then hurry back. The beasts won't notice a thing... I hope,
he thought and gulped nervously as beads of sweat began to
pop up on his brow.

And then suddenly, before he even really realized it, he
was running across the dark clearing as fast as he could,
adrenaline and sheer terror pulsing through his body as he
scurried past the bobcat. Looking like no more than a shifting shadow in the night, Ono darted from behind a mound of
dirt to a stack of pipes, then around a deep trench, all the
while feeling as if a thousand hungry eyes were watching him
and frothing at the mouth.

Although the oak was gone and replaced by bare, packed
earth, Ono still knew the exact location of his father's
grave in the dirt with more of a gut feeling than by any
other means. When he arrived to it he glanced nervously a-
round him, then knelt down and cupped his hands on the
ground.

"Father! It's me!" he whispered as loud as he dared to.
"I'm sorry for not coming in so long, but humans have taken
over everything and I'm here all alone! I'm okay though, so

don't worry about me." A breeze gusted through the clearing
then, and somewhere off in the distance a piece of metal
rattled and tapped. "Oh! I must go now dad! I love you!" Ono
said quickly, then stood up and sprinted off.

He could have sworn he was being pursued as he ran across
the clearing, so when he came to the forest's edge he dove
headlong into the underbrush, crying out in relief at having
made it to cover. Still shaking like a frightened puppy, Ono
stood up and brushed himself off and carefully watched the
clearing for any sort of movement. None of the beasts had
made so much as an attempt to move, much less chase after
him, so he felt a little better knowing that such beasts
weren't nearly as sharp-witted as he had once feared them to
be.

Having had enough of them for the night, he tucked his
dagger and wand back in his robe and turned to leave for
home, satisfied with himself now that he had visited his
father. But then a strange and sudden urge came over him,
and before he could think twice about what he was doing he
spun around and hopped back out in the clearing.

"Snakes to you!" he yelled at all the orange beasts. Then
he made a gesture at them, one considered quite rude and
obscene by gnome standards, before turning and scampering
off into the shadows.

CHAPTER THIRTY THREE

The days that followed dragged by like tired feet for Ono, for it was a period of transition into a new and lonely way of life for him.

To avoid the humans' ugly racket and stench that the daylight hours brought, he began sleeping during the afternoons to escape them. At first it was difficult for him to fall asleep because the roars and beeps of the beasts penetrated all the way down into his den, and he had tossed and turned and grumbled curses at them as he tried to get his rest. Then one afternoon, frustrated and desperate for peace and quiet, he had torn two chunks of moss from his pillow and screwed them down into his ears with the tip of his finger. After that he had no trouble at all falling asleep.

He started waking in the early evenings just as the humans quieted their beasts and left for the day, and as the sun began to sink behind the mountains he would go out to gather in the woods by the pale glow of the moon and twinkling stars. The summer was beginning to mature, and the nights were always clear and cool as he waddled through the underbrush with his pouch hung from his shoulder.

It was the season where all the berries on the bushes were full and ripe, and the insects were large and fat and many; the pine cones were packed with nuts and dropping from the limbs above like giant brown raindrops, and the mushrooms sprouted conspicuously up from the cracks and crevices on

the forest floor as if to present themselves for the picking.

Since there were not any other gnomes or a noticeable a-
mount of wildlife to share in this abundance of food, Ono
reaped much more on his nightly hikes than ever he had done
before. Never once did he return back to his burrow without
his pouch full and weighing down his shoulder. He ate well
and often, sometimes gorging himself out of sheer boredom
until he could not eat another bite. His modest potbelly began to push out against his robe, and he was soon looking
like himself again, although he never smiled, his ears hung
low, and his eyes never showed even a glint of the happiness
that had once come so easily.

Although he was adjusting altogether well enough to his
new neighbors and the changes they had brought along with
them, he still missed everyone with a fierce longing and
would have eagerly given almost anything to see them again.
But more than anyone else he missed Bej, and he often
stopped in the middle of whatever he happened to be doing to
think of her while blinking back his tears. For him, it
seemed like years had passed since she had turned and walked
out of his life, and the memories of her pained him greatly.

Ironically enough, it was the humans and their beasts that
kept Ono from spiraling back into the depression they had
caused, for their bizarre activities in the meadow were far
more than enough to keep his mind busy. Even though he still

hated their kind with a deep passion, he could not for the life of him figure out what it was they were doing over the mountains, and after a time his gnomish curiosity began to get the best of him.

From the top of the mountains looking down, the humans looked like a colony of worker ants, all of them scrambling around busily. It was difficult for Ono, even with a gnome's keen eyesight, to make out in any clear detail what it was they were doing, so over those weeks he began to gradually creep further and further down the slope for a better view of them in the early mornings before he retired back to his burrow for the day.

He was of course frightened at first of venturing so close to a crowd of real living, breathing humans, because in some of the tales he had heard about them he had been told that they could smell the scent of a gnome from far away, and that the aroma would drive them into a wild killing frenzy like that of a pack of ravenous wolves on a rabbit. But Ono quickly learned that like the orange beasts that he navigated safely around on the nights he visited his father's grave, they too were not terribly sharp like the stories had made them out to be. Still, he did not completely dismiss all the old notions either, and whenever a human strolled by his hiding spot at the edge of the clearing they did so with a wand trained directly on them and held in a ready hand.

Sitting quietly in the concealing shadows of the underbrush, Ono saw many things that he did not quite understand nor comprehend as he nibbled on whatever he had gathered that night, the gawking look on his face much like that of one seen in a theater.

He watched the humans lower large pipes into the holes in the ground, then wave at their beasts to push dirt in over them; he saw them swinging picks, thrusting shovels, and smoothing out the earth; heard them grunting and yelling to one another; and when the wind blew just right he also smelled them, which was not at all pleasant, for they were all very sweaty and dirty.

On one of the more baffling of days, Ono had watched with wide eyes as a giant gray beast rolled up the meadow, trailing a billowing cloud of dust behind it. It was not the majestic size of the beast that had amazed him, but rather that its massive, elongated rump was actually turning slowly over and over again on its back like some sort of alien beetle's.

Intrigued, Ono had dropped a half-eaten berry back down in his pouch and leaned forward, squinting curiously at the beast with his ears perked up.

It was, of course, a cement truck that he was watching drive into the construction site, but he certainly had no way of realizing that. The situation quickly got stranger for Ono when several humans gathered around the back end of the gray beast and, quite rudely he thought, fastened a

large hose to its behind. And if that was not odd enough, a
thick brown substance had soon there after begun to flow
down through the hose and plop wetly to the ground in large
glistening piles where the humans eagerly began to shape
and mold them with an assortment of tools.

"Oh! Ooh, ugh!" Ono had gagged quietly into his hands,
for he had never before witnessed such an unsightly and unmannerly act in all of his life. Having seen enough for that
day, Ono had turned and hurried back to his burrow with an
upset stomach and a troubled mind.

The bizarre spectacle only piqued his interests further
for what they were up to though, and after that incident he
sometimes caught himself lingering in the construction site
on the nights he visited Proi's grave just a bit longer than
was necessary to look around a little. The mounds of what he
had taken to be beast dung had been formed and dried into
blocky foundations, and tall stacks of lumber were piled
everywhere. There were blue tarps and tools, buckets and
plastic sheeting scattered across the ground along with many
other strange items Ono couldn't have imagined, and they
were all horribly intriguing and tempting to him.

But he always stayed a careful distance away from all of
those things, for he told himself repeatedly that he would
gather nothing from the humans, for everything they possessed was surely to be as wicked and as cursed as they
were.

Still, his eyes occasionally strayed to all the strange things and his fingers wiggled greedily as he came and went to visit his father.

CHAPTER THIRTY FOUR

On this day Ono was sound asleep in his burrow, laying sideways across his bed with the covers kicked on the floor and his limbs splayed out at all awkward angles. His head was nowhere near a pillow and his mouth hung wide open while he let out shrill, wavering snores that seemed to take much effort to produce. He had been dreaming earlier of uncomfortable things, and had spent the afternoon tossing and turning in bed until the dream had trailed off to a more pleasing one. He could have slept contently for several hours more, but a rather powerful snore abruptly turned into a harsh snort that startled him from his slumber.

Suddenly awake, he sat up and looked around his dark burrow with a sleepy frown on his face. Realizing it had been nothing, Ono grumbled to himself and wondered for a moment how he had ended up in such an odd position before feeling the painful kink in his neck.

"Ohhh.. " he mumbled and rubbed the side of his neck as he scooted to the edge of the bed. Wincing, he turned his head from side to side to loosen the cramp and noticed his blanket laying in a pile on the floor. Well, this is certainly the start of a good day, he thought grumpily. Deciding it was time for him to get out of bed anyway, Ono picked up the blanket and dusted the dirt off before getting dressed. Then he took his wand off the shelf and picked up his pouch and headed from his burrow, rubbing his neck and yawning.

Outside the sky was still a light blue, but the sun was far in the west and the early evening shadows were just beginning to fill the forest.

Ono climbed out from the tunnel and straightened his cap on his head, then pushed through the brush and began waddling up the mountain side to see what the humans had accomplished since he had been asleep. He could hear the sounds of them working as he traveled through the underbrush, which meant he had awoken earlier than he had normally been doing, for they were usually done by the time he came out to gather.

The horrendous roaring sounds of the orange beasts was seldom heard anymore because most had been taken away, but they were now replaced by the screaming whine of power saws and the clapping of hammers on wood, which was just as equally irksome and incessant.

Ono traveled over the mountain top and twisted through the brush down the other side towards his usual sitting spot at the very edge of the clearing. It was a small space hidden amongst a clump of ferns and tall grass and moss covered stones, and once Ono nestled down between them he could hardly be discerned from the rest of the green tangles. He rested his feet on an acorn in front of him and began watching the humans with his usual irritated glare of interest, which was an odd combination of expressions that put both a scowl on his face and bent his eyebrows together in curiosity.

Out in the construction site the workers were cutting and drilling, lifting and positioning, nailing and screwing long planks of wood together that were just beginning to form the skeleton frames in the rows of homes that were being built on the foundations. The workers crawled up and down ladders with an assortment of tools hanging from their tool belts and white hard hats on their heads, while others dragged boards from the stacks of lumber and yelled out instructions to their coworkers and pointed in all directions.

There was a boom-box with a crooked antenna placed on top of a pile of cinder blocks not far from Ono's hiding spot, and from its speakers a hostile and angry sounding voice was attempting to scream over violently beat drums and an electric guitar.

Even though the humans were painful enough on the eyes with their round ugly faces and their ridiculous clothing, the horrid racket they made was far worse, and as Ono sat there he was glad he hadn't taken the moss out of his ears when he awoke, for even the muffled echoes he was hearing were terrible.

The construction crew continued working and building for another half hour while Ono observed them and their strange habits, and just as the sun began its descent behind the mountains a shrill and powerful whistle blew from the far end of the site. When it came, Ono covered his ears and grumaced, for the earsplitting sound was even worse than the others.

But the humans, in their perpetual strangeness, all seemed to enjoy the horrid sound for the brief moment it lasted, because many called out and laughed to one another when they heard it. They began climbing down their ladders and putting their tools away, all of them obviously happy to be done for the day. Then they started trickling out of the construction site, wiping the sweat from their faces and waving good-bye to one another with gloved hands as they walked to their trucks and left. Several walked just feet from where Ono sat, but not one of them seemed to acknowledge in anyway that they had picked up so much as a whiff of his smell. Still, Ono kept his wand trained suspiciously on them and a spell ready on his lips as they went by.

After a time he thought they all had left, and was also getting ready to leave himself, when he heard a pair of deep voiced grumbling back and forth to one another somewhere in the construction site. They sounded as if they were headed in his direction, so he sat back down and cocked his ears forward, wondering curiously why they hadn't left with the rest of their pack.

From behind a large tarp hanging down from the beams of a home not far away pushed two burly-looking workers one after the other. The two had on dirty blue jeans and white sweat-ringed shirts that bulged and strained with massive bellies.

They lumbered over on booted feet, laughing heartily about a filthy joke that I would not dare to write, and sat down on the pile of lumber nearest Ono, making the boards beneath them squeak and moan in protest.

Oblivious to the small pair of gray eyes looking out from the underbrush behind them, they opened up a red ice chest and pulled several cans of beer out. Appearing to be quite parched from the long day's work in the hot sun, they quickly drained their drinks as if they were racing to finish them, then crumpled the cans and tossed them nonchalantly over their shoulders.

Ono had to duck down behind a rock to avoid being pelted by one, and his robe was splattered with beer foam when it hit the ground beside him. Red-faced and angry, he frowned up at the broad backs of the two humans and considered for a moment zapping them both in the ample top half of their rears that hung rudely from their pants. He quickly dismissed the idea as foolish though, and he sighed quietly and wiped the blotches of froth from his sleeve and side. They are just lucky none got on my cap! Oh! Indeed they are! he thought and glared up at them.

The two humans continued to talk and laugh and drink for some time while the sky gradually got darker, and Ono soon got bored with them, for they weren't doing anything worth spying and he was beginning to feel the compelling urge to use a bush. So, quietly and carefully, he stood up and

picked his pouch off the ground and turned to tiptoe off in
to the shadows.

But then he caught the glimmer of something from the corner of his eye, and he looked back to see what it was.

In the dying light of dusk the set of keys that poked up
from the human's back pocket gleamed like beautiful trinkets
of silver, and when Ono saw them his jaw dropped down and
his eyelids lifted up. I have certainly never seen such mag-
nificent treasure in all my life! he thought as he stared in
wonder at the finely crafted ridges and angles of the keys
and the perfect circle of polished metal holding them all
together.

Awe-struck, he stood there staring at the set of keys for
a time, wondering what the ugly creature would want with
such beauty and thinking of how rich he would surely become
if ever he was to possess them.

Then, as if to lure him in, the human leaned over to reach
down in the ice chest for another beer. When he did, the set
of keys slipped out from his pocket and fell to the ground
where they landed almost noiselessly in a pile of sawdust.

Ono gasped when he saw them fall, then quickly slapped a
hand over his mouth, his eyes darting back and forth to the
two humans and his ears tall and trembling.

The one on the left sat back up and handed his friend a
beer and laughed about something, apparently unaware he had
lost anything.

It must be a trap! It has to be, no one would be so care-less with treasure. Now run away you fool! Ono's caution squawked in his thoughts. But the beautiful keys were less than a yard away, and he couldn't quite make_up his mind of what to do. After a moment he sat his pouch on the ground and pulled the moss plugs out of his ears, then slowly crept forward to the very edge of the clearing, his heart beating like a hammer in his chest. Oh! I don't know about this, I really don't! he thought and wrung his hands nervously as he looked up at the two mountains of human before him with big round eyes.

Then Ono looked back down at the keys in the sawdust and swallowed uneasily.

CHAPTER THIRTY FIVE

"Come on Mike, are you serious? You really think your
Niners have a chance at the play-offs next season?" Frank
asked incredulously, then made a farting noise. "Please," he
snorted and took a swig of his beer.

Sitting to his right, Mike nodded his bald head and
burped. "Oh yeah. Let me tell you, that new running back
they have is going to change it all man. They had him
benched most of this last season 'cause they were letting
their starter finish his last year before they trade him to
the Rams. But next season," he pointed a declaring finger in
the air, "-he'll be starting, and the sky's the limit with
that kid. Probably make it to the Super Bowl."

Frank sputtered and coughed out a mouthful of Budweiser on
the ground when he heard this, then wiped his mouth on the
back of his hand and turned to look at his friend. "And you
have done and convinced yourself beyond all reasonable doubt
that such a miracle could truly happen, haven't you? My good
god, all you Niner groupies are stupid."

Mike shrugged his shoulders and polished off his beer.
"Just sayin' it could happen is all. And why are all you
Raider fans so hostile anyway hugh? Have you ever seen your
kind in the stands on tv? Man, all them skulls and horns and
evil paint on all of you. Shoot, I guess I'd be yelling my
head off too if I was so ugly," he said, then crumpled his
empty can and tossed it over his shoulder. "Wanna' get me

another there Frank-o? I'm on empty."

Frank threw his can away also and reached down in the ice chest. Coming up with two fresh cans held in one meaty hand, he handed one off and began drinking. Mike tapped suspiciously on the top of his before he popped it open though, because Frank loved to shake people's beers when they weren't looking and then laugh hysterically at them when foam was spit all over the front of their shirts. He was just one of those guys.

After a moment Mike held the can out from his body and opened it. He was fairly surprised that it didn't erupt.

The two sat on the wood pile for a time in thoughtful silence as they drank. It was becoming nighttime, and the chirp of crickets and the croaks of frogs were sounding in the dark mountains around them.

"So what's up with you and that Sherry broad? Man, she is fine. Don't know how you landed that one. By the way, you still seeing her or.. ?" Mike asked after a while.

Frank spit in the dirt and shook his head bitterly. "Hell no. I'm tellin' you man, I've been having this streak of bad luck lately. Listen to this: first I get the flu last month and I'm stuck running to the toilet every five minutes on our first date. Well, I should have told her I was sick instead of kissing on her like I was, 'cause she came down with it too." He stopped to take a gulp from his beer before continuing. "Anyway, she got all mad at me 'cause she works at a school or whatever, and they wouldn't let her near a classroom until she was rid of it. A few weeks pass, and it blows over right? No big deal. We even laughed about what a bad first date we had. Then, just last week, she came over to my place for dinner."

He stopped for another drink and Mike frowned at him with a confused look on his face. "Why in the world would you do that? Your place is a dump. I don't even like it there. It stinks like feet."

Frank waved a hand impatiently in the air at him. "I got it cleaned up first you genius. Anyway, we were having a good time, barbecuing steaks in the back yard, and she took a liking to Hank. You know, petting on him and playin' with him."

Mike tipped his beer and clucked his tongue. "Hank is a good ol' hound dog," he said.

"Yep, yep he is god love him. Anyhow, I guess poor old Hank had himself a little infestation of lice or fleas, or some little bug thing like that, and they ended up in her hair. Well, to make a long story short, she passed it around to some of her students and got fired. So she blames me, of all people, and won't talk to me anymore," he said and shrugged before taking another swig. "I see it as her loss."

Mike was glad it was dark because he rolled his eyes at him and shook his head. "Yep, sure is."

The two finished their beers and Mike pushed the glow but-

ton on his watch. "Whoa. Dang it, it's almost nine thirty.
Hey, I gotta get goin' man, my wife's probably wondering
where I'm at," he said and got up from the lumber pile and
dusted himself off.

Frank snorted and got up also. "See, that's why I'm not
married right there. I could never be at the beck and call
of some woman. I gotta have my freedom."

"No, you're not married because you spread fleas," Mike
said as he began walking off.

Frank picked up his ice chest and followed after him. "No
stupid! I just told you that I didn't give 'em to her, Hank
did!"

They walked through the construction site without need of
a flashlight because the moon was three-quarters full and
cast down enough light to see by. They bickered back and
forth the entire way, then arrived at their trucks which
were parked side by side next to a row of porta-potties at
the far end of the clearing.

Frank put the ice chest in the bed of his truck, then
pointed a finger-gun at Mike as he dug in his pocket for his
keys. "Hey, how about fishing next saturday? I found a nice
little hole on the river filled with rainbow trout. I'm telling you, last time I went I caught my limit."

Mike flipped through his keys until he found the one he
wanted, then shook his head. "I can't on Saturday. Katie's
got that dance rehearsal thing and I said I'd watch her.

Maybe on Sunday though."

Frank shook his head with disgust. "See? This is why I gotta start finding Raider friends to hang out with. All you Niner fans are too uptight. A dance rehearsal? Man, crap on that."

Mike got in his truck and started it up and rolled down the window. "Hate to break it to you buddy, but I think I'm pretty much the only friend you have. See you tomorrow Frank."

"Yeah, dang it. See you tomorrow."

Mike backed up and began driving off down the rough dirt road that led out of the construction site and through the mountains.

Frank burped and scratched the back of his head. Then just to be sure, he held his hand up to the moonlight and checked beneath his dirt blackened nails for lice. He couldn't make any out. "Yeah, thought so," he mumbled and walked around to the driver's side. Then he reached to his back pocket and frowned. "What the.. ?" he said, suddenly realizing that his keys were missing. Patting himself down and cursing, he looked on the ground around him, then back up at the road where Mike's taillights were winding through the darkness.

"Hey! Stop! Come back! I lost my keys! Hey, I need a ride! Mike!" he yelled and waved his arms. But Mike was too far a-way, and the truck's taillights disappeared around a bend and were gone. "Dang it! Come on!" he shouted and kicked up a cloud of dust, not at all believing his luck lately.

He paced back and forth for a minute, wondering what to do, until finally he stopped and looked up into the starry night sky. "Are you punishing me or something? Is that what this is lately?" he yelled. He waited for a moment and sighed, then stuffed his hands down in his pockets and began walking.

"He must be a dang Niners fan too," Frank grumbled as he went.

CHAPTER THIRTY SIX

Ono scurried through the dark forest with the set of keys
jingling and clinking on the ground behind him. Fueled by
adrenaline and terror, he hurtled over rocks and plowed
through bushes, repeatedly glancing over his shoulder and
expecting to see the two humans charging after him with wild
eyes and hooked fingers reaching out to snatch him up and
tear him to shreds in a rage.

But in the shadows behind him he saw no pursuers and heard
no following footsteps, and spread across his sweat-sheened
face was a big excited grin as he realized that he had made
off freely with a human's treasure in tow. I cannot believe
it! Yes! Serves them right. Ha ha! Right out from under
their big ugly noses! he thought as he hurried up the mountain.

Too high-strung to notice yet how tired he was, he didn't
stop running until he came to his burrow and dove quickly
inside and pulled the slab of bark down behind him. Waddling
down into his burrow on rubbery legs, he set the keys on the
floor and lit a candle to admire his new treasure.

When the flame's glow lit the room, Ono's widening eyes
shined with the dazzling gleams that winked off the keys.
"Oooohhhh..." he cooed in amazement and reached his hand out
to touch them. He slid his fingers delicately over the curve
of the key ring, then down to a large copper passkey that
looked to be well used and worn. Greedy goose bumps prickled

his arms and he giggled happily, for he had never known such riches as the ones he now had.

Further down the ring were several stainless steel keys of various lengths, widths, and styles, and Ono lifted each one carefully in his arms and slid them apart to admire them separately. On a smaller one in the collection there was a word etched in its side, so he turned his head and squinted curiously at it as he sat kneeling on the floor.

"Mas... mast.. ter, Master," he sounded out the letters, figuring that the word must be a very important one to the humans for them to engrave it on such a treasure. "Master... hmm," he said, then shrugged his shoulders and continued fiddling with them and admiring their strange beauty.

All the rest of that night Ono positioned the keys all throughout his burrow, trying to find the best spot to hang or prop them so the light from the candle would wink off them just right. He moved a few items to put them in the near corner, then stood there for a time pulling the hairs on his chin and staring at the keys, wondering if that was the right spot for them. After a while he shook his head though, then drug them across the den and placed them beside the tunnel's opening. He thought they looked well enough there, but then he narrowed his eyes. That will not do! It would be much too easy for someone to come in and make off with them without my knowing, he thought jealously and moved then again.

It took a very long time and a wearisome amount of work, but he finally found just the right spot for them as the morning sun rose over the mountains. After he had, Ono stripped off his robe and sat it beside his cap, then flopped down on his bed with an exhausted yawn. he folded his hands behind his head and wiggled his toes happily, then was fast asleep within minutes, a hint of a smile pulling at the corners of his lips for the first time in over two months.

As he slept the day soundly away, the set of keys dangled from above, hung from a gnarled root in the ceiling like a sparkling chandelier over his bed.

CHAPTER THIRTY SEVEN

Over the next few days Ono kept a cautious distance from
the construction site, for he feared that the humans would
be desperately scouring the land for their missing treasure
and salivating with rage for the one who took it. So during
that time he decided it wise to stay on the far side of the
mountains until the matter had blown over or been forgotten
by them.

He spent some of that time going out at nights and picking
through the forest for his usual meals, but he always ended
up returning promptly back to his burrow to admire his new
treasure. He couldn't quite bring himself to believe that he
had found the nerve to do such a thing as steal from a human, for such a feat would certainly be worthy of many generations of tales whispered in wonder and amazement, and he
found it difficult to part with the keys for any length of
time.

So Ono had mostly laid in bed looking up at the beautiful
new treasure he owned with a smug grin on his face and feeling a satisfying sense of retaliation against the monsters
that had put him through so much. He knew it wasn't an equal
pay back of course, but he felt as if he had scored at least
a minor point against them, and to a body as small as Ono's,
that in itself was a considerable achievement.

Unfortunately for him though, there was no one left in the
woods to brag to about his amazing act of bravery. This was

very frustrating for him, for he felt like an overinflated balloon that was expanding and about to burst with boastfulness.

Knowing that he should wait longer to go visit his father and tell him about what he had done, Ono had tried his best to stay away from the construction site. But on the fifth day he wasn't able to restrain himself any longer, because he knew Proi would have been proud of him and he couldn't wait a moment longer to tell the story of how he had so stealthily snatched their treasure from right out beneath them.

When he left that evening, he waddled up the mountain and peered down into the construction site, suspiciously watching the land below for nearly half an hour until the sun was gone from the sky. Having seen no humans lurking or sniffing about in search of their missing treasure, and figuring that the ordeal must have been forgotten, Ono quietly snuck down the slope. As he came to the edge of the clearing he pulled apart a clump of tall grass and stuck his face between the gap to look out into the construction site and pricked up his ears to listen.

The early night was dark and quiet, and the only thing that moved out there was a white plastic bag caught in the breeze that twirled and tumbled across the bare ground.

The rows of framed houses were beginning to take shape with the peaked roofs, doorways, and windows all outlined

in a network of angled lumber, and the strong smell of sawdust hung in the air. There were now stacks of cement bags,
cinder blocks, fence posts, wheelbarrows, and rolls of black
plastic laying about along with the general construction
rubbish. Judging by the new materials, it appeared as though
the workers were about to begin a new phase in their pro-
ject.

Ono waited for a moment until the plastic bag tumbled by
and faded off into the night, for he did not entirely trust
it. When it was gone, he stepped quietly out into the clearing with less fear and hesitation than ever he had done before and began waddling quickly through the construction
site, his wand held out in front of him. He hurried around a
giant stack of plywood sheets, through a long culvert pipe,
climbed over a pile of red bricks, then turned right and
walked the rest of the way on smooth, perfectly level dirt
that felt strange beneath his feet.

He soon came to the bare patch of ground beside a pair of
dusty old work boots where Proi had been laid, and stopped
with his hands on his hips. He glared menacingly at the
boots and warily poked at them both with his wand, but
quickly realized the only threat they posed was their pungent odor.

"Plah! Phew!" Ono spat and waved the smell from his nose.
He sat down on the toe of one of the boots and set his gathering pouch beside him, then leaned over and gently patted

the ground with his hands.

"Father! It's me Ono. You won't believe this, but-" he said, then sat up and looked carefully around for any eavesdroppers, his ears swiveling from side to side. Detecting none, he leaned back down and whispered through cupped hands: "I snatched up a human's treasure just a few days ago! And from right out beneath them!" he snickered quietly. "Oh, I do wish you could have seen it dad. There were two of them, giants! sitting down with their backs to me, and one of them dropped a whole ring of big, beautiful trinkets right on the ground. Can you imagine?" he said, then hopped up off the boot and crouched down. "Seeing my opportunity, I snuck forward ever so quietly.. " he whispered as he acted out the approach, "-and when I was just beneath the two monsters I bent down and whisked their treasure away without them noticing a thing!" he said and backpeddled, reenacting how he had pulled the keys into the underbrush. He giggled again, then sat back down on the boot and cleared his throat. "That's been all the excitement there is to tell about lately I suppose, other than what's going on here... " he said and flicked a hand towards one of the homes and rolled his eyes.

For the next half hour or so, Ono continued babbling and rambling on, mostly about inconsequential things, for he had been terribly lonely for a long while and it felt good to talk again. Among the topics, he told Proi about what berries were the best to pick that year, where the best log to find begs was, and how well he was doing now. He spoke about the weather for a while and about how warm it was getting, but after a time his words trailed off into silence.

He sighed heavily, then put his elbow on his knee and rested his chin in his palm. "Father, I miss Bej terribly. I try my best not to think of her, but I always do." His eyes watered at the mention of her, and he sniffed through a nose that had suddenly become runny. "Now that she's gone, it's.. it's like there's a part of me missing that I can't seem to find again. And I'm always worrying about her, but I can't think of leaving my home. What should I do?" Ono whined and hung his head down.

His cap slipped off and fell to the ground, but he made no move to pick it up. He just sat in silence for a time on the toe of the boot, thinking and wondering and remembering. Behind him the white plastic bag tumbled by, but he paid it no attention.

After a while he grabbed his cap off the ground and dusted it off, then stood up and put it on. He slid his pouch on his shoulder and dried his eyes on his sleeve, then cleared his throat.

"I'm trying my best father, but I just loved her so much.. .. " Unable to finish, he shook his head and waddled off in to the night.

CHAPTER THIRTY EIGHT

Wanting desperately to occupy his mind so the thoughts of Bej and the feelings of loneliness weren't so hurtful, Ono decided to explore the construction site. For him to do so earlier would have seemed like lunacy, but after stealing the human's treasure the idea was no longer quite as frightening as it once was.

He waddled carefully and quietly along when he first began his snooping, but after a while he loosened up a little and let his gnomish curiosity take hold of him. When it did, all of the depressing thoughts he had were drowned out and quickly forgotten, at least for the time, because there were certainly enough odd items around for him to ponder over.

His first stop was at a large generator that sat on the ground beside a shovel. It was big and blocky and smelled of oil, and Ono wondered what use it could be to the humans as he paced around it pulling thoughtfully on the hairs of his chin. On one side of it there was a control panel with a choke lever, a cracked voltage guage, a primer button, and a pull start. He spent some time fiddling with them, all to no avail or reaction.

"Worthless thing," Ono mumbled and then kicked it before moving on.

Waddling further into the construction site than he had ever gone before, he looked from side to side as he passed by the framed homes. On his way he found several nails that

had been dropped in the dirt, and he discreetly picked them
up and dropped them in his pouch with a sly look around and
a mischievous smile on his face, for he was beginning to
like stealing from the humans.

He went on to see extension cords snaking across the ⌐
ground, power tools sitting on buckets, hard hats that stunk
of human sweat, and many long steel bars stuck end-up in the
ground. He did not understand what any of it was, was used
for, or was going to be, and he felt as if he were a lone
explorer venturing deep into an alien territory.

Further on he passed by a stack of cinder blocks, and when
he did he caught a sudden flicker of movement in the shadows
beside him from the corner of his eye. "Egh!" he squawked in
surprise and jumped back, his wand out and aimed in a flash.

But instead of using it, he hesitated for a moment and
then frowned, for he was puzzled by the blurry figure staring back at him. It was a small and hazy thing, about the
size of himself, standing quietly in the darkness beside the
cinder block pile. "Hel.. hello?" he called out nervously to
it and have it a quick, unsure wave.

The vague figure said nothing in response, but returned
the same hesitant gesture.

Ono narrowed his eyes suspiciously at it, then stuck his
leg out from his side and wiggled his foot.

The figure in the shadows did the same.

"Hmm," he wondered, still not entirely sure of what to

make of it. With his wand held at the ready, Ono snuck carefully forward. As he did, the dark figure seemed to twist
and morph fluidly in the shadows as he neared.

The coffee thermos had been left on the ground beside the
pile of cinder blocks by a forgetful worker earlier that
day, and its shiny surface was a strange thing for Ono to
encounter. When he came to it, he slowly and cautiously
reached out with his pointer finger to touch its surface,
and the hazy reflection before him leaned forward to meet
his finger with one of its own. He tapped on it, and the
thermos gave a hollow clunk.

Ono poked at it several more times with the same result,
then snorted out a nervous laugh and looked around him, as
if to make sure no one had spied him talking and waving to
his own reflection. Seeing no one to heckle him, he shuffled
closer to the thermos and leaned in towards it.

"Blaaa," he said, letting his tongue roll out of his mouth
and wiggle on his chin. Ono giggled at himself and shook his
head, then turned to leave for more interesting things than
his own reflection.

It was when he took a few steps past the thermos that he
noticed the white styrofoam cup sitting on the ground behind
it. Intrigued, for he had never seen such a thing before, he
turned back to inspect it.

The styrofoam cup was short and squat like the ones generally found around an office water cooler, and Ono came to it

and leaned over the rim to peek down inside. When he did he saw a brown, murky fluid pooled within that gave off a strong musky odor that held just a tinge of sweetness.

He inhaled deeply through his nose and closed his eyes, savoring the new smell for a moment. I wonder if it tastes as good as it smells? he wondered after a moment and shook the rim of the cup so the cold coffee rippled and sloshed against the sides. No! Don't you dare even think of it! It could be human poison for all you know! his thoughts shouted back.

He pondered on what to do, then reached into his robe and pulled out his dagger. Leaning down in the cup with it in hand, he dipped the blade in the coffee and brought it back up to inspect it. When the blade didn't sizzle and wilt and melt away like he imagined it doing if it were to be dipped in human poison, he quickly touched the tip of his tongue to it. Smacking his lips and liking the taste in his mouth, he then lowered his face down in the cup and began slurping up the coffee with pure delight.

After drinking his fill he wiped his mouth on his sleeve and patted his belly, then headed off once again to explore.

It was perhaps twenty minutes later that Ono first felt the effects of a strong dose of caffeine. He was in the middle of stuffing discarded scraps of plywood down into his pouch when it hit him like a punch to the bladder. "Ugh-oh," he frowned and put a hand low on his stomach, suddenly feeling in strong need of a private area. Then his heart began to flutter and his body to tingle. He shook his head and rubbed his face in his hands, puzzling over the queer sensation before hurrying off to the shadows where he did his business beside an empty Gatorade bottle with a long, relieved sigh. When he finished, which was a surprisingly long while later, he felt remarkably refreshed and rejuvenated.

Waddling back to his pouch and picking it up, Ono then looked around the construction site as if wondering where to start first. There is so much to be gathered here! But I must hurry before the humans come back! he thought and rubbed his hands together with an eager smile on his face.

And with that, he darted off like a shot in the darkness, his greedy gnome instincts intensified by a powerful caffeine high that lasted the rest of the night.

It would be difficult to explain in any sensible order and detail what Ono did during that time, for he was but a fleeting shadow in the construction site, zipping this way and that as he rushed about trying to gather as much as he possibly could before the dawn came, the rustle of plastic and the skittering pitter of little feet the only sounds to be heard in the night.

When a golden glow finally did begin to rise on the horizon and the construction workers were just beginning to pull up in their trucks to start the day, Ono was dragging a bulging pouch behind him off through the underbrush and snickering to himself. Those humans certainly are fools if they leave such treasures just lying around for the taking! Ha ha! They're all mine now! he thought as he made his way up the mountain side.

Among the treasures filling his pouch was a snapped pencil, a single dark sunglass lens, a dried piece of chewed gum that still smelled of mint, a red soda cap, and a broken drill bit.

CHAPTER THIRTY NINE

The construction continued on over the next few months, and where a lush meadow had once been, a subdivision quickly began to take shape. The framed homes were fitted with windows, covered in siding, roofed, and painted; fences and streetlights were erected; and the streets and sidewalks were paved. The construction workers were still working at plumbing, wiring, carpeting, tiling, flooring, and finishing the inside of the homes, while the landscaping crews laid grass in the lawns and planted rows of spindly young trees along the streets.

Winter, like the workers' deadline, was soon to be coming, and so far the workers were on track to be finished before either arrived.

They no longer had the bulldozers bulldozing, or the backhoes digging, or the bobcats winding about among them, and the screeching beeps and guttural roars of their engines could no longer be heard. Less frightened now that the terrible ruckus was gone, the smaller animals of the forest, such as the birds, chipmunks, and squirrels, gradually and cautiously came back to the surrounding mountains. They were wary and cagey for some time, but seemed to adjust well enough to the humans' presence.

When Ono noticed the returning wildlife he had hoped dearly that it was a sign that his loved ones might come back as well. Hopeful, he had spent many mornings and evenings wondering along the borders of his land calling out in his shrill voice all the names he knew. But to his disappointment his calls were never answered and he eventually quit trying altogether, for it seemed clear enough to him that the other gnomes were not returning. Neither had the larger animals, such as the bear, deer, coyotes, or mountain lions that had once roamed the mountains.

So during this time, Ono tried his best to make friends with the smaller creatures that he had once squabbled with over nuts and berries and bugs. Desperate for some kind of companionship and even the slightest bit of interaction with another animal, Ono had waddled through the forest following them around, trying his best to imitate their whistles, chirps, and chitters in a vain attempt at conversation.

But the birds had only ruffled their feathers at him and the chipmunks growled shrilly, for they wanted no part of him nor his strange antics. Confused and annoyed with his queer behavior, most had quickly departed in their various methods of travel, leaving behind a rather forlorn-looking gnome in their wake.

The most interaction he received was from a little brown mouse he ran across while out gathering among the underbrush one evening. It had sat up on its hind legs when it saw him, then wiggled its nose and squeaked sweetly.

Excited, Ono had crouched down and wiggled his nose and squeaked back at it, more thankful than you could imagine for having finally found a friend.

To his utter disappointment though, it soon became obvious that the cute little mouse had only one interest in him, and that had been the pouchful of berries hanging from his shoulder. Defeated, Ono had sighed and handed the mouse a berry, then watched it scamper off through the ferns with sad eyes.

Feeling as lonesome as ever, he managed to keep himself more than busy by gathering amongst the humans' things at night and decorating his burrow with the items he found. Soon his home became quite a sight to see, for he invested every spare moment he had into it with gnomish cleverness.

He covered the entire floor of his den, which had always been dirt, with thin scraps of plywood that he fitted to- gether like puzzle pieces. Of course, he had never seen such a thing done before, but he thought it would help keep down the gophers, which had on several occasions suddenly popped their heads up from his floor and scared him nearly to death with their beady eyes and buckteeth.

In the far corner was a small table fashioned from a blue slab of tile set on top of a short section of p.v.c. pipe, and beside it was a little wood block that served as a chair; placed on top of the table like a platter was the sunglass lens now piled high with pine nuts; a row of nails were pushed into the opposite wall that served as robe and cap hangers; and a shiny quarter was propped up on a soda cap beside the tunnel's opening with George Washington's stern face looking down the wall at a blue pen cap with snippets of colorful wire shooting out its top like a vase filled with exotic reeds. He had drug out his old bed of grass and lumpy moss, and replaced it with a new one made from scraps of foam and carpet. It was much more pleasant to sleep in than the last, and pinned up like a poster on the wall behind it was a bright red Skittle's wrapper.

Many other treasures that he had gleaned from the construction site lined the shelves in the walls, and almost the entire back corner of his den was piled high with the miscellaneous items that he had no plans for, but certainly had no plans for getting rid of either. Indeed, no other gnome had ever had such an elegant looking burrow than what his had become, and it helped Ono pass the time away, for he enjoyed looking greedily over his things and fiddling with all of his new found wealth.

But although snatching things away from the humans for his personal gain did well to occupy his mind over that time, he always returned back to his burrow completely alone, with nothing more to greet him but his treasures that were filling up an otherwise empty home.

CHAPTER FORTY

On this day Ono was fast asleep in bed, curled up in the folds of carpet like a flea in fur and snoring soundly. His legs were pulled up to his chest in a tight fetal position, and his arms were wrapped around his midsection. The tip of one ear was flopped across his eye, and his little nostrils flared with each breath he took. Occasionally his stomach would gurgle, and when it did Ono would wince and mumble sleepily, then pull his knees up higher.

Even though he was asleep, he was not feeling at all well today, for he had foolishly eaten a pill bug earlier the night before. Every gnome knows that it is always a gamble to do so, but he had been craving an insect horribly and that was the only one he was able to capture. Unfortunately for him, he had been unlucky with his choice of meal, and wicked stomach cramps had plagued him since.

After a time a rather bubbly rumble came from his belly, so he rolled onto his back and cringed. "Ohh, not now," he groaned, hoping the urge to use the bush would go away so he could finish his sleep. But his stomach gurgled again insistently and the pressure grew worse until it was nearly painful. "Ughhh.. " he grunted as he sat up, unable to take it anymore.

Pressing a hand to his bloated stomach and bitterly cursing pill bugs of every kind for all eternity to come, he got up and took his clothes off the nail hangers and dressed. He pulled his cap down on his head, and with his eyes still sleepy and half closed, he grabbed his pouch and wand from the tabletop and hurried towards the tunnel.

When he pushed the bark aside and stepped out he realized he hadn't gotten but a few hours of sleep, for the sun was directly overhead and blazing in the clear blue sky above. It was a beautiful day out, but he could have cared less for it because he didn't feel well and he just wanted to get back to bed and sleep the rest of it away.

With the pressure in his stomach gradually getting worse, Ono whined and waddled off through the brush to find a suitable place to do his business. He hurried down the mountain side as quickly as he could with beads of sweat popping up on his forehead and his eyes darting about looking for a good spot, for gnomes are much too modest to do such things in the view of others.

Nearing the bottom of the slope, Ono hurried around a hummock and saw a pair of mossy logs slanting across one another among a grove of ferns. "Oh thank goodness!" he cried, then began untying his sash as he ran over to them. Feeling as if he couldn't possibly hold it for even a second longer, he quickly ducked into the small space beneath the last log to fall and disappeared in the shadows.

Ono stayed in there for quite some time before finally reaching his arm out and tearing off a piece of fern leaf growing nearby. After a moment he stepped back out into the daylight, smoothing his robe and looking very relieved indeed.

The creek was not far away down the slope from him, and the sound of its gentle babbling suddenly made him thirsty as he was making to return back to his burrow for more sleep. So he turned around and climbed over the log and headed down the mountain side for a drink. When he arrived he knelt down on the bank between two large rocks and drank from the cold water until he no longer could. It felt good in his belly, and when he finished he splashed a handful on his face and stood up, feeling awake and refreshed.

It had been quite some time since he had last been out in the woods during the afternoon hours, and he had nearly forgotten how good the sun's rays felt on his face and how bright the colors of the forest were when not dulled by the nighttime shadows. He took a deep breath and smelled the day's scent, then pricked up his ears to listen to the sparrows' chatter being chirped and whistled from the tree branches above.

Perhaps a short walk and some sun would do me well before I went back to sleep? I certainly do miss this wonderful daylight, he thought for a moment and turned a hand palm-up in the air as if to touched the sun's rays that tingled warmly on his skin.

Ono's new bed was like sleeping on a warm, fluffy cloud, and it beckoned him back with the promise of pleasant dreams and a deep sleep. But although it was warm out, Ono could sense that the change of seasons wasn't far away, and he knew that perfect days like this one wouldn't be around in a few short months, so he decided to enjoy it instead of sleeping it away. And so, feeling much better in both mood and belly, he waddled off into the underbrush, whistling for the first time again without even noticing.

CHAPTER FORTY ONE

Ono felt increasingly better about the day as he wondered
north along the creek. He was in no hurry at all to go anywhere or do anything but enjoy the forest that was left a-
round him, which was something he had not done in quite a
while. He stopped at a cluster of yellow daisies growing a-
longside a boulder, and sniffed each one carefully before
letting out a shrill sneeze that knocked his cap crooked on
his head. He wiped his nose on his sleeve and chuckled, then
fixed his cap and waddled on.

On his leisurely way, he saw a large water snake slither-
ing through the moss and ferns, its sleek black and yellow
scales shining in the sun. Its middle bulged with some unlucky lump, and Ono watched it slither by from a careful
distance and glide into the creek without so much as a ripple on the surface. He had never been one to appreciate
snakes of any variety, but he smiled at it nonetheless as it
swam off down the stream.

Further on Ono came to a berry bush. He pondered for a moment if he should eat anything yet, for his stomach was
feeling well again and he didn't want to upset it. He almost
decided against it, but then noticed that some of the red
berries dotting the tangle of branches were beginning to dry
up and shrivel away, which was a waste not often seen in
lands where gnomes gather. Oh, I might as well. They won't
be around much longer either, he thought, then picked a few

of the finer looking ones and dropped them in his pouch before waddling off.

Nearing the bottom of Mud Hill he slid on his rump down a
small drop off, then dusted himself off and was walking away
when he suddenly stubbed his toe.

"Agh!" he squawked as he stumbled and fell to the ground
clutching his foot. "Snakes! Oh, snakes to it!" he whined
and cursed and blew on his big toe, which was very large and
red now indeed, and seeming to grow larger with each pulse
of pain that went through it. "I was finally having a nice
day for once, and it gets ruined! Oh! I should have expected
as much!" he grumbled bitterly and glared around him,
searching for what he had tripped over. At that moment he
couldn't help but feel glad that no one was around, for a
gnome who stumbles is often gossiped about and labelled as
clumsy, which is a rather hurtful insult to a people who
pride themselves on their silent travels.

But when Ono saw what it was that had caused him to fall,
his eyes widened and a smile stretched across his face. "Ah-
haaa.. " he said and wiggled his fingers, apparently forgetting all about the wicked pain in his toe. Standing up
quickly, he limped over to the sparkling column of quartz
and knelt down beside it.

The crystal was poking up from the forest floor at an odd
angle, and was partially obscured by the thick blanket of
pine needles laying all around it.

Ono brushed them away, then wrapped his hands around the crystal and began greedily tugging on it with all the strength his little body could muster. The crystal did not budge at first, but Ono kept pulling with his teeth bared in effort and a vein bulging in his forehead. "Come on! Come on! Up and out you!" he grunted as he tugged.

It took a moment, but then, as if giving up the struggle, the crystal suddenly popped up from the ground and sent Ono reeling backwards into the ferns. When he gained his balance he held the quartz up to the light to get a better look at his new treasure. In the perfectly formed spear of crystal, the sun's rays seemed to become trapped, and when he turned it in his hands they shifted and twinkled and sparkled within like a kaleidoscope.

For the next few minutes Ono giggled happily as he played with the crystal, completely engrossed with watching the colors inside dance and gleam, its rays of light sliding over his face and dazzling in the reflection of his eyes. But then a squirrel chittered from somewhere nearby, and he quickly hid it in his arms and shot an askant look into the underbrush around him.

"Dirty, thieving rodents," he mumbled after a moment of hearing nothing more, for he had never trusted their kind and was still bitter with their rejection of his attempts at friendship. Discretely slipping the crystal into his pouch and grinning smugly at his new find, he turned and continued on with his stroll.

It was perhaps an hour later that he came hurrying around the other side of Mud Hill in hot pursuit of a white moth, his arms stretched up in the air and his hands snatching hungrily at it. Under any other circumstances he would have most likely captured the savory insect, but his pouch was heavy with gathered items and it slowed him down considerably. He chased after if for a couple of yards more, then slowed to a stop and gave up to catch his breath.

Terrified, the moth fluttered and twisted away through the trees and disappeared.

After getting his wind back, Ono wiped the sweat from his face and pulled a berry from his pouch. "I would rather have one of these than choke down those chalky wings anyway," he puffed to himself and took a bite, sending red juice dripping down in his beard. He wiped his hand across his chin and rested his shoulder against a rock as he chewed.

While he ate his berry he looked at the forest around him and wondered how in the world he had traveled so far without even realizing it. He was on the far slope of Mud Hill now, and from just around the bend he could see a glimpse of the construction site through the trees ahead. Looking at the last two rows of homes on the edge of the subdivision, he pricked up his ears and cocked them forward to listen to the humans' noise.

Oddly enough though, besides the rustle of leaves in the breeze and the occasional bird chirp around him, all was quiet. None of the banging hammers, blaring music from radios, power saws, or electric drills could be heard. Nothing at all.

Ono narrowed his eyes suspiciously, for the humans never left so early in the day.

"That's strange..." he wondered, thinking it unbelievable that they would just up and leave after doing so much work to change the meadow into what it now was. He chewed slowly and thoughtfully for a time while he waited patiently for some kind of movement or noise to be heard. But he ended up finishing two more of his berries and becoming quite full before either came.

By then his curiosity was all aflame and nearly burning him up, for he had steadily grown accustom to their presence day in and day out, so to find them suddenly gone greatly unnerved him. And by that, of course, I do not in any way mean saddened, just uneasy by the sudden change in their normally predictable behavior and the ominous silence.

Wary of what was going on, Ono pulled his wand from his sash and began creeping along the hillside. Rounding the bend of the mountain, the view of the subdivision gradually opened up and gave him a clear sight of the entire area. He snuck silently into a nearby bush, then once inside and hidden in its green tangles he pulled a branch down just enough to peer out.

A hundred feet down the slope from him was a tall wooden fence that had been erected within the past week, and it now encompassed the entire patch of land that the humans had claimed as their own. Within its borders were four giant rows of homes that stretched nearly the entire length of the meadow. These rows were sectioned off into square parcels, each with six homes built on them and separated again by more fences and gates.

Black paved roads crisscrossed along and through these rows, and were outlined by the lighter concrete of the sidewalks and spindly saplings. On every corner there was a streetlight that gleamed in the afternoon sun, and most of the lawns were green with grass and newly planted hedges, although a scant few still remained bare.

In the driveways of some of the homes were rolls of carpet, stacks of lumber, boxes of tile and other items, and there was also the occasional large dumpster sitting at the curb. To our kind it would appear that the subdivision was in its final stages of completion and was only being touched and finished up, which it obviously was.

But Ono couldn't have known that, and he wondered if maybe there was some significant reason behind the humans' desertion, for they had labored away like clockwork for the entire summer and never once missed a day. Except this one.

Perhaps I should go take a look around and see what I can

find down there? maybe then I'll discover what they're up
to, for this is certainly queer of them and I do not like it
in the least! he thought. Ono had never once been down among
the humans' things without the company of nighttime shadows
to hide him, and the thought of doing so now made his heart-
beat quicken in his chest and his ears stand up straight and
twitch nervously.

He pondered on what to do for a moment, then decided that
he wouldn't be able to sleep well, if at all, until he had
at least nosed around a bit into what was going on. Ono took
a deep breath and pushed out through the bush, then scanned
the subdivision once more for any humans or their beasts before waddling down the mountain side.

CHAPTER FORTY TWO

Ono came to the bottom of the mountain and stopped at the base of the fence. It looked to him like the Great Wall of China would to one of our kind, for it separated two vastly different worlds and seemed to stretch on forever into the distance in either direction. He looked around once more, then slid his gathering pouch off his shoulder and knelt down. There was a small space between the fence and the ground, and Ono first stuffed his pouch under and then got on his belly and crawled through to the other side.

When he stood up and brushed the dirt from his robe, he was standing on the lawn of a large back yard and facing the rear patio of a big white house. The sun's rays gleamed off the windows of the second story like the blazing eyes of a giant, and although he knew the homes were harmless, Ono did not at all like how vivid they appeared in the daylight.

Holding his wand at the ready, Ono bent down for his pouch and then cautiously scooted sideways with his back against the fence and into a row of hedges. The hedges were still new and young and not nearly as thick as he would have liked them to be, but he figured he would have to be thankful for what cover was available to him in such a place. His heart was thudding like a drum in his chest and his legs were weak as he began tiptoeing through the bushes, causing not even a rustle or shake of the leaves as he went.

The row of hedges went along the side of the house and

down the length of the driveway where they ended abruptly at the sidewalk. Coming to the end, Ono pulled the branches aside and stuck his head out to look down the street both ways, seeing nothing but more lawns and the shimmering heat waves that hovered just above the pavement. A light gust of wind blew the scents of blacktop, fresh turf, and wood to him, but the musky scent of the sweaty humans was gone.

Nothing moved.

Ono gulped down a large knot that had suddenly swelled in his throat and wiped his sweaty forehead across his sleeve. "Ono... two... " he counted quietly as he prepared to venture further into the neighborhood, rocking back and forth on each count.

On three, Ono shot out of the hedges and scurried across the street as fast as his legs would carry him. But instead of jumping up onto the sidewalk and running for cover in the hedges across the street, he fell back on his rump and slid into a drainage pipe like a baseball player desperate for home plate would and vanished from view.

In the shadows of the pipe, Ono stood up and took off his cap and tucked it beneath his arm. Then, with one last wary look over his shoulder at the street-level circle of daylight behind him, he turned and waddled off into the depths of the drainage pipe.

Many weeks earlier, while out stealing the humans' treasure in the construction site, Ono had stumbled across this network of pipes and culverts by sheer accident.

There had been a small aluminum can that was filled with nuts and bolts and washers sitting at the curb beside a stack of cabinet doors, and the moon's shine on its surface had caught his eye as he came waddling around the side of a home nearby. Intrigued like he always was by shiny objects, Ono had hurried over to the can and peeked down in over the rim. "Wooooowww.. " he had said with a big smile when he saw the things inside, for he enjoyed even better shiny things he could carry away with him. He reached in and picked up one of each nut and bolt, then had to stretch his arm down for a washer near the bottom. He didn't get a good grip on it though, and when he pulled it over the lip of the can it slipped from his grasp.

The washer had fallen to the ground, clicked off the curb, then flipped out into the street.

"Hey! Oh no you don't! Get back here!" Ono had called after it when the washer began to roll down the street and in to the gutter. Not willing to let his new treasure escape him so easily, Ono had hopped down off the curb and chased after it.

The washer rolled along through the gutter, wobbling and bouncing over the gaps in the pavement with Ono's greedy hands grabbing at it from behind. Then it turned and rolled into the shadows of a drainage pipe, and without even noticing where he was going, Ono went in after it.

The washer had rolled around many dark twists and through several intersecting pipes before he finally caught up with it. "Ha! I got you!" Ono laughed and snatched it up. He had been running after the washer crouched over at the waist like a parent does when hurrying after a fleeing toddler, so when he straightened up to drop it in his pouch he felt his cap crinkle on his head.

It was then that he suddenly realized he was in a very unfamiliar and dark place, and didn't know how he had come to be there.

And so Ono had spent the next several hours trying to find his way back out again, and in the process of doing so discovered that the pipes led almost everywhere throughout the neighborhood. Since that time he had explored and memorized them like we do with our streets, and he found the pipes to be a much more preferable way to travel about than darting from cover to cover on the surface and constantly worrying over being spotted.

Coming back to the present now, Ono waddled through the maze of pipes for a time, then turned a corner and headed towards a patch of light at the end. When he came to it he stuck his head out from the shadows and pricked up his ears.

All was still quiet in this part of the neighborhood, and nothing moved along the street but a small lizard that scampered off into the heat waves when it saw him.

After a moment of listening, Ono stepped out into the road

and put his cap back on, then hopped up on the curb and darted into the hedges that ran alongside a driveway. He waddled several yards up through the bushes, then stepped back out and hurried to the middle of the driveway where he quickly got down on his hands and knees. He rapped his knuckles against the pavement, then cupped his hands around his mouth.

"Hello father! It's me again!" he called down loudly, for ever since the humans paved over Proi's grave Ono had worried that his father would have a difficult time hearing his voice under there. "I know it's awfully early for me to be here, but all the humans have just up and gone all of a sudden. Isn't that strange? I sure hope it's because they've left for good, but I certainly won't get my hopes up for that quite yet. But wouldn't that be just wonderful if they did?" Ono said.

He spoke for the next few minutes about what treasures he had collected between the time of their last visit until now, and also attempted to describe in uncertain detail what the houses around him looked like, occasionally stopping to look around and listen for a moment before continuing on.

When he was finished, he lightly patted the concrete with his hand. "I suppose I should be off now father! I'm going to go look around a little more and see if I can get to the bottom of what's going on here. I'll be sure to be careful though, so don't you worry! I love you dad!" he called down.

Then he stood up, waddled back into the hedges, and made his way down to the curb.

Placed in the middle of the driveway was a single red berry Ono had left behind for his father.

CHAPTER FORTY THREE

Ono waddled along through the maze of twists and turns in the drainage pipes for the next hour or so as he made his way beneath the neighborhood, occasionally popping his head out from the gutters to look suspiciously around before ducking back down again.

Oddly enough though, each time he peeked out from the gutters he saw absolutely nothing but an alien ghost town, devoid of even its normally hideous noises and replaced by an unnervingly hollow silence that hung like a thick fog in the air. His ears strained and leaned and cocked from side to side, but they could pick up nothing.

Ono traveled throughout nearly the whole neighborhood, and was beginning to consider that perhaps the humans really had left for good, for he figured that any break in their normally routine schedule must be a significant sign. Happy and hopeful that they were indeed finally gone, he began to quietly hum a merry tune as he waddled through the pipes with a grin on his face. Oh I do hope it's true! I've finally waited them out and they're gone forever! Please let it be true! he thought as he walked along, thinking of how much better his life would be without the humans around anymore. A slight bounce even began to show in his waddle, and it became more prominent each time he came to the end of a pipe and saw nothing but desolate, abandoned rows of homes either way down the streets.

His enthusiasm was interrupted though, when he waddled through a long curving pipe and came to its end. Ono tiptoed towards the opening, then carefully stuck his head out and peered around with his ears tall and alert. He heard nothing and saw even less, and was more than happy to do so as he turned to leave.

But then, from across the street, a brilliant twinkle of light flashed in the sunlight, and it instantly caught his attention. Turning back around and shielding his eyes from the glare, Ono squinted into the distance and tried to make out what it was.

Beside the garage of a single-storied blue house, there appeared to be some kind of workbench piled up with lumber. Among the stacks of boards was where the glimmering object sat, but the bright glare winking off of it made it nearly impossible to make out what it was other than its vague, rectangular shape.

Wow! I wonder what that could be? Something beautiful surely! Ono thought to himself as he looked between his fingers at the dazzling glints of light coming from atop the workbench. After a moment of staring at it he blinked away the stinging spots from his eyes and decided to go see what exactly it was that could shine so. With greedy expectation apparent on his face, Ono set off to stake claim to whatever he could of the shiny object.

With the first step he took out into the street though, he

suddenly felt that there was definitely something wrong with the situation, so he instinctively retreated back into the shadows of the pipe with a shiver on his spine and a worried cramp in his belly. What can it possibly be? There isn't any humans or beasts out there, at least none that I can hear or see anyway. And I must know what that thing is! he thought as he peeked from the darkness with his gray eyes round and his big ears twitching nervously.

Don't be a fool! Can't you feel that? It's bad and it's terrible, whatever it is! So go home and be gone this moment! his caution chimed in, for it did not at all like the strange things going on in the first place and wanted to return back to the comfort of the forest as quickly as possible.

Ono chewed his bottom lip for a time with his eyebrows bent together in worry and his fingers wiggling slowly as he stood at the threshold of the pipe, wondering what to do. The feeling in his stomach was indeed an ominous one that made both his heart quicken and his legs reluctant to move. Nonetheless, the dazzling shine from across the street held his interest like a flashing lure would a hungry trout's.

After a time, and as I'm sure you could have already guessed he would, Ono put on his cap and took a big nervous breath. Just a quick peek wouldn't hurt, I'm sure. But that is it! Then I'll leave as quickly as I came! he thought before hurrying across the street towards the brilliant shine.

It is not often that a gnome of any sort will chastise itself for its greed, but little did Ono know that he would soon be cursing himself for his in a wicked and nasty way.

CHAPTER FORTY FOUR

Ono hopped up on the curb, darted across the sidewalk, and dove into the hedges where he stood trembling for a moment and looking warily around for any sudden movement coming in his direction. But after a few minutes of seeing nothing but a bluebird land in the yard nearby and begin casually pecking the grass for worms, he rolled his eyes at himself and rubbed his forehead with a sigh, for he figured that he must have been put on edge by the humans' sudden departure and was jumpy for no reason at all.

Ignoring the urgent feeling in his stomach telling him not to do so, he waddled up through the hedges towards the side of the garage. When he got there he pulled the branches aside and looked out at the workbench.

It was four feet high with four steel poles as legs, and a thick slab of wood for a tabletop. Looking up at it, as Ono was, a long narrow metal tray with vertical slits along its side and bottom could be seen fastened to the underside of the table, and dangling down over the far edge was a black power cord that swayed back and forth in the breeze. The ground around the workbench was coated in a thick layer of brown powdery sawdust, and scraps of discarded wood bulged beneath it like rocks under a blanket of snow.

Nothing seemed especially threatening about what he was looking at, so after a minute he stepped out of the shrubs and waddled over to the nearest table leg. When he got there

he found that it had a row of holes drilled up its length
for adjusting the table's height, and they were just the
right size to give him a good hand hold.

Ono took a deep breath and looked up at the tabletop, hes-
itating for a moment as he worked up his nerve. I'll just
climb right up, see what there is to see and gather what
there is to gather, then come right back down before anyone's the wiser. Nothing to it at all, he thought to himself. Then he hoisted himself up and began climbing the
table leg hand over hand, much like one of our kind would on
a ladder.

It was when he was nearing the top with only three holes
more to go when he felt a sudden shift in the waist of his
robe. Alarmed, Ono looked down just in time to see his wand
slip out from under his sash and go tumbling through the air
and land end-up in the sawdust below. "Oh snakes! Snakes!"
he squeezed his eyes shut and cursed under his breath.

Although four feet is not a significant height to us, to a
body as small and delicate as Ono's it was certainly not a
simple matter of jumping back down to the ground again, for
he would have most likely broken one of his feet, or a leg,
or perhaps even worse, on the uneven scraps of wood below.
He would instead have to climb back down to retrieve his
wand, and with his heavy pouch on his shoulder weighing him
down, it would take much longer to get to the shiny object
on the tabletop.

And for some reason, his stomach was now telling him that time was of the essence.

Ono glanced back down at his wand poking up from the saw-dust with a worried look on his now sweaty face and whined uncertainly, for he did not like the idea of leaving it be-hind, especially in such a place as this. I can get it on my way back! I'm already at the top and it would be a waste of time and effort to climb down just to come back up again. Now go!" he thought to himself.

So with one last nervous glance around, Ono decided to leave it and began climbing once more. He quickly came to the bottom of the table, then with one hand still gripping a hole in the leg he reached his other arm out and up over the side. Once he found a good grip he slowly let his other hand slide away from the leg until he swung loose and was dang-ling by a single arm. "Agh.. erg, come.. on," he grunted with effort as his legs kicked in the air and he struggled to stretch his free arm over the ledge. It took a tense mo-ment, but after he finally managed to get his forearms on the workbench's top he was able to make it over quite easi-ly. Once he had, he stood up and wiped the sweat from his brow and looked out across the table.

What he saw in front of him made his eyes stretch wide with awe and his mouth drop open, for he couldn't quite be-lieve what it was he was standing before. "It's... it's a giant treasure chest!" he whispered in wonder.

On the workbench was a simple red tool box that had been left open with the lid propped up against the stack of lumber behind it. The bottom side of the lid was polished metal, and the sunlight reflected off of it like a mirror and lit up the rows of sockets, wrenches, ratchets, and other steel tools within like gleaming treasure.

Sitting just to the left of the tool box was a large power saw laid on its side, the edge of its sharp blade lined with hooked teeth that winked in the sunlight.

What are those things? Whatever they are, they're beautiful and I must have them! Ono thought greedily, the ominous feeling in his belly completely dismissed and forgotten. Waddling towards the gleaming tool box, Ono hopped over a board and then carefully stepped over a long, narrow gap splitting the workbench's top that showed the metal tray hanging beneath. He gave it but a fleeting downward glance as he went, then came to the tool box and stood on his toes to look over the edge.

The tools within gleamed and shined like a chest full of silver. "Ha ha! Oh yes, look at it all! And all here for my taking! How lovely!" he said and giggled excitedly, then stepped up on the saw's blade and hopped into the tool box.

So for the next several minutes the only thing that could be seen of Ono was the brown tip of his cap poking up from within the tool box as he rummaged through the tools, humming and laughing over the clinks and tings as he moved

things around inside. Indeed, he was having such a delightful time that the sound of an approaching truck did not even
register to his ears.

Off in the distance a dusty black Ford pulled into the
neighborhood, then drove slowly down the street and turned
right on the second block. It passed several more homes,
pulled in the driveway, and came to a stop. Then its engine
shut off, and the truck sat quietly before the garage for a
moment.

Oh, wouldn't this look great beside my bed? Or perhaps e-
ven by the table next to the wall? I suppose it doesn't matter, since I'm taking it anyway and can figure it out then!
Ono thought with a big smile as he struggled to get a socket
to fit in his pouch. It was horribly heavy and cumbersome,
but he couldn't imagine leaving without it and was intent on
getting it back home with all of his other valuables.

He had just managed to get the socket's end in his pouch
and was working to pull the cloth up around it when he suddenly heard the truck's door open and then slam shut.

Instantly terrified, Ono popped his head up from the tool
box with his ears trembling and gasped in shock when he saw
a stocky human only yards away leaning over the bed of the
truck and grasping for something within. Most of the truck
was hidden behind the corner of the garage, but he had a
perfect line of sight to the back of it where the human
stood.

See you greedy fool?! **Do** you?! I told you not to come, but you just had to! Now what are you to do? the voice in his thoughts shouted at him as he frantically began thinking of a way to get out of this situation with all of his skin still attached an unpunctured. His first reaction was to reach for his wand, but his hand grabbed nothing but the cloth at his waist.

"Ohhhhh!" Ono whined pitifully and looked around, desperate for someplace to hide. Moving as fast as any gnome ever had, he dropped the socket back in with the others, grabbed his gathering pouch, and hopped out of the tool box. Then he darted across the table and hid on the far side of the stack of boards, gasping for breath as quietly as he could.

After a time that felt like agonizing hours to him, he heard the sounds of heavy footsteps approaching from up the driveway. Beads of sweat were rolling down his face, and he gulped nervously as he watched the giant shadow slide across the ground off to his left. His knees were knocking together beneath his robe, and his ears trembled like leaves in the wind as the human approached.

Just behind him the worker walked up pulling his gloves on and stopped at the edge of the workbench. On his head was a yellow pair of headphones, and he drummed his hands on the tabletop and mumbled along with the words for a moment before reaching down for an extension cord half buried in the sawdust and plugging it into the power saw.

"Boo-bababa oooh, wow wow!" he hummed off-key as he reached across the workbench and put his hand on a board at the top of the stack. When he pulled it away, Ono ducked further down on the other side just in time to go unnoticed.

This will not do at all! Oh! I'll surely be found if I stay here any longer! Ono thought and wrung his clammy hands together, his heart thumping almost painfully against his ribs. His eyes darted all around, but all he saw was the table's ledge and the ground far below him. Stranded, he began to feel like an appetizer hopelessly alone on a deserted plate. Come on! There must be some way out of this! Please! Think Ono! he thought to himself as frightened tears began to well up in his eyes.

The worker reached into his tool box and rummaged around, then pulled out a tape measure. "'Cause I'm TNT, I'm dynomite!" he sang as he stretched out the tape and squinted an eye at it. His booted feet took turns tapping their toes to the ground, and his shoulders teeter-tottered to the beat. "Watch me explooooode! Da-dum!" he continued on as he took out a pencil from his pocket and marked the board.

After a moment he walked around the side of the workbench and picked up the stack of lumber with a grunt. Then he turned and knelt down and sat it on the ground beside the garage so it was out of the way of his work area.

And, suddenly, Ono was gone.

CHAPTER FORTY FIVE

But he was nowhere near away from trouble yet.

At the last second before the pile of lumber had been moved, he had remembered the split in the top of the work-bench that he had stepped over earlier. So he had scrambled on his hands and knees over to it and squeezed down into the crevice just as the human had come around the side of the workbench. He dropped down into the metal tray beneath with his gathering pouch in tow, and sat huddled and trembling as he watched the narrow slit of light above.

Ono's cramped hiding spot was filled with sawdust and wood shavings that tickled his nose, so he pinched his nostrils shut to keep from sneezing. Snakes! This is it, I can go no further! he thought as he looked around him. The slits in the tray were much too small for him to fit through, and both ends of it were capped. If the human discovered him, he would have no defenses and nowhere to run.

The worker, obviously having not yet noticed the gnome's presence, went about more measuring and marking and humming for the next few minutes. Once he was done he tossed his tape measure back in his tool box and inspected the board.

"Ain't got no gun! Ain't got no knife! So don't you start no fight! Da-dum!" he sang as he laid the board back down on the workbench and slid it into position to be cut.

In the tray below, Ono nearly squawked in terror when the board came sliding directly over his head and covered the

gap above, blocking out all but the meagerest of light filtering in from the slits. Oh! What's happening now? This is
not good at all, I know it isn't! he thought and waited nervously in the shadows, wishing dearly that he really had
stayed in bed that morning and that this whole mess was but
a terrible nightmare he would soon awake from.

It was quiet for a long moment, then a sharp click! came
from above.

Ono cocked his trembling ears upwards and bit his bottom
lip and squeezed his little fists in frightened suspense,
for he had never been so terrified in all of his life.

Then a shrill mechanical scream suddenly sounded, and the
noise was so horrifically piercing that Ono covered his ears
and cried out with pain as his eardrums threatened to burst.
It felt as if a thorny blackberry vine was being yanked
through his ears, and as he grit his teeth in pain he
thought that there could surely be nothing in the world
worse than it.

But then, at the far end of the tray, he saw the spinning
saw blade sink down from the crack above and slowly begin to
come towards him, its razor sharp teeth slicing through the
board with ease.

"Oh no.. No! nonono!" he whined as he struggled to back a-
way from the advancing saw blade through the thick wood
shavings, his legs kicking desperately out in front of him.
Then his back bumped against the end of the tray, and all he

could do was watch it come steadily closer with his eyes

wide with horror. Once the gleaming blade was nearly upon

him, he threw his hands out in front of him as stinging

chunks of wood began to pelt his face.

The agonized screams that followed were drowned out by the

shrill power saw and the worker's headphones.

CHAPTER FORTY SIX

"Ba-ba, wooo hoo! Yeah! Yeah!" Owen sang and nodded his head with the beat as he pushed the saw along the line he had drawn down the board's middle. He leaned further and further over the workbench as he did, and was stretching his arms forward to cut through the last foot of board when the shrill whine of the power saw suddenly cut out. Without power, its blade made several more revolutions before its teeth bit deep into the wood and stopped with a jerk.

"Come on you piece of garbage, not now," he mumbled and jiggled the saw to loosen its blade from the board. But the blade had buried itself quite deep and wasn't about to budge so easily. Frustrated, he grunted and slipped off his gloves then smacked the side of it with his palm before squeezing the button in the saw's handle again. Nothing happened.

"Oh but honey, we can't afford the expensive one right now. I'm sure this one's juuust as good. Psh, yeah, right," Owen grumbled in a mocking voice, then wiped the sweat from his face and hung the headphones around his neck.

He had wanted to buy himself a new set of good tools for his birthday several weeks earlier, but before he had, his wife Shelly had announced quite happily over dinner that she was pregnant. Again. For the second time in two years. And so he had been forced to settle for the cheaper brand so they could save their money for the coming baby, which was due sometime in April. It was a girl to be exact, which

would make the family ratio three to one in gender now. This
he was not entirely excited about, for he knew that in about
twelve years he would be living in an utter war zone.

Snorting back a ball of phlegm and spitting it on the
ground, Owen picked up the power cord and traced it back to
where it met the extension cord. He pulled the connection a-
part, then blew hard on each plug before pushing them back
together. If that doesn't do it, I'm driving straight to the
hardware store to get a new one. Don't care what she says a-
bout it either, he thought as he slipped his gloves back on.
Then he grabbed hold of the saw's handle and depressed the
power button. It came instantly to life.

"Dang it!" he said and shook his head, for he had been hoping for an excuse to replace the thing since he had bought
it. He sighed, then was just beginning to push the saw once
more down the board when he heard his name being shouted o-
ver its loud whine.

"Owen! Ow-en!" the voice called out from behind him.

Getting annoyed with all the interruptions, Owen turned
the saw off and spun around. "Yes?! What is it?" he shouted
over the dying whine.

Standing beside the garage with his hands in the pockets
of his blue jeans was Bob, the construction companie's su-
pervisor. He had on his usual cowboy hat, plaid shirt, and a
cigarette hanging from the corner of his mouth. "What are
you up to?" he asked evenly, then plucked the cigarette from

his mouth and flicked off the ashes before sticking it right back in.

Owen looked puzzled. "Ugh, finishin' up the cabinets sir. Ain't I supposed too?" he asked, then reached to his hip and snapped off his Walkman.

Bob chuckled and took off his hat, revealing matted brown hair beneath. "Well, yes, I guess you are eventually, 'cause that's why I'm paying you. But today's a holiday son, we only worked a half-day today. Unless of course you wanna work for free, that'd be okay with me," he said with a pinched smile, then scratched his head and put his hat back on.

Owen shook his head and cursed. "Hell! I though everyone was just late coming back from lunch."

"No.. no, you were just a few dozen hours early," Bob said, then pointed a thumb over his shoulder. "Hey, all the guys are down at Tommy's place gettin' ready to watch the game. You wanna tag along?"

Owen thought about heading home instead, but quickly decided against it. Shelly was already in her "nesting" stage, and she'd more than likely want him to do something new to the nursery. "Yeah, might as well," he said, then took off his gloves and began walking towards his truck.

"You just gonna leave your tools there like that? Some hoodlum might come around and steal 'em," Bob said and nodded his head towards the saw and tool box on the workbench.

"Yeah, that's kind of what I'm hoping for," Owen said as

he walked past, "That or rain."

Bob opened his mouth, but then figured he didn't want to know. "Well alright. Let's go see that game," he said, then turned and followed him away.

After the two got into their trucks and drove off, the neighborhood became silent once more.

Beneath the workbench, Ono was pressed nearly flat against the back of the metal tray. His hands were covering his eyes and his mouth was stretched wide open in a silent scream, for he was still too frightened to move. He sat there frozen for a time with his brain spinning in shock and his ears trembling until finally he slowly bagan to come back to his senses. Am I still alive? Or perhaps I'm dead already and don't yet know it? Oh, I hope not! he thought.

It took him a moment to work up the nerve to open his eyes, but when he did he had to cross them, for the teeth of the saw blade had stopped just a hair's width away from the tip of his nose. So close, in fact, that he could feel the blade's heat radiating off its gleaming edge.

"Ohh.." Ono sighed with more relief than I could ever explain, then wiped the sweat from his face with a weak and clammy hand. Still feeling harried and dizzy, he managed to squeeze and scoot around the side of the saw blade and work his way back down the length of the tray. The end of the board covering the gap in the tabletop had been knocked out

of line when the human had left, and a small crack of sunlight shined down from above.

Ono stood up and pushed his gathering pouch through, then
pulled himself up after it. When he climbed out and stood up
he brushed the sawdust from his back, then looked over at
the shiny tool box to his right. He narrowed his eyes at it,
then waddled across the table on unsteady legs. When he came
to the edge he let his pouch fall to the ground, then slid
down on the extension cord like a fireman on a pole.

When his feet touched down he saw his wand still sticking
up unharmed in the sawdust, and he pulled it out feeling a
tremendous relief at having it back in his hand. "I won't
ever leave you behind again! I swear to it!" he said, then
planted a firm kiss on it before tucking it back in his
sash. Then, with one last unbelieving look around, Ono
picked up his pouch and slowly waddled back towards the
mountains in a haze.

But before he went home though, he planned on stopping by
the creek so he could wash away the big wet stain covering
the front of his robe.

CHAPTER FORTY SEVEN

Understandably, Ono was not exactly chomping at the bit to return back to the neighborhood soon after, for he had had his fill
of the humans and everything related to them, at least for the
time being anyway. So over the next couple of weeks he stayed in
the mountains where life was normal and mostly predictable.

Autumn had begun to stealthily creep into season, and soon its
subtle presence could be seen as much as it was felt in the
chilled mountain breeze. The forest leaves started showing
splashes of its touch in brilliant oranges and yellows and reds
that painted their borders, and the puffy clouds in the sky above
began to drift lazily by more often and in much greater quantity.
The bright patches of wild flowers on the hillsides steadily wilted and drooped, their pedals curling in on themselves and dark-
ening as they laid down for the long rest of the coming winter.

But as the forest seemed to become increasingly drowsy and
listless, the creatures that lived in it were becoming quite the
opposite, for they all had much hoarding and stockpiling to do
before the winter came. In the trees above the gray squirrels
bounded and raced, ducked and leapt through the branches as they
sought out the last of the pine cones, and nearly all the birds
turned south and departed by way of wing, chirping and whistling
farewells as they went.

The forest floor was even more of a hasten bustle, and if one
were to sit quietly in a nook there would certainly be much activity to be watched. The chipmunks fussed and squabbled with one
another as they scurried about frantically stuffing their mouths

with nuts and berries until their cheeks were comically round
and full and nearly about to burst. The occasional rabbit
would go hopping past in search of the next sprout to be
found, and the mice scurried through the underbrush wiggling
their whiskers in the air and squeaking. Quails ran awkwardly
along from place to place looking for good ground to scratch
and peck at, and a scowling porcupine lumbered past with a
fallen oak leaf impaled on the quills of its back.

Luckily for Ono though, there was much less of this sort of
traffic during the nighttime hours when he ventured out, so
he didn't have to deal with the confrontations and quarrels
like he once had to during this time of year. He instead waddled leisurely along through the dark forest, whistling merrily as he picked the last of the berries from the bushes and
pulled up mushrooms and whatever else was edible to store a-
way for the coming months.

You see, gnomes do not hibernate during the winter like
many other creatures in the woods do, but act much like our
kind does during the chilly season; when it's rainy and nasty
outside, they prefer to lounge in their burrows and eat all
day with their feet propped up, or to have warm get-togethers
with their friends and families while the storms pass on. The
last thing they want to be doing is to be out gathering food
and getting muddy and wet, so they are sure to be well-
stocked before the rains or snow arrive.

On this evening, Ono had just pulled his head from the pillow with a wide yawn and a stretch of his arms. Still groggy and tired, he reluctantly sat up and swung his feet to the wood floor. Then he rubbed his face and cast a longing glance over his shoulder at the warm, snugly folds of carpet. He thought seriously about going back to sleep for a moment, but then looked across his burrow at the neat stack of food lining the far wall. It was nowhere near what it should have been, for he had spent most of the summertime fooling around with the humans' things and concerning himself with their shiny objects of wealth instead of gathering and storing food away like a sensible gnome should.

"Ohh fine, I'll go," Ono mumbled as he reached over for his wand and lit the candle. Deciding to eat a bit of breakfast before he left for the night, he stood up and pulled the candle off the root. Forgetting to put on his robe, he then waddled sluggishly across his burrow and plopped down on the wood block beside the table with a grunt. Sitting the candle down before him, Ono reached out and chose a pine nut from the platter and began to crunch on it.

While he chewed he willed his puffy eyes to open, for it was just one of those mornings that his eyelids felt heavy and cumbersome and wanted to stay closed. He took another bite from the nut and shook his head to clear the sleep away, then put his elbow on the table and leaned his cheek against his palm.

As he ate he watched the yellow flame of the candle dance

and shimmer on its wick. The flame was a ghostly blue at its
curved bottom, then as it tapered up to its flickering tip it
faded into a gentle yellow that cast a warming glow on his
face.

The dancing flame had an almost hypnotic affect on poor
Ono, and as he gazed into it his eyelids gradually crept back
down again until they were both nearly closed. After a few
minutes he began to breathe heavily and steadily, and from
his open mouth half-chewed bits of pine nut began to spill
out onto the table. The deep breaths soon turned to snores,
and he was once again fast asleep before he even had a chance
to fight it away.

Luckily enough for him though, all thoughts of napping
would soon be completely gone from his mind as if they had
never even been there in the first place.

While Ono slept, he gradually leaned forward over the table
in a slow collapse, and as he did its top began to tilt under
his weight. The other end of the table began to rise up, and
the candle gradually slid down the tile towards him until it
came to a stop beneath his chin.

The candle's wavering flame licked at his sparse beard, and
most of the hairs that it touched only singed in a thread of
smoke and curled away from it. But then one caught, and a
finger of fire began to crawl up his chin.

From the look on his face, Ono had been having a pleasant
dream. Then the pungent odor of singed hair crept into his

nostrils, and he awoke with a frown. What is that smell? Oh
is it nasty! Is something burning? he thought to himself as
he rubbed his eyes with his fists and looked around his burrow with sleepy suspicion.

Then he noticed the rising tendrils of smoke and the rather hot sensation on his chin.

"Aaaah! Oooohhh!" he screamed in a shrill panic and began
frantically slapping himself about the face to put out the
fire. He fell backwards off the wood block and hit the floor
squirming and squawking and flailing at himself like a mad-
gnome until the flames puffed out.

Once they had, he stood up and glanced around with a look
of utter bewilderment on his face and with smoke still rising from his beard, for he had no idea how he had come to be
in the middle of his burrow without a stitch of clothing on
and his face mysteriously alight. It took a moment for the
shock to wear off, but when it did he suddenly remembered
waking earlier and carrying the candle to the table for
breakfast.

"Snakes! This will take forever to grow back!" Ono
shrilled belligerently and stomped his feet.

Rubbing the tender patch of red hairless skin on his chin,
Ono huffed angrily one last time, then waddled over to the
row of nails in the wall and got himself dressed. Then he
got his things together, and on his way out he stopped at
the table and leaned down to the candle's flame. He glared

bitterly at it, then stuck his tongue out and blew it a
raspberry that sent drops of saliva spraying until the flame
hissed out and went dark.

Feeling none the better, Ono grumbled under his breath as
he waddled up the tunnel, already in a very bad mood.

CHAPTER FORTY EIGHT

Outside it was already nighttime, with not even the faint-
est hint of the sun's dying rays in the west. The moon was
full and bright in the black sky, and the scattered wisps of
clouds that slid over the twinkling stars looked like dark,
ghostly forms drifting silently through the night above. The
wind had become stronger, and it carried with it a chill as
it rattled through the leaves and made the tree limbs sway
so that the forest was a gently shifting collage of shadows.

When Ono pushed aside the slab of bark and popped up out
of his burrow he shivered at the crisp air, then rubbed the
goose bumps from his arms and hopped out onto the hillside.
He cocked his ears up and around for a moment to listen to
the forest noises, then pushed past the brush and began
waddling through the shadows of the underbrush down the
mountain. He didn't whistle a single tune, or even so much
as hum as he went, for his chin still stung wickedly where
the flame had licked away the patch of hair from his beard,
and he was not at all happy about it.

As I have explained earlier in this tale, a gnome's beard
is quite important to him, for it represents the knowledge
and wisdom that he has accumulated along with the length of
his chin hair. For such an odd looking patch to be missing
from it would certainly bring many wagging tongues to whisper and point and giggle in huddled groups, for it would be
gossiped that there must also be a sizable hole in one's
common sense to let such a thing happen.

Rubbing his chin and scowling, Ono climbed over a log and pushed through a bed of ferns, then came to the stream's edge. Kneeling down beside the twisting branches of a scraggly bush, he lowered his face to the water's surface and squinted at his reflection. The moon's pale light shining off the water was just enough to see by, and as he turned his head to the side he could make out the oblong patch of bare skin among the brown of his beard.

Cursing miserably at himself, Ono began scooping up handfuls of water and carefully patting them on his chin to cool the burn. Once the pain began to recede, he stood back up and grumbled as he looked both ways along the creek. He wondered in what direction would be best to start his gathering for the night, for the nuts were better up it where the trees were tall, and the bulbs better down where the ground was softer.

While he was debating on where to go several small bats darted and flicked through the air above him as they pursued the flying insects hovering around the creek. Their clicks and squeaks and the soft beat of their flapping wings were small noises in the babble of the stream and the wind through the creaking branches.

After a moment of thinking, Ono made up his mind and headed south towards where the bulbs were good and many. He traveled along the stream for quite a time, pushing through the undergrowth and treading over the occasional newly fal-

len leaf without so much as a brittle crunch to be heard a-
long the way. When he finally came to the far side of Pine
Ridge, he waddled over a vine-tangled hummock and begun to
work his way down the slope towards where the bulbs grew.

This small area at the foot of the mountain seemed somehow
sunken down into the ground compared to the area around it,
if only be several inches or simply by the lay of the land,
and was filled with every sort of lush plant and grass that
thrives in marshy soils. There was a spring somewhere deep
below it all, whose water seeped up through the ground and
fed this odd little patch of ground with far more moisture
than it required, for it stayed a bright green every season
through.

Ono picked up a small twig off the ground, then stepped
out on the spongy earth and begun pushing his way through
the thick grass and large leaves, grunting in labor as he
went. He spent some time rustling around in the shadows and
unwieldy foliage before he finally discovered what he had
been searching for: a cluster of thin green shoots sprouting
amongst the blanket of moss, their jointed stems resembling
accusing fingers pointed sharply up at the heavens.

In normal times there would have been far less of them
here, for the herds of deer enjoyed them just as much as the
community of gnomes once had. But with them both gone now,
there were certainly more than enough for Ono to retire on
for the coming winter.

Judging that one night of hard work would net him quite a
profit in this area, Ono spit into each palm and rubbed his
hands together, then took the twig and waddled over to the
nearest shoot. There he began scratching the twig's end in
the dirt around the base of the stalk like one of our kind
would with a hoe, his tongue wiggling from the corner of
his mouth as he worked. The dirt was soft and easily moved,
and within just a matter of minutes there was a fair sized
trench dug that showed the top half of a pale bulb that
resembled a miniature onion.

Once that was done, Ono tossed the twig aside, then
crouched down and wrapped his arms around the stalk in a
tight bear hug. Getting a good grip on each forearm, he then
began to pull up on the shoot with all the strength he had.
The shoot held itself stubbornly in the ground for a moment,
then with a wet sucking noise it slid up and out of the
moist soil to reveal a bulb perhaps the size of a small ap-
ricot, which to a gnome is quite a hearty amount of food.

Ono released the plant and let it topple over, then
reached in his robe and pulled out his dagger. At the bottom
of the bulb was a patch of thick tangled roots that he me-
thodically trimmed away like his father had shown him so
many years earlier. Then he tossed it away over his shoulder
before moving on to the nest stalk and repeating the same
process.

He worked diligently for the next several hours, digging

and pulling and trimming and stacking, stopping only every
so often to wipe the sweat and soil from his face and to
catch his breath before continuing on. His grumpy mood
lightened considerably as does usually happen when one works
with their hands, and soon he was back to whistling a shrill
wavering tune, for he figured that if there was ever a time
to wear a mutilated beard, then it was certainly now that
there was no one else around to laugh and point at it.

Once the stack of bulbs had become quite a sizable pile
and the ground was pocked with many holes, he decided that
he had dug all that he would need to last him the winter. So
he tucked his dagger back in his robe after trimming away
the last patch of roots and prepared himself for the long
night of work ahead. Now he had to take the bulbs all the
way back to his burrow and make many trips while doing so,
for he was only strong enough to carry two at a time along
with him.

Getting started, Ono waddled around to the front of the
pile and grasped a stem in each hand, then with a grunt
pulled them away through the thick underbrush with the bulbs
dragging on the ground behind him. And so for the rest of
the night he came and went, went and came, and the moon
gradually traveled across the sky and dipped behind the
mountains just as the sun began to peek over the ones in the
east.

The brilliant glow of the early rays brought with it a

sparkle to the stream's rippling surface, the awakening
chatter of chipmunks, the fresh smell of an autumn morning,
and also a work-disheveled Ono who was panting for breath as
he made his way home with his last load. His hands and robe
were dark with soil stains and his cap was crooked on his
head and ringed with sweat.

"Just a little... further, come on!" he grunted through a
grimace as he pulled the last two bulbs up the side of the
mountain. He made it back to his burrow and rolled the bulbs
down inside, then put his hands on his hips and leaned back
with a pained grunt, his spine popping and snapping from the
heavy load. Relieved to finally be finished, he then sat
down at the base of the tree to rest for a spell.

He took off his cap and wiped the sweat from his forehead
with a sigh, then reached out and plucked a leaf from the
bush beside him. It was dotted with beads of dew, and when
he folded it in half they all ran together and puddled in
the center of the leaf. Instead of traveling all the way
back down the mountain for a drink, Ono opened his mouth
wide and poured the water in, which was enough for one satisfying swallow. He smacked his lips and wiped the damp leaf
across his face, then crumpled it up and discarded it.

It was when he was leaning over to pull another from the
bush that he heard the sounds of scampering feet from above,
so he shot a suspicious glance up into the branches and
pricked up his ears.

High in the limbs of the old pine tree there was a gray
squirrel that was worrying over the last pine cone to be
seen around. Its big fluffy tail twitched eagerly as it
pulled and pushed at the cone with its little paws, struggling mightily to get it to break away from the branch. After a few minutes of hard labor the little animal had the
pine cone swinging back and forth in perfect rhythm before
it finally broke loose with a dry snap! and fell from the
branch. "Chit chit chit! Chit chit!" it chittered happily,
then began scurrying down the tree after it to collect its
prize.

The pine cone smacked the ground several yards away from
Ono, and the impact knocked loose several small brown nuts
that spilled out onto the ground around it. The thought of
running out with his wand drawn and claiming it as his own
crossed Ono's mind, for life in the forest occasionally
calls for such filching, but he was much too tired and had
done too well for himself that night to be in any real need
of it. He simply sat there with his hands folded in his lap
instead, content with watching the squirrel go about its
business.

The gray squirrel scurried down the side of the tree and
hopped to the ground, then bounded over to the pine cone.
There it began quickly plucking the nuts out from between
the bristles of the cone and stuffing them eagerly in its
mouth. This made Ono smile as he watched, for he always

thought their kind looked silly when they were round-faced
and lumpy-cheeked.

The squirrel picked all the nuts there was to pick on the
top half of the cone, then stood up on its hind legs and
rolled it over to begin with the next side. But before it
could continue on, there came a soft chitter from above.
Suddenly, the squirrel stopped what it was doing and looked
up into the branches with an odd look on its furry face.

Ono frowned curiously at it, then followed its seemingly
worried gaze up to the next tree over.

Lumbering awkwardly along a branch above was another gray
squirrel, but this one had a large round belly that bulged
out at its sides as if instead of just eating the nuts it
had swallowed the entire cone. Obviously pregnant, the new
arrival came to the base of the limb and began making her
way carefully down the side of the tree, paw over paw.

"Chit! Chit chit chit!" the squirrel on the ground chittered nervously and twitched its tail about as it watched
the other come down the tree's trunk and step delicately to
the forest floor.

The new arrival slowly lumbered right past Ono towards her
mate and snuggled her face into the fur on his neck, chittering quietly and sweetly. As if forgetting all about the
pine cone he had worked so hard for, the other squirrel
closed his eyes and nuzzled her back and returned her chitters, which could not have possibly been any other thing but

loving words whispered in their quaint squirrel language.

Ono rolled his eyes and stuck his tongue out distastefully when he saw the two beginning to fawn over one another, but as he continued to watch them a much different look came a-cross his face. His eyes slowly began to soften and his eye-brows steepled together into a look of deep envy as he pic-tured in his mind what the winter was going to be like for the two squirrels. He imagined them cuddled up next to one another in their small den high up in a tree somewhere, their warm tails curled lovingly around their mewling off-spring as the rain and snow swept by unnoticed outside.

Ono sighed heavily as he watched the two snuggle one an-other, for he suddenly felt a deep longing for Bej again that made his heart ache like it hadn't done in quite a time. Remembering the sight of her beautiful face and the sound of her lovely voice, Ono's eyes welled up with tears as he slumped over.

Oh... I do miss her terribly, he thought to himself and whined as his chin began to quiver beneath his beard.

Before the tears could spill down his cheeks though, Ono suddenly clenched his teeth bitterly and narrowed his eyes at the squirrels, for he found it to be nowhere near fair that they could be so content when he would surely be miser-able and alone the whole winter through. Red-faced and angry he sprang to his feet and pointed a hateful finger at them.

"You two! Stop that this instant or else! You make me

sick!" he squawked and stomped his foot.

Looking like two teenagers being barged in on unexpected-ly, the squirrels turned and looked at Ono with shocked stares and agape mouths that revealed their white buckteeth.

Enraged, Ono reached in his robe and pulled out his wand. "You heard me! Leave and be gone! And-don't-let-me-see-you-here-ever-again!" he shouted and jabbed his wand at them.

Knowing full well what a gnome was capable of with such a thing in its hand, the squirrels looked to one another and chittered nervously, then turned and scampered off into the underbrush.

Ono watched them flee with a menacing glare, then stuffed his wand back in his robe and pulled his cap back down on his head with a huff. Then he turned and stomped back to his burrow and slammed the slab of bark shut behind him just as the tears came in a long and hurtful flood.

CHAPTER FORTY NINE

During the next two weeks Ono continued on in the forest with his gathering and storing not out of necessity any longer, but rather to stave off the dull boredom and dreariness that hung over him like a cloud.

The reason for his dolefully drab demeanor was of course due in part to his renewed longing for Bej, but also because the dark clouds were steadily rolling in over the mountain tops and the rains were soon to be following them. But it was not the coming downpours that had him looking so gloomy though, but was instead the fact that Autinter would no longer be celebrated like it once had, and the thought of it did nothing to lift his spirits in the least.

Autinter, which was called so by the gnome folk because it was celebrated during the last few days of autumn leading in to winter, was quite a merry and joyous affair where the whole community got together to trade and peddle with one another for things they needed for the coming months. For Ono to be stranded and alone during this time was quite hard on his heart, for it would be like one of us having to sit out from Christmas or Thanksgiving while stuck at home to twiddle our thumbs and think of how great it would be to have all of our friends and family around.

And think he did, for one of the last few memories Ono had of his father was the first time he had gone to Autinter with him. He thought of that day many times while out gathering during those two weeks.

Proi had awaken him early that morning by gently tugging on the tips of his ears as he slept. Ono had groaned and lazily batted his father's hand away, then rolled over in his bed of moss and squinted his sleepy eyes out at him from over the fern leaf.

Already dressed with his green robe and cap neat and clean, and his beard combed straight and proper, Proi had crouched down beside him with a big smile on his face. "You wake up Ono, I've got a special treat for you today," he had whispered, then patted his cheek and stood back up to light a candle.

Ono had whined in protest, for even as a youngster he was never much of a morning gnome, then jerked the leaf over his eyes to escape the candle's glow. "Ohhhh! But father, can't it wait for just... just another moment, or... or two... " he trailed off in a yawn and snuggled back down for more sleep.

Proi had blown out his wand and tucked it in his sash, then waddled back over to Ono's bed. When Ono had jerked the leaf over his eyes his feet were left bare without covers, and his stubby little toes wiggled slowly and contently as he slept. With more than a little cruel enjoyment, Proi had reached down and snatched up one of his son's legs by the ankle and began mercilessly tickling his foot.

Instantly awake, Ono erupted from the covers thrashing about like a hooked fish on a river's surface. "Yeeeea! Father! I'm awake now! I promise I am! Aahaa! Let go!" he had squealed and giggled as he flopped and struggled to get away from his grasp.

Proi smiled down at him. "That's a good son!" he laughed and released his foot. "Now get up and dress yourself in your good robe, then wash your face and comb that nest of hair of yours. Today is Autinter! And you must be looking your best for it. No up, up!"

Excitement had lit up little Ono's eyes into gleaming circles of wonder, and he shot out of bed in a flash. Then he quickly slipped on his robe, which matched the green of his father's and was just slightly too large on him so he could grow into it. Tying his sash and rubbing his hands together happily, Ono hurried over to the walnut shell basin in the near corner and crouched down beside it.

"Oh! What's it going to be like? Is there lots of others there? And will there be honey? Oh I hope so! I do love honey!" he babbled excitedly as he scrubbed his face, for he had been gnome-sat all the years before by the decrepit old Wumble and didn't know what to expect.

On the far side of the burrow Proi was working in the dim light with his back turned. "There could possibly be some to be found Ono, just as long as you stay on your best behavior and mind your manners. Remember: no running, or yelling, or throwing anything of any sort at anyone. I would certainly hate to take you back to Wumble's home and have

him watch you while I gobble up all the sweets there are to

be had," he said, then glanced back over his shoulder at him

with a raised eyebrow.

Ono smoothed his wispy hair down on the top of his head,

then nodded solemnly. "I promise! I'll be the best ever!"

"Good, that's what I was hoping to hear. Now come over

here and let me have a look at you before we go."

With his ears trembling with excitement, Ono waddled over

to him with a big crooked smile stretched across his face.

Proi knelt down before him and adjusted the front of his

robe and dusted off his shoulder before giving him an ap-

proving nod.

"There you are. You look quite handsome, you do. But there

just seems to be something missing... hmm," he said, then

rubbed his chin with a feigned look of puzzlement.

Ono shifted nervously from foot to foot and looked down at

himself with a worried frown. "I don't think I forgot any-

thing father. I.. I tied my sash just like you showed me to

and I washed up and I-"

"Aha! Yes of course! **That's** what it is!" Proi had laughed

and snapped his fingers as if suddenly remembering what he

had forgotten.

From behind his back he had then pulled a small green cap

and set it carefully on his son's head with a warm smile. It

was the first cap he had ever worn, and Ono's knees had

nearly given way in bliss when Proi snugged it on his head, for it was certainly a special privilege for such a young gnome.

"There. That's much better I'd say. What do you think?" Proi asked.

Ono hadn't been able to reply through his happiness, but instead squealed in shrill delight and hugged his father as tight as his slight arms could squeeze.

"Well then! I'm glad you should say so!" Proi had laughed and then picked up a large basket filled with various odds and ends and took Ono's hand as he led him outside.

It was comfortably overcast on that day, with the sun nothing more than a glowing haze behind a thick blanket of gray clouds. The bright leaves were falling like snow from the branches above, and the breeze made them twirl and dance and frolic on the air as they twisted down from above.

Side by side, the two waddled down the slope of Pine Ridge then began traveling north along the creek bank, laughing and smiling as they went. On their way they saw many other gnomes popping out from the nooks and crannies along the forest floor getting ready to leave, and all waved and called out joyful things and promised to see them at the celebration.

The celebration itself was traditionally held year after year in the grove of willow trees beside the stream at the foot of Mud Hill. As the two neared, Ono straightened up his ears and puffed out his chest with a smile, for he was more than proud to be at his father's side and wearing his very first cap for everyone to see. They came to the screen of dangling willow branches where the sounds of the festival were coming, and Ono looked anxiously up at his dad.

"Is this it? Are we there yet?" he asked.

Proi nodded his head, then reached out and pulled the willows aside. "After you my son. And remember, only your very best behavior will be suitable in that cap. Now come, let's go find some honey shall we?"

Ono had squirmed with excitement and wiggled his fingers, then stepped through the threshold and into his first Autinter celebration.

Inside, it was like walking into a giant domed tent, for in the center of the area within the trunk of the willow rose high up in the air where its limbs begun to branch away and spread far out overhead. Then they gradually tapered off into thin vinelike ropes that fell gracefully to the ground all around them like a green curtain that hid the celebration from the rest of the forest.

And quite a celebration it was, at least by their standards that is. Amongst the bustling crowd of waddling bodies, tall pointed caps, and the babel of shrill voices talking and laughing merrily, there could be seen many business transactions taking place between the gnomes as they traded and peddled and bartered with one another in their vigorously greedy fashion. The wiser of them had arrived early to claim a good spot to show their goods, and most vendors had their wares displayed neatly on tabletops of moss covered stones, or laid out on a cloth for the passersby to see.

Nearly all of the browsers carried along with them baskets and pouches filled with things for trade. Among them, Ono saw several unfamiliar faces of those who had traveled from far down the creek to attend.

"Follow along with me son, and do your best to keep up! We mustn't let all of the good things be bought before we can get to them, can we?" Proi asked over the voices and laughter.

Feeling as if he had been brought to a very exclusive party, Ono had looked up at his father with a face that showed little more than a smile with ears. "No! Never!" he chirped.

"Then off we go!" Proi said, then led the way through the crowd with his son following his every step. Proi was not very tall at all, and the tip of his cap came to where most began, and Ono's was nowhere to be seen amongst the groups of bodies as they waddled to the far end of the gathering.

"Proi! Hello my dear friend! And a merry Autinter to you!" Trellit called out from up ahead and waved.

Trellit was a kindly soul with a brown, chest length beard. The top half of his left ear was sliced clean off and covered in a nasty scar that wound around the back of his

head and disappeared under his cap. The fox that had left
him in this condition many years before would have no doubt
taken much more from him if Proi had not come in at the last
moment with his wand blazing and fended it off.

In his hand he was holding firmly a bundle of long grass
blades whose ends were tied around the midsections of several plump beetles that clicked and fought to get away. He
looked much like one of our kind does when attempting to
walk several unruly dogs all on leashes.

"Why hello Trellit, I was hoping to see you here. Selling
your beetles I see?" Proi asked as he stopped before him.

"Oh yes. The secret place I go to find them was nearly o-
verrun with them this year, and these are the very best pick
of the bunch. Mighty tasty morsels, let me tell you. Worth
whatever you have in trade," he said, then sprang up his
eyebrows in surprise when he saw Ono peeking bashfully out
from around Proi. "Ono! Well well, growing up fast are we?
Lovely to see you on this fine day, and with such a smart
looking cap as well! Welcome, little one," he said and
tipped his cap down to him.

Ono blushed like a rose in bloom and tipped his cap in
return, then went back to standing just slightly behind his
father.

"For what price would you be willing to part with the June
bug? We would like a feast tonight, my son and I, and that
one there looks fit to go in our bellies," Proi said and be-

gan rummaging a hand in his basket, making sure to tilt it just so so that it couldn't be seen what he had in it.

All business now, Trellit pulled on the grass leashes to keep the beetles from getting too far and appeared to think it over while his eyes drifted cleverly along the rim of the basket. After a moment he relented trying to peek and gave Proi a sly look.

"Well I'd say with a rare and especially tasty beetle as my Junie is here, I'd have to ask... oh, about a clear crystal's worth. But that's only because you're a special friend of mine, so don't go about telling everyone that I practically gave it to you. I'd be cleaned out in a blink and wouldn't make a red berry off of my efforts!"

Proi had looked up from his basket and cocked his eye at him. "Unfortunately, I haven't any crystals with me, but I do have something else you might be interested in.. "

The two had proceeded to haggle and wrangle over the price of the June bug and the value of the things to be traded for the next several minutes as if they were enemies; cleverly fencing with one another by pointing out flaws, claiming hunger and impoverishment, theatrically rolling their eyes and shaking their heads in disbelief until finally a deal was reached: one June bug in trade for two bitter roots and a dried water nymph.

"I would only let you take advantage of my soft heart in such a way! But surely no one else!" Trellit exclaimed as

Proi dropped the payment into his palm and he reluctantly handed over the June bug's leash.

"Thank you for your generosity my friend, and I'll be sure to tell everyone I meet that I was more than happy to purchase it for triple what I really paid. Good day, and a happy Autinter to you!" Proi said and tipped his cap before turning around and waddling off.

As they made their way through the crowd with their new purchase scurrying out before them, he handed the leash down to Ono and snickered to himself. "Were you listening well to me back there son? Ha ha! That's the way to talk any price down if you value your wealth. I would have gladly paid double that amount if I had to, and now we have enough for twice the honey! Did you see how that worked?"

Ono struggled to keep the beetle at bay and nodded his head eagerly. "Yep! The less you spend the more honey you get!"

"Exactly! Always remember that and you'll be fine forever!"

The two continued on for the next several hours, browsing what there was to be browsed and stopping to talk to friends about the winter and what it might bring. Ono listened intently to it all with tall ears and watched everything with his eyes wide with wonder, for he saw hardly anyone else his age there and felt suddenly grown up and very important. The old gnomes fussed over him and pinched at his cheeks and

said he looked very handsome in his new cap, and Ono loved
every minute of it, sucking it all up like a dry sponge.

Among the other things being traded off and bartered for
was a whole mess of hand-worked daggers and polished crystals of many shapes that belonged to Deblo, who watched the
items being handled very closely and suspiciously; a big
beautiful arrangement of bird feathers of all colors and
sizes that Quinep fussed over and generally did not want to
part with but at the highest of prices; several tall stacks
of Kifol's egg shells, some spotted, some brown, some white
and others tan, and he bragged to anyone that stopped to
look at them that he had climbed many tall trees and battled
more than a few ferocious raptors to retrieve them; many
baskets filled with dried, twisted up earthworms that Corvil
crunched on as he spoke, which resulted in more than a few
stray morsels dotting folk's robes and dresses when they
walked on; a neat row of wands and staffs that Hafel explained had mysterious powers when used properly and at just
the right moment; and Nez, who smiled sweetly as she sold
whole dried flowers and her sweet-smelling potpourri by the
pouchfull.

There were lots of other items being offered of course,
but gnomes are both imaginative and resourceful and it would
take up many pages to explain all of the different things
their crafty little hands had produced from the forest.

"Can we get some honey now? Pleeease father?" Ono asked

once they had made several laps around the festival and were
both carrying quite a load of things that they would be
needing for the winter. Even the June bug had a bundle of
candles tied to its shell.

"Of course my son, and I'm glad you asked. I always save
the best for last, now come along," Proi said, then waddled
over to the base of the willow where Mippel sat amongst his
profits with his buckets circling him like pots of gold.

"Proi! And little Ono! Well, what would do me the honor of
seeing you two here on such a darling of an Autinter?" he
asked as he stood up and greeted them with a bow, his impressive beard nearly dipping in the honey.

"Hello to you today Mippel! Ono and I have finished with
our trading, and we might have just enough for a few helpings of your fine honey here. What do you say we strike a
bargain?"

Mippel had smiled beneath his beard and rubbed his hands
together happily, for he knew Proi to be a fine haggler and
quite enjoyed his company at these festivals. "That I'm sure
we can do my friend. And just how much might you have to
spend on these helpings of mine?" he asked.

Proi had then raised a finger in the air and smiled proudly. "Aha! That I cannot yet say, because my son here is
growing quickly and needs to learn the spirit of Autinter
for himself. So I am happy to say you must ask him that
question instead of me. A word of warning though: he's been

learning from his father today, so do be careful you don't loose your cap in trade," he said with a wink.

Ono's mouth had fallen open as he looked up at Mippel and his intimidating beard, for he hadn't yet a single hair on his chin and was positive he would loose everything they had just to dip his finger once in the honey.

Proi crouched down beside him and cupped his hands over his ear. "Be strong Ono, it's alright. Now listen, we have four pine nuts, a dried grasshopper, two more bitter roots, and a handful of deer hair. That's more than enough, and I'll let you keep whatever you can save. Now go get us some honey!" he whispered, then took the beetle's leash from his hand and replaced it with the basket before scooting him forward.

"So, little Ono, I get the pleasure of dealing with you first do I? That is quite the honor if I do say. Now what have you got in exchange for the last of my very hard-earned and supremely delicious honey?" he asked with a smile and crouched down to Ono's height.

"Ah.. um, well," Ono bumbled and stammered, his face red and his ears twitching nervously. The basket was large and cumbersome as he held it, and although he was trying his best to hold it high and tilt it away like he had seen his father do, he wasn't quite able because the weight of it threatened to topple him over.

Mippel could see clearly what he had to trade with of

course, and he gave Proi a knowing wink as Ono fumbled for
words.

"I... I have two bitter roots that are very, ugh, tasty
and hard to find this time of year... ?" he finally said
with an adorably bashful smile and a hopeful raise of his
eyebrows.

Mippel chuckled heartily and patted his belly, for he
could certainly tell that Ono had been listening to his
father and also shared his cunning tongue. He stroked his
beard and squinted an eye at him. "And how much, would you
say, might that buy you of my honey?"

Ono struggled to get the basket to rest on his hip, then
pointed a twig of a finger at the largest of the buckets.
"That one!" he said and greedily smacked his lips.

"Ha ha! You have good and hearty taste my young friend,
but unfortunately I could not part ways with it for quite
so cheap. You see, I am in need of practical things for the
bad weather and have more than enough bitter roots, as you
can see," he said and swept a hand towards his pile of profits beside him. "What else have you?"

Ono frowned for a moment as if he was stuck, then snapped
his fingers. "I have the bitter roots, a grasshopper, and
half of a handful of deer hair in trade for the smaller
bucket of honey and the two front legs off the praying mantis right there," he said and pointed to the dried insect
curled among the stack of goods. Then he glanced over his

shoulder at his father, who gave him a quick thumbs-up.

Mippel narrowed his eyes and thoughtfully brushed a hand down his beard, pondering and weighing the little one's offer, for it was not a bad price, but certainly not one he had hoped for. After a time of bouncing it through his thoughts, he decided that he couldn't let it go quite so easily and would need at least the other half of the deer hair left in the basket to make a deal.

"Well, Ono.. " he began almost reluctantly. But then he saw how the bucket of honey shined gold in the little one's hopeful eyes, and he paused for a moment to reconsider.

"Yes?" Ono asked and pricked his ears up, leaning forward with a big crooked smile matching that of his father's standing behind him.

Mippel smiled, revealing two missing teeth and many crooked ones, then turned and snapped the front legs from the praying mantis and stuck them end-first into the honey bucket. "It was not easy for me in the least, but you have yourself a deal my little friend, one that even seasoned hagglers would be proud of," he said and pushed the bucket towards him.

"Aha! Thank you! Thank you thank you!" Ono had squawked, then paid out his due quite happily.

Soon there after, he and Proi had pushed out of the willows one after the other and began waddling back home, each with a honey covered mantis leg in their hand and the burdened June bug scampering out in front.

"Oh I loved Autinter! I did good back there, didn't I Father? Will you take me again next year?" Ono asked as they waddled along.

Proi had nodded his head and smiled. "I will take you every year from now on son, I promise," he said and playfully fiddled with the tip of Ono's cap. "And I will be more than glad to do so. You're growing up now, and I'm very proud of you."

Ono had smiled and licked his mantis leg like a lollipop, deciding then and there that Autinter was his favorite time in the whole entire world.

He didn't know it then, but his father wouldn't live to take him the following year.

CHAPTER FIFTY

The memory of that perfect day made Ono miss his father
something terrible, and although the first rain had already
sprinkled the afternoon before, he decided on this evening
to go back to Proi's grave and wish him a happy Autinter, as
he had done every year since his passing. Of course, his
fear of the neighborhood still lingered from the last incident he had had there, but he promised himself that he would
never again do such a ghastly and foolish thing as gather
there in the broad and revealing daytime hours when the humans were up and about.

He was already awake and dressed, and was standing before
the wall of stacked food that now covered the entire length
of the far wall from floor to ceiling. He had his hand on
his chin and was rubbing the new bristles growing back in
his beard as he pondered over what he wanted for breakfast.

Hmmm.. a dried grub perhaps? No, I should save those for a
stew later. How about a.. he thought to himself as he slid
his gaze over the large stash of food. Ah, yes! A mushroom
would be nice, and I certainly have enough of them for later.

He pulled the mushroom cap ever so carefully from the others so as not to cause a small avalanche, then waddled a-
cross his burrow and sat down at the table to eat it. He
finished nearly half if it, then patted his belly and let
out a small burp. He stood up and put the rest of the mush-

room back to save for later, then began getting his things together to leave for the night. He took his pouch off one of the nails in the wall, then slid his wand in his sash and grabbed his dagger off the shelf just for good measure before blowing out the candle and waddling out.

Now that the seasons had changed, the sun was sinking behind the mountains sooner and it was already dark out. There was not a single star to be seen in the ink-black sky, and the breeze hooted through the trees on its sporadic gusts through, bringing with it the scents of fresh rain and the musky smell of damp forest and wet earth.

When Ono popped up from his tunnel he shivered with the cold, then tugged his cap down further on his head and pulled in the sides of his robe before hopping out on the hillside and beginning his hike over the mountain. The crispy leaves that had fallen to and blanketed the forest floor the previous weeks were now moist and flimsy, and Ono traveled silently through them, humming quietly as he went. He waddled through the underbrush and crested the mountain, and when the view of the subdivision began to rise over the shrubs he suddenly stopped in his tracks and cocked his ears forward.

"What the... ?" he puzzled, then squinted curiously down at the neighborhood below at the strange, yellow dots of light.

What he was seeing was the streetlights that had just been

hooked up and connected with the new power lines. The pools
of light they cast down splashed circles on the street corners and sidewalks in neat, evenly spaced rows that
stretched the entire length of the subdivision. The clusters
of homes between them were vague, shadowy shapes that were
difficult to discern from one another.

Ono was baffled by the queer sight and didn't know whether
to be frightened by the odd phenomenon or inquisitive of its
nature, for he figured that it must surely be a kind of magic producing such strange light out of the sheer darkness.
He was caught between the two, and was stuck in an uncomfortable interest for quite some time as he stood watching
from the shadows.

I wonder if it's like candle light? he pondered and stood
up on his toes and craned his neck to peek over the ferns.
It must surely be, being that the sun is gone now and that
is the only other kind of light there is. But I wonder,
should I go down there? I'm not certain that I trust this
new business in the very least of way.

Ono debated on whether or not to venture down the mountain
for the next ten minutes, and if it hadn't been for his
lonely Autinter he would have most likely swallowed his
curiosity and waddled away. There is still plenty of shadows
down there, and I'll be mostly in the tunnels anyway, coming
and going. But if anything queer happens, then that will
surely be it! No more of this sneaking about in the humans'

land! he thought, then began his silent trek down the mountain side.

As fluidly as a fleeting shadow, Ono slipped under the gap in the fence and hurried through the shrubs towards the sidewalk. When he came there he slowly stuck out his head and suspiciously peered around with his wand in one hand and his dagger in the other.

From where he stood, he could see two large pools of light on either side of him down the street some forty yards in separate directions so that he was in the dark space between. They were splashed down on the glistening blacktop from what looked like giant, unblinking eyes atop tall metal poles. Ono had to gulp down a knot in his throat when he imagined them suddenly turning their bright alien gaze on him and exposing him to the world like a stunned deer in the headlights.

Cautiously, Ono parted the shrubs and stepped out on the sidewalk, his ears flicking this way and that as he tiptoed to the curb. Looking both ways down the street and seeing that the lights had not moved in the least, he hopped down and waddled across the street and disappeared into a drainage pipe on the other side. sighing with relief, he took off his cap and tucked it under his arm, then began strolling through the twists and turns beneath the neighborhood, his feet plopping and sloshing through the rain water caught in the ridges of the pipes.

After a time he peeked his head out from the curb on the
other side of the subdivision and looked around. There was a
streetlight further down the road and one at the corner, and
both were staring just as stupidly at the ground as the
first pair. Deciding that they weren't much of a thing to be
frightened of as one to be avoided, he stepped out of the
pipe and snugged his cap on, then hopped up on the curb and
scurried towards his father's grave. Then he knelt down in
the driveway and cupped his hands on the pavement.

"Happy Autinter father! I know I'm late in coming, but
better late than never right? I would have come by sooner,
but I had a wickedly close call with a human and was far too
frightened to come back so quickly," he whispered, then went
on to tell him about the shiny tools on the tabletop and the
loud, spinning blade coming to a stop at the very tip of his
nose. He giggled nervously, for it made him uneasy to even
talk about the incident, then cautiously looked back over
his shoulder at the nearest streetlight before telling him
about those as well. "They're like giant eyes stuck on top
of shiny poles that cast the light of a thousand candles to
the ground in big round patches. Isn't that odd? And there's
lots of them around! I could have never imagined such a
thing..."

So for the next half hour Ono went on about various
things, rambling on about his store of food for the winter
and how well he had done in his gathering, how the weather

was beginning so sour and darken, and of course reminiscing

on their last Autinter spent together.

"That sure was a great day huh father? I just wish we

could have had a few more of them is all. I got much better

at bartering you know, and even wise old Mippel couldn't

hold a price against me the year after. Oh, I do wish you

could have been there," he sighed and patted the pavement.

"Well, I suppose I should be off and back to my burrow be-

fore I catch my death of cold in this chilly weather. I'll

come back again soon. I love you!" he said as he stood up

and waddled down the driveway and slipped into the gutter.

He strolled back the way he had come through the pipes,

then hurried across the street and began making his way a-

round the side of the white two-storied home he had passed

earlier. He paid the giant looming structure little mind as

he waddled through the hedges, but as he was crouching down

and slipping off his gathering pouch to slide it under the

fence, something caught his eye about it that he hadn't no-

ticed before.

There was a small opaque doggy door placed at the bottom

of the back door leading to the deck, and it almost seemed

to glow in the shadows of the rear lawn. It did not do this

on its own like Ono thought it to be doing, but was instead

revealing the streetlight's glow being beamed on it through

a side window from within the home.

Ono stood back up and pulled his wand from his sash more

out of instinct than fear and stood there studying the
strangely subtle glow of the odd little square, waiting patiently for his gut to tell him to turn and flee. But the
worried cramps didn't come, and his curiosity began to come
alive as his ears stood straight up.

Picking his pouch off the ground, he waddled across the
lawn and climbed the three steps to the top of the patio,
then snuck across the porch and stopped several inches from
the doggy door. He leaned forward and squinted his eyes, and
through its thin sheet of plastic Ono thought he saw vague
angles and shadows of things within.

This night just keeps getting stranger by the very minute!
First it's those queer lights, and now this... thing! I wonder what it is? he thought and sniffed the air, his little
nostrils flaring and flexing. He smelled nothing but rain
and wood and paint, so he reached out with his wand and
poked it against the doggy door.

It swung back and forth on top-mounted hinges, and Ono,
for some reason, wasn't at all surprised to see that it was
a passageway of some sort. A very small, luminescent, passageway in the humans' land. It was a queer night indeed.

Ono chewed his lip for a moment, still waiting for his
common sense to tell him to run as fast and as far as his
legs would take him, for it all seemed much too odd and
strangely out of place. Once again though, his gut told him
nothing but that it could stand to be sent down a bite or

two, but grumbled about nothing more.

"Well, okay then," he shrugged, then pushed the doggy door open and curiously stepped through.

CHAPTER FIFTY ONE

The first thing that Ono noticed as he pushed through and stepped inside was the smooth, cool feeling of tile beneath his feet. Then he ducked under the flap and straightened back up, and as the doggy door swung shut behind him his eyes grew as big as saucers and his mouth fell open into an unbelieving o.

"Ohhhh, my... " he whispered in a tiny voice as he tilted his head back to take it all in.

He was standing in what would most likely be used as a laundry room, for it was completely floored in light gray tile from wall to wall, which like the exterior were also painted white. There was a row of oak cabinets off to the right, and the bare window on the left filtered in the streetlight's glow and cast it down on Ono like he was a lone performer on an empty stage. The walls, besides two e-lectrical outlets, were otherwise bare, and a dark hallway lay directly ahead.

What **is** this place? I don't... I can't even.. Ono thought bewilderedly, his mind spinning like a windmill in a storm and his ears twitching and swiveling nervously. The house was deathly silent, and he had to strain to even pick up the muffled sounds of the wind sweeping by outside.

As you could have imagined, Ono stood there in awe for quite some time, his gaze sweeping this way and that in utter disbelief, for he never would have guessed that there

was an interior to these strange structures. He had always
seen them as giant ugly lumps that consisted of nothing more
but their solid form, like small mountains or boulders on an
alien planet. It was a very difficult concept for a gnome's
mind to grasp, for he didn't know and could not even begin
to guess what it was that he had just discovered.

After a while, and with his brain feeling almost numb beneath his cap, Ono took his first uncertain steps forward
with his wand held tightly in his fist. The hallway ahead
looked to him like a giant yawning mouth beckoning him to
venture down into the dark abyss of its throat, and the ele-
gantly curved molding above it looked like sinister serpen-
tine eyes watching him hungrily from above.

Ono gulped down what little saliva he had left in his
mouth, then waddled quickly through the threshold before he
lost the nerve, his feet pitter-pattering softly across the
tile and then going quiet on the light colored carpet in the
hallway. Keeping close to the wall and running his hand a-
long the base boards, he waddled further into the home, puzzling over everything he laid eyes on, for none of it seemed
natural in the least bit of way.

He traveled over no dirt or grass or mud, nor saw no bushes or trees or ferns. There were no rocks or weeds, or even
a single pebble anywhere. Everything, from the floor to the
walls to the ceiling, was instead clean and smooth and precise, and the oddity of it all amazed Ono to no end.

A door on his side of the hallway caught his attention
when his fingers came to the end of the base board, and he
stepped back to look up at it. The door was tall and wide
with a flowing design carved into the dark wood and a big
brass doorknob halfway up. It smelled strong and sweet of
fresh lacquer.

Ono looked it carefully up and down with his eyebrows bent
curiously, then noticed that it was just slightly ajar on
the far side where it was an inch or two from meeting the
door jam. Intrigued, he shuffled over to it and squeezed between the door and the wall and stepped again onto more
tile.

This time he had discovered the bathroom, and he didn't
know what to make of any of it either.

In it, there was of course a gleaming white toilet
straight ahead with its lid up, and a shower on the right
side of the room with a shower head that looked like a wilted sunflower made of silver protruding from the tiled walls
within. On the left side there was a marble counter top with
two sinks. On the wall above it there was a large rectangular mirror that, from Ono's view, only reflected back the
light fixture in the ceiling. Below the counter top was a
number of drawers, each dotted with a small shiny knob that
gleamed like pearls in the shadows.

"Aaaha," Ono cooed quietly, then pitter-patted quickly a-
cross the bathroom to claim one as his own. He came to the

bottom drawer and set his things on the floor, then rubbed his hands together greedily. I must certainly have one of those! They're beautiful! he thought, then jumped up and wrapped his arms around the knob in a tight embrace.

Whatever he had expected to happen, either it breaking off or coming loose under his weight, didn't occur, and he hung there foolishly for a moment waiting for it to budge.

"Oh! Come on you! Off this instant!" he grunted as he walked his feet up the side of the cabinet and began pulling and jerking out on it with every bit of his strength. Unfortunately for Ono though, the screw holding it in place was much stronger than he was and his grip failed before its did.

"Waa!-Ugh!" he squawked when he fell and hit the floor with a thud. "Oh, never mind then. Not all that pretty anyway," he grumbled as he rubbed his bottom and picked himself up off the floor.

Abandoning the knobs, he picked up his things and waddled across the bathroom to explore the shower, which looked to him like a sheer cliff face of polished stones sunken into the wall. Looking longingly up at the two curved water levers high above, Ono was quite surprised when he suddenly bumped his forehead into a very solid and unseen surface blocking his passage to the shower.

What the? Oh, now this is getting very strange indeed, he thought to himself and rubbed his forehead with a frown.

His face had left a small smudge on the glass of the shower's door, and Ono reached out and rapped his knuckles against it, amazed that something so big and sturdy and unwieldy could be practically invisible. On any other occasion he would have been likely to spend many hours fiddling with and pondering over such a phenomenon, but on this night it was just one of the many mysteries surrounding him, and he turned and waddled back out into the hallway with a perplexed frown on his face.

He passed by several other shut doors, then the hallway came to an end at two arched walkways that branched off in separate directions. Ono stopped and put his hands on his hips for a moment, then turned left and wandered to the end of a short hall. Once there it opened up into a living room, which was by far the largest area yet.

There were large exposed beams slanting across the cavernous, vaulted ceiling high above, and a big bay window that showed the dark hedges in the side yard. There was a brick fireplace on the wall nearest him, while all the others were tall and broad and bare.

Looking at the room, Ono had the feeling that he could cup his hands around his mouth and shout out a greeting and that the same voice would echo back to him a few moments later. He didn't do it, but he was nearly tempted to try.

He strolled further out in the living room, liking very much how the soft carpet felt beneath his feet and even beginning to find himself thinking that it was quite amazing that the horrendously ugly humans could create something so majestic with their barbaric, blood-stained hands.

Perhaps they're not as addlebrained as I first took them to be. Hmm. Now there's an odd thought! he pondered as he waddled beneath the bay window, thoughtfully sliding his hand across the wall. He stopped when he came to a power outlet at eye level beside him. He squinted curiously at its three odd shaped holes, for he had seen a few others just like it in the other rooms and wondered what use they could be to the humans.

In the forest, dark little holes are a welcoming sign that there is a meal to be had at its bottom, whether it be in dirt, wood, or even stone, because there is almost always a grub or a worm of some sort hidden within. Seldom, if ever, does a gnome of any age knowingly pass by one without first poking and prodding and worrying over what could be inside, and Ono decided not to start now.

Wiggling his fingers greedily, Ono pulled his dagger from his sash and bit his tongue in concentration as he aimed his blade for the larger slit on the left. Ha! There must be something great in there! Perhaps it's a cache filled with treasures? That would be something! he thought as he brought his dagger in closer.

The tip of the blade was just sliding into the darkness of the outlet when from the corner of his eye Ono suddenly noticed a subtle irregularity on the far wall beside him. Distracted for a moment, his dagger stopped mid-plunge while he cast a curious glance across the living room.

What he had first taken to be a solid wall when he first waddled out of the hallway was instead two different walls overlapping, and from his angle he saw a shadow slanting down between them from above and ending at the floor near the corner.

But that's strange, I haven't seen anything like that yet. Is there a crevice hidden in that shadow I wonder? he thought to himself as he studied it.

After a moment he decided to come back later and explore the mysterious little holes, then tucked his dagger back in his sash and waddled over to where the shadow came down from above and met the floor. As he neared he saw that the closest wall was set far apart from the other, and he peeked around it to find a flight of stairs between them stretching down like a rippling tongue from another dark hallway high above.

Ono frowned and took a deep breath, then reached up and hooked his fingers on the top of the first step and pulled himself over. There were many to be climbed and it took him quite a deal of time to reach the top, so when he finally did it was with heavy breath and a sweat sheened face. "Whoo!" he sighed when he stood up and wiped his forehead on his sleeve and stopped to catch his breath and look around.

The second story looked much like the first in its general design, with several brass-knobbed doors lining the hallway and a tall window at the end that looked out over the street. There was a dark skylight in the ceiling above, and the hallway bent to the right and disappeared around the corner.

Knowing he was very high up from the ground's natural level, Ono cautiously tapped a foot on the carpeted floor in front of him, then nodded his head and began waddling down the hallway, looking for gaps around the doors as he passed them. All of them were shut and had not even a crack to squeeze through, but when he rounded the corner in the hall he saw at its end a door standing wide open like a silent invitation.

The room inside was faintly illuminated by the ghostly pale glow of a streetlight out front that came in through a window, and Ono thought he could see a rhythmic shifting of shadows from somewhere within. Perturbed, Ono narrowed his eyes suspiciously at the shadows filling the room, then pulled his wand out and began to creep silently down the hallway with his back pressed against the wall.

When he came to the door frame, the first thing to peek around the corner was the tip of his wand, followed by a cocked ear, and then a single gray eye which darted back and forth around the room.

Although bare of any furnishings, it was obvious that this

would be the master bedroom, for it was nearly as big as the
living room was. There was a row of recessed lights in the
ceiling above and two large slotted closet doors on the
right. Two other doors leading to separate bathrooms stood
ajar far across the room, and the big window that the
streetlight's glow came filtering through was on the left
casting its shape down on the carpet like a weak spotlight.
What had been making the shadows in the room ebb and flow so
eerily was a small red dot of light on the round dial of a
thermostat high up on the far wall that blinked steadily on
and off without a sound.

Ono didn't like the looks of the thermostat, but didn't
suppose he needed to be frightened of it either, for it was
much less threatening than the lights along the street and
far less bright. Still, he kept his wand ready, just in case
it suddenly did something queer.

He came out from around the door jam, then waddled quickly
through the pool of light in the center of the room and
headed over to the first door on the left. Squeezing past it
and the door frame, he found himself standing again in a
bathroom filled with gleaming tile. Like the last one he had
explored, it had a toilet, sink, cabinets, shower, and mirror. But it also had something else, a very strange and awkward looking thing mounted on the wall beside the toilet
that made Ono frown and thoughtfully tug on the hairs of his
chin.

The urinal looked to him like a big elongated, toothless
mouth with its bottom jaw jutting forward. The thick pipes
curving out from under it and into the wall added more to
its odd appearance, for they almost seemed to make up a
crude, skeletal neck.

Ono felt a stitch of apprehension while looking at it, but
shook it off when his curiosity gently nudged him forward.
Pitter-pattering across the tile, he came to the underside
of its curved bowl and timidly tapped his wand against it.
The white porcelain gave a sharp and solid click! click! in
return. He sighed in relief when it didn't move, for he had
expected a giant tongue to loll out and come wiggling and
slurping after him like a hungry pink snake. When one didn't
he slid his wand back in his sash and peered up at it, for
he wanted to see what it looked like inside but was much too
short to simply stand on his toes and peek over the rim.

"Hmm," he wondered as his eyes began to drift cleverly o-
ver it, trying to find a way to climb up. The urinal itself
was smooth and offered no handholds of any sort. Ono was
stumped for a moment until he looked at the wall beside it.
Oh! Now that will work just fine! he thought and hurried o-
ver to it.

Hopping up on the narrow ledge of the base board, he
reached over his head and wiggled his nimble fingers into
the slight crack between the tiles on the wall. With shrill
grunts of effort, he managed to pull himself up several

tiles, then swing his leg over the rim of the urinal and hook the ledge with his knee. Then in one quick movement he pushed off from the wall and came to a rest straddling the rim.

Inside the urinal the shallow bowl swept down on a gentle curve that surrounded a watery hole at the bottom, its surface shining in the shadows. When Ono saw the pool of water at the bottom he smacked his lips, which suddenly felt horribly chapped and sandy, and threw his other leg over the rim. He had not drank so much as a drop of water so far in the night, and the sight of the sparkling water reminded him that he was nearly parched.

Carefully, Ono lowered himself into the urinal's bowl and crouched down beside the water. He sniffed at it cautiously, then eagerly puckered his lips and began slurping up the cool water. When he had drank his fill he patted his belly and smacked his lips, then climbed back out and hopped to the floor.

And so for the rest of the night Ono continued on with his exploration of the home, wandering curiously here and there and stopping several times to do his business in the dark corners of the rooms. In the next bathroom over he found a bathtub, and he managed to scale up its pipes and slide down inside it on the fabric of his pouch like a sledder down a slick slope. He spent quite a while doing this, running up its side and giggling as he slipped back down, and by the

time he got tired and climbed out again the morning's glow
was just beginning to pierce its golden rays through the
windows.

Seeing that he had lost track of time and overstayed his
visit, Ono hurried back the way he had come, then quickly
hopped down and rolled across each step in the flight of
stairs. When he came to the bottom he darted through the
living room and down the hall, then dove out of the doggy
door like a shot from a cannon. Slipping quickly under the
fence, he then disappeared into the underbrush with a crooked smile on his sweaty face.

As the sun continued to rise and shine down through the
slits in the broken clouds above, a number of small birds
flew chirping from the mountains and into the neighborhood
to land on the damp lawns and peck for worms. One of them,
a brown-feathered little sparrow, did especially well for
itself early on, and it tugged up a fat earthworm from the
grass and quickly flew off with its prize before it could
be stolen by the others.

The sparrow flew down the street, flicking between the new
trees for a time, before coming to perch on a large orange
sign at the front of the subdivision. It tilted its head
back and gulped down the worm in one laborious swallow, then
turned around and wiggled its bottom and lifted its tail
feathers in the air. Relieving itself with a squirt of

white, it then chirped happily and flew off in search of another worm.

The bird's watery droppings slowly oozed down the front of the sign, which exclaimed in big, bright blue letters:

MOUNTAIN MEADOW ESTATES

OPEN HOUSE THIS FRIDAY

HOMES ARE GOING FAST!

FRIDAY! FRIDAY! FRIDAY!

CHAPTER FIFTY TWO

Friday was just another day for Ono, one that seemed every bit as normal in its routine tedium as any other. As the sun came up on that morning he was just returning back to his burrow from treasure hunting in the forest. That night, although quite chilly, had been clear of clouds and sparkling with stars, and he had gone out to enjoy it before the next rains came and found him lounging lazily in his burrow again.

He pushed through the brush with his pouch hung at his side, then hopped down in the tunnel and shut the bark behind him. Waddling into his den, he upended the pouch on the table, then grabbed a bitter root from his stash and sat down to inspect his new things. There was a short, downy gray feather that he had found laying amongst the mossy stones on Pine Ridge, and as he crunched on a mouthful of root he eyed it suspiciously, for it looked to him awfully like that of an owl's.

Now there is one animal I do not miss in the least. Goodbye and good riddance I say! he thought as he set it aside and took another bite.

The other two items consisted of an unusually large acorn cap that would serve as a perfect bowl to make his soups in, and a small, bleached-white bird's bone that he planned on stirring them with. He finished the root, then brushed the crumbs off his robe and stood up. Putting his things away

with the others on the shelf in the wall, he then took off
his clothes and hung them on the nails and waddled yawning
over to bed. He laid down with a sigh and pulled the scrap
of carpet up to his chin, then smiled up at the set of keys
dangling from above. Then he closed his eyes and rolled on
his side, and was fast asleep within minutes, his mouth hung
open and letting out soft, wet snores.

It was perhaps an hour later that Ono groaned sleepily and
pulled the covers over his head, for in his dreams he was
hearing faint garbled noises that disturbed his rest. Half
awake, he rolled grumbling over to his other side and buried
his face in the scraps of foam, trying his best to ignore
the strange, muffled sounds and fall once again back to
sleep. But the noise persisted, and Ono let out a frustrated
sigh as he sat up and threw back the covers, his sleep-
puffed eyes irritated and grumpy.

Ugh! The humans are back at it again! Snakes! And to think
I was hoping for a peaceful winter? Ha! How absurd! he
thought as he got up and stomped across the room to his
clothes, wondering what the humans could possibly be doing
now to disturb him from a pleasant day's sleep.

He yanked his robe and cap off the hangers and dressed
quickly, mumbling curses at them beneath his breath as he
did. Then he snatched his wand off the shelf, and, huffing
angrily, stomped out of his burrow and began waddling up the
mountain side.

The sounds Ono was hearing as he went were vaguely busy
ones that were garbled together in a babel of unorganized
noise. He heard several of the familiar beep-beep-beeps echoing up from over the mountain, but the rest were indistin-
guishable from one another. Ono didn't like, or trust them,
nary a bit.

He pushed through the underbrush and crested the mountain
top, then climbed up on a stump and looked down at the subdivision with his ears cocked forward. When he saw what was
going on, his angry frown slowly lifted from his face and he
rubbed his eyes, not quite believing what his tired brain
was telling him.

When he opened them again, the scene down there hadn't
changed.

It was busy in the neighborhood below, with cars and mini-
vans of all shapes and sizes and colors pulling in and out
of driveways and zipping about like beetles in a hurry.
Several bulky moving trucks rumbled oafishly among them as
they came and went, beeping shrilly when they stopped and
backed up to the open garages to be unloaded.

The humans, coming also in many shapes and sizes and colors, far outnumbered the cars, and they dotted the subdivision like scurrying ants in a bustling colony. Among them
there was a gray-haired elderly couple strolling casually
hand in hand along the sidewalk, pointing at and discussing
the homes they passed; a smart-looking woman in a blue busi-

ness suit showing an eager young family around a front yard
with gestures of her clipboard; a curly-haired woman was
struggling to get a wailing infant fastened into a stroller
while her two other kids ran squealing and clapping around
her; a large dark skinned man pulled up a for sale sign from
a yard and snapped it in half over his knee, then held up
the pieces in triumph while his family laughed and clapped
at the curb; a young blonde headed boy was running and playing with his twin brother in a back yard; and a skinny bald
man with a gleaming head was pounding a mailbox in the
ground at the foot of his new driveway.

Ono was completely and utterly confounded by what he was
seeing, and the look on his face showed it as clear as crystal. The humans he had grown accustom to were big, sweaty,
dirty beings that traveled together in large packs, and the
beasts that accompanied them were giant orange monsters with
blades and black, smoke belching horns.

Ono didn't know what to make of this group of new arrivals
or their strange new beasts, but as he watched them with his
mouth agape and his eyes squinted quizzically, he had one
thought travel through the shocked, empty plain in his mind:
Oh my. Things are going to get... interesting, I'm sure.

And how very, very right he was.

CHAPTER FIFTY THREE

Over the next few weeks people steadily continued to move into the subdivision, pulling behind their luggage-stacked vehicles moving trailers packed full with furniture and appliances, and soon the neighborhood lost its appearance of a ghost town altogether.

The dull, empty stare of the windows were filled with curtains and shutters and drapes, and porches were decorated with flowerpots and bird feeders and wind chimes. Cars were parked in the driveways, and front yards were lined with ornaments and birdbaths and childrens' bicycles. Trashcans and recycling bins sat at the curbs, and back yards were filled with swing sets and lawn chairs and barbecues.

The people moving in went to one anothers' homes to meet and greet their new neighbors, often bringing with them cakes or pies along with their smiles and handshakes and friendly chatter. It was a happy time for the people moving in, because they were all excited and satisfied with their new homes and pleased by the tall green mountains rising beautifully around them and the fresh, piney smell of the place.

But while they were going about getting settled in and acquainted with one another, there was one neighbor none of them had ever met or even knew existed at all watching them curiously from the forest slopes all around them. During those weeks Ono got little rest or sleep, for he spent the majority of his time intently watching this new group of

humans from the underbrush and puzzling over them, for they
and their beasts did none of the things that the construction crew had. Never once did they tear anything down, rip
anything out, build anything up, or clear anything away, and
Ono was absolutely stumped.

That's what they always do. Everyone with any kind of
sense knows that. But why aren't they doing it now I wonder?
he thought suspiciously and pulled on his beard as he
watched them.

So determined was he to catch one of these new humans in
their notoriously detestable behavior that he sat patiently
through several downpours with a fern leaf pulled down over
his head to escape the pummeling drops. These humans seemed
to almost be of a different sort than the others though, and
never once did he see the monstrous behavior they were known
for.

Indeed, and most baffling and bewildering of all, Ono saw
what appeared to be quite the opposite. It was that, of all
things, that kept him coming back each day, for he almost
didn't believe some of the things he witnessed down there.

One rainy day as he sat huddling on the slope of Pine
Ridge, he had squinted down to see a young boy in a hooded
Scooby-Doo rain slicker skipping playfully along the sidewalk. Giggling and stomping through the puddles in his yellow rubber boots and catching rain drops on his eager
tongue, the boy had been having such a delightful time in

the downpour that he hadn't watched where he was going. His boot had squeaked off the curb, and he fell back on his bottom into the gutter with a splash. "Mooomee!" he had wailed and cried.

Almost immediately, a woman had thrown open a door and come running barefoot from across the street and crouched down beside him. She had cuddled and comforted and coddled the boy, then after a moment led him giggling once more back inside for some hot chocolate.

On a different and dry day, he had spied a very old blue-haired woman with large round glasses struggling feebly to pick a moving box up out of the trunk of her car. She had managed to get it most of the way out, but when she grasped the bottom and lifted, the box had toppled over and spilled silverware clinking and clacking down the driveway. "Ah hell!" the old woman had cursed, then bent down with a grimace and a hand pressed to her lower back as she begun to gingerly pick up the utensils one by one.

It would have likely taken her most of the afternoon if two small girls had not come peddling by on their frilly-handled bikes and noticed her struggling with the mess.

"Do you need some help ma'am?" they had asked sweetly, and then proceeded to pick up every fork, spoon and knife within just a matter of moments. By the time they were done the old woman had come back out with a fresh platter of baked cookies held in her arms and a thankful smile on her wrinkled face that flashed gleaming white dentures.

One evening, when Ono had just arrived and the sun was sinking behind a wall of red-orange clouds, there had been a young couple sitting hand in hand on their back porch watching the sunset together. They were talking quietly and laughing softly like those capable of love do, occasionally leaning over in their chairs to plant a kiss on the other's cheek. They had sat out there until it was dark and chilly, then went inside one after the other, laughing and joking the whole way.

A father and son playing baseball in a back yard caught his eye another day, and he puzzled over them and the odd game for quite a time.

"Okay, you ready for this? 'Cause here.. comes..a.. fastball!" the dad had called out, then tossed the ball underhanded across the lawn. The little boy had been wearing a Giants cap that was much too large for him, and when he swung the cumbersome bat it spun sideways on his head. The bat connected to the baseball with a crack! and sent it rolling across the yard where it bumped against the fence and came to a stop.

"Home run! Go! Go! Go!" the dad had cheered and jumped and began windmilling his arm in the air. The boy took off like a rocket and rounded a diamond of paper plate bases, then sprinted to home where his father was waiting with his arms held out wide. The boy jumped laughing and hooting into his grasp as the dad spun him around. "Yeah! Just like that! Next year you're going to have little league whipped Robbie! Good hit boy!" he said and squeezed him.

But one of the most shocking and confounding incidents that Ono saw was when he was just standing up to leave for the afternoon when the sound of a dog's bark echoed up the mountain side to him. Alarmed, Ono had ducked back down and pulled his wand, then began searching for the animal with his ears tall and twitching. When he saw where it was his heart had nearly stopped and he leaned forward in the underbrush to get a better look at what was happening.

In the back yard of a large blue house below, a big black Rottweiler was wagging its stumpy tail and growling at a teenage boy with long sideburns who held a stick tauntingly high up in the air. "What are you gonna' do? You can't get it! You can't get it Buddy! No you cannot!" he teased and made silly faces down at the dog as it advanced on him across the grass.

Then the animal suddenly sprang up in the air with its mouthful of sharp teeth snapping and knocked the kid down on his back and stood growling on his chest over him.

Ono had stood up and gasped in disbelief when he saw that, then had to stick his fist to his mouth and bite anxiously on a knuckle to keep from cheering out accolades to the brave animal for finally standing up to a wicked human.

But then, both to his utter bewilderment and disappoint-

ment, the animal had began wagging its nub tail and swiping
a drool dripping tongue all over the boy's face while he
laughed and sputtered and scratched behind the dog's floppy
ears.

Ono had stood there for quite some time puzzling over
those two as they continued to play together in the back
yard, for he never thought such a thing could ever be possible. A human being **nice** to another animal? Well, I certainly have never heard of such a bizarre thing, and it
would surely never be believed by anyone else if I was to
tell them, he thought to himself as he recalled all of the
whispered tales he had ever heard about the humans being
bloodthirsty maniacs, killing every creature they encounter
with cruel delight.

Down there in the yard though, the dog seemed to be enjoying the boy's presence as if he was one of their own.

Well... perhaps some of those stories weren't quite...
Suddenly remembering again his hatred for their kind though,
Ono cut himself off in mid thought and glared bitterly down
at the two. Of course they're all true! Every single one!
That poor animal is either a brainwashed fool or has joined
their ranks and become one of them. There is no other explanation to be said. Period! he thought with an angry huff and
stomped off through the underbrush.

Still, the possibility often nagged at him later.

CHAPTER FIFTY FOUR

As he had done with the construction crew, Ono became increasingly curious about the new humans, and he found himself sneaking further and further down the mountains to
watch them until he was literally squinting through the
cracks in the fences of back yards as they mowed and barbe-
cued and played between the rains. And soon, of course, even
that became tiresome and inadequate to satisfy his gnomish
curiosity, and he often stopped to stare down at the gap beneath the fence and debate on whether or not to slip under
and investigate what it was they were up to in there.

Ono held himself at bay for a time, but then the urge to
have a go at it became nearly overwhelming one evening. He
was sitting on a low sapling branch on the mountain side,
swinging his feet slowly beneath him and watching the glowing windows in the homes below go dark one by one as those
inside snapped off the lights and went to bed for the night.

The wind was gusting and cold and the thick blanket of
rolling clouds above blacked out whatever light the stars
and moon had to offer. Not a drop of rain fell, and it was
nearly pitch-black in the swaying, whispering forest. Soon,
all the windows were dark and the only light around was that
of the occasional streetlight's shining down in yellow pools
on the sidewalks.

"Hmm," Ono wondered as he sat there studying the subdivision. No beasts traveled along the streets, and everything

appeared calm and peaceful.

You know, if you were going to snoop around down there, now would surely be a perfectly good time to do it... a small voice whispered in his thoughts, stoking his curiosity like a poker in a flame.

Idiot! No, don't you dare even ponder it! A whole clan of humans are sleeping down there. What if they awake and discover you hmm? Then you will have hordes of grumpy, hungry humans after you! Oh! And that would certainly be just great and well! a different voice chimed in shrilly.

Ono thought about it for a time as the two voices took turns bickering with one another. While they did he thoughtfully nibbled the ends of his fingers and spat bits of his nails into the underbrush.

Snooping around when the humans were there was not a wise sounding thing to do in the least. But neither had been stealing the keys from right behind the two that were awake either, and he had gone away from that unscathed.

Yes! Exactly! Those humans were dumb and unaware! But what of these ones? You don't know anything about them!

Aha, but there is one way to learn, Ono thought with a smile. Before he could think better of it, he hopped down off the limb and picked up his gathering pouch and hurried down the mountain side. When he came to the fence he crawled and squirmed under it on his belly, then stayed flat on the ground with his wand pointed out before him for a moment when he emerged out the other side.

He was in the back yard of a green, single-storied home
that had a square patio with a covered hot tub on it. A red
riding lawn mower was parked around the side of the house,
and a big round trampoline was in the center of the yard to
his left.

Ono gulped nervously and his ears twitched and flicked one
way to the other, alert for even the slightest sound. The
only thing he heard was the hiss of the wind through the
power lines above and the tinny clinking of a wind chime
somewhere in the distance. Everything else was either still
or hidden in the breeze.

On shaky legs, he carefully got to his feet and scurried
across the lawn and around the side of the house. He darted
around a bucket and squeezed through the spokes of a mountain bike, then slid under a wooden gate and shot into the
hedges lining the front yard. Already breathing heavily and
looking all around him for pursuers, Ono hid there for several minutes without hardly moving a muscle.

There was at least one car or truck or SUV parked silently
in each driveway all down the street in either direction,
and the streetlight's glow shined dully off their dark windows.

Ono suspiciously eyed a white Explorer parked at the curb
through the screen of brush, then bent down and combed his
fingers through the soil. Finding a pebble, he crept down

through the hedges where they ended at the sidewalk and squinted an eye shut in careful aim. Then he stretched his arm back and hurled the stone with a shrill grunt.

The pebble flew out of the hedges and sailed across the sidewalk, then clicked off the Explorer's front fender. It sat there impassively just like the bobcat had months before.

Ono sighed with relief and wiped his sweaty face on his sleeve. After a moment he crept carefully out of the bushes and snuck past the Explorer with his wand trained on its smiling, shiny grill, then sprinted across the street and vanished in the drainage pipe. Once inside Ono took off his cap and glanced over his shoulder, then waddled off down the pipe, feeling much better knowing he could make it this far with his life and limbs still intact.

Now that the humans had moved in, the pipes were not as clean as they once were, and Ono stepped over discarded gum wrappers and cigarette butts and many other small pieces of rubbish that had been carried in with the rains as he waddled along. It smelled musky and sour in the dark, damp space, and when Ono came to an intersection in the pipes he turned left and headed for the first opening he saw to get some fresh air through his nostrils.

Coming to the pipe's end, he slowly stuck out his head and looked around the empty street for any dangers. Seeing none, he then took a long deep breath that smelled deliciously sweet compared to the pipe's odor. So sweet, in fact, that after a moment Ono frowned at its strong aroma.

What in the world is that smell? And what could be making it I wonder? he thought as he stepped out in the street and snugged his cap back down on his head. He looked up and down and across the street, then turned around and looked over the sidewalk behind him.

There was a driveway some few yards away that sloped down and across the sidewalk, and at the corner of the two was a large green plastic trashcan whose lid was propped up by bulging garbage bags within. Piled high right next to it was a stack of cardboard boxes, and beside them was a recycling bin filled with crumpled aluminum cans that gleamed in the faint glow of the nearest streetlight. It was these strange things that the sweet aroma seemed to be drifting away from on the gusts of wind.

Ono narrowed his eyes as he sniffed at the breeze, not quite trusting anything that smelled so good in the humans' land, but not wanting to leave before he found out what was making it either. He stood there undecided for a moment, then snapped his fingers and pulled his wand and hopped up on the curb to investigate.

Waddling over, he first stuck his nose out to the recy- cling bin and gave it a quick sniff. Of course, he had never smelled the musky, sour scent of stale beer before, and he frowned at it and waved a hand before his face, not liking

it one bit. "Blah!" he spat and moved on. The pile of cardboard boxes had little smell, and he was left looking up at
the lip of the trashcan with his hands on his hips. Yes,
that surely has to be where that delightful smell is coming
from, I'm almost positive, he thought to himself and nodded
his head.

The pile of boxes was just slightly shorter than the
trashcan, so after he scaled them Ono had to leap up and
grasp the lip with his fingertips and pull himself over,
struggling and straining and kicking. When he finally made
it he threw his legs over the edge and squeezed beneath the
open lid, then lowered himself down onto a slick, smooth
surface that crinkled beneath his feet.

The sweet aroma was strong and hung thickly in the still
air within the garbage can, and the sound of the wind blowing by outside was muffled and hollow. It was mostly pitch-
black inside, but a hazy shaft of yellow streetlight was
cast in from the slight gap beneath the lid, revealing to
Ono the huge mounds of awkwardly bulging garbage bags that
he stood among.

Not knowing what to think or even guess at what alien
things he had just discovered, Ono stepped very carefully
and nervously across the garbage bag he was standing on and
over to the round side of another. The sweet smell seemed
to be stronger in that one, and he put the tip of his nose
to the plastic and began sniffing anxiously all around it

until he found the spot it was closest to. Getting excited
about what he was going to find inside, he pulled his dagger
from his sash and stabbed it in the bag, then pulled the
blade down, opening up a long slit in its side. When he did,
the sweet smell within came wafting out over him in a soft
gust that made his mouth water and his tongue tingle.

Oh! It has to be something excellent! I must find it and
have it this very instant! he thought and reached both arms
eagerly through the slit and began groping around inside
with greedy, snatching hands.

At first, feeling blindly by touch, his hands brushed over
nothing but crumpled wads of paper and other bits of junk
that rustled loosely around inside. Then Ono's fingers
plunged into something soft and sticky. Startled, he yanked
his arms back out and frowned down at his hands, which were
both covered up to the wrists in a glistening, dark tacky
brown substance that looked sickeningly familiar.

"Oh, please don't let it be.. Oh!" he whined uneasily and
stomped his foot on a milk carton, then grimaced when he
smelled his hands. But to his surprise it was this unsavory
looking goo that was the source of the deliciously sweet a-
roma he had been hunting down. He took several long pulls of
it through his nostrils, enjoying the smell of the chocolate
frosting very much indeed.

Hesitantly, he then stuck out his tongue and quickly
touched it to his palm. He rolled the taste around in his

mouth for a moment with a brooding look on his face, then
smacked his lips and smiled. Excellent, whatever it is! The
best I've ever had! he thought as he quickly licked his
hands clean and plunged his arms back in the garbage bag for
another helping. This time he was able to get a grip on the
big soft thing inside, and he managed to work the half-eaten
donut out from the slit and set it down at his feet with a
grunt.

"Aaaaha!" Ono said and rubbed his hands together, his
stomach rumbling eagerly to start feasting on the strange
new delicacy. Before he took even a first bite though, a
sudden thought came to him that made him pause for a moment
with a queer look on his face. "I wonder.. ?" he said quietly to himself and stroked a hand down his frosting-clumped
beard. Then he turned around and stood up on his toes to
peer over the rim of the trashcan and out into the night.
What Ono saw out there made a crooked smile slowly stretch
across his face until the ends of it were nearly touching
his ears.

And that was many more trashcans, rows and rows of them,
stretching down both sides of the street and bulging with
countless, unknown wonders.

CHAPTER FIFTY FIVE

When the dawn began to fall gray and cloudy the next morning, the subdivision began to stir with activity like an a-
wakening beehive. Men in ties were carrying briefcases and
sipping down mugs of coffee as they kissed their wives good-
bye then hurried out to their cars and drove off, and elderly retired folks in bathrobes strolled leisurely down their
driveways to pick up the day's paper and wave to them as
they went. Mothers came out herding and shooing groggy children off to school that ambled along to the bus stop, and
the early joggers huffed and puffed their greetings to those
walking their dogs as they passed them on the sidewalks. The
mailman went putting by on his tedious stop and go, stop and
go route, and a green garbage truck followed close behind
him collecting the morning's trash.

While all of this was going on, an exhausted and filthy-
faced Ono was struggling to drag back the last load for the
night of pilfered goods he had crammed in his pouch.

His ears were flaccid with fatigue, and sweat rolled down
his face in beads and soaked his robe in a dark collar. The
veins stood out in his neck as he stumbled and staggered
down the mountain side on weak, shaky legs, and his arms
felt as heavy as lead as he pulled the pouch along behind
him through the underbrush. Grunting and groaning almost
painfully, Ono somehow made it back to his burrow and waddled down inside, so tired that he forgot to shut the slab

of bark behind him as he went.

"A won... derful night... indeed!" he panted with a weak
smile as he came out into the den and left the pouch laying
on the floor. Thoroughly and completely exhausted from the
night's work, he didn't stop to undress or even wash up, and
he staggered across the room towards his bed for what would
surely be a long and much needed rest. But before he got to
it, an overworked muscle in his leg suddenly cramped up and
gave out beneath him and sent him toppling over.

"Waa..!" Ono squawked and flailed his arms through the
air. There was nothing around to steady himself on though,
and he fell face first to the ground, his forehead making a
sharp crack! against the plywood floor. Knocked instantly
unconscious, he groaned once and twitched, then went completely still and silent as a purple lump began to swell a-
bove his left eye.

Piled all around him in heaping mounds were the things he
had discovered in just a few of the trashcans he had been a-
ble to get into that night. Feeling as if he had stumbled a-
cross a gold mine of treasures, he had made many trips back
and forth over the mountain to get as much of it as he could
before the daybreak came.

Ha! these humans **are** just as dumb as the last ones! Only a
fool would leave these things just lying about for the taking, and I'm more than happy to do it to them also! he
thought to himself many times as he rummaged snickering

through the trashcans.

Among the many things he found that night, there was a half-eaten granola bar; a sticky blue lollipop; stale bread crusts; moldy cheese; an old hot dog bun; a pile of spaghetti noodles; a broken section of mirror; a plastic ring; and a bent spoon.

Splayed out on the ground, Ono smiled pleasantly in his dreams as he imagined what he was going to do with it all. From the corner of his mouth a thread of drool oozed and stretched and soon became a puddle on the floor.

CHAPTER FIFTY SIX

Weeks passed by, and the lonely, humdrum winter that Ono had expected so gloomily was instead a time of great wonder and interest for him. The longing thoughts for Bej and all the others he loved did not come often or frequently during this time, for he was quite busy with his new discoveries. Nevertheless, they still came up on occasion though, like a sore's pain beneath a new bandage. When they did, he would stop in the middle of whatever he was doing and sigh heavily with wilted ears. He would think of them for a moment and reflect back on the memories he had, then rub his misty eyes and shake his head, then begin with his tasks once again with a new determination.

During this time Christmas came and went for the humans, and the strings of twinkling lights and dazzling tinseled trees and flowing ribbons were quite a sight in the new neighborhood. Young carolers sang and skipped from one house to the next, and cheerful parties were held where cups of eggnog and warm apple cider were sipped from laughing mouths while presents were generously passed around and graciously accepted.

Ono knew nothing of Christmas or any of the other human holidays of course, and he didn't much care about their bizarre antics either, for during those weeks the trashcans were nearly overflowing with goods and it was difficult for him to pay much attention to anything else that was going

on. He went out to rummage and gather nearly every night
when the trashcans were set out and the weather was bear-
able, and it was a blissful time of feasts and treasures for
him.

Ono took back with him on many nights the leftovers of all
sorts of festive pies and cakes and cookies and candies, and
he snacked on them while lounging in his burrow with sheer
delight painted across his face. There was also bits of tur-
keys and hams and roasts to be found, along with steaks and
mashed potatoes and gravy and rolls that he sampled curiously when he came across them in those wonderful cans. Never
once was he in the least bit hungry, and his store of forest
food was hardly touched yet.

The strange, brilliant treasures he discovered were just
as delightful and satisfying to him as his constantly full
belly was, and he displayed them all around his burrow in
the meticulous way we decorate our own homes. There were
several scraps of colorful gift wrapping paper pinned up on
the walls around the den like paintings, and a tall knight
from a chess set stood by the entranceway like a noble
statue; a child's plastic bracelet with little trinkets of
Sesame Street characters dangling from it hung on the far
wall like an odd looking reef, and a layer of bubble wrap
was added to the scraps of carpet and foam in his bed; a
new robe and cap made from the black fabric of a pair of
socks hung on the row of nails, and a ripped section of a

lacy garment covered the table like a dainty tablecloth; a shiny silver watch with a cracked face hung clicking away on the wall beside his bed like an elegant grandfather clock, and a large square piece of red flannel fabric from a ripped shirt laid neatly folded on the floor like a rug.

There was also a sharp, wickedly gleaming shard of broken glass that he had found in the trashcans and then sewn a black cloth handle around, and it stood propped up in the corner like a lethal looking sword. Ono wasn't sure why he had ever wanted such a vicious looking thing to sit amongst the inviting beauty of his burrow, and he had often stopped to look at it curiously while pondering over whether to throw it out or not, for such a threatening thing looked far out of place in a gnome's burrow.

Why did I ever bring this disturbing thing back to my home? And what use could it ever be to me? I have my wand and my dagger, and those would surely be enough in even the worst of situations, I'm sure. I should just bury it far a-way and be done with the awful thing! he had thought over and over in that newly prosperous and busy time.

But for some odd reason, while he was squinting closely at its fine, razor edge, he got a very strange and unpleasant feeling that stirred ominously in his belly urging him to keep it. And he did, although grudgingly and skeptically.

He knew, on some vague and detached level in his mind, that he would be in dire need of it one day. That feeling sometimes troubled him during those mostly happy and busy

weeks.

CHAPTER FIFTY SEVEN

When Ono awoke from his dreamless sleep it was in a fresh, sprightly mood, and he sat up and stretched his arms and looked around his burrow with a greedy smile already on his face. I've got much to gather tonight and so little time in which to do it. Oh! The plight of the rich indeed! he thought happily as he sprang out of bed and skipped whistling across the room.

The cause for Ono's merriment was because the trashcans were going to be set out tonight if the humans kept by their schedule, and he looked forward to what he was going to find very much. He hadn't been down there for several days, and he had been waiting for this night with tickling anxiousness.

Eager to be off and on his way, Ono slipped into his new robe and tied a wide black shoelace snugly around his waist. Then he pulled on his cap and stopped for a moment to mug before the chunk of mirror hung on the wall directly above the nails.

His new outfit made him look nearly like a mini-ninja, for the black material was thin and sleek and the ends of his sash hung down from a knot at his belly like that of a black belt. Thinking himself to look quite handsome in his new clothes, Ono pulled in the sides of his robe and stroked his chin, noticing with a smile that the patch of hair missing on it was finally beginning to grow back in and fade away.

He cocked his thumb and pointed at his reflection. "Looking sharp you. Now let's go pilfer some of the humans' things shall we? Ha! They must all be nearly famished and poor because of me!" he laughed as he waddled over to the table and sat down to eat a quick breakfast, which consisted of half a Fig Newton and a handful of crumbs from the crust of a pumpkin pie. When he was done he stood up and took his dagger to the end of a candy cane and chipped off a small piece to suck on while he worked, then grabbed his wand and pouch and headed quickly for the tunnel.

Before he went out though, he stopped to look back over his shoulder at the shard of glass in the corner. He frowned at it for a moment, wondering whether or not to bring it along with him. Figuring it would be much too cumbersome to carry around, he shook his head at it and continued on without a worry. The humans did not frighten him nearly as much as they once had anymore, and he was quite confident he could go about undetected all he wanted. And so he left, skipping and humming and smiling out into the night with the minty morsel rolling around in his mouth and clicking on his teeth.

Outside it was cold and damp on the forest floor, and a light mist drifted on the slow, steady breeze that made the tall trees creak and groan as if they were complaining to one another about the drizzly winter in their old wooden voices.

On his way up the mountain side, Ono was waddling along through the ferns and ducking through the brush when he suddenly made out several large, shadowy figures moving quietly along the ridge above him. In a flash, Ono had his wand out and was hidden in the shadows of a tangle of vines. With his eyes round and wide and his ears tall and swiveling, he watched the group of dark figures slide between the columns of trees, their shapes vaguely silhouetted against the night sky above the mountain.

One of the shadows that had what looked like a tall, elongated head turned and uttered a low powerful snort to the others behind it, then began crunching through the underbrush in his direction.

Ono's heart began to thump in his chest as the group came down the mountain side, but then it began to slow again when he realized what they were. Deer? I thought they had all left and weren't coming back. Now how curious is that? he thought and shook his head as they came near.

The one with what Ono had thought was an elongated head was just a tall-horned buck leading his heard, and several does and spotted fawns followed closely behind him. Looking up at them from the ferns as they trotted by only yards away, Ono smiled and waved, for he was happy to see another one of his old forest neighbors again. The herd of deer trotted down the mountain with a rustling of brush and disappeared in the shadows, and Ono sighed happily as he

watched them go. Well, that was certainly unexpected. I figured they would never return. Hmm, imagine that, he thought
with a shrug and began again on his way in an even better
mood.

He zigzagged up the slope, then crested the mountain and
began down the opposite side, keeping a watchful eye on the
neighborhood for any movement as he went. He saw none, but
did make out the rows of tiny trashcans dotting the sidewalks below like dark spots against the cement.

"Ha ha! The blundering morons have left them out once a-
gain! When will they ever learn? Never I hope!" he giggled
quietly as he hurried down. Soon coming to the fence, he
slipped silently under and crept through the back yard of a
familiar white home and around to the front hedges. He snuck
down through those, then came to the sidewalk and peered out
either way along the street.

There was a trashcan at the foot of nearly every driveway
that he could see down the block, and he smiled and wiggled
his fingers greedily, for he saw several whose lids were a-
gape or sitting like flat, round hats on top of the garbage
bags within.

Carefully and quietly, he stepped out of the hedges and
began waddling down the sidewalk to the nearest can. There
was a streetlight just across the road, and Ono's small,
pointy headed shadow waddled silently on the cement next to
him as he went. When he arrived at the trashcan, Ono stopped

at its base and looked around cautiously and warily like a mischievous child about to snatch a cookie from a cookie jar. Nothing moved along the rows of homes but a sitting bench on a front porch that swung slowly back and forth on its creaky chains, and a cluster of pink balloons tied to a mailbox that danced and bobbled in the breeze.

Since there were no boxes around to climb up on, Ono reached down in his gathering pouch and pulled out an old treble hook and began unwinding the dental floss wrapped around it. Once finished, he bit his tongue and then began windmilling his arm around and around while squinting up at the rim of the trashcan and judging the distance and height he would need. When he got the treble hook spinning so fast that it was hissing through the air, he let it go and watched it sail up and over the rim of the trashcan with the white dental floss trailing behind it. It landed within, so Ono yanked on the floss and felt the hook snag solidly against something inside.

And on my first toss! Ha! I'm getting much better at this every time I come, he thought happily, crunching on his candy. He slid his pouch over his shoulder and looped the floss around his hand and put a foot against the side of the trashcan. Then he began pulling himself up hand over hand and walking up the side of the can like a mountain climber on a sheer cliff face.

When he came to the top he pulled his upper half over the

rim, then kicked his feet in the air and squirmed until he slipped beneath the lid and vanished from view. And just to be careful to cover his tracks, he reeled up the floss behind him, and everything looked just as it had been before.

Inside the trashcan it smelled of damp rubbish, and Ono, who was very intrigued by that scent by now, rubbed his hands together excitedly and looked around at all the bulging garbage bags with a big smile on his face. I don't even know where to start! They all look so promising! he thought and took out his dagger and waddled across the top of a lumpy, uneven plastic bag to another that had been stuffed down on top of it. He sniffed around at it a little, then sliced a long vertical slit down its side. Tucking his dagger back in his sash, he then pulled the slit open and reached in and began feeling around.

His fingers brushed over a juice carton and a burned out lightbulb, then closed over something that was long and narrow and curious feeling. Ono pulled out the Q-tip and frowned at it, then twirled it and tossed it away behind him. Reaching back in he felt around some more, and after a time he managed to pull and jerk and wrestle out a nearly whole slice of combination pizza.

Ono crouched down and squinted at it, then peeled off what looked like a mushroom and dangled it in front of his nose. He sniffed at it curiously, then spit the chunk of candy cane in his palm and took a small testing nibble from it.

Delicious! I must have it! I've only been here a short
time and have already found by first load for the night.
That is a wonderful sign if I ever saw one, he thought with
a smile and popped the candy back in his mouth as he jostled
the cumbersome slice of pizza to the side of the trashcan.
He hoisted it up by the crust onto his knee, then got an arm
beneath it and lifted it up, straining and struggling and
grunting until he pushed it out over the rim.

Out on the sidewalk, the slice of pizza fell to the ground
and slapped the cement as if the trashcan had not liked the
taste of it and spit it back out again.

Ono tossed down the bundle of floss after it, then climbed
out and repelled down the side of the can. When he came to
the ground he shook the treble hook loose and wound the
floss neatly back around it, then dropped it in his pouch
and went to work dragging the heavy slice of pizza back to
his burrow. It proved to be not an easy job, but the smell
of the mushrooms and onions and cheese were irresistible to
Ono, and he thought it was more than worth the labor for
such a feast.

He drug the pizza along the sidewalk, then turned up the
first driveway he came to and pulled it around the garage
and through the bars of a metal gate. There was a new brick
walkway leading to the back yard, and he made his way down
it in the shadows and stepped out on the lawn and drug his
prize through the grass. Then he parted the shrubs and came
to the back fence, and was pushing the slice of pizza be-

neath it when he glanced cautiously back at the house just
as he was getting down on his knees to follow it under. He
thought nothing of it at first, but then did a double take
when he suddenly remembered which house it was.

It was the same white two-storied home he had explored
months before, but its appearance had changed quite a bit in
that short time. The back porch was now littered with colorful flowerpots sprouting all sorts of plants with odd looking ornaments standing among them. There were gaudy little
bird statues at each end of the three steps leading down to
the lawn, and a large birdbath stood on the far side of the
grass. On the other side of the porch was a big canvas um-
brella spread over a round table, and several bird feeders
hung from tacky bamboo poles. The windows were draped with
lacy curtains, and a pink flamingo was standing awkwardly
in a large flowerpot by the back door.

The doggy door still looked the same as it did before
though, and Ono ignored all the other strange things to
squint at it through the tangled branches. "I wonder.. " he
whispered curiously and got back up to his feet and pulled
the shrubs apart for a better look. He cocked his ears forward and began to puzzle over what it would look like inside
there now that the humans had moved in.

I bet there's all sorts of bizarre things to be seen in
there, things no other gnome in all of history has ever laid
eyes upon, that's nearly for sure! His heart quickened and

his stomach cramped at the thought, but the urge to sneak up and quickly steal a peak inside nonetheless fell over him like the bothersome itch from a poison oak's leaf.

He shifted nervously on his feet and brushed his fingers over his wand as he rolled the thought around in his mind for a moment. Oh! I don't know about this! That's a human's dwelling now! Surely they're more dangerous there than anywhere else!

Ono whined and his ears twitched.

It's just a harmless peak! The dumb humans will be none the wiser, I'm positive of it. They haven't noticed their missing valuables you've taken yet have they? I think not, and I think the same about this. So go on then, have at it! Ono thought and nervously swallowed the chunk of candy cane with an audible gulp.

CHAPTER FIFTY EIGHT

Abandoning the slice of pizza and his better sense telling him not to, Ono pushed through the shrubs and crept across the lawn with his heart feeling as if it were beating in the middle of his throat. He hurried over and pressed his back against the side of the birdbath, then peered apprehensively around the bend to the back door.

The entire rear lawn was dark and filled with overlapping shadows, and when the breeze gusted by overhead they slid and shifted and morphed fluidly, and Ono was nearly invisible as he hurried through them to the bottom of the porch. Not quite trusting nor liking the looks of the strange, glossy-eyed bird statues at the ends of the steps, he climbed up the center of the first two, then slowly rose his head up over the top of the last one and squinted down the porch to the doggy door.

The big, quiet house suddenly seemed much more menacing than he remembered it being, as if it were holding its breath and waiting for him to venture inside. The white lacy curtains on both of the second story windows weren't pulled together all the way, and the slit of dark, gleaming glass between looked like elliptical eyes staring down at him with sinister patience.

Ono's knees shook beneath his robe and the tips of his ears flexed nervously back and forth. I'll just hurry over and push in the flap and peek inside, then be off as quick

as I came! Nothing to it but to do it! Now let's go! he
thought as he hopped up and threw his knee over the last
step.

Standing up, he looked warily around at all of the weird
ornaments scattered along the porch for a moment and pulled
out his wand suspiciously. He saw what looked like a giant
green toad with its mouth stretched wide open with a spindly
plant growing out of it, and a pair of porcelain swans with
their long necks arching down towards one another so that
they made a heart shaped space between them; there was a
frozen faced Dalmation with its head cocked stupidly to one
side with an ear flopped down, and a miniature wooden wheel-
barrow with lush, thick leaves spilling over the edges; a
large tortoise on the other side of the porch seemed to be
smiling a wrinkled, toothless old smile, and a white bunny
rabbit sat on its button tail with its paws folded neatly in
the air as if begging sweetly for a carrot.

Many others stood crowded in the shadows behind them, and
Ono shivered uncomfortably under their blank, glossy gazes,
for he didn't know what to make of the strange things and
didn't want to know how the poor animals had come to be in
such a state. He only wanted to peek inside the human's
dwelling and see what there was to see, so he begun creeping
across the porch with his wand held tightly in his grip.

When he came to the doggy door, he got down on a knee and
slowly reached out to push it open with a trembling hand.

Right before he touched it he squeezed his eyes shut and sighed as a trickle of sweat ran down his temple.

"One... two... three," he counted quietly to himself, then pushed the flap open and quickly peeked through the gap at the bottom. Whatever it was his gnomish imagination had conjured up and been expecting, either tall piles of sparkling treasures or gutted corpses hung from hooks on the blood-smeared walls, wasn't there at all. Ono frowned in disappointment, for he felt that he had gone through much for very little in return.

On the left hand side of the room was a wicker clothes hamper with a white tube sock dangling over the side, and on the floor beside it was a long row of sneakers, boots, and tennis shoes. There were two blue little dishes in the corner with the name Special painted in pink on the sides, and a little aluminum scooter was propped up against the wall with a black helmet hung on its handlebar. On the other side of the room there was a washer and dryer beneath the cabinets, and a blue box of laundry detergent sat on top. Some of it had been spilled and was sprinkled white on the gray tile. Directly ahead the hallway was dull and empty and dark except for a nightlight's weak glow just above the base board at the far end.

Is this it? Is this how the humans live? he thought and pushed the doggy door further open to get a better look inside. There's hardly anything interesting in here! Where's all the amazing wonders or horrible terrors? Snakes! Well, I was certainly hoping for much more. What a stale bore of a tale this would make!

He shook his head and was letting the flap close to leave when another thought suddenly slid through his mind: of course there's nothing interesting in here! Do **you** leave your valuables by the entrance of your burrow for just any-one to snatch away? Certainly not, so why would you think the humans would? No, it's in the big den at the end of that long passageway where you'll find them, mark my words.

Both intrigued and disturbed by the daring notion, Ono lifted the doggy door again and glared down the length of the hallway with his eyebrows pinched together. The hallway was perhaps twenty five feet long to its end, and completely clear of any obstructions. Everything was quiet except for the tiny whisper of the wind coming through a cracked side window and hissing in the gently swaying curtains.

It's not too far I suppose, to just hurry down and peek a-round the corner and run right back. But that's it and no more! he thought and took a big breath of air. Then he wiped the sweat from his face and stepped quietly inside, careful-ly easing the doggy door shut behind him.

This is positively the single most foolhardy thing you have ever done! You must be begging to die a horrible death! an urgently shrill voice squawked in his mind, sending down uneasy cramps to his belly. Ono ignored them, but pulled his dagger from his sash and held it at the ready along with his wand.

Just down and back, then out and far away. That simple, he thought, then pitter-patted across the tile and hurried down the hallway.

Each dark door he passed as he darted by sent a flare of cold goose bumps rippling down his spine and along his arms, for he half expected a snarling, drooling human to reach out and snatch him up and crush his little bones in its giant hand like brittle twigs. Luckily though, that didn't happen, and he came panting to the end of the hallway and turned the corner, his shadow sliding quickly over the wall as he passed the nightlight. When he did, he came to a skidding halt and gasped at what he saw before him.

What had once been a vast, cavernous room was now filled with every sort of strange oddity imaginable. Across the room the big bay window was adorned with sweeping curtains and decorative flowerpots with climbing vines snaking over, and beside that was a massive entertainment center filled with a giant television screen and other sleek looking elec-tronics where several small lights blinked steadily on and off; a long, neatly organized desk was along the wall with the stairs, and on it was a computer whose screen saver was a colorful ball bouncing around off the sides of its screen as if it was trapped inside; a black, L-shaped leather couch filled the corner beside it, and a glass coffee table stood gleaming in the center of the room with a small crystal bowl filled with a rainbow of M&M's sitting on top of a dainty tablecloth; beside the brick fireplace was a tall green vase, and an elegant sparkling chandelier hung from the exposed beams above; a cluster of framed pictures of smiling human faces grinned grotesquely from the nearest wall, and a shelf full of knickknacks was just above them.

Ono was quite taken back by what he saw, and he absent-mindedly lowered his weapons and waddled out into the living room, looking in awe all around him. What is this place? And what do the humans do in here I wonder? he puzzled as he made a slow circle around the room studying everything he saw.

Distracted for the time from his fear by his overwhelming curiosity, he stopped to watch the computer screen for several minutes with his hands on his hips, nearly put in a trance by the colorful, soundless ball bouncing so beautifully around inside. Wow... It's, it's magic! Gorgeous human magic like none I've ever seen before! How do they do that? Ono thought to himself as the computer screen's reflection dazzled in his wonder-filled eyes.

He moved on and slid his hand along the smooth leather of the couch while starring longingly up at the chandelier until he came back around to the glass coffee table. He slid his greedy little hands all over its shiny brass legs, then looked up beneath it at the crystal bowl placed on top.

"What are those..?" he wondered and stroked his beard when he saw the candies, for they were colorful and small enough for him to carry away in his pouch, which made them all the more intriguing to him.

He eyed the table cleverly for a moment, then waddled over to its end where the thin strip of lacy tablecloth draped down from over the edge. It was still quite high up for Ono to reach, so he tucked his wand and dagger in his sash and backed up across the room. Then, with a running start, he sprinted across the carpet and leapt as high as he could up in the air. His hand closed over the tablecloth and he swung precariously back and forth from it for a moment before pulling himself up and onto the coffee table with an excited grin on his face.

Ha ha! More of the humans' treasure I get to steal! Oh, are they going to be livid when they discover it gone! he thought as he waddled across the table and began eagerly plucking the M&M's out one by one and dropping them in his pouch as fast as his arms would work.

His pouch was lumpy and heavy by the time he snatched the last one from the bowl with a triumphant smile, and he drug it back across the table and let it drop to the floor. It landed with a muffled thud that made Ono wince. He waited there frozen for a moment with his ears tall and an expectant grimace on his face, but after hearing nothing but more silence he hopped down after it and landed on the soft carpet.

Feeling a sudden urge to leave now that he had stolen something, he got up and quickly began dragging his pouch off towards the hallway. He had just turned the corner and was snickering quietly to himself as he passed by the night-light when he heard the quick pittering of small feet on carpet and the jingle of a little bell coming from around the corner.

Oh no! Snakes! Ono thought as his ears sprang up and he began frantically pulling and tugging his heavy pouch down the hallway. He made it perhaps five feet from the tile's edge and was looking desperately back over his shoulder at the doggy door when a high, angry growl made his head snap forward with a look of surprised terror on his face.

Creeping around the corner at the end of the hallway was a hunched, scruffy looking shadow with two gleaming eyes glaring wickedly out at him. The thing's growl was shrill and furious, and it became more incensed as it advanced towards him until it was nearly a continual herrrr-herrrr-herrrr that made Ono's knees weak and his ears tremble.

Horrified, for he had nowhere to go and nowhere to hide, he froze in his tracks and dropped his pouch as he watched the shadow shrouded animal come slowly towards him down the length of the hallway. His shaky, sweaty hand reached slowly and carefully into his robe and clutched the hilt of his wand, but didn't pull it out.

The animal came closer, and as it did it passed by the nightlight's glow, revealing a ragged, mangy looking little gray terrier. Its mouthful of bared snaggled teeth shined yellow in the light, and its ears were laid flat against the sides of its head, which was held low to the ground with its dark eyes glaring menacingly out from beneath its furry brow. A bright pink collar was fastened around its neck, and from it hung a little golden bell that tinkled with each step it took closer. Its hackles were bristeling, and its upward-curving tail was rigid and tense like that of an angry scorpion's.

What is this odd little trespasser doing in my territory? I marked this area just yesterday! Oh am I angry! How dare it come here! I'm going to get it and tear it to pieces and show it to my masters! And they will surely pet me and feed me and call me good for doing it! the terrier thought as it approached. It passed through the nightlight's glow and was once again shadow-faced as it advanced down the hallway.

Trembling, Ono pulled out his wand and aimed it at the terrier's nose. "Do not come any closer, please. I, ugh, was just leaving and will not ever return. I swear to it," he said in a tiny pleading whisper, for he didn't want to alert anymore attention than he already had in the house.

Bewildered by what it heard, the terrier suddenly stopped its growling and cocked its head curiously to the side with its ears up. Ono took this as a good sign from the animal, and slowly bent down to grab the pouch's strap while keeping the wand trained carefully on its nose.

"Thank you. Now I'm just going to grab my things here and be off. Good-night to you," he said gently as he straightened up and began dragging his pouch off down the hallway.

The terrier stood there blinking in confusion while it watched Ono back away, for it had never before seen a gnome and didn't know quite what to make of it. What is this little trespasser? And why can it talk like that? I've never had... Wait! It's getting away! The trespasser's getting away! the dog thought and yelped before rocketing off down the hallway after him.

Ono had made it to the tile and was nearly in the middle of the washroom when the terrier came barreling at him with its snaggled teeth snapping. The stubby animal came as fast as a bullet, and Ono had hardly enough time to think before it was already upon him.

"Blemmit osil utix!" he squealed and dove to the side. As he fell to the tile, a bright green flash shot from his wand and struck the terrier directly on the forehead, sending a shower of multi-colored sparks bursting up into the air and brilliantly lighting up the whole room for just a fraction of a second. The shot caught the terrier in mid stride, and it suddenly yelped and went stiff as if having been seized by a powerful jolt of electricity.

Ono landed on the floor rolling for cover, and the dog hit

the tile like a limp ball of fur and slid by only inches a-
way, coming to a stop in a gray, crumpled heap.

And just as quickly as it had all begun, the room was suddenly dark and silent again.

Panting for breath, Ono got up on shaky legs with his wand
ready and aimed for another spell. But the terrier was out
like a snuffed candle's flame, and as he watched warily the
dog's tail slowly uncurled and flopped limply to the floor.

Ono sighed a great sigh of relief, then picked up his
pouch and crept around the terrier's limp body and pushed
through the doggy door and was gone. I will surely never do
that ever again! he thought as he hurried across the back
yard and slipped beneath the fence.

CHAPTER FIFTY NINE

"Joey! Joey, come down here for a minute would you?"
Joey's mom called from somewhere downstairs. She had a high,
nasally voice that carried throughout the entire house, and
as Joey finished brushing his teeth he rolled his eyes. Then
he stood up on his toes and leaned over the countertop and
spit a glob of toothpaste in the sink.

"Sure mom! Hang on, I'm getting ready right now!" he
called back.

After he was done rinsing he checked his spiked red hair
in the mirror and peeled his lips back in a snarl to check
his new braces for bits of breakfast. Finding none, he
clicked off the bathroom light and opened the door and went
out into the hallway. He turned left, then walked down the
stairs sliding his hand along the rail. "What's up?" Joey
asked as he went.

His mom was sitting on the couch in the living room wearing a white bathrobe with yellow daisies spotting it, and
her red hair was in rows of curlers. In her hand was the
small crystal bowl that usually sat on the coffee table,
and on her face was a tight, exaggerated smile.

"Come on down here and have a seat son," she said and gave
the cushion beside her a few gentle taps. Her fingernails
were especially pink today.

"Ugh, okay," Joey said, knowing something was wrong before
he even made it to the bottom of the stairs. She was always

curt and smiling like a shark when he was in some kind of trouble, and he began racking his brain for what he had done wrong as he walked hesitantly across the room with his hands stuffed nervously in his pockets. There were a few things, of course, but he thought he had covered up for them well e- nough weeks ago.

"Yeah? What's going on mom?" he asked as innocently as he could and plopped down on the couch beside her with a gleam- ing smile full of metal.

She handed him the bowl and turned sideways to face him. "Why don't you tell me what's wrong with that?" she asked pleasantly. She hadn't done her makeup or even had her usual cup of coffee yet, and the sleep lines on her face and the puffiness around her eyes hadn't been smoothed out. The cur- lers encircling her hair made her head seem much larger and looming than it really was, and her smile did not match well at all with her one cocked eyebrow.

Joey thought she looked a little like a scary monster, so he turned his attention down to the bowl. He flipped it in his hands, squinting for chips or cracks. "I don't... No- thing?" he said after a moment and handed it back.

She took it and shook it over the table like she was try- ing to pour something out of it. "Sure you do dear! It's empty. Now how do you suppose it got that way?" she asked and set it down again.

Joey scratched behind his ear and looked down at his

sneakers. The left one wasn't tied all the way, and the loop had come undone. "I don't know," he mumbled. He wasn't looking at her, but he sensed the smile drop off her face like a wall of ice breaking off the end of a glacier.

"Joey...?" she warned sternly.

He turned and looked at her with his palms up. "Mom! I don't know, honest. I didn't take all the candy," he whined.

She huffed and stood up wagging a finger at him. "Do you know how much we spent on those teeth of yours mister? Eighteen hundred dollars! That's one thousand, eight hundred dollars that we could hardly afford along with this new house. Do you remember what the orthodontist said? **No** candy for the first two weeks. And what do you do? You eat a whole bowl of chocolates the very next day!"

"No I didn't! I went to bed after the Spider Man movie was over! They were still there when I went upstairs weren't they?" he asked.

His mom put her hands on her hips and frowned at him, then turned her head and shouted around the corner to the kitchen, "Honey! Did you eat all the M&M's last night?!"

What sounded like a pan went clattering to the floor and was followed by a muffled curse, then, "No! Lot's of ice cream but no M&M's. Probably a few too many beers too..." his voice trailed off in the clinking and clacking of dishes.

His mom thoughtfully ran her tongue along the inside of

her cheek and tapped her foot on the floor, looking down at him expectantly. Her toenails matched the bright pink of her fingernails. "So? Who ate them then?" she asked after a moment.

Joey's eyes had begun to water, and he wiped his nose on the back of his hand and sniffed. "Not me," he mumbled. Then he heard the sound of the dog's bell tinkling, and he straightened up and pointed to the terrier as it trotted in to the room. "Maybe it was Special? He eats **anything** mom! Remember that one time when we caught him in the back yard eating his own-"

That was the wrong thing to say.

His mom gasped and covered her mouth like he had cussed at her, then bent down and scooped up the terrier and clutched it like a baby to her bosom.

"Joey! I am very disappointed in you! First you won't admit to it, then you try and blame it on Special? Over chocolates! He doesn't even like chocolates!" she said and glared at him. Special seemed to be enjoying the attention very much, and he wagged his tail and licked eagerly at the corner of her mouth, which she didn't pull away.

Joey sighed and hung his head as his chin began to quiver and bob. This is not fair! I didn't do anything wrong! It probably was that stupid mutt! he thought and crossed his arms bitterly.

"So? What do you have to say for yourself now young man?"

she asked.

"Nothing," Joey said with an angry pout.

"That's what I thought. Now go get your backpack and get to the bus stop before you're late."

Dejected, Joey stood up and moped across the room and started dragging his feet up the stairs. But before he got halfway up his mom called out his name again and he looked back at her.

"And on your way down, why don't you bring all your video game stuff with you. You won't be needing it for the next two weeks," she said.

Joey's face paled. "But mom! I swear I didn't-" he began to protest, but his mom jabbed a finger in the air and pointed up the stairs.

"Now." She pronounced the word very slowly and clearly.

Knowing it would do no good to argue, Joey slumped over and glared at Special as he went up to his room. In his mom's arms the terrier's dark beady eyes followed him up the stairs. The corners if its mouth were pulled back into a grin, and its tongue hung over its teeth and slid in and out as it panted. Special looked very sinister indeed at that moment, and he seemed to be snickering quietly at him for the trouble he had caused.

Joey stomped down the hallway and slammed his bedroom door shut and flopped down on his bed crying. I'll show them! I'll catch that stupid dog doing something wrong, and they will feel **so** bad for this! he thought while pummeling the

mattress with angry little fists.

CHAPTER SIXTY

The next several weeks it rained or hailed nearly every other day, and the dark clouds hardly seemed to ever move but to grudgingly let the occasional column of sunlight squeeze through while they hung over the mountains. It even begun to snow one afternoon, but the flakes were thin and icy and melted away and disappeared as soon as they touched the ground.

Undaunted, Ono kept on with his gathering in the neighborhood late at night, but was sure to save his pilfering for the trashcans only, for after the close call with the terrier his curiosity for the humans' dwellings had flown from his mind and out of his ear and been forgotten. He eyed them cautiously when he crept by them now, and began carrying the shard of glass along with him just in case, wearing it slanted across his back like a sword in a tidy little black sheaf he had sewn. It was cumbersome at first and quite a pain to carry while dragging back heavy loads, but after a few nights he grew accustom to it and felt much safer with it also.

It was a smooth, busy time for him, and the winter seemed to be passing by very quickly.

On this dark, late night, we find Ono waddling through a drainage pipe, already on his third trip back to the neighborhood and very pleased with himself. It had rained earlier that evening, and dirty water flowed over his feet as he splashed through it, humming merrily to himself with a smile on his face. He went straight for a long while and traveled far into the subdivision, then turned right and poked his head out from the gutter and peered out at the road.

The blacktop was wet and shined with the glow of a nearby streetlight, and a small stream of water carried a candy wrapper along the sidewalk before turning the corner of the gutter and flowing between his feet and disappearing down the pipe behind him. Across the street a blue minivan was parked before a big white house, and on the curb an aluminum trashcan gleamed beautifully in the darkness. Its lid was askew, and a mountain bike with a bent front wheel leaned up against it.

Ono rubbed his hands together happily, then pulled his cap back on and looked once more down the street both ways before hurrying across. He hopped up on the curb, then waddled over to the bicycle and looked it up and down. After a moment of thinking he snapped his fingers and grinned, then went to the rear wheel and climbed up the spokes and stood up wobbling on the tire with his arms held out for balance. Then he hopped up and wrapped his arms around the seat and nimbly threw his legs up and over with a shrill grunt. Once he was standing on the seat, he hopped down in the trashcan between the gap of the lid and landed softly inside on his rump on the top of a garbage bag.

"Aaaha... What could be in here I wonder?" he whispered to

himself and got to his feet. He reached over his shoulder and pulled out his sword, then used it to slash a few quick gashes through the side of the garbage bag. Then he slid it back in its sheath and pulled the slit open and began rummaging around inside.

There were more than a few crumpled tissues and empty medicine bottles and boxes that Ono flung out over his shoulder as he dug, and it wasn't long before he discovered a half-eaten roll with strawberry jelly smeared on its top. He rolled it out of the bag and sniffed at it, then poked the congealed jelly and licked his finger. He smacked his lips for a moment and frowned. "Mmm... na," he said, then pushed it away and continued on.

To turn down a meal of any kind is a truly odd and almost unheard of thing for a gnome to do, but Ono had more food than he could possibly hope to eat squirreled away in his burrow, and he could afford to pick and choose from the things he wanted now. He even found himself doing the same with the shiny treasures he discovered, which was something he could never have imagined himself doing, for his burrow was becoming cluttered with all sorts of wealth and there wasn't much room left along the walls and shelves to place it anymore.

Humming happily, he continued to dig as the pile of loose garbage behind him grew with empty wrappers and soup cans and dingy cotton balls. There was something round and smooth somewhere inside that his fingers slid over as he worked, and it took him a moment to get his hands around the thing before pulling it out to inspect it.

When Ono realized what it was, he gasped and dropped it like it had suddenly burned his hands and backed away in horror.

The severed doll's head landed on the plastic bag and slowly rolled to the side, coming to a stop against the edge of the trashcan where it sat up on its jagged neck and stared lifelessly from the shadows at him. All of its hair had been ripped from its head, and tiny holes pitted its scalp where it had once been. The doll's eyes were colored in with waxy black crayon, giving it a gleaming, skeletal stare that seemed to lock onto Ono through the darkness. The thing's mouth hadn't been mutilated though, which made its appearance even worse, for its prim little smile and bright red lips were eerily unsettling.

Disturbed by what he had found, for the head was nearly the size of his own, Ono pulled his sword and crept forward with its point held out in front of him. Shocked and shaking, he crouched down in front of it and curiously poked his blade at it.

The head first tipped on its side and then rolled face-down. Relieved at not having that blank stare following him anymore, Ono reached out his hand and timidly touched it before yanking his arm back.

"What..?" Ono puzzled with a confused grimace, then reached out again and patted it once more. He did not feel cold, dead skin like he had thought he would, but instead felt dull plastic that clunked hollowly when he tapped on it. Setting his sword aside, he picked up the head and turned it in his hands, wondering for a moment why something so ugly and distasteful could ever be wanted. The thought made him shiver, and he dropped the doll's head and picked up his sword and turned his back to the frightful thing.

Having found all he wanted to find in the disagreeable trashcan, Ono gladly climbed out and scaled down the bicycle and hopped to the ground. He stood at the curb for a moment and looked around, then saw at the far end of the block the driveway where Proi was buried. Suddenly feeling horribly guilty, he sighed and looked down at his toes.

Even though he had dearly wanted to, he hadn't been able to bring himself to visit his father's grave in an awfully long time, for the humans' beasts were always parked over it like giant sentries and he was much too frightened to sneak beneath them where he would surely be crushed into a red puddle if they were to discover him.

Are you just going to forget all about him then? Is that it? I must say, if you were brave enough to sneak into a human's home and battle a fierce, wild monster for a pouch of sweets, then you're brave enough to do this or much too selfish not to! his thoughts badgered him.

Ono shifted on his feet and gave the trashcan beside him a mistrustful glance, for he still felt offended by what he had found in it. Then he looked back down the block and picked up his chin. "Yes, I do suppose a visit is long over-due, and I will just have to deal whatever way I will with the rotten beasts," he whispered to himself, then puffed out his chest and began waddling down the sidewalk.

He passed by several homes and was nearing the driveway when suddenly a bright glow began to spread at the end of the block, lighting up the stop sign at the corner and gleaming off the wet asphalt.

Ono pricked up his ears and gasped, then darted into a row of hedges nearby for cover where he pulled his wand and waited quietly. A moment later a black, sleek looking car turned the corner, and its bright headlights shined down the street and made the shadows before it slide and dodge elu-sively away. Ono winced when the light struck his eyes, then shaded them with a hand and ducked further down in the bush-es, squinting curiously to see what the beast was up to.

The car drove slowly down the street as if it were creep-ing sinisterly along, the pools of light cast down from the streetlights sliding up and over it. As it neared, a muffled Boom Baba, Boom-Boom-Boom noise could be heard from within as the speakers thumped out the loud music.

Ono turned in the brush to watch it go by, but before it passed it slid up beside the curb on the opposite side of the street and came to a sudden stop. Then the headlights blinked off, and the car went completely silent.

Oh! I don't like the looks of that beast one bit! What's it doing out so late, and why has it stopped so close to me? Of all places? Ono wondered and tightened his grip on the wand as he glared suspiciously at the car.

After a moment the driver's side door opened, and a tall, lanky teenager stood up out of it and looked around the neighborhood. He had on a white sweater that almost seemed to glow in the darkness, and his baseball cap was turned a-round backwards. He shut the door and carefully tiptoed a-cross the lawn of a blue home and disappeared around the side of the garage.

Intrigued by the human's strange behavior, Ono leaned for-ward in the hedges and began to pull on his beard. That was awfully queer. I wonder what it's doing sneaking about so late? he thought as he waited for the human to return again.

It didn't take long, and just a few minutes later he heard hushed giggles and laughter coming from across the street. Then the lanky boy came hurrying out of the shadows holding the hand of a much shorter girl who followed quickly behind him. She had long dark hair and was wearing a short skirt and a halter top with healed shoes that clicked on the side-walk. They came to the car giggling, and she playfully slapped his shoulder as he dug in his pocket.

"Brandon! You are nuts! Do you know what my dad will do to

us if he finds out we went to a party together? I'll be grounded forever, and you'll be **soo** dead. Seriously!"

Brandon pulled out the car keys and held them up in the air and gave them a jingle. "Come on Becky! My parents are out of town and my mom left the keys to the Volvo. We have to go! This kind of thing only happens, like, once in a lifetime! You're not chickening out are you?" he teased and opened the door.

Becky put her hands on her hips and smiled. "Okay, but you better have me back before he wakes up, or else this will be the last thing we do in our lives," she said and clicked around to the passenger's side.

"Yeah! Par-tay!"

"Shh! Quiet Brandon!"

Both doors shut, and the headlights and loud music came back to life as the car made a quick u-turn and sped off.

Ono leaned out of the hedges to watch the glowing taillights disappear around the corner, then stepped out on the sidewalk and fixed his cap. Hmm, that's odd, he thought and slid his wand back in his sash. Who would have thought to call a beast a Volvo? Volvo! What a curious sounding name!

Shaking his head in disbelief, Ono continued on down the block with a puzzled look on his face.

CHAPTER SIXTY ONE

When he came to the bottom of the driveway and peered halfway out from around a mailbox post, Ono studied the two beasts sitting in the driveway with a wary eye and a cocked ear.

The one on the left was a blue pickup truck with a shiny roll bar and a tool box in the bed, and the other on the right was a newer green Mustang with a small basketball sticker in the rear window. Neither moved or made even the slightest hint of noise while they sat parked before the garage except for the truck's tall antenna that wobbled in the wind.

With his heart thudding frightfully in his chest, Ono crouched down and began crawling on his belly with his wand held in his teeth up the driveway towards the rear of the truck. I hope it doesn't come alive and run me over and smash me into a puddle of gnome pulp! Oh! I hope not! he worried as he went.

Feeling nearly like a bug must when watching the bottom of a shoe step down on it, Ono crawled beneath the rear bumper and into the huge shadow the truck cast down. With his eyes round and his ears tall, he glanced up at the beast's underbelly as he crawled over the driveway. There was a large spare tire tucked up under the bed, and an exhaust pipe ran beside it and bent crookedly out to the side. A small oil leak was glistening on the rear transfer case with a dark

puddle beneath it, and nearly everything was coated in dried
mud.

How disgusting are these creatures? My goodness is that
unpleasant! Ono thought and wrinkled his nose distastefully,
for he thought he was getting an unwanted view of the
beast's unmentionables. He shook his head to rid himself of
the graphic sight, then kept his eyes down the rest of the
way.

He stopped hesitantly near the spot in the driveway where
Proi was buried, for it was just behind the front right tire
of the truck. The tire was tall and wide with deep, knobby
treads, and Ono was quite scared to go anywhere near it, for
he suddenly pictured his mangled, broken body twisted up and
caught in the grooves as it rolled along down the street.

You've already made it this far haven't you? Now go on! Go
already! It's nearly been months since your last visit! he
thought. Flustered, Ono whined and wrung his hands together.
After a moment of debating, he crawled forward and propped
his sword point-up against the tire so that if the beast did
decide to roll back on him it would get quite a sting for
its evil efforts. Then, with his wand ready in one hand, Ono
timidly knocked on the driveway with the other and lowered
his face down until the tip of his nose touched the pavement.

"Hello! It's me father, Ono! I am terribly sorry about not
coming to speak with you in so long, but Volvos are right o-

ver your grave! Oh, what huge, dirty creatures these Volvos
are! If you could only see them!" he whispered, then glanced
upward and shivered with disgust when he saw a bulging
transmission hanging above.

So for nearly the rest of the night Ono filled his dad in
on all of the strange new things that had been happening in
what had once been the meadow. He explained all about the
humans moving into the homes and their strange behavior a-
mong one another and how he had yet to figure them out. Then
he went on to talk about the herd of deer he had seen and
how he felt that was a good sign that maybe the other gnomes
would someday return also, and gone into quite a bit of detail when telling about his adventure stealing the M&M's and
his close call with the terrier. The Volvos were quiet and
dormant the whole time, and he gradually loosened up and
quit worrying so much about them, and while telling about
the trashcans he became excitedly animated.

"You wouldn't believe it, but-" he said and hopped up to
his feet, "-the humans leave out giant containers full of
sweets and feasts and treasures and beautiful riches for the
taking! You wouldn't imagine some of the marvelous things
I've discovered!" Ono said, then suddenly realized he'd
nearly been shouting. He clapped a hand over his mouth and
froze for a moment to look around, then crouched back down
again.

"Perhaps I should get going now father. It's getting to be

late and I've been here for quite a time. But I'll be back soon now that I know these Volvos are heavy sleepers. I love you!" he said, then picked up his things and hurried down the driveway.

He came to the sidewalk and waddled to the end of the block where the nearest drainage pipe was, and as he was getting down off the curb to step inside he noticed a trashcan that was overflowing with garbage just around the corner. Its lid was pushed several inches up by bulging plastic bags, and a squat recycling bin filled with glass bottles sat on the ground beside it, twinkling in the streetlight's glow from across the road.

Hmm, perhaps I have just enough time for one more? Ono wondered and turned around to look towards the east. He knew it was getting close to morning time, but it was still as dark as night and he couldn't make out the glow of dawn over the tops of the homes yet. It wasn't a hard decision for him to make really, and after a moment he was scurrying eagerly down the sidewalk to see what he could discover.

When he arrived at the bottom of the trashcan he unwound the floss from the treble hook, flung it over the top, and then climbed up the side with expert skill and was gone from view a moment later.

Inside the trashcan, Ono cut open the top bag and begun to hurriedly rummage around. There was a pair of broken headphones and a scratched CD and a yellow toothbrush that he

impatiently shoved aside as he searched. "Come on, there
must be something good in here. Now where is it?!" he said
to himself as he continued to comb through the trash.

After pulling out a snarled ball of fishing line and nearly tangling himself in it, Ono discovered a little silver
earring in the shape of a teddy bear stuck on a scrap of
duct tape. "Ohhhh... Well, I could certainly use this somewhere at home," he whispered with a smile as he reached out
and pulled it off to inspect it. Yes, it would look especially nice stuck in the wall beside my bed where that dreadfully empty area is, he thought and dropped it down into his
pouch.

He was preparing to leave for home with his new treasure
when a strong, intriguing smell drifted to his nostrils. Ono
sniffed at the air curiously, then began digging further in
the bag to search for what could make such an odd scent. He
moved aside a jagged tuna can lid and found a narrow little
bottle that had a bright red sauce dripping from its opening.

Ono reached out his hand and hooked a gob of the bizarre
sauce on his finger and brought it under his nose for a
closer smell. Its aroma was a pungent spicy one that tickled
his nose. Ono frowned at the stuff, then shrugged and put
his finger in his mouth and sucked it clean.

At first, smacking his lips and rolling his tongue around,
Ono liked how the hot sauce tasted very much, for it tingled

and heated his mouth like a warm mug of pine water did in
his stomach on a cold day. But then, much to his surprise,
the hot sauce gradually began to heat up, and then to sting,
and finally to burn like a raging furnace.

"Oooh! Aaak!" Ono panicked and fanned his mouth as his
eyes began to water and his nose to run. Panting and
scratching the taste off his tongue with his fingernails, he
whined and choked and spat as he picked up his things and
left as quickly as he could to find something to drink that
would relieve the torturous taste that was spreading down
the back of his throat like molten lava. He repelled down
the trashcan and hurried across the sidewalk and looked down
at the gutter, hoping to find the same trickle of rain water
flowing along the edge of the street. But the gutters had
long ago carried the water away and drained the curbs, and
all that was left was damp pavement. Frustrated, Ono stomped
his foot and fanned his mouth.

"Hakes! Hakes oo id!" he cried with his inflamed tongue
hanging from his mouth.

He turned and looked down the sidewalk through blurry eyes
and noticed the recycling bin. Laying sideways on top of the
pile was a brown, long-necked bottle with the label torn
off, and inside of it was a pool of amber liquid that was
settled at the bottom corner.

"Ank hoodness!" Ono shrilled, then hurried over to the recycling bin and began climbing up its side.

The bottle's opening hung out over the edge, so while clinging to the side of the bin Ono reached up with his free hand and grabbed the lip and pulled down. The bottle teetered stubbornly for a moment, then began to tip down as the puddle of liquid swayed forward. Desperate, and not thinking of or even caring what the liquid was, Ono opened his mouth as wide as it would stretch and wiggled his tongue pleadingly in the air. The liquid came spilling out and splashed over his face while he gulped and sputtered and choked as much of it down as he could without even tasting it, but loving every precious drop it had to offer nonetheless.

When the flow finally stopped Ono swallowed the last mouthful, then sighed in relief when the burning in his mouth subsided. His tongue felt oddly numb from the burn it had received, but felt much better than it had only moments before.

Well, if I ever come across that devil sauce again I will run away as fast and as far as I can! he thought as he climbed back down the bin and let out a loud belch that tasted strangely bitter and musky. Ono smacked his lips and wondered about the taste, then waved a dismissive hand in the air and picked up his things.

I have done more tasting and smelling of things tonight than was good for me, and it is time to leave before I do any more of it! he thought and hopped down off the sidewalk and ducked into the gutter.

As the horizon began to glow several minutes later, the Volvo came speeding down the street and went squealing a-round the corner and sped off down the block.

CHAPTER SIXTY TWO

Ono began to feel the effects of the beer he had guzzled
while waddling back through the twists and turns of the
drainage pipes towards the end of the subdivision. Suddenly
his scalp began to tingle and his head seemed to float up
off his shoulders like a balloon on a string. Then the darkness around him took on an attractively soft velvety texture, and reality became as smooth and relaxed as if he were
walking through a pleasant dream.

Thinking that the long night's work was beginning to take
its toll, Ono smiled lazily and yawned as he strolled along
on feet that seemed to just barely brush over the ground. It
has certainly been a good night, all in all I suppose, he
thought gaily as he drifted along through the pipe, suddenly
happy and content with all the world. He gently patted his
gathering pouch on his hip and felt the earring through the
cloth, and he decided that that was a very good thing also.

Of course, poor Ono had not even the slightest inkling
that he was becoming intoxicated, for he had never before
encountered alcohol of any sort and didn't know what it
could do. He only knew that he felt smooth and comfortable
and that he liked the feeling very much. What he also didn't
know though, was that alcohol has very profound effects on
little bodies such as his, and that he was only enjoying the
first swallow or two that he had taken of the beer.

There was much, much more to come.

"Hum-dee-de-doo-de-dum..." he began to sing merrily and
dance his arms in the air before him like a conductor as he
waddled along. His head was starting to swim and his knees
felt like loose hinges.

He turned left down an intersecting pipe, but took the
corner much too soon and bumped his shoulder on the corner.
He spun around and stumbled and nearly lost his balance, but
put an arm against the side of the pipe and caught himself.
"Whoa there! Watch what you're going you clumsy squirrel!"
he said to himself, then found it rather funny that he would
call himself such a name and snickered behind his hand. Then
he hiccupped and pushed off from the pipe and began to waddle towards the mouth of the gutter. He could see the dim
street at the end of the pipe, but as he walked towards it
the pipe seemed to stretch and the opening to get smaller
until it was just a tiny dot in the darkness.

"What? Nooo, you get back here you! Thish very inshtant!"
Ono shouted and pointed at the end of the pipe. For some
reason he found that hilarious as well, and he doubled over
laughing and lost his cap. Once the fit had passed he picked
it up and wiped the tears from his eyes, then stuffed it
down in his pouch and continued on.

His waddle gradually became a wavering stagger, and as he
heel-toed along he had to put out his arms to steady himself
against the sides of the pipe. By the time he made it out of
the gutter and to the street some several minutes later, he

was no longer feeling smooth and comfortable, but rather drunkenly lethargic and increasingly uncoordinated. His head wasn't floating pleasantly above his shoulders, but was instead reeling in a nauseating spin that made it difficult to keep his balance.

Holding on to the curb for support, Ono belched and smeared a hand down his face, then looked around as if he were lost.

The neighborhood around him was still dark, but at the tops of the mountains surrounding it was the morning's glow turning the clouds a light shade of gray. Somewhere down the block a dog barked impatiently to be walked and fed, and the early sparrows were beginning to land in the yards and peck for worms.

"Tiiime to gooo..." Ono grumbled, then pulled himself over the curb and got unsteadily to his feet. The house before him was a tall white one, and as he squinted at it the home seemed to ripple and shimmer as if he was looking at it from under water.

"Stupid, human.. thing," he slurred, then took a few unsteady steps towards the front hedges. But before he got there he stopped in mid stride and frowned curiously at the home. Suddenly, it leaned over on its side as the ground rushed up and struck the side of his head.

Ono didn't realize he had fallen over until the pain flared a moment later and his ear started to ring. "Oohh..."

he groaned and rolled over and got to his hands and knees.
Then his throat tightened and his mouth began to water as
his stomach tensed and rumbled.

"Oh no, no, no, NAAAAGHHH!" he started to protest, then
spewed forth a great stream of vomit on the pavement before
him. Much more came out in several agonizing waves, and once
the last had passed Ono spat and wiped his mouth and stood
up.

Groaning and miserable and teetering unsteadily on his
feet, Ono looked quite the drunken mess. Without his cap on
his hair was in wild disarray, and his normally clear,
bright gray eyes were bloodshot and glossy and half open.
Chunks of vomit were clumped in his beard, and his left ear
was red and swelling.

"Gotta get home... Humans'll be up soon," he mumbled, then
leaned forward and stumbled across the sidewalk and went
crashing head first into the hedges. Usually when he snuck
through the tangle of branches he would duck and slide and
step silently through the tangle of branches as he slinked
along. But he was much too inebriated for such a task at the
moment, and he made quite a racket as he went snapping and
rustling and cursing up the side of the yard. He made it to
the gate and gingerly squeezed between the rails, then
climbed out of the brush and stepped out onto the walkway.

The side of the house was just to his right, and a pyramid
of small paint cans were stacked against it beside a five

gallon bucket. Ono paid them little attention as he stumbled along the walkway towards the back yard, but when the bricks before him began to course and flow like a red stream he again lost his balance. His arms flailed as he tipped to the side, and he went reeling into the stack of paint cans, sending them falling and clacking to the ground around him.

"Snakes! Too loud! Too loud!" Ono giggled as he picked himself up and stumbled as quickly as he could across the back lawn. He half fell, half dove beneath the fence, and when he crawled out the other side and into the underbrush he sighed with relief. "Finally made it, just... almost there," he panted and laid splayed out on the ground beneath a fern for a moment. It was comfortable for him there in the dirt, and he seriously considered sleeping there until the underbrush began to spin like a tornado all around him and a cold sweat beaded his brow.

"Ohhh.. please, not again," he groaned as he rolled over and began to heave dry, painful retches that produced nothing but burning bile. Then, just when he thought it could not possibly get any worse, he heard the sound of a human's voice near the fence behind him. Still retching, he crawled away on all fours further into the underbrush to get away.

Once the wave of nausea ended and the human's voice trailed away behind him, Ono stumbled and staggered up the mountain side, grasping on to branches and stones and ferns for support. The forest was a blurred, reeling green haze,

and the ringing in his ear seemed to be the sound the trees
made as they spun mercilessly around him. More miserable
than he could ever remember being, Ono just wanted to get
back to his burrow and fall asleep in his soft bed and escape this horrible illness.

On his way he collapsed and fell quite a number of times,
and by the time he reached the top of the mountain he was
covered in mud and had sticks and pine needles poking out at
all angles. It was well into the start of the morning by
then, and the forest creatures were beginning to stir.

"Kaw! Kaw! Kaw!" a crow squawked from the branches above.

Ono winced when he heard the sound, then glared upward and
saw a black smear in the branches of the tree. "You! you
thing... thing this ish funny? Hugh?! **Bird?!**" he slurred
angrily. "Ha! Well, I got, have something for you!" He
reached over his shoulder for his sword, but his hand could-
n't find the hilt and he begun to turn in slow circles as he
grasped for it.

The crow eyed him bewilderedly for a moment, then ruffled
up its feathers and flew away.

Ono fell down again and forgot why he wanted his sword in
the first place, then hiccupped and began to stagger down
the mountain side, which proved far more treacherous than
going up it. He tripped and tumbled and rolled most of the
way, and he somehow made it back to his burrow relatively
unscathed and with all of his things. Somewhere along the

way he had picked up a handful of leaves, and he frowned curiously at them for a moment. His eyes wouldn't seem to come into focus though, so he dropped them and staggered through the brush and pushed aside the slab of bark. "Aahh.. home.. " he mumbled before his eyes rolled back and he fell forward.

The last thing he saw was the dark opening of his tunnel rushing up to swallow him like an earthen mouth.

CHAPTER SIXTY THREE

When the sound of cans crashing and clacking on the walk-way suddenly awoke him, Joey sat up in bed and rubbed his eyes and squinted at the Garfield alarm clock on the dresser beside him. His red hair was twisted and snarled on one side, and he wore an awkward looking headset that had two curved, thin metal bars that encircled his mouth and hooked onto the front of his braces.

The round clock held in Garfield's gaping mouth read 5:47 in big orange numbers that glowed in the darkness of his room.

Groggy and half asleep, he turned and looked over at the window on the furthest wall. The drapes weren't pulled in all the way, and the window was propped up on a football. Somewhere outside the tinny clinkclinkclink of cans rolling across the walkway could be heard, and a slight sliver of daylight could be seen hinting in the distance.

It took Joey a second or two to realize what was going on, but when he did he threw back the covers and hurried across the room in his Sponge Bob tighty-whiteys. He jumped over a bean-bag chair, pulled aside the drapes, slid up the window, and stuck his head out and looked down.

Even in the feeble glow of early morning, he could see clearly enough from the second story to make out several of his mom's small paint cans scattered across the walkway. One had rolled off into the grass, and another had broken open

and spilled a puddle of bright yellow paint on the red
bricks.

Joey narrowed his eyes and smiled wickedly behind the
gleaming bars of his headset. "Spethel, thad sthupid dog's
gonna ged id now!" he lisped, then rushed off for the door
to tell his mom. When he did, his elbow bumped against the
football and knocked it out of the window and sent it falling to the walkway. It bounced twice, rolled through the
paint, then came to a stop against the side of the bucket.

Joey ran down the hall, thumped down the stairs, and hurried across the living room towards the lit kitchen where
the smell of brewing coffee was coming. "Mom! Dad! Come
quick!" he said as he came sliding out across the tile.

His mom was behind a cluttered countertop whisking a bowl
of eggs with her hair up in a messy bun, and his dad was
sitting at the table in his underwear reading the paper and
sipping from a steaming mug. Both stopped what they were doing and frowned sleepily at him.

"What? What are you doing up so early for dear?" his mom
asked.

Joey pointed down the hall. "I'll thow you! Come on!" he
said and hurried towards the back door.

"Honey! It's not good to shout when you're wearing your
headset! Joey?!" she called after him, then put down her
whisk and sighed. "Come on Allen, let's go see what the boy
wants."

She shuffled across the kitchen in her slippers and Allen grunted and laid the paper on the table, then stood up and followed after her with the mug in his hand. He was a lanky, balding man with glasses, and his white, stork-like legs were bright in the dark hallway. The back door was open when they came to it, so they stepped out on the back porch and saw Joey standing on the walkway to the left of the yard, pointing around the side of the house.

"Look! Look ad whad thad sthupid dog did!" he kept lisping through the bars of his headset.

Allen shivered and took a sip of his coffee. "Son, isn't it a little early for all this? Can't it wait at least until the sun comes up?" he asked and shifted uncomfortably on his bare feet. It was cold and damp, and the back porch was littered with his wife's tacky lawn ornaments that she refused to put out in the yard until the rains stopped.

"Nod uleth you wan the spilled paind to dry!" Joey replied and smiled when his mom gasped.

"Spilled paint? What spilled paint? It better not be my ornament latex!" she said and hurried down the steps pulling her bathrobe around her. She shuffled over to Joey and covered her mouth with a pedicured hand. "Oh no! Damn it! That stupid dog!" she cried when she saw the yellow puddle spreading over the bricks. "Allen! Where's Special at? Go find him and bring him out here so I can rub his nose in this mess!"

Joey folded his arms and nodded his head as he watched his mom shuffle down the walkway and start gathering up her paint cans. Ha ha! That's what you get for grounding me! Now you'll know that precious Special's up to no good, and you'll feel so bad that you'll have to buy me the new Alien Slaughterer game! he thought smugly as he listened to her curse at the dog while cleaning up the mess.

A few moments later Allen came out of the back door with an odd look on his face. "Honey! Ugh... I found Special!" he called out around the corner.

"Good! Bring him out here and let me spank him! Do you know how expensive this paint is? Damn! And bring some paper towels with you! Paint's everywhere!" she huffed.

Joey was standing at the corner between the two looking back and forth with an obscured grin on under his headset until his dad called out, "Well, sweetheart, I found him locked in the garage! He couldn't have gotten out. I must have accidentally locked the poor little guy in there last night after work without food or water. Don't worry though, I'll get those paper towels!" he said, then looked at Joey and shrugged before going back inside.

Disappointed, for he was truly looking forward to seeing Special with a yellow nose and a red rump, Joey slumped over and turned to follow his dad inside when he heard his mom practically growl his name. He backed up and looked curious-ly down the side of the house and saw her sitting hunched over the yellow mess.

She slowly reached out and picked up the football from
behind the bucket and turned it dripping in her hand to ex-
amine it. Then she tilted her head back and looked directly
up at his open window where the curtains swayed in the
breeze. **"Joooeey?!"** she growled again and looked over her
shoulder with one blazing blue, angry eye.

Although it was chilly and damp and overcast, and he was
only in his underwear, Joey suddenly felt like he was about
to break out in a sweat. "Mom! No mom! I did nod do thad!"
he said and began to back away in horror.

She turned and stood up with the football clutched in her
hand as if she were trying to squeeze the air from it. "You
drop your ball out of the window and spill my paint? And
then try to blame it on my poor little Special? Again?!" she
said as she stomped towards him down the walkway. A thick
s-shaped vein was pulsing across her forehead, and her bared
teeth glistened frightfully in the early light.

The burning freckles on Joey's ghost-white face stood out
like spots on a Dalmation, and his eyes were round with panic. "Mom! Please! I swear thad I did nod do thad!" he tried
to explain with his hands waving in the air.

"I don't want to hear it!" she squawked, then grabbed him
by the ear and began dragging him towards the porch. "You
are grounded for two months! Two months this time, do you
understand me? No phone, no nothing! And this is all coming

out of your allowance! What is with you lately?!"

Then she pulled him into the house and slammed the door shut so hard that several of the lawn ornaments rattled and clinked together on the porch.

CHAPTER SIXTY FOUR

Since it had been Ono's first encounter with alcohol, it was also his first time experiencing a hangover as well, and the next day following the incident he truly believed he was about to perish from some wicked disease. His head pounded like a drum and throbbed as if it was about to crack open like a nut, and his eyes stung at even the slightest glow of candle light. He was weak and sluggish and moaned miserably with nearly every breath he took, and his stomach immediately sent back everything he sent down. His left ear was bruised and purple, and a scratch had scabbed across his forehead from one of the many tumbles he had taken.

"Ooooh, if I live through this, I'm never going to drink that horrid human poison ever again! Never!" he whined many times while splayed out in bed and laying in a puddle of his own sweat.

By the next night he had slept most of it off though, and Ono rolled out of bed feeling much better and very happy to still be alive. The first thing he did was clean up the splashes of dried vomit from the floor around his bed, then eat a light breakfast of stale muffin crumbs and a few nibbles of a mushroom cap. Afterwards he felt fit enough to go out gathering again, but before he did he headed down to the creek to wash up first, for he could hardly stand the sour smell of his own beard.

It was as dark as a night could get outside, and the

winds were whipping through the mountains and swaying the
forest in a tree leaning, limb shaking dance that rattled
the leaves and trembled the bushes. The heavy smell of coming rain was thick in the air, and the thunder's occasional
rumble boomed down from the black, stirring clouds above.

Ono waddled down to the stream, his cheerful whistling
being carried off by the wind and hidden in the creaks and
moans of the trees around him. He pushed through the undergrowth and set his things on the bank, then got down on his
knees and cupped the icy water in his hands and splashed it
on his face. Scrubbing himself until he once again felt
clean, he drank his fill and dried himself on a fern leaf.
Then he slid his sword across his back and picked up his
pouch, and as he was leaving he glanced up at the sky.

This is quite a storm that's coming! Yes, the big ones always seem to come towards the end of the winter for some odd
reason. Well, I'd better get in what gathering I can before
it arrives, because this storm will surely be a nasty long
one, he thought as he hurried around the side of the mountain.

Ono arrived at the fence sometime later and slipped beneath it, then crept through the back yard of a big blue
house. It was quite noisy, for the house had several wind
chimes hung from its eaves, and they all spun and twirled
and clinked crazily in the gusting wind. There was a bird
feeder swinging along with them, and it sprinkled seeds on

the porch every time it swung back and forth.

Not as worried as he normally was about what little dis-
turbance he might make in the night, Ono made his way down
to the sidewalk and stopped in the shadow of a fire hydrant
to look around and pricked up his ears to listen.

A potato chip bag tumbled crinkling down the street to
his right, and the hiss of the wind through the power lines
came from above. All of the windows in the homes were dark
all the way down the block, and a lawn chair had been blown
off a front porch across the way and laid folded in the
yard. There was only one trashcan that Ono could see anywhere near, and it was all the way down at the far end of
the street. It was a large metal one, and it laid on its
side across the sidewalk. Its lid had rolled into the street
and a bulging garbage bag sat half out of it.

Well, that's certainly convenient, Ono thought happily
and hopped down off the curb. He waddled along the gutter
with a hand holding his cap down on his head and leaning
forward into the wind, then came to the trashcan and climbed
back up on the sidewalk. The wind was broken by the blown o-
ver can, and Ono wiggled his fingers greedily and began with
his rummaging. He cut a slit in the bag and pulled it apart,
then eagerly reached in and started feeling around.

Inside, it felt as if it were mostly discarded clothes
filling the bag, and Ono pulled out several socks and shirts
and shorts to inspect before either tossing them over his

shoulder or rolling them up like a rug and stuffing them in
his pouch. Then he discovered a dog-eared baseball card, and
he picked it up and tilted it towards the streetlight to get
a better look at the strange thing.

On the glossy card, the top half of a dark-skinned human
grinned a big white smile while holding a menacing club over
its shoulder. His forearms were thick and lined with tense
muscles, and his biceps and chest bulged almost unnaturally
beneath his uniform. Arched above his head was a name in red
letters, and Ono tilted the card to squint at it.

"Bar.. ry, Barry. Bon.. onds. Barry Bonds," he sounded out
the name, then wrinkled his nose at the frightful picture
and dropped it face down on the sidewalk so he wouldn't have
to look at it. Then he reached back in the bag and felt a-
round some more.

His fingers brushed over a TV dinner tray, a juice carton,
then slid over something small and round and smooth. Picturing the mutilated, evil-looking doll's head, Ono gasped and
pulled his hands away. I hope it's not another one of those
awful heads! I'll surely have nightmares for weeks if I see
one again! Oh did I hate that ugly thing! he thought to himself and shivered.

He took his wand from his sash with one hand and pulled
the flap of plastic aside with the other, then leaned forward and peered cautiously in the garbage bag.

It was dark inside, but a pale orb of some sort could be

seen sitting amongst the other rubbish.

Ono reached out and curiously poked at it with his wand, then after a moment slid it back in his sash and pulled out the weird orb. It was not what he had feared, but only a Ping-Pong ball with a dent in its side. Ono turned it in his hands and frowned at the peculiar thing, then let it fall to the sidewalk. The ball clicked off the cement and, much to his surprise, bounced right back up into his hands.

"Ha ha! That's awfully strange. What could it be I wonder?" he puzzled and dribbled it at his side like a basketball. After a minute of playing with it he became bored, so he held it out and kicked it away before resuming his rummaging while humming merrily to himself.

Behind him, the dented Ping-Pong ball rolled clicking away down the dark sidewalk. Pushed along by the wind, it rolled past a driveway and bounced over a crack in the cement, and as it rolled past a row of shrubs a pair of golden eyes watched it go by. Then the eyes shifted back down the block at Ono and narrowed into sinister slits that shined in the darkness.

Yes... that strange little creature will do just fine for a late night snack, the white cat thought as it slipped silently from the shrubs and began to creep up behind him.

CHAPTER SIXTY FIVE

Ono was pulling out an empty toilet paper roll and wondering what on earth it could possibly be when the rain suddenly started to come down. It begun first with a few scattered drops that pattered gently here and there on the cement, then with a rumble of thunder the clouds seemed to break open and wring themselves out like sponges. Fat drops of rain came down in sheets and buckets, and the glow of the streetlights became yellow halos in the downpour.

"Snakes! Oh, this is just fine!" Ono cursed up at the sky when the drops began to pelt him and soak through his robe. There was still much left to be found in the garbage bag, and if the rain hadn't been quite so heavy he most likely would have stayed to see what he could discover in it. But the drops were big and falling fast, and to a body as small as his such rain can soon become painful and bothersome to be struck by. Grumbling at the storm, Ono dropped the toilet paper roll and bent down to pick up his pouch.

And that was when he saw the sudden flash of movement from the corner of his eye.

Caught off guard, Ono flinched and ducked down just as a big white paw came hooking out of the dark rain and tore the cap off his head, sweeping so close over him that its claws raked painfully through his hair. Terrified, his first reaction was to run for cover in the garbage bag. He spun around and pumped his legs, but the cat was much quicker and was already upon him.

It twisted around him and stopped him dead in his tracks with its ears laid back and its needle-like teeth bared and glistening. Its eyes were angry slits of gleaming gold, and when it hissed Ono felt warm droplets of its saliva spray his face.

"Eeeegh!" he shrilled in horror and ran for the curb, hoping desperately for a drainage pipe nearby. Hearing the cat's claws scraping on the wet sidewalk as it scrambled after him, Ono hurtled over the pile of garbage he had tossed aside and jumped down off the curb with his heart hammering in his chest.

Everything happened very quickly.

When he jumped, the cat reached out and swiped his legs out from under him. Ono's arms flailed wildly in the air and he bellyflopped in the street, his face splashing in the water and smashing hard against the pavement. Behind him, the cat slid gracefully down off the curb and licked its teeth as if to prime them for a meal.

Odd little thing. I wonder how much more fun I can have with it before it finally gives up and dies? the cat thought and smirked down at Ono as it paced nonchalantly around him in the rain.

Ono got up on his hands and knees sputtering out water and the blood that ran from his nose and busted lip. Water blurred his vision, and when he rubbed his eyes he saw that the nearest drainage pipe was far down the block. He'd never make it.

The cat's shadow slid over him as it paced expectantly around in a tightening circle, and Ono reached to his sash for his wand to deliver the very worst spell he knew. But before his hand closed around it, the cat swiped at him again with a flash of its paw. The powerful blow caught him in the ribs and sent him rolling and tumbling into a pool of streetlight in the middle of the road like a rag doll being tossed carelessly away. Before he could recover, the cat then batted it paw down on his stomach so hard that it drove all the wind from his lungs.

"Ough! Please! Stop!" Ono whined pitifully as he clutched at his side and gasped for breath with an agonized grimace on his blood-smeared face. It was raining heavily, and he splashed in the street as he struggled to get up and get away.

Very much enjoying the fun it was having tenderizing its meal, the cat advanced slowly, and as it sauntered into the streetlight its eyes glowed with wicked pleasure.

Holding his throbbing ribs and pleading for mercy, Ono slipped and fell in the water, then got up again as the cat suddenly arched its back and pounced. The cat seemed to hang amongst the raindrops for a moment with its needle-teeth bared and its hooked claws presented, and Ono let out a panicked squawk and dove to the side. The cat landed with a splash where he had been only a moment before, then lashed

out at him as he backed away stumbling.

Ono saw it coming and ducked the blow, but wasn't expec-

ting it when the cat immediately swiped out with its other

paw. It was intending to disembowel him, and Ono threw back

his hips and sucked in his belly as its claws slashed

through the front of his robe and tore it to tatters.

It's going to kill me in seconds if I don't do something

soon! he thought desperately as the cat advanced on him with

its head held low and scowling between its shoulders. Not

knowing what else to do, he faked like he was going to run

to the left. The cat flinched to head him off, and Ono made

his move. He spun to the right behind the cat, pulled his

wand and shrilled, "Nerhi, vitheling mor-"

He was only one syllable away from finishing the spell

when the cat spun around and swiped blindly back at him. He

had the wand held out away from his body like a pistol, and

the cat's claws raked across the back of his hand and batted

it out of his grasp.

"No!" Ono cried out in pain and clutched his bleeding hand

as his wand tumbled through the air and splashed in the gut-

ter. Doomed and devastated, he watched as it was carried off

down the street and disappeared. "Noo... " he sobbed and

fell to his knees, knowing he was as good as dead without

it.

Getting impatient and tired of the rain, the cat growled

deep in its throat and began to circle him again as it tried to decide in which fashion to kill him. Should I just pin it down and chew out its innards? Or perhaps pull it to pieces and save bits of it for later? Hmm.. the cat wondered as it eyed him hungrily.

Bleeding with his head bowed and his ears limp in defeat, Ono began to shiver under the glow of the streetlight as a whole lifetime of memories flashed like flipped pages before his eyes.

He saw each and every one of his old friends' smiles and heard their individual giggles and gossips; he saw Ezquit and Nez holding his little hands and smiling down sadly at him as they took him back to their burrow for the first time; he heard Bej's sweet laugh as she swung her feet over the creek and batted her green eyes at him; he remembered every joke and prank pulled by Sked and Kei; the kind comments and waves and gifts given to him from the older folks as he grew up; he saw his father laying weak and dying in bed, and remembered all the fun he had with him while playing in the tall grass of the meadow.

And then he realized that his cherished memories were all he had left of them, for everyone had been scared away by the humans and the meadow paved over, and even those were about to be stolen away from him by the murderous claws of a cat. Taken, just like everything else he once had, and never given back.

Suddenly, Ono was madder than he had ever been before. "It won't happen anymore! Not again!" he shouted as he reached over his shoulder and pulled out his sword and got to his feet.

Perplexed by the sudden change in its victim's demeanor, the cat stopped its pacing and curiously cocked its head to the side. Now what has gotten into this strange little creature? Just a moment ago it was half dead! it thought as it watched Ono turn the shard of glass readily in his hands.

"You heard me! Now come on! Let's have at it, if that's what you want!" Ono yelled and planted his feet beneath him.

The storm was in full swing by then, and the water in the road was up to his ankles and seeming to boil as more rain fell. The wind was whipping about and howling noisily, and the thunder boomed and rolled overhead.

The cat no longer seemed amused. The rain had plastered its fur to its body, and its face was a matted skull with a dripping white beard and angry eyes. It bared its teeth and hissed, then began to advance with its tail twitching eagerly as it came towards him.

Ono glared back at it and tightened his grip on the sword.

The two began to circle one another, feinting this way and that in the pool of light like two fighters in a ring. The tense stare down lasted a few long moments, but ended when the cat's paw shot out and slapped Ono across the face, slicing a jagged gash that opened up his cheek from ear to

nose. Ono spun around and nearly lost his footing, and before the pain of the blow came the cat swiped at him again.

This time it was trying to take out his legs, so Ono
jumped up in the air and swung his sword as hard as he could
as its paw swiped beneath him. "Aaeee!" he screamed and sunk
the blade so deep in the cat's cheek that he felt it clunk
against bone.

The cat screeched and flailed away shaking its head, then
looked at him and growled a high, angry growl as blood
stained the side of its face red. I've had enough of this
strange creature! I'm going to kill it and be done with it
already! it thought and charged.

Ono was ready for it, and as the cat came closer he stood
as still as stone. Then, when it was nearly upon him with
claws swiping and teeth snapping, he ducked down and hacked
the sword at its legs like he was swinging an ax at the
trunk of a tree. The blade cut deep, and the cat went
splashing and sprawling to the pavement.

"Do you want some more?! Huh?! Come on and finish it then!
Come on!" Ono squawked and shook his fist angrily.

As if understanding the challenge and not taking kindly to
it in the least, the cat flipped back up on its feet and
came at him once again. This time, Ono lifted his sword in
the air and met its attack screaming wildly in a rage.

The two clashed and turned into a struggling ball of swiping claws and swinging sword that rolled and splashed in the

street. At one moment Ono was on the bottom with his robe being slashed off his body and ripped to tatters as the cat tried to dig a hole in his chest, and the next he was on top with his blade chopping and hacking and flinging droplets of crimson blood in the air. And then, with one last piercing caterwaul, the cat turned tail and ran limping away with its tail tucked low.

Gasping for breath and covered in cuts and what little robe was left on his blood smeared body, Ono dropped his sword and wavered unsteadily on his feet. He watched the defeated cat slink off into the night and disappear in the dark downpour with an exhausted look of disbelief on his bleeding face.

Then he raised his arms and threw back his head and squealed in shrill victory up at the streetlight.

CHAPTER SIXTY SIX

The weeks of gloomy-gray storms and downpours came and
went like tides in the sky, and by the time the winter began
to fade and spring to brighten, the subdivision had become
as busy as an ant farm. There were mothers in round hats
digging in their gardens for weeds and planting flowers and
vegetables while their husbands rode around on their lawn
mowers drinking beer and pretending to wipe sweat from their
brows. The children proudly brought out their new bikes and
scooters and skateboards and hurried about doing tricks a-
long the streets, and the older folks stood scowling on
their porches wagging fingers at them and warning them to be
careful. The fond smell of barbecue sauce sizzling on hot
grills floated along in the breeze during the cool evenings,
and gum-smacking teenagers jabbered and exclaimed on their
tiny phones while washing their cars in the driveways.

The animals even seemed to rejoice in the start of spring,
and dogs of all shapes, sizes, and colors ran yapping and
capering in the back yards. The birds swooped and circled a-
round the feeders and pecked vigorously in the lawns, and
even a few gray squirrels bounded precariously along the
power lines without a care in the world. On clear nights
when the moon was full and high, a coyote's cry could sometimes be heard in the distance, and on others the hoot of
an owl came questioning from the darkness. Even the skittish
deer had calmed some, and they could often be seen among the

columns of trees on the mountain sides quietly chewing their shrubs and puzzling over the humans below with their ears tall and wide.

Over this time Ono's cuts and gashes healed and turned to scars, and he continued on with his gathering, although much wiser and carefully. He and the white cat occasionally crossed paths with one another late at night, but the cat, sporting its own set of fur-parting scars, thought it smart to keep its distance and did well to avoid him. It still glared its wicked golden glare and hissed at him as it slinked away though, and Ono was always sure to flash his sword and make unsavory gestures back as he watched it leave.

With the new weather came all sorts of new foods and treasures, and Ono passed through those many weeks very quickly by decorating his burrow and feasting like a gnome-king. His home gradually became even more luxurious as he swapped out old items for the shiny new ones he found. His modest potbelly grew to be quite a hearty bulge beneath his robes, of which he had sewn several more from the fine fabrics he discovered in the cans.

His once sparse beard had grown quite a bit since we have known him, and although it was nothing quite like Ezquit's masterpiece, it had filled in considerably and covered the candle's burn and most of the cat's slash on his cheek. The curly brown hairs looked much like Proi's had, and he kept

it neatly combed and bragged about it when he made his weekly visits to his father's grave.

It had nearly been a year since his world had been so dramatically flipped upside down, and without ever realizing it
Ono became something near content with his new life, for he
had everything and more of what he needed there. That is,
all but his friends and family and Bej of course, but he had
long ago accepted their choice to leave and his to stay, and
he did his best not to dwell on it as the time passed on.

Still, and as any elderly person that has spent their life
in labor will so begrudgingly assure you, injuries that have
seemingly been healed over and forgotten can still ache and
throb and flare something terrible far after they have been
acquired, and Ono spent many lonely hours in the darkness of
his burrow crying over his lost loved ones.

Some wounds, it would seem, heal much slower than others
and never seem to go away no matter how you try to ignore
them.

PART THREE

BLOOMS AND BLOSSOMS AND BERRIES

CHAPTER SIXTY SEVEN

"Whew! I say, that was certainly a good night!" Ono grunted happily to himself as he drug his full pouch up the side
of the mountain. Earlier that night he had come across a
whole box of discarded cinnamon rolls that were still sticky
with frosting, and after tasting one he had made several
trips back and forth to the trashcan to carry home as many
as he could. He had snacked on them along the way to lighten
his load, and stuck in his beard were more than a few crumbs
and clumps of frosting.

The sun was just beginning to rise over the mountains in
the east, and its rays were bright and bold in the clear
spring morning. The air was crisp and fragrant with blooming
plants of all sorts, and the neighborhood below was just beginning to stir with waking humans and beasts.

Smiling, Ono pulled his pouch behind him through the underbrush, the colors around him once again a brilliant green
that was dotted with a rainbow of fresh wild flowers. The
sparrows were whistling from the branches above, and Ono was
in such a good mood that he pricked up his ears and whistled
back. He waddled his way over the mountain and down to the
old pine tree, and as he pushed through the brush and shuffled down into his burrow his whistles were muffled and disappeared beneath the ground.

Inside, he set his pouch down beside him and pulled out
his wand to light a candle. Since his father's old wand had

been lost during the fight with the cat, he had fashioned a-
nother from the fallen limb of an oak tree. It wasn't as
nice as Proi's had been, but while recovering from his
wounds Ono had carefully polished it and carved his name in
its side in scraggly, lopsided letters.

As the candle's flame grew, he slid his wand back in his
sash and pulled out the cinnamon roll from his pouch. Then
he rolled it across the den and propped it up beside the
others and licked his fingers clean. He finished tidying up,
and as he was reaching over his shoulder to take off his
sword the smell of his own armpit came drifting up to his
nostrils.

Oh... oh no, that's not pleasant at all, he thought after
a few curious sniffs. Deciding that a bath before bed time
would do him well, he picked up his things and blew out the
candle and waddled back outside. He made his way whistling
down through the ferns and came to a willow beside the
creek, then glanced modestly around before getting undressed. The water was still very cold, and when Ono dipped
in a toe to test it he shivered and rubbed his arms and
pulled it right back out again.

Knowing there was only one way to go about it, he stood
at the very edge of the creek bank and took a few quick
puffs of air to ready himself. Then he jumped out over the
water with a wet Ka-Ploop! and came up splashing and sputtering shrilly. With teeth chattering like a dog biting at

fleas, Ono scrubbed his fingers through his beard and cleaned himself with a handful of moss. He had gone completely numb by the time he finished, so he climbed shakily out of the water and dried himself on a fern leaf.

"Aahh, yes, that is much better," he sighed as he slid back in to his robe and pulled on his cap. He tied his sash and picked up his pouch, and as he was turning to leave for home he heard a small noise through the waking sounds of the forest that made the tips of his ears suddenly twitch.

A hushed gnome's voice, whispering behind him.

Stunned, Ono perked up his ears and spun around with his gray eyes round and hopeful and his mouth hung wide open. In the underbrush on the hillside across the creek, the tops of the ferns and shrubs shook and trembled as something pushed down through them.

Can it be? Oh let it! Please! Please let it! Ono thought excitedly and held his breath.

The hushed whispering came again as the trail of wobbling ferns neared, and as he stood there frozen on his feet Ono began to feel a flicker of hope deep in his heart that hadn't been there for quite some time. A big toothy grin slowly spread across his face as the hushed voice neared, and he dropped his pouch to the ground and joyously held up his arms to welcome whoever it was back just as the ferns burst aside.

"Ha ha! Wel... " Ono began to say, but trailed off when he

saw what it was making the commotion.

The quail came loping awkwardly out of the underbrush as if it were dumbly pursuing the odd little feather dangling from its forehead and came to a skidding halt. Then it turned its head to look at him, blinked curiously, and then ruffled its feathers and ran off ah-hooing.

"...come back," Ono sighed quietly as he watched it go. His cheerful smile melted away and his ears flopped down in disappointment as he bent over and grabbed up his things.

You should have known better! That's what you get for thinking such foolishly hopeful things! None of them will ever come back! he thought and bitterly kicked an acorn out of his way as he slumped back towards his burrow.

CHAPTER SIXTY EIGHT

A moment later as Ono moped away grumbling a fern leaf was
pulled slowly aside where the quail had come running, and a
single brown eye peered cautiously out from around it and
squinted into the forest. It scanned suspiciously back and
forth, then noticed Ono slumping off up the mountain side.
Surprised, the eyeball sprang wide open, and Corq pushed
through the ferns with a big smile on his face calling out
his name. He would have waved his arms happily at the sight
of his friend, but he was carrying Igit on his back and a
stack of baskets in his arms.

"Ono! Hi! Hi! Hello there!" Igit chirped and waved from
her mate's shoulders as he eagerly carried her down towards
the stream. She looked her usual self, with fresh yellow
wild flowers braided in her hair and her green dress neat
and proper. Beneath her, Corq looked the same as well, with
his cap crooked and his brown robe patched and disheveled.
"Ono! Over here! We've missed you! And worried so!" they
called as they stopped at the stream's edge.

Ono froze in his tracks again, not quite believing what he
was hearing and almost afraid to turn around. If I'm hearing
things again, then I have finally gone crazy! Oh! I hope
they're really there this time! I really do! Ono thought and
whined, shifting nervously on his feet. Then he slowly
looked back over his shoulder with his eyebrow cocked and
uncertain.

Igit was climbing down off Corq's back, and he was waving
and smiling and gesturing for him to come near. "Have you
forgotten all about your old friends already Ono? Or have
those big floppy ears of yours stopped hearing? Come over
here and greet us already! It's been much too long!" Corq
called out and brayed with honking laughter.

Ono's face went pale as he dropped his things and turned
around. He suddenly felt weak and his ears trembled happily.
"Corq?... Igit?" he managed to choke out through a growing
smile.

"Yes! Yes, of course it is! Who else silly?" Corq cried
and took off his cap and swept it across his feet in a bow.
Igit clapped and waved and curtseyed at his side.

Ono squealed with absolute joy and darted down the hillside. Too excited to stop at the creek bank, he sprang up on
to a rock and jumped out over the water and grabbed a hold
of a dangling willow branch. "Woo-ha!" he cried out as he
swung over the stream and dropped onto the other side.
"What?! Are you two?!... Ugh, do you want? Ha ha! Oh!" Ono
stammered and fumbled as he ran to them. He was so overjoyed
at seeing another gnome that he could hardly speak, for he
wanted to say many things at once and his tongue twisted and
wagged wildly in his mouth trying to say them all.

Igit met him first, and she squealed and hugged him like
she was trying to cut him in half. Corq set the baskets
down, then pulled Ono away from her and hugged him closely

for a long while. Then he grasped Ono's shoulders and looked him up and down with an astonished look on his face.

"Ono! I must say, you certainly look to be in good health, I'm glad to see. And look at that beard! It wasn't half that when we saw you last!" he exclaimed with Igit chiming in shrilly.

"Aha! Thank you my friend! And it is good to see you again! I was just about to say the same about that nose of yours! Oh how I've missed it!" Ono said, making them all cry out and double over in laughter.

The morning sun had risen well over the mountains, and its warm glow was cast down in golden shafts throughout the forest, sparkling on the creek's ripples like brilliant diamonds were being carried off in its current. There was nary a cloud to be seen in the blue sky above, and Ono was so happy with it all that he could have wept a flood of tears and made quite a puddle. The three eagerly exchanged more pleasantries and kind comments and laughs and giggles than my hand has the strength to write, and they stood there by the stream for quite a while getting caught up with one another.

"I thought my eyes would never be laid upon another gnome for as long as I lived! Oh, you wouldn't believe how lonely I got here some times. I've missed everyone so much and have had to do some mighty outlandish things to keep myself busy!" Ono said with a gleaming smile and trembling ears.

Corq honked and tipped his cap. "Did I not tell you that I would return to visit some time? Of course I would! It took me nearly all winter through to persuade Igit here to let me make the journey, but I finally cajoled her into it when I offered to carry back all of her things we had to leave behind when we left."

"That's right! This namby-pamby made me abandon some very precious and valuable treasures that could surely never be replaced again. I hope they haven't been looted, for his sake Ono," she said and playfully nudged her mate with her elbow. She smiled, but it was obvious that she was quite serious about retrieving her treasures.

"I'm sure your things are still right where you left them and all accounted for. By the way, where was it everyone left to anyhow?" Ono puzzled.

Corq snorted and flicked a hand through the air and Igit rolled her eyes. "Bah! That wretched, deplorable place is just awful! We all traveled through unfamiliar lands for days on end to finally settle amongst a mountain range filled with nothing more but tall bare trees, jagged boulders, and prickly-thorned bushes that seem to reach out and poke at you when you pass by them. It's nothing like home used to be of course, but I must admit that the lack of humans certainly adds a welcoming touch to it, for I'm sure even they would not want to live there," Corq said, then glanced uncomfortably up at Boulder Mountain and shivered.

Ono smiled at this, and was about to explain that the humans weren't quite what the stories made them out to be, when Igit suddenly leaned forward and squinted curiously at him.

"Is that...? Is that a scar on your face?" she asked, then gasped behind a hand and pointed her finger at it. "It is! Corq! Look at that horrendous wound! Ono, you must have been nearly killed, whatever could have happened?" she shrilled, then turned her ears towards him and held her breath with her eyes wide, waiting intently for a juicy tale about a death-defying encounter with a bloodthirsty human.

More than happy to oblige, for he hadn't had the chance to tell a good tale in quite a time, Ono puffed out his chest and lifted his chin hairs. "Well! It all happened.. " he began and wiggled his fingers ominously in the air, making both of his visitors lean anxiously forward with their mouths hanging loose.

But before he went on he suddenly thought better of it, for he didn't want to frighten them away with stories of teeth and claws and blood and have them leave any earlier than was necessary. Disappointed that he couldn't tell his greatest tale ever, Ono sighed and shrank down again. "I, well, it's embarrassing to speak about really. Just a little wound that came as a result of my carelessness. Nothing worth bragging on, I'm sure," he said and shrugged.

They both frowned at him, then snapped their mouths

closed. Igit even pouted, for she felt she had been robbed of an excellent piece of gossip to tell about when they returned. No matter! I'll just make one up on the trip back! she thought to herself.

Corq's forehead wrinkled with worry at his friend's scar, and he frowned up at the surrounding mountains and pricked up his ears. "How have things been here Ono?" he asked, suddenly very solemn. "Did the humans finish with their merciless killings and depraved acts of barbaric cruelty and depart? I certainly hope so, but even if they did, this once beautiful land will forever be tainted with their nightmarish essence. Such a pity. I don't know how you stayed so near them my friend, for I shudder at the very mention of their name," he said, looking very uncomfortable. Beside him, Igit clutched tightly to his elbow and nodded vigorously with her eyebrows bent together in fright.

Ono bit his lips together and tried his best no to laugh, for he had once shared their all-consuming fear of the humans and understood well how they must feel. But since that time he had learned so much about the humans that he just couldn't help it. His cheeks puffed in and out as his belly began to shake and bounce beneath his robe, and the sputters soon followed. Then he covered his face and laughed into his hands until his ribs began to hurt.

Corq and Igit couldn't have appeared any more bewildered even if they had tried to. She glanced up at him with a puzzled look and he glanced down with the same as if they were

silently asking the other what to make of him. They both

shrugged, then looked curiously back at Ono.

The fit passed, and he wiped his eyes with one last chuck-

le. "I'm sorry for that, really I am. Please pardon. It's

just... Well, I go out among their dwellings nearly every

night and snatch their treasures away while they sleep! Ha!

They're completely oblivious to my theiving!" he bragged and

clapped happily. "And such wonderfully brilliant things the

fools leave out to be taken. Come! I've passed the time by

decorating my burrow with hoards of their wealth and have

dreamed of showing it. You'll be the first to see it! Come!

Follow me!" he said as he picked up his things and waddled

towards his burrow, more than eager to brag on his riches.

Still standing beside the creek, both Corq and Igit's

faces were twisted up in utter confusion. After a moment Ig-

it shook her head and blinked. "Did I just hear him right

dear? Did... did he say that he gathers among the humans'

dwellings? They **live** here?" she asked incredulously.

Corq pondered on it for a moment, then scratched his chin.

"Yes, I believe that is what he said," he answered.

"What?! Has he gone mad?!" she squawked.

Corq bent down and picked up the baskets. "Yes... I be-

lieve he has, that poor, poor Ono," he sighed, then followed

after him up the mountain with his mate reluctantly in tow.

CHAPTER SIXTY NINE

When they came to the base of the tree and pushed through
the green brush, Ono was proudly standing beside the tunnel
with the bark slab pulled up on its side and his elbow resting on top. "After you!" he said and gestured downward,
nearly squirming with delight.

Not knowing quite what to expect in there, Corq pulled off
his cap and tucked it beneath his arm and waddled inside.
Clinging to him like a tick, Igit was much more apprehensive
than he was.

"Do you think this is wise? He claims to have humans'
things in here! He's crazy!" she whispered as they went
twisting down through the tunnel.

"Shh! Don't be rude! I'm sure he's gone through a lot in
this past year, and he may just have the right to be so if
he was!" Corq whispered back.

Behind them Ono danced a merry jig and quickly shut the
slab of bark as he followed them down.

Inside it was pitch-black, and their eyes had yet to adjust from the bright daylight outside. The first thing that
Igit and Corq noticed when they stepped out into the den was
the sweet, cinnamony aroma that filled the burrow and made
them sniff curiously at the air. Then they felt a hard flat
surface beneath their feet that felt nothing like dirt
should. Not sure what to make of it they stopped immediately, feeling quite uncomfortable.

Giggling happily, Ono waddled past them, lit a candle, and

then held it up so its glow left not a shadow anywhere in the den. "What do you think? Marvelous isn't it?" he smiled as his burrow came alight.

Igit gasped and Corq dropped both his baskets and his jaw to the floor in amazement. They could hardly believe what it was they were seeing. Before them, the entire den seemed to sparkle and shine in the candlelight as their round, dazzle-filled eyes swept this way and that.

Across the room they saw the twinkling set of keys dangling like a chandelier over his bed of soft foam and carpet; the shiny quarter propped up against the wall and the stern looking chess piece beside it; the red pen cap with colorful snippets of wire shooting out its top; the blue tile tabletop to the right and the whole wall behind it stacked with strange foods; a bright red Skittle's wrapper pinned up along the wall along with other neatly cut scraps of beautiful gift wrapping of all colors; a large, cracked-faced wristwatch clicking like a shiny grandfather clock on the far left side of the den; a fragment of mirror over the row of nails where several robes and caps made from fine cloths hung; and placed neatly along the shelves were rings, thimbles, beer caps, earrings, a pair of tweezers, a broken drill bit, a ball bearing, a pog, a butterfly hair clip, and many other wondrous, shiny things that glinted in the candlelight.

"Ono! This... this is amazing!" Corq managed to stutter in

awe as he took it all in.

"Aha! Wait until you see this! Come, come!" Ono said and pittered across the jigsawed floor to the watch hung on the wall.

More impressed with his friend than you could imagine, Corq followed him shaking his head in wonder. He had to nearly drag along his mate though, for she was gawking at everything around her and seemed to have become uncoordinated with awe.

They all stopped before the watch and Ono blew out the candle. "Brace yourselves to see amazing magic!" his excited voice said in the darkness. Then came a small click, and a blindingly green light suddenly flared from the watch's cracked face and lit up the burrow.

"Egh!" they both squawked with surprise and threw up their hands before their faces.

A moment later the light flicked off again, and when Ono relit the candle he found that Igit had leapt up into Corq's arms and was trembling like a leaf in a storm. "Ono! Howdid-itdothat?!" she shrilled with her arms cinched tightly a-round her mate's neck.

Ono chuckled and nonchalantly batted his hand at the watch. "Oh this? This is nothing! The humans have many more treasures that are far more amazing than this, let me assure you. But I've only taken what I thought would be tasteful. I certainly wouldn't want to overdo it!" he bragged and stroked his beard.

Corq set Igit down, and then cautiously reached out his hand and ran his fingers across the stainless steel wristband and whistled in amazement. "The humans, they don't notice their missing treasures? How could they not? Look at this! Why haven't they tracked you down and killed you yet?" he asked, nearly to himself. Beside him Igit was touching the watch also, but with a bright red look of deep envy on her face that pulled down the corners of her mouth.

"That's a good question my friend, and it will take quite some time to explain. Have you two eaten breakfast yet? Good! We'll discuss it at the table then," Ono said.

They went to the table and sat down on the blocks of wood, and Igit seemed jealous of that as well. While Ono was picking out a meal for his guests she was sliding her little hands over the glossy blue tile and looking around with a frown on her face. This is not at all fair! What is **Ono**, of all gnomes, doing with all this wealth? I should have all these things as well! she thought and pouted at her mate. Corq was much too awe-struck to notice her displeasure though, and he paid her no mind.

A minute later Ono came rolling a cinnamon roll over and set it on the table with a grunt. Then he slapped his hands together and licked his lips. "Dig in! I just gathered these last night, and they're excellent!" he said and tore off a large sticky piece. He had already eaten and wasn't espec-

ially hungry, but the chance to dine with friends again suddenly made him ravenous.

Corq leaned forward and sniffed at it curiously, then
poked at the frosting and cautiously licked his finger. "My
word Ono! This is excellent, whatever it is!" he cried in
surprise and pulled a piece away for himself.

At first, Igit stubbornly crossed her arms and stuck out
her tongue in a haughty snub. "Blah! I draw the line at ever
eating human food! It's unnatural, and I would rather eat
stink-bugs!" she huffed and turned up her nose.

Apparently not hearing her or choosing not to, Corq and
Ono finished with their pieces and reached laughing for more
with sticky clumps looking ridiculous in their beards.

"Where do you discover these things? I dare say, I have
never had such a delightful tasting meal in all my life!"
Corq exclaimed, licking his fingers clean and reaching for
more.

"You wouldn't believe where!" Ono replied, "the daft humans put all their treasures and feasts into giant buckets
and bags, and then just leave them carelessly lying about
for the taking! Ha! Those fools. It's harder trying to catch
a wingless moth than it is to gather a meal like this on any
night."

Corq seemed puzzled by this, nearly to the point of disbelief. "Buckets and bags you say? With things like **these** in
them?" he asked and looked around at the sparkling burrow

before slipping another piece of the cinnamon roll into his
mouth with a confounded frown.

"Oh yes! And more! This is only what I was able to carry
back by myself!" Ono laughed.

"And what do these buckets and bags look like? Surely
they're locked away and guarded by vicious spells, sharp
blades and the such?" Corq asked.

"You would think! But no, not in the least. The buckets
are tall and wide and open at the tops. The bags are inside,
and once you climb up and in all there is to do is cut them
open and take what you want from within. It's that simple!"
Ono said, then twisted a clump of frosting from his beard.
He frowned at it, then popped it in his mouth with a flick
of his thumb.

"All this gathering goes unnoticed by the humans? Can't
they smell you among them? Like... like a fresh wound among
a pack of hungry wolves?" Corq asked.

"My friend, let me assure you, the humans are nowhere near
as acute as you have been told. For example, I snatched
those," Ono said and pointed across the den to the set of
keys dangling from the ceiling, "-right out from under two
humans' behinds while they were jabbering with one another
just inches away, and I strolled away with them none the
wiser. I gather at night now, because that's when they're
asleep, and it makes it even that much simpler..."

While the two went on talking, Igit glanced at the center

of the table where the partially eaten cinnamon roll sat. I must admit, it at least smells intriguingly pleasant, she thought to herself and leaned over for a quick sniff. To her surprise its sweet aroma made her mouth water and her stomach tingle. Hmm... perhaps I should try just a nibble. But surely no more than that! she thought, then glanced slyly over at Corq and Ono.

They were both very deep in conversation. Corq was alternately asking questions and nodding his head in amazement, while Ono made wild gestures with his hands and laughed and bragged. They seemed much too enthralled with their discussion to notice much else.

When she was sure they weren't looking, Igit quickly reached out and pinched a piece of the cinnamon roll off. Then she discretely raised her hand to her mouth like she was politely covering a yawn and took a tiny, curious bite. When the taste of baked bread and sweet frosting filled her mouth her eyes sprang open in astonishment, and she quietly gobbled down what was left in her hand and licked her fingers clean.

"So you say they **live** there now? Where the meadow was? In what? Towering huts fashioned from bones and the rotting skins of their victims?" Corq asked and leaned forward over the table with an apprehensive curiosity gleaming in his eyes.

Ono grabbed his belly and chuckled. "Not at all! Their

dwellings are peculiar..." he began, then frowned for a moment to think of how best to explain them. After a moment he
spread his arms as wide as they would reach. "Picture a
small mountain," he began, "with four sheer cliffs on every
side and a bare, sloped peak on top. Now imagine that it's
hollow on the inside, with many soaring passage ways leading
to giant caverns filled with unimaginable wonders..."

Ono went on like this for quite some time, making more
than a few outrageous similes that contorted Corq's face in
all bewildered directions. He described carpet as, "wonderfully soft, white grass that tickles your feet as you walk
along," and a urinal as, "a dazzling pond protruding high up
on the wall with fresh, tasty water inside," and stairs as,
"a stack of giant sloping stones that raise you high into
the air." He then went on to describe a window, a computer,
and a television set, but was interrupted when Corq, seeming
to have become overwhelmed, waived his hands in the air and
shook his head.

"Just how do you know all of this about the humans' dwellings?" he asked in utter confusion.

Ono frowned and wiped a hand down his beard. "Well that's
a silly question. I've been in one, twice," he said evenly.

Corq's eyes nearly popped out of their sockets with shock.
"You've been **in** a human's dwelling?! Holy snakes Ono! Are
these the kinds of things you've been up to since we've been
gone?" he gawked.

Ono snickered and shrugged his shoulders. "What else was I
to do? I got horribly lonely here you know! And besides,
their dwellings aren't the half of what's down there!" he
said, then went on to describe the fences, lawns, mailboxes,
streetlights, stop signs, fire hydrants, and all sorts of
other strange, marvelous sounding things. While he spoke
Corq listened intently and eagerly nodded his head. He was
more than impressed with Ono's bravery, and he couldn't seem
to hear enough of the humans' strange ways and their wondrous possessions.

Then Ono began to talk about the network of drainage pipes
beneath the neighborhood. "They're great! I can travel all
through their village in those tunnels and just go from
bucket to bucket at my leisurely choosing," he said, then
leaned forward and raised his eyebrows. "Believe it or not
my friend, I find it much safer than gathering in the forest. I've been attacked by animals many more times, and much
more efficiently, than by the humans."

Corq was shocked to hear this. "Are you serious?" he asked
and wrinkled up his forehead. "It's really that simple to
get treasures like what you have here, and such meals as
well?"

Ono, who of course was enjoying flaunting his wealth to
his company, leaned back and folded his arms behind his
head. "Much simpler. Why don't you two come out with me over
the mountains tonight and see for yourselves? I'll give you

the grand tour, it'll be great! You might even decide to stay!" he said happily.

Corq thought about it for a time, then cringed. "Oh Ono, I just don't know about all that. The idea of being so close to a village full of humans..." he trailed off and glanced around at the burrow. "I'm not sure if it's even worth all of this."

Suddenly, the two heard a loud SLAP! that rattled the table. Surprised, they both flinched and glanced over at Igit. There were crumbs scattered on the table before her, and her face was bright red with anger. The entire cinnamon roll was gone.

"Oh yes it is too worth it Corq!" she shrilled and stood up shaking a frosting glazed finger at him. "I want things like these as well! And more!" she squawked and then began pointing wildly all around her. "I want floors like these! And clothes like those! And treasures like his! And meals like that one every night! And if anyone deserves them, then it is me! Me! I refuse to go back to that horrid land again when such wealth can be had here! I won't, I won't, I won't!" she finally ended in a belligerent huff. There was a ring of frosting around her lips, and she almost seemed to be foaming at the mouth with greed.

Corq turned to look at his mate with a perplexed look on his face. "Are you saying you want to stay here? To live here, with the humans as your neighbors?" he asked in disbelief, for he was the one that had to bribe her to even come back in the first place.

"Yes! That's exactly what I said!" she squawked, then pointed at Ono. "If he can do it, then so can we! I'm tired of living like a pauper in that wasteland Ezquit has led us to!"

There was a long moment of silence that followed, because Igit was catching her breath and Corq was in what looked to be deep thought. Ono leaned forward with a crooked, hopeful grin spreading over his face, for he had been happy when he had thought that they had only come to visit. But now that the possibility of them staying there with him had come up, well, that was a whole better thing altogether. Come on Corq! She knows best! She surely does! Come on! Ono pleaded with his friend in his thoughts.

Corq, looking quite flustered, frowned at her and cleared his throat. "My dear, it is not often that I put my foot down on something that you want, but this? Living a mountain over from a village of humans?" he asked incredulously, then turned and looked at Ono from across the table with a taut, pained face. "I am sorry my friend, but although it pains me to do so," he sighed heavily, "we just cannot make such a rash decision. Not, at least, until you've shown us around and proved what you claim about these humans."

It took a second for his words to seep in, but when they did both Ono and Igit threw their hands into the air and let out shrill cries of joy. Igit hopped up and down and clapped her hands, imagining all the treasures and luxuries she was sure to soon have, and Ono rushed around the table and threw his arms around Corq's middle in a tight bear hug.

"Oh! You'll see Corq! I'll prove that the humans aren't so bad! You'll see! Ha ha!" he shrilled and spun him in a circle, so overjoyed at finally having his friends back that tears threatened to burst from his eyes.

Corq hugged him in return and honked with laughter. "I hope so Ono! I do hope so! And we've much time to make up for!" he laughed as he began to feel dizzy.

CHAPTER SEVENTY

That night, after Corq and Igit had been reacquainted with their old burrow and had rested from their travel, Ono led them up the mountain side for their first look at what the meadow had become.

"What's it like? Are we going to be shocked? It's not too frightening is it? Oh! What should we expect?" Igit kept asking as they waddled up through the underbrush. She was quite nervous, as Corq's aching hand could attest to, but was also very eager to start finding treasures to decorate her home with.

"Just a little further and you'll see for yourself, I don't want to spoil it for you!" Ono smiled back over his shoulder as they went.

The night was especially quiet, with hardly a breeze to be heard rustling through the leaves, and the crickets' chirping sounded loud and distinct in the darkness. The air was crisp and chilly, and the stars sparkled and shined brilliantly. The moon was bright and nearly full, and it looked almost close enough to touch as it hung over the tops of the mountains.

The three kept walking quietly through the underbrush as the mountain began to level, until Ono suddenly stopped before a wall of fern leaves and turned back to them with a big smile on his face. "This is it! This is where the humans live, and also where they suffer my stealthy pillagings. Are you ready to see it?" he asked and cocked an eyebrow at them.

Corq and Igit exchanged queer glances and shifted uncertainly on their feet, then nodded their heads.

"Okay then," Ono began, then pushed the fern leaves open like he was making a dramatic entrance through two large doors. "Here it is!" he said and showed them the neighborhood below with a presenting sweep of his arm.

Now Ono's shock at witnessing the meadow being transformed was set upon him gradually, over several slow, long months as it were. He saw the clearing, the digging, the building, the paving, and every step in between take place before the neighborhood took the form it had now. And even then it was quite difficult for him to believe what was happening.

But poor Igit and Corq! The last time they had come to the mountain top and looked down, there had been a lush meadow filled with tall green grass. It was as if a pair of magical fingers had suddenly snapped it all away and in its place made appear something completely and utterly alien. They saw the rows of homes lining the streets; square patches of fenced in yards; the pools of yellow on the sidewalks from the streetlights; telephone poles and telephone wires stretching here and there; stop signs and street lights; and many other odd things that were absolutely bewildering.

Ono squinted down at the neighborhood and saw that all the windows were dark in the homes and that everything seemed to be still. The beasts were parked and quiet in the driveways, and no humans were moving about. Eager to start showing his old friends how good he had gotten at his pilfering, Ono adjusted the pouch's strap on his shoulder and snugged his cap down before looking back at them. "Are you two ready to-" he began to ask, then cut himself off when he saw the expressions on their faces.

Corq and Igit both wore the same frozen mask of surprise. Their eyebrows were raised high over round, bugged eyes that didn't blink. Their mouths were perfect circles, and their ears were tall and alert. Neither moved, or seemed so much as to breath.

Ono shook his head and sat down on the ground. Oh, I suppose this could take a while, he thought to himself and waited.

And for quite a while, as it turned out. The two stood there for nearly an hour, occasionally turning their heads to look down at something else or to work their lips in silent questions as they squinted below. Their eyes were trying to take it all in, but their brains couldn't seem to process what was being relayed to it.

Bored, Ono simply sat there twiddling his thumbs and counting stars in the sky.

It was only when the car of some late-night driver pulled into the neighborhood and began weaving itself along the streets that Corq finally discovered his tongue again.

"What.. what is that thing?" he puzzled and pointed at it.
The car's headlights were bright in the darkness, and as it
pulled into a garage they shined off the taillights of a
pickup before the door rolled shut behind it.

"That, my friend, is a Volvo," Ono yawned, then got to his
feet and stretched his back.

Igit frowned. "A Volbo?" she asked.

"No, a Vol-vo. That's what the humans call them anyway.
Such a silly name isn't it? They may look frightening, with
those glowing eyes and whatnot, but once they're asleep
they're nothing at all to worry about," Ono assured them,
then picked up his pouch and dusted off his bottom. "Ready
to go?"

Corq's face paled and his ears twitched. "Ugh... perhaps
we should wait until another night, since we've only just-"
he began, but was cut short when Igit shoved him forward and
smiled at Ono.

"Yes Ono, we are. And we trust that you won't lead us to
our death as well. Now let's go find some sparkling treasure!" she said and rubbed her hands together, the greedy
sparkle in her eyes clear even in the darkness.

Ono tossed his head back and laughed. "That's the spirit!"
he said as he led the way down the mountain.

CHAPTER SEVENTY ONE

The three gnomes soon arrived at the fence.

"This is the barrier that separates our land from the humans'. We'll have to squeeze under to get through," Ono whispered to them as he crouched down and began rummaging in his pouch.

Corq reached out and lightly knocked on the wooden planks with a frown on his face. "Awfully strange way to mark their territory isn't it? Considering all the other ways to do it," he whispered to his mate and leaned back to look up at the fence.

Igit wasn't paying attention to it, for she was busy craning her neck and squinting curiously at what Ono had in his pouch. She watched him move aside a tangled ball of twine of some sort, then pull out a long object neatly wrapped in a black sheath that matched his robe. There was a thin strap that ran the length of the sheath, and he pulled it apart and slid the strap over his head so the sheath slanted across his back. Then he closed up his pouch and stuffed it under the fence.

"Ono, what is that thing you've just put on? What's it for?" she asked.

"Oh, this?" Ono asked as he stood up and reached over his shoulder. "It's just something I carry with me when I gather. It comes in handy every now and again," he explained and pulled out his sword. In his hand the shard of glass winked

in the darkness as it was slid out of the sheath, and its
sharp edges shined and gleamed when he turned it for them to
see.

"Whooa!" Corq gasped when he saw the blade. "What, I dare
ask, does this weapon come in handy for Ono?" he asked with
an unnerved tinge in his voice, for it was quite disturbing
that such a vicious looking blade could possibly come in
handy often enough to carry along.

Ono shrugged and slid the sword back into the sheath. "Oh,
you know, nothing really. Cutting open bags," he said and
flipped a hand vaguely in the air, "and a few other things,
on occasion."

Igit and Corq gave each other a queer glance for a moment,
then looked back at Ono. "And what other few things might
I -" she began to ask, but before she could finish the question Ono's feet disappeared beneath the fence.

"Come on you two! We're almost to the treasures!" he whispered back at them.

The two hesitated for an awkward moment before Corq nudged
Igit forward. "Ugh... females first, it's only polite," he
said and gulped nervously.

Igit narrowed her eyes up at him, then flipped a pigtail
over her shoulder. "Fine, but you're carrying all of our
treasures back home. And you'd better hope my dress doesn't
get dirty, because you know who'll be cleaning it if it
does!" she said, then pulled up her hem and got down on her

hands and knees and crawled under.

"And you'd better hope we don't all die because of your
incessant jealousy," Corq mumbled as he bent down.

"What did you just say?" her voice snapped from the other
side.

"Nothing! I said I'm coming!" he whispered and squeezed
under.

When all three of them were through, they found themselves
in the back yard of a tall green home. On the back patio
there was a barbecue and several chairs, and in the lawn was
a plastic wading pool with smiling, colorful fish portrayed
on its side. Around it, the grass was littered with squirt
guns and water toys.

"Okay, we're going to hurry over there to those shrubs,
then make our way around the humans' dwellings to the tunnels," Ono explained as they stood huddled together. Before
he could lead the way though, a worried Corq pulled his
wand and pointed it over Ono's shoulder.

"Nobody move! I, I see a giant orange snake!" he stammered. He was as jumpy as a cricket, and his ears were tall
and trembling beside his cap.

Ono turned and scanned the lawn, then saw what Corq was
aiming his wand at. A water noodle. He shook his head, then
reached up and lowered Corq's hand. "Don't worry about that
Corq. I can assure you that it won't attack us, as nearly
every frightening looking thing here won't."

Corq tucked his wand back in his sash, but didn't appear entirely convinced that the water noodle wasn't a snake, for he kept a cautious eye trained on it. Ono picked up his pouch and pressed a silencing finger to his lips, then pointed to the shrubs. Then he waved them along to follow him and began waddling across the lawn with Igit closely in tow and Corq bringing up the rear. One after the other they scurried into the shrubs, then quietly rustled their way along the side of the fence to where the hedge met the sidewalk. There, three pairs of wary little eyes peered out into the street and looked around.

"The tunnels I've been telling you about are right across the clearing there, in the shadows. Do you see the opening?" Ono asked and pointed across the street to the gutter.

Igit nodded her head and wiped the sweat from her brow. Her ears swiveled back and forth, and her knocking knees made the fabric of her dress ripple. And yet, she still managed to have a look of greedy excitement on her face. "We travel through those to get to the treasures and feasts right? It won't take long will it?" she whispered anxiously.

"Exactly. It won't take us but a few minutes to find a good gathering spot," Ono replied and glanced up and down the street for oncoming beasts. The streets were empty and quiet, and there wasn't even a breeze to tinkle the wind chimes.

Corq stuck out his leg from the hedge, tapped his foot on

the sidewalk, then pulled it back in again. "Ono, what in the world is that covering the ground? A giant flat stone?" he asked and peered down the length of the sidewalk, which seemed to stretch on forever into the distance.

Ono's mouth dropped open to reply, but quickly snapped shut again when he remembered how the rude beast with the spinning rump had come and done its business all over the place. Its thick droppings plopping wetly to the ground and the humans clamoring eagerly after them were not an attractive memory. Ono shivered at the thought and grimaced. "You don't want to know," he said, "now get ready to hurry across! Corq, you may have to crouch down once we get inside the tunnels, so be careful of your head when we go in,"

The three of them scurried across the street in the shadows between the streetlights and darted into the gutter one after the other. Within the darkness of the drainage pipe, Ono took off his cap and looked back to make sure they had made it inside. Igit was sniffing distastefully at the damp, sour smell of the pipe, and Corq was hunched over like he had a heavy weight hanging from a chain around his neck.

"Stay close to me. We're almost there!" Ono whispered and began leading the way through the dark twists and turns and intersections in the pipes.

Seeming to be more comfortable in the small space, Igit and Corq began to chatter nervously in hushed voices. "I can't believe you're taking us to steal humans' treasures!

My word, not even in my wildest dreams would I have ever imagined doing such a daring thing! I feel like a stealthy
burglar! You'll be a legend one day Ono, surely!" Corq said
as they walked. There was a Hershey's wrapper that had been
blown into the gutter, and their feet pitter-pattering over
it sounded loud and obvious in the darkness.

   "Yes! And we'll all be rich soon! Unimaginably rich, won't
we Ono?" Igit asked when they took a corner, getting herself
all worked up.

   "Very soon indeed," Ono smiled happily as they came to the
end of the pipe and peered out from the gutter. Across the
street at the foot of a driveway before a yellow home stood
a large green trashcan. Its lid was pushed up several inches
by promising garbage bags, and a squat recycling bin filled
with bottles sat on one side with a red fire hydrant on the
other.

   "Is **that** where the humans hide all their treasures? Right
in there? In between those two other strange things?" Igit
puzzled.

   "Yes, but stay far away from that thing on the left. It's
filled with containers that hold a wicked poison that makes
the world seem to spin all around you until you're deathly
ill. It's not pleasant in the least," Ono warned them, then
pulled his cap on and cracked his neck. "Are you two ready?
This is it!"

   Igit and Corq took big deep breaths and looked to one another, then nodded their heads. Their eyes were as round as saucers and their ears were trembling.

"Excellent! Let's go!" Ono said, then waddled across the street and hopped up on the curb. His friends were close behind, and they all came to a huddled stop in the shadow of the trashcan where he bent down and began rummaging in his pouch again.

Igit clung tightly to her mate's robe and glanced apprehensively all around at the dark homes, wanting very badly to get out of the open and start with the gathering. Obviously feeling the same way, Corq whined and shifted nervously on his feet and glanced up at the top of the trashcan. It seemed awfully high, with no possible way of getting up its sheer, smooth sides.

"Ono, how are we ever supposed to get inside this thing? There's nothing to climb!" he said, then flinched when a bat went squeaking by in the night sky overhead.

"Aha my friend! With this!" Ono said and stood up with the treble hook in his hands and began unwinding the dental floss from around it. Bewildered, the two simply stood there with their eyebrows bent together as he then proceeded to windmill his arm around and around. Once he got it going in to quite a spin, he let go of the hook and flung it high in to the air with a shrill grunt.

"Wooa!" Corq and Igit gasped and tilted their heads back as they watched it sail over the top of the trashcan with

the dental floss trailing behind it like a ribbon. When it
landed, Ono gave the floss a smart tug and felt the hook
catch. Then he picked up his pouch and rubbed his hands together.

"See? Simple as a slumber spell," he smiled proudly.

His friends were staring incredulously at him.

"Ono! That was amazing! I say, what a shot!" Corq gawked
and shook his head in wonder as he looked up at the floss
hanging down from above.

"Well, I have had plenty of practice," Ono shrugged, then
looped the floss around his hand and put his foot against
the side of the trashcan. "Now this is how you climb up:
hand over hand and foot over foot. Easy as walking I suppose, just be sure to have a good grip on the rope before
you start," he instructed, then began pulling himself up.

Corq and Igit were quite taken back by Ono's professional-
ism, and watched as he made his way up. He suddenly seemed
supremely confidant and at ease with himself, even in the
midst of gathering in the humans' village. They could have
never pictured the Ono they left behind doing such a daring
thing.

My goodness! He has changed so! Nearly into another gnome
altogether! they both thought to themselves.

Ono scaled to the top and glanced back down at his friends
to see them still on the ground below, looking up at him
with strange expressions on their faces. "Are you two coming

or not? The treasures won't gather themselves you know!" he
whispered down to them.

They both seemed to snap from their thoughts, and Corq
waved his hand. "Sure thing Ono! Coming right up. Just a
bit uneasy, being as it's our first time and all," he whispered back and gave him a thumbs up.

"Fair enough. I'll have the bags cut open by the time you
get up. I have a feeling this will be a good one!" Ono said,
then disappeared over the top of the trashcan and went
rustling down inside.

Igit turned to Corq and cocked her head to the side. "Was-
n't that just impressive? And he made it look so easy as
well! Who would of thought that little Ono could do such a
thing?" she puzzled.

Corq snorted and rolled his eyes. "Give me a few days to
practice, and I'd do it just as well, I'm sure," he said,
then bent down and laced his fingers together. "Come on,
I'll follow you up so you won't fall."

Excited to begin gathering, Igit took hold of the floss
and stepped on her mate's hands. With a grunt he lifted her
up, and she looped the line around her hand and put a foot
against the trashcan. Its top was quite high up though, and
she hesitated for a moment before starting to climb as she
stared at the floss disappearing over the ledge.

Holding her other foot, Corq squirmed impatiently. "Would
you hurry up? I don't think it's wise to just stand out here

in the open!" he whispered.

"Hush up you! I'll go when I'm good and ready, and not a
moment before!" she snapped back down at him in a huff.

Corq grumbled under his breath and glanced over his shoulder as he stood there holding her up. The yellow home across
the lawn from them was dark and quiet. There was a neat
flower garden around it that ended on either side of the
walkway leading to the entrance, and a big glass jug of sun
tea sat just to the left of the front door. An uncollected
newspaper laid folded on the welcome mat, and all the windows were filled with drawn curtains like lids over sleepy
eyes.

Looking at the alien structure, Corq got an eerie feeling
that he was being watched by it. He shivered as goose bumps
prickled the back of his neck, then turned his attention
back to his mate.

"Do you want to find treasure, or do you just want to dan-
gle from that rope all night? Because I'll be more than happy to let you stay here and do it by yourself!" he whispered
impatiently.

"Oh quit your whining already! I'm going! And you had better not let me fall!" Igit warned, then pushed off his hands
and began pulling herself unsteadily up the side. Ono's smiling face appeared over the ledge as she worked her way up,
and he held down a hand to her and pulled her into the
trashcan.

Once she was to safety, Corq took hold of the floss and looped it over his hand, then put a foot against the side of the can to follow her up. He took a deep breath, then glanced once more at the yellow home with a suspicious frown before he went.

It still sat there, quiet and unmoving.

If I do decide to stay here, I will certainly have to get used to those strange things, he thought uncomfortably as his eyes slid over the home, still feeling as if he were being watched.

Then Igit poked her head out over the ledge and pointed down at him. "And look at you, you frightened dangler! It's not so easy, now is it?" she whispered.

"Oh be quiet! I was coming, until you broke my concentration!" he said, then pulled himself up and followed them in.

CHAPTER SEVENTY TWO

In the flower garden of the yellow home, the white cat's face slowly materialized out of the shadows as it pushed through the begonias. It had smelled something unfamiliar drifting in the air a moment before, and was quite curious as to what it could be.

The little brown mouse hanging limply in its jaws was in its final death throes, and it twitched silently as the life drained from its body. Slanting across the cat's cheek was a part in its fur where Ono's sword had left its scar, and its golden eyes slid back and forth as it searched for what was out there.

The cat glanced carefully up the street and back down again. It saw nothing unusual at first, then noticed a small shift in the shadow of a trashcan standing at the curb. Intrigued, the cat lowered its head down between its shoulders and squinted across the lawn.

It waited patiently for a time for the movement to came again, and when it finally did the cat made out a long, thin silhouette standing in the darkness. The shape was puzzling at first, until a small pair of voices came whispering from it and the silhouette suddenly morphed in half. The dark little figure on top went climbing up the side of the trashcan and rustled down inside. The other, wearing a tall pointed cap, seemed to fidget nervously and glance around, its shadowy face wary and hesitant.

Not wanting to be noticed, the cat quietly ducked down in
the flower bed, squinting curiously out from the darkness.

After a moment filled with silence there was a hushed,
shrill exchange of words between the two silhouettes, and
the figure on the sidewalk began to scale up the trashcan
after the first.

Oh my.. It's more of those strange little creatures again,
the cat thought to itself as it watched the figure scamper
up into the trashcan. Ever since its battle with Ono the cat
had been cautious of his scent and stayed far away from him
and his nasty little sword. Not wanting another dispute like
the last, the cat bitterly thought it best to leave the new
creatures alone to go about their business.

Before it turned to leave, the cat raised its pink nose
and sniffed at the air to memorize their scents for later.
When it did, the cat smelled something very strong coming
off of them that it hadn't smelled on Ono since their fight.

It was fear, pungent and plentiful like a sweet perfume.

Well, that certainly changes things for the better, the
cat thought and narrowed its eyes into sinister, golden
slits. It had been wanting revenge on Ono for quite some
time, and figured that these two would be much easier tar-
gets than dealing with that horrid little creature again.
Yes, much easier indeed, the cat thought as it savored
their scent.

Deciding to abandon the mouse for the other two morsels,

the cat peeled its lips back from its teeth. The impaled mouse dropped silently to the ground, leaving behind streaks of its glistening blood as it slid off the cat's fangs.

Seeming to smile a wicked, crimson smile, the cat then slid back into the begonias and disappeared into the darkness.

CHAPTER SEVENTY THREE

After Ono helped pull Corq into the trashcan, he reached
over his shoulder and slid out his sword. "These sacks are
what the humans put all of their treasures in, and all we
do now is cut them open and take what we want! It's that
simple! Silly creatures, aren't they?" he giggled happily
as he pittered over to the bulging side of a black plastic
bag.

Igit had pinched her nose shut and looked dubious. "Are
you serious Ono? The humans keep their most valuable riches
and delicious feasts in these... things? Plagh! They smell
absolutely rancid!" she said, looking reluctant to touch
anything around her. Corq was tapping his toes on the plastic bag, his eyebrows bent together curiously.

Ono sliced a long cut in the bag, then slid his sword
back in its sheath and snapped his fingers as he turned his
back to them. "Yes, the odd smells do take some getting
used to I suppose, but they're well worth it once you find
something like... like, ugh," he trailed off as he rustled
in the bag, his elbows working as he dug inside.

Corq and Igit watched him as he rummaged around tossing
out crumpled tissues and food wrappers for the next two minutes with queer looks on their faces, for they were beginning to wonder what they had gotten themselves into as they
stood in the cramped musky space. They had each been expecting piles of glittering treasure and platters of mouth-wa-

tering food, and were so far unimpressed. Corq scratched his
ear and shrugged when Igit pinched her lips at him and
turned her palms up.

Then Ono siad, "Aha! Here we are!" as he pulled out a big
brass coat button. It had an eagle with its wings stretched
out on the front, and it glimmered in the darkness when Ono
turned and held it out for them to see.

Igit gasped, then shoved rudely past Corq to get a look at
it. "Oh my Ono! What is that?! Let me have a look!" she
shrilled, then snatched it from his grasp and held it up to
her face. "It's absolutely fabulous! Look at it Corq! It's,
it must be some type of amulet or something of the such! And
the detail! Oh, we must have this for our home Ono! We must
indeed!" She squealed with delight as Corq ogled it over her
shoulder.

Ono laughed and graciously tipped his cap as his friends
fussed over the button. "Of course you can have it, it's
yours! That is why I have brought you down here haven't I?
But there are many more things waiting to be found in here,
I can assure you, if you two would care to join me...?" he
asked, then pulled open the flap of plastic and raised his
eyebrows with a smile.

Both Corq and Igit's ears sprang up, and they glanced at
one another with wide, happy eyes. It's true! There really
are treasures to be found in here! they thought. Then Igit
shoved the button at him and began rummaging eagerly into

the bag. Corq quickly slipped it in his pouch, and a moment later was at his mate's side, digging and pulling and tugging and flinging and laughing joyously.

Sure that his friends would be pleased enough to stay, Ono danced a quick jig and pumped his fist in the air, then squeezed into the bag and began rummaging beside them.

For the next hour the garbage bag rustled and bulged and trembled as the three gnomes dug around inside. Together they discovered a shiny cap from a perfume bottle; a long chain made of paper clips; a broken zipper; a white shoelace; a frayed telephone cord; a tiny bent spoon; a red Hotwheels car; a single chopstick; and a sliver of green soap that smelled clean and fresh, stopping only once to sit around and snack on a half-eaten waffle.

The two pouches were quickly filled, and as he was trying to stuff in a blue marble Ono called out to the piles of rubbish around him, "Corq! Igit! We don't have anymore room!" he laughed, "Come, let's carry these back to your burrow and return for the rest!"

A moment later Corq's head came popping up from the garbage like a gopher's beside a bright cereal box. "Already? But we've hardly just begun! I bet there's all sorts of more things left to be found, and I'd hate to stop here!" he whined. There was a fruit sticker stuck to the side of his cap, and his sweaty face was like an excited child's, giddy and hesitant to leave.

Then Igit came crawling out from the end of a paper towel tube clutching an infant's lacy sock. Her hair was in disarray, and her dress was splotched with what looked to be yellow egg yolk.

"Oh Corq! These humans have such fabulous things! Just look at this fabric! What a perfect night!" she cried happily and pressed her cheek to the soft material. "Will we come right back Ono?"

"Of course we will, if that's what you like. But we must work quickly if we want to make more than a few trips back and forth. Now that the weather's getting warm the humans are waking earlier you know, and we must get what we can. So let's get these treasures back to your home!"

Igit clapped and fluttered at the idea, and Corq pulled himself up from the rubbish and brushed off his robe, then picked up his pouch and followed Ono up. They climbed over a milk carton and a shoe box, then squeezed through the slit in the bag and stepped out on top of the pile.

"Alright, I suppose it would be easiest of you go down first Corq, and then you follow him Igit, then I'll toss the pouches down to you. Ready?" he asked.

Corq nodded and slipped off his pouch, then waddled to the ledge and threw his leg over. Then he grasped the floss and carefully lowered himself down to the sidewalk below. Eager to get back for more treasures, Igit hurried to the ledge and followed him down. Once Corq had helped her to the sidewalk, Ono leaned over the side of the trashcan and held the pouch out by the strap.

"Look out below!" he whispered down and released it.

Corq caught it, but just barely, and received an earful from his mate standing at the curb with her arms crossed. "If you break anything in there you will be sorry! I did not get this filthy for nothing! Now be careful, do you hear me?" she whispered.

Corq seemed much too happy with the new treasures to notice her squawkings though. "Got it Ono! Send down the next one! Ha ha!" he laughed and waved his hands in the air.

Grunting, Ono leaned out with the last pouch and held the strap in both hands. It was the biggest and heaviest of the two, and bulged awkwardly with pilfered goods.

"Get ready! This one's heavy!" Ono warned.

"And all the better that way!" Corq smiled.

Then, just as Ono dropped it down to him, Igit screamed a shrill piercing scream and pointed across the sidewalk. Startled, Corq snapped his head to the side and saw a streak of white coming across the lawn towards him. Other than its color, all he could make out was a pair of golden eyes gleaming hungrily in the darkness.

"Ahh!" he squawked and reached into his robe for his wand. But before he could pull it out the falling pouch struck him and threw him back onto the sidewalk, knocking the wand from his grasp and driving the wind from his chest. Terrified, and not knowing what else to do, Igit shrilled and held the little sock up to her face as if it would shield her from danger.

Seeing that its prey would be easier than it had imagined, the cat slowed to a trot as it came across the lawn. It licked its needle teeth and glared at the strange little creatures, its tail twitching eagerly for revenge. Which one should I kill first? Hmm, perhaps I'll just eat them both at once? Now that would certainly be fun to try! it thought as it neared.

Laying on the sidewalk, Corq coughed and pushed the pouch off of him, then sat up and frantically looked around for his wand. He couldn't see it, and the cat was nearly upon him. "Igit! Run for the tunnel!" he yelled and jumped to his feet as the cat closed in.

But just when the cat arched its back to pounce on his friend, Ono leapt off the top of the garbage can. "Aaaeeee!" he shrilled as he tucked himself into a ball and went flipping down through the air. He cleared the sidewalk and landed rolling in the grass, then sprang up to his feet with his sword drawn. "You again!" he said and glared at the cat as it came to a skidding halt only inches before him. Having had enough of the bothersome animal, and quite angry that it had come after his friends as well, Ono slashed the blade as hard as he could across the cat's neck.

Luckily for it though, the cat recoiled at the very sight

of the sword and barely missed being killed when it sliced clean through its red collar. "Reeerrr!" it screeched as it spun and darted off into the dark neighborhood.

Ono huffed angrily as he watched it go, then bent down and picked up the collar off the ground as it disappeared around the side of a house down the block. There was a little brass tag fastened on it, and he squinted at the name engraved a-cross it.

"Muf-fin. Muffin. Huh," he grunted and tossed it aside. Then he slid his sword back in its sheath and turned around to face his friends. "That was Muffin, who obviously didn't know that you two were friends of mine, because it wouldn't have dared-" he started to explain, but stopped when he saw the looks on their faces.

They wore the same gawking masks of surprise they had had on when they had first seen the neighborhood, except this time their bugged eyes were trained on him in sheer disbe-lief.

Ono smacked his forehead and sighed. Snakes! Not this a-gain! he thought and cringed.

CHAPTER SEVENTY FOUR

The three gnomes made two more trips back and forth into the neighborhood, and the rest of the night passed quickly by. They rummaged and pilfered and giggled together in the darkness, and were quite happy with themselves as they made their way up the mountain side as the morning sun began to rise.

"So this is what you've been doing this whole time Ono? My word, no wonder you didn't come running after us once we left! You've had a gold mine all to yourself, you devil!" Corq panted as he drug his pouch along.

Behind him, Igit was struggling with a crumpled ball of black fabric from a torn scarf. "A gold mine indeed! Imagine what Autinter would be like here! Oh! So many wondrous things to buy and sell I bet!" she said as they went, picturing all the profits she could make sewing dresses from the fine fabrics.

The two weren't saying it in as many words, of course, but Ono could tell from their excited jabbering and babbling that they wanted to stay, and as he led them up the mountain he smiled very happily to himself.

They made their way laughing down through the underbrush to Corq and Igit's burrow at the bottom of Pine Ridge where they stopped at the green wall of ferns before the entrance.

"My friend, I would invite you in and show my gratitude with a hearty meal, but I'm afraid that your tour has pushed me to exhaustion, and I doubt that I could keep good company while snoring," Corq said, then took off his cap and gave Ono a bow. "But your generosity will be repaid, and until it is, I am gratefully in your debt," he said and flipped his cap back on.

"Yes Ono! Thank you so very much! Is there anything I can make for you? A new robe or cap perhaps? Whatever it is, don't you hesitate to ask!" Igit chirped.

Ono smiled. "That will not be necessary at all! I'm just happy to have friends to share it with, especially as good ones as you two," he said, then took the pouch off his shoulder and set it on the ground. Corq honked with laughter and shook his hand, and Igit squealed with delight and hugged him.

When they parted ways they made plans to meet up again the next night, and the two stood before their burrow waving him good-bye as he left. "Thank you again Ono!" they called out.

Ono laughed and waved back at them, then made his way skipping along the creek towards his burrow. He was tired from the long night's work, but was still giddy with excitement at the idea of his old friends staying there with him. Finally! Someone to talk to! he thought as he went.

The morning was clear and beginning to brighten, and the branches above were musical with waking birds. A vulture circled lazily in the blue sky, and a brown lizard clinging to the side of a stone watched Ono waddle past with big round eyes.

Ono came to the bottom of Boulder Mountain, and as he was making his way up the slope he heard a small squeak from the underbrush beside him. Curious, he pricked up his ears and peeked around a bush to see what it was.

Beside a tall clump of grass, a little brown mouse twitched its whiskers and sat up on its tail. It squeaked sweetly as if it were glad to see him, then scratched at the air with its tiny paws.

Ono smiled curiously at the little rodent, for its behavior was certainly queer, and he wondered what it could want. Then, after a moment of pondering, he remembered the mouse. It was the same one that had taken his berry months before when he had been out friend hunting, then gone scampering off into the underbrush, leaving him lonely and sad and without another moment's company.

Ono smirked at the mouse as it squeaked and pawed at the air, then huffed and turned his nose up in a snub and waddled on whistling. He arrived back at his burrow a short time later and went down inside. He came out into the den and yawned, then pulled his wand from his sash and lit the candle. In its yellow glow he undressed and hung his clothes on the wall and propped up his sword in the corner, then rubbed his eyes and drug his feet over to bed.

Laying down with a sigh, he smiled and wiggled his toes happily. The keys hanging above glittered and gleamed in the flickering light, and they looked even prettier than before. The scraps of foam and carpet were warm and soft, and Ono felt as if he were sinking in their comfort as he closed his eyes. Things are perfect... Just perfect, he thought as he drifted off to sleep.

Forgetting to blow out the candle, it continued to burn and the beeswax to roll down in slow milky drops as the wick darkened and curled. Ono's lazy smile stayed stretched across his face as the candle slowly got shorter, but when Bej's face appeared in his dreams hours later he whined and rolled over in bed.

CHAPTER SEVENTY FIVE

When Ono awoke that evening, it was to the sound of an urgent fist rapping on the slab of bark. "Ono! Ono, are you awake in there?! Ono!" Corq's muffled voice called from outside.

Groggy, Ono rolled over in bed and wiped the drool from his cheek, then got up and shuffled through the darkness over to the far side of the burrow. There he slipped into his black robe and pulled on his cap, then lumbered up the tunnel towards Corq's insistent knocking.

"Ono! It's getting dark! Are you awake in-" he was calling out when Ono pushed the bark aside and squinted out at him with puffy eyes. There were wrinkles etched on the side of his face from the folds of covers, and several strands of untucked hair curled out from beneath his cap.

The sun had set behind the mountains, and the sky was just beginning to darken. Corq was already dressed and wide awake with an excited grin on his face and a gathering pouch on his shoulder. Greedy anticipation lit up his eyes, and his ears were tall and alert.

"Ha ha! There you are my friend! What are you doing asleep? There are riches and feasts to be found! Time is treasure, and we mustn't waste either!" he said, wiggling his fingers and shifting eagerly from foot to foot.

Ono sighed and rubbed his face, then mumbled under his breath and waved for him to come down inside.

"I must've awoken ten times today just to hurry outside and check to see where the sun was! I even dreamt of what riches we would discover tonight. Oh, I just cannot wait until our burrow looks like yours Ono! Perhaps then Igit will let me rest!" Corq said as they came out into the den.

Ono waddled over to a shelf in the wall and picked up a fresh candle, then lit it with his wand. "Where is she anyhow?" he yawned as he sat it on the table and shook out his wand.

"Oh, once we got back this morning she realized how dirty she had gotten, and she refused to sleep until she had cleaned every last stain from her dress and scraped all the grime out from beneath her nails. You know how Igit gets. Needless to say, she decided quickly that such jobs are best left to the males. Happily, it'll just be you and I tonight! Now I only have to see her when I'm coming and going! Fabulous!" he honked.

While Ono went about getting ready, Corq continued to babble on, for he felt as if he had suddenly stumbled across a very good thing. Not only did he have his old friend and home back, but all of a sudden there were more treasures and feasts than he knew what to do with just waiting to be snatched away from the humans, who were suddenly nowhere near as frightening as they had once been.

"Did you know that I saw a raccoon and a deer on the way over here? My word, I figured they would have fled with the

rest of us and never returned. Ha! Well, I suppose that
shows what the rest of us know!" Corq said.

Awake now, Ono slid his sword over his back and picked up
his pouch, then pointed at Corq and smiled. "Ready to go?"
he asked.

Corq's ears perked up and he rubbed his hands together.
"Yes! Yes indeed!"

The two left out into the forest and began making their
way over the mountain. The stars were beginning to sparkle
in the dark sky, and the moon was full and bright, casting
down vague shadows throughout the woods with its pale glow.

When they crested the mountain top the two gnomes stopped
for a moment to peer down through the trees at the neighborhood below. Several windows were still alight and flickering
with the glare of television sets throughout the subdivision, so they sat down beneath a log and waited for them to
go dark. After several minutes of silence and watching for
any movement along the streets, Ono suddenly frowned and
cleared his throat.

"Corq, I've been meaning to ask," he began, fiddling with
stick beside him, "how has Bej been? I mean, you know, ever
since..?"

Corq sighed and leaned back on his hands. "Oh, she still
misses you terribly Ono. When we all left here, all she
could do was mope around with red eyes, hardly talking to
anyone at all when she came out of her burrow, which wasn't

often. Everyone was worried for a time that she was simply
going to wither away, for she quit eating altogether and
didn't look at all well, not even like herself," he said,
his dark face somber. "But we all got together and pitched
in, and one morning we left ten baskets full of food before
her burrow and scratched get-well greetings in the dirt a-
round them. That must've been just what she needed, for she
laughed and clapped and cried when she came out and discovered them. After that she began looking better, healthier,
going about her business again with a smile and the such.
But once when I was out gathering I saw her though, sitting
atop a large rock and looking at the rows of mountains in
the distance with a grim look on her face and tears on her
cheeks. I never asked what it was she was doing, or even let
her know I saw her, but I imagined she was worrying over
what you were up to over here."

Ono nodded his head thoughtfully. In the neighborhood below the windows were gradually blinking off one by one, and
a breeze rustled the underbrush around them.

"But why didn't she come back to visit with you and Igit?"
he worried.

"Honestly? She thought you might have been killed, and she
couldn't bare to think of discovering you in such a state.
Before we departed though, she pulled me to the side and
told me that if I found you alive that she would pay me
whatever it was I asked of her if I would stuff you in a

gunny sack and drag you back to her," he said and snorted
out a laugh. "She was quite serious about it you know."

Ono smiled fondly as he watched the neighborhood below.
"That does sound like her," he agreed.

"Oh, and I nearly forgot, what with all this excitement
going on," Corq said and snapped his fingers. "Everyone
wants you to know that they all miss you and love you. Ezquit and Nez asked me to tell you that they've had a burrow
dug and waiting for when you come to your senses, and old
Koilli sais that she'll have a feast-pot full of mushworm
stew ready when you return. Ofil told me to ask you about
the humans and whatnot, and old Bruffit grumbled what sounded like a greeting. Let's see... who else? There were so
many," he wondered for a moment and tugged the hair on his
chin. "Oh yes! Sced and Kei! Oh Ono, you should see how
they've grown. They wanted to come along with us, but of
course their parents wouldn't have any of that. Anyway,
they've promised never to throw another mud ball at you if
you return with souvenirs,"

The two laughed quietly, and the nighttime breeze blew
warmly through the pine trees. A coyote howled from somewhere far off in the distance of the mountains, and was answered a moment later by the whiny yap of a dog below. Then
the laughter trailed off, and Ono sighed.

"I do miss then all Corq, and in a terrible way. But I
can't just leave, especially not after all the trouble I've

gone through to stay. No, but I do hope they'll understand," he said sadly.

Just then Corq honked with laughter and sprang to his feet. "That's the thing my friend! Ha! They won't understand! Not at all and not one bit!" he exclaimed happily.

Ono scowled up at him. "And just why is that a thing to be happy about?" he puzzled, much to Corq's delight.

"Because! Can't you see Ono? They won't understand unless we show them, like you did with Igit and I! We thought you were absolutely mad until you gave us a tour, but look at us now!" he cried, flipping his hands happily in the air around him. "We don't want to leave at all! Not with all the treasures to be had!"

Hesitantly, Ono's crooked smile began to spread across his face. "Go on," he said and sat up straight.

"Oh Ono! If only your brain were bigger than those ears of yours!" Corq said and began to pace and shake a declaring finger in the air. "If you want everyone to return back, then what we must do is this: load up every piece of treasure we can carry back with us to that awful land, then pass them around to everyone to ogle and envy. Oh! And we'll treat them all to a feast of delicious foods like none they've ever tasted while we do it. Then, once we've gotten them all worked into a fuss, we collect all our wealth, tip our caps, and bid them farewell until we return again for another visit! Oh yes! They won't come scrambling after us right away I'm sure, but give them all a few days to stew in

their envy, and they'll begin to trickle away one by one un-

til finally everyone returns! Genius! And you'll have your

Bej back, as sure as the sun shines!"

Ono, whose ears had begun to tremble with excitement,

stood up and shook Corq by the front of his robe. "You're

right my friend! Why didn't I ever think of such a thing?

That is a plan, if I have ever heard one! Let's do it! Let's

do it!" he shrilled as Corq honked with laughter.

Imagining what it would be like to see Bej's beautiful

face again, he then turned his head and squinted down at the

neighborhood. All the windows were dark, and many trashcans

sat at the curb.

He looked back up at Corq and grinned. "Come! We must have

only the finest of things to take along with us when we vis-

it, and we mustn't wait any longer than necessary! Follow a-

long!" he squawked and hurried off down the mountain.

CHAPTER SEVENTY SIX

The two went whispering and rustling down through the ferns, then grew quiet as they came to the fence. Corq was especially eager to get started, and he got down and wiggled under first. Ono followed close behind him, and the two crawled out into the back yard of a squat, tan home.

Off to the right there was a tall metal pole sticking up from the lawn, and at its top an American flag swayed flaccidly in the weak breeze. On the porch was a rickety rocking chair, and beside it was a small table where an ashtray full of cigarette butts sat. Backed up against the fence on the left was a wooden dog house, and over the arched entranceway was the name Rover. In the shadows below it there could be seen the wrinkly face of an old hound dog resting on its paws as it slept, its ears and jowls drooping and sagging to the dirt.

Ono pulled his wand and pointed it at the dog for Corq to see, then pressed it against his lips and gave a silent, "shhhh," before tiptoeing across the lawn and around the right side of the home. One after the other they squeezed through the bars of an iron gate, then slipped into the hedges and made their way down to the sidewalk. Once there, they stood side by side and pulled down a branch to peer out into the street.

Ten yards down the sidewalk a black motorcycle was parked at the curb, its single headlight peering like a cyclop's eye off into the night and its handlebars arching down like horns. Corq didn't like the looks of the queer beast, but Ono didn't seem entirely concerned about it, so he said nothing. Across the street two metal trashcans sat abreast at the curb, their shadows stretched down the sidewalk by the streetlight at the corner of the block. Neither were overflowing with garbage, but the one on the right had its lid askew, and a small crescent gap curved at the rim.

Looking like a good place to start, they pushed through the hedges and hopped down off the curb and waddled across the street. When they came to a stop in the shadows of the trashcan, Ono reached down in his pouch, pulled out the treble hook and began unwinding the floss from around it.

"Ono, can I throw it this time? For the practice?" Corq asked.

"Oh, yes, or course. Here you are," Ono said and handed him the hook. "But just remember to grab the line when you spin it, or else it won't go as high."

Corq hefted the hook in his hands, then pushed his cap back on his head and squinted up at the rim of the trashcan. He judged the distance for a moment, then began to windmill his arm around and around like he had seen Ono do. Once the hook was hissing through the air, he then released it with a shrill grunt and watched as it sailed up over the edge. It went further than was needed though, and it landed on the metal lid above with a sharp Ting! that made both gnomes

cringe and look around. Nothing in the neighborhood seemed
to take notice of the tiny noise though, so Corq tugged
gently on the floss until the hook slid off the lid and fell
down into the trashcan and snagged.

"Ha! Good shot my friend!" Ono said and pulled his pouch
on.

Corq scaled up first, his feet pittering up the side of
the metal can as he climbed. When he reached the top and
disappeared over the rim, Ono heard a startled squawk and
the crunch of something landing within.

Concerned, Ono perked up his ears and cupped his hands a-
round his mouth. "Corq! Is everything alright in there?!"
he whispered up.

There came several muffled curses, then two rows of fingers hooked the rim of the trashcan as Corq pulled himself
up and peered down at Ono. "Just fine! But be careful when
you let yourself down, this one's only half-full, and it's
quite a drop if you're unaware!" he warned.

Ono snorted out a laugh and shook his head at his clumsy
friend, then took hold of the line and pulled himself up. At
the top he pulled himself over the rim, then slowly slid
down until his feet crinkled on the white plastic of a garbage bag. It smelled of musky rubbish and faintly of old
fish, and the dim glow of the streetlight spilled in weakly
from the opening above.

There were only two bags filling the can, and Corq had

already cut a slit in the furthest one over and begun to dig inside. He was a silhouette in the darkness, and was humming merrily as he rummaged. Ono reeled in the line, then waddled across the bag and got down on his knees. He cut a slit in the plastic and sat his pouch beside him, then eagerly reached in with both hands snatching and began to search for what there was to be found.

The two worked intently for ten minutes, for they were each picturing the envious faces of the other gnomes as they returned back to flaunt their wealth to the community, and they wanted to find only the best of things to take along with them. Ono was especially anxious, for he wanted to impress Bej more than anyone else, and he felt that this would be his one shot in which to do it.

After a time of working in silence, Corq honked with laughter and popped up out of the garbage bag. "Ono! Look at this odd thing I've just discovered! What do you suppose it could be?" he puzzled as he held the cracked, rectangular lens from a pair of reading glasses up to his face. When he did, his head doubled in size and his eyes seemed to bulge out from their sockets, while his toothy smile in the bifocal below was pinched and tiny.

Ono thought he looked much like a happy praying mantis with a big nose, and he doubled over in shrill laughter when he saw him. "Corq! Oh! I wish you could see yourself! You look absolutely absurd!" he giggled and pointed.

Corq squinted his bugged eyes through the lens at Ono, who suddenly seemed very fat. His face was stretched wide like someone had grabbed his cheeks and pulled them apart like putty, and the crack in the lens put one eye high above the other. In the bifocal below his legs looked like scrawny twigs that would surely buckle beneath his inflated body.

"I look absurd? You should see yourself! Ha! What an odd thing this is!" Corq laughed.

The two passed the lens back and forth and made silly faces at one another for a time, then grew bored with the thing and stuffed it down in a pouch before continuing their dig. Although there wasn't a terribly large amount of garbage in the can, there were certainly quite a few treasures to be found within. Over the next hour and a half the two gnomes found a shiny battery, a thimble, a single cufflink, an orange shot glass, a number of brilliantly colored fish pebbles, a chrome tire-pressure guage, and a thin copper tube.

Towards the bottom of the bag Corq discovered a whole mess of potato chips scattered amongst crumbled fast food wrappers. Curiously, he leaned forward and sniffed at one, then broke a small piece off and nibbled it with a brooding look on his face. It was salty, and it crunched pleasantly between his teeth as he chewed. "Ono! I've found us a tasty snack! Come, we've been working hard and are in need of a break!" he called out.

Ono's voice, sounding tiny and muffled and far away, called out a moment later from behind the wall of plastic, "Excellent! I was hoping one of us would find something soon. Where are you?!" he asked.

"Just follow my voice! Over here! Over here!" Corq called out.

It took a minute, but Ono's sword finally pierced the bag and cut a long slit down. Then he pulled it apart and squeezed through from the other bag and stepped inside. He was panting for breath and sweating from the labor of wrestling his way through the rubbish, but looked quite happy to see the potato chips scattered about.

"Oh, good find Corq! I've discovered these things on a few other occasions, and I've enjoyed them each and every time!" he said and licked his lips. Corq already had a mouthful of the strange delicacies, and was busy crunching away on them as he crushed pieces in his hand and slapped them to his mouth.

The two ate as if they were famished for a time, and after their bellies were full they gleaned what chips were left and sat down to rest for a spell. Ono had his feet propped up on a pickle jar, and Corq had splayed himself out amongst a wad of crumpled tissues with his hands folded behind his head. Both had loosened their sashes to let their bellies bulge, and after being in there for so long the trashcan's musky aroma was no longer noticed by either of them.

Ono burped and patted his stomach, then glanced over at Corq. "How long do you suppose it will take us to get there?" he asked, for his mind couldn't seem to stray from the topic for even a moment.

Corq picked a morsel from his teeth and flicked it away, then folded his hands back behind his head. "Oh, I'd say four days' travel, perhaps five at the most, depending on how much we carry along with us," he explained. "It's a gruelingly wearisome way, and the travel is slow over steep foreign mountains and across rickety logs bridging raging rivers. I still can't believe I cajoled Igit into making it again, but she missed all her things terribly and forced me to carry her nearly the whole way."

Ono twiddled his thumbs as he thought to himself for a moment. "How about we set off to make the trip next month? The weather should still be nice, and it'll give you two some time to get settled in before we go," he proposed hopefully.

Corq nodded his head. "Yes, I was just thinking the same. Of course, I still have to check with Igit first, but I'm sure she will nip at the idea of flaunting our wealth in front of all those envious eyes. Oh yes! I'm sure she would. Can you imagine? Mark my words Ono, this will all work out in the best of way for all of us," he said, sounding both eager and hopeful.

Ono sighed and smiled, for he was sure his friend was

right.

You see, gnomes are easily made jealous by the sparkle and shine of other's treasure, and tend to become very agitated and unpleasant when they won't be bartered or traded for. When they won't, gnomes have been known to go to far lengths to acquire them anyway.

Once, many years before, Fobil had uncovered an especially attractive chunk of iron pirite beside the creek, and he had made quite a show of rolling the sparkling treasure through the forest back towards his burrow. As he had, the residents of the community had come hurrying from all directions like fluttering moths to a flame to catch a glimpse of what could shine so.

"I've got seven clear crystals for that!" "Nonsense! I've got nine!" "My dear friend Fobil! Would you accept this robe and all my appreciation for it?" "Do you remember last Autinter when I practically gave you my best of walking sticks? That would surely make us even! It's only fair!" many shrill voices had chirped and squawked at Fobil as he struggled to roll it along.

He had laughed and waved and enjoyed the attention that his new found wealth was bringing him very much, but was so intent on getting the heavy thing back to the safety of his burrow that he had quickly tuckered himself out. As evening had come to the forest he was forced to sit down with his back against the sparkling pirite and sleep until the morning time to finish the rest of the trip back to his burrow.

Much to Fobil's surprise though, he had awoken to the feel of a strange something poking his back, and had soon realized with dawning horror that some deplorably clever thief, or thieves, in the night had replaced his beautiful treasure with a worthless pine cone.

"Egh! Thieves! Thieves have robbed me! Somebody help! There's a thief on the loose!" Fobil had shrilled as he stomped his feet and flailed his fists and spit curses from his beard.

The treasure was never seen again, but a round stone was later found in the mud alongside a trail of roll marks, and old Bruffit had soon thereafter begun throwing ones just like it at those who ventured too close to his burrow. It was strongly suspected but never proved that he had snatched it away, and beside their suspicion the rest of the community held a bit of envy towards Bruffit, for it had certainly been a wonderfully beautiful piece of pirite.

Imagine what they would do to own some of the things I've discovered! Ha! They'll probably arrive back here before I do! Ono thought to himself. His stomach fluttered with excitement at the idea, and he looked over at Corq. "Ready to get back to work?" he asked.

Corq sat up and rubbed his hands together. "Of course I am! I was wondering when you were going to ask!" he said.

Eagerly, the two gnomes grabbed their pouches and began to rustle back up through the rubbish, laughing and jabbering about the future as they went.

CHAPTER SEVENTY SEVEN

Out in the night Corq dropped the last pouch down to Ono, then threw his legs over the lip of the trashcan and re- pelled down to the sidewalk. Once there he shook the hook loose and wound the floss around it, then handed it back to Ono.

"Whatever became of Proi's grave? I remember it was at the foot of the old oak in the corner of the meadow, but with the humans' dwellings scattered about I can't seem to picture quite where it was anymore," he said, picking up his pouch and squinting curiously both ways down the street, trying to imagine just where he would be standing in the tall grass of the meadow if it were still there. Everything was so strange and unfamiliar though, and he couldn't seem to place himself no matter how he tried.

Ono stuffed the hook down in his pouch, then picked it up with a grunt and hung it on his shoulder. "Oh, I'll show you. It's just down the way a bit. Come, we've still got much work to do tonight, but on some other soon we'll have to stop and visit him. I'm sure he would be delighted to hear that you and Igit are back," he said and started off down the sidewalk with Corq waddling at his side.

Avoiding the glowing pools cast down from the streetlights along the way, the two hurried to the end of the block, cut across the front lawn of the home on the corner, then slipped into the shrubs lining the driveway. They rustled

through them to the other side, then pulled down a branch
and peered out at the two beasts parked silently before the
garage. This time the blue pickup truck was nearest them,
and the green Mustang was on the other side of it.

"His grave is under the hard-earth beneath the second
beast over, towards the thing's front," Ono whispered and
pointed under the truck to the Mustang. Several oil stains
dotted the driveway around where Proi laid, and the underside of the car was only several inches from the ground.

Corq was quite intimidated by the two vehicles, and shifted uncomfortably on his feet and rested his hand on his
wand as he eyed the tall, knobby tires of the truck. Its
windows were tinted nearly black, and dark splotches and
streaks of mud had been flung up the side of the fenders
like gruesome morsels on the cheeks of a gorging beast.

My word! Ono must truly love his father, for I would surely never have anything to do with such Volvos! They're giant
and horrid looking! he thought as he gaped up at the beasts.
He had never been so close to one before, and found them
quite frightening.

Ono noticed his friends round eyes and tall ears, and he
thought for a moment of explaining to him again that they
weren't much of a thing to be frightened of. But then he
smiled and sat his pouch down, then nudged Corq with his elbow. "Wait here!" he said before pushing out of the hedges
and pitter-pattering across the driveway towards the truck.

"Ono! What are you..?" Corq whispered after him.

Ono hurried into the shadow of the pickup, then stopped and turned around to wave. Then, much to Corq's shock, Ono pulled back his leg and kicked the front tire with a dull thud. "Wake up you dim Volvo! My friend and I are here to challenge you! Come on then, come to and face us!" he said, pistoning his fists in the air.

Horrified, Corq backed up in the hedges to hide. "Ono! Are you trying to get us killed?! You're crazy! Stop that this instant!" he whispered.

Ono slapped the side of the tire and stuck out his tongue for good measure, then hurried back into the hedges. "See? Volvos are the heaviest of sleepers. They don't notice a thing when the humans aren't around. I'm telling you, they are nothing at all to be scare of!"

Seeming ruffled, Corq adjusted his pouch and cleared his throat. "Yes, well, it would certainly seem so. Nonetheless, I think I'll keep my distance for now. I'm afraid I'm not as insane as you seem to have become. Tell your father that I said hello for me though," he said and quickly rustled away through the hedges.

Ono bent down and picked up his pouch. "Oh you ninny! Come back and tell him yourself!"

"Absolutely not! Besides, we've got work to do, remember? And you're holding it up!" he squawked back.

Snickering to himself, Ono glanced over and sent his father's grave a loving wink, then pushed through the hedges after his friend. At the foot of the lawn Corq was already standing in the shadow of a mailbox post, looking cautiously up and down the street.

"Which way do we go now?" he asked.

Ono waddled down to him, then pointed up the block. At the curb near the corner was a small dark shadow where the mouth of a grainage pipe opened to the gutter. "Right down there. That tunnel will take us to the other side of the humans' village and back to the forest," he said and began walking towards the end of the block. He made it ten feet down the sidewalk before noticing that Corq wasn't with him though, so he frowned and turned around to see where he had gone.

At the foot of the hedges, Corq was still standing in the shadow of the mailbox post, having not moved a muscle. He was completely silent, looking across the street with a queer look on his face.

Concerned, Ono followed his gaze across the street to the familiar white two-storied home. Nothing appeared especially threatening about it, Ono puzzled for a moment. But then he saw the two cars backed up in front of the garage off to the left, and he sighed and shook his head. There was a street-light not far away, and its yellow glow whined off the cars' headlights like the eyes from a pair of hungry cats.

"Corq! I already told you, they're asleep! I was fooling around. Now come along!" he said.

Corq flapped an impatient hand at him, then pressed a finger to his lips and waved for him to come over. Shaking his
head, Ono waddled back.

"You do know we're never going to get any gathering done
at all if we don't-" he began to say as he neared, but cut
himself off when Corq whispered urgently, "Ono! We're being
spied on as we speak! Be quiet and look over there!" he said
and pointed across the street.

His finger was aimed past the side of the house to the
metal gate separating the back yard from the front. The
streetlight's glow was weak there, and everything to the
back fence was draped in overlapping shadows. The only movement came from a sapling in the front yard of the blue house
next door that bristled when the wind blew past.

Ono bent his eyebrows together and squinted into the darkness. He saw nothing worth such concern at first, and was a-
bout to ask Corq what exactly it was he was worrying over
until he suddenly made them out from the surrounding shadows.

Three small dark figures, all wearing tall pointed caps,
standing abreast in the back yard.

Their vague silhouettes could hardly be noticed but from
the corner of the eye against the back fence, but it was e-
nough for Ono to make out several distinct details. The figure on the left was resting patiently on some sort of thick
club, and the one in the middle seemed to have its hand out,

pointing right back at them. The one on the right had some
large thing hanging from its fist and was bent down at an
awkward angle, as if trying to peer curiously past the bars
of the gate to get a better look at them. They appeared to
be gnomes, but were awfully bulky and unfamiliar.

And why would they just hide from us in the shadows I wonder? Hmm, that's awfully strange of them, Ono thought with a
frown.

Corq was just as puzzled as he. "Who are they Ono? Do you
know them?" he turned and whispered, keeping his eyes
trained on the three strangers.

Ono shrugged. "No, I don't. At least I haven't seen them
here before," he said and tugged thoughtfully on his chin
hairs. Then after a moment of pondering he snapped his fingers and looked up at Corq. "Perhaps they're travelers that
have been run from their land and are in need of help? Can
you imagine traveling through the mountains to suddenly
stumble across a place such as this? Oh, I'm sure you'd be
frightened as well! Come, let's be polite and greet them
instead of rudely gaping at them all night," he said happily, then hurried across the sidewalk and hopped down off
the curb.

As Ono went pittering across the street, Corq frowned to
himself and hesitantly raised his arm in a wave to the three
strangers. They did not return the greeting, but only stared
blankly back at him with shadowy faces.

Suddenly feeling very uncomfortable with the situation, Corq pulled his wand from his sash and hurried across the street after his friend.

CHAPTER SEVENTY EIGHT

The two rustled through the hedges, scurried across the front lawn, then squeezed past the bars of the gate and began waddling down the brick walkway along the side of the house towards the three figures standing quietly in the back yard. As they neared, they passed by a collection of colorful potted plants placed in a neat row to the right, and a large bird bath in the grass to the left. The strangers ahead made no attempt to wave or tip their caps, or even to acknowledge their very presence in any kindly way. They just stood there, side by side and as still as stone.

Figuring that the poor travelers must be as awe-struck with the humans' village as Corq and Igit had been, Ono stopped several feet before them in the grass and swept his cap across his feet. "Greetings my friends," he said quietly, then straightened back up and pulled his cap on. "How do you all do? My name is Ono, and my friend here is Corq,"

Suspicious of the newcomers, Corq eyed each of them carefully, then pulled off his cap and gave it a half-hearted sweep before putting it right back on again. "Greetings. How do you do?" he asked.

Unresponsive, the three figures simply stood there and said nothing. Their faces were shrouded in darkness, and their blank, shadowy stares were quite unnerving.

There was a long awkward silence for a moment until Ono cleared his throat. "H-Hello? It's okay, we don't mean you any harm at all. You see, we live close by in the mountains and come down here to gather. If you need help or directions of any sort, why, we'd be more than happy to assist you," he said, hoping for some response.

There was none, from any of the three.

Getting irritated with the strangers' unmannerly silence, Corq took a step closer and squinted at the dark face of the figure with its elbow propped up on a club. "Hello, we said, how do you do? we asked. Have any of you any manners?" he asked and wagged his wand like an angry finger, becoming quite perturbed.

Again, not a thing from any one of them.

Ono frowned and shifted on his feet. "Well, if you three insist on being like this, then that is all fine and fair by me. We have better things to do tonight than help you anyway. Good luck trying to make your way through the humans' land with your lives intact though, as I'm sure that you'll be in dire need of it! Good-night to all three of you!" Ono huffed, then spun on his heels and begun stomping away through the grass towards the back fence, aghast that the strangers could be so discourteous. I hope they keep moving, for I would rather be neighbors with the humans than those rude fellows! he thought as he went.

Corq glared at the three stubbornly silent silhouettes for a moment waiting for some apology, then turned up his nose when one didn't come and made to follow Ono under the fence.

But before he did he turned back and pointed his wand at the figure in the center. "Here's a bit of advice: being polite is always better than not-" he began to say, but suddenly went quiet and pricked up his ears with a puzzled look on his face.

In his irratation, Corq had accidentally poked his wand in to the chest of the shadowy stranger before him. It wasn't a hard or hurtful poke, and instead of eliciting an indignant squawk there came a sharp Click! from the stranger. Confounded, Corq poked his wand at the stranger's chest again.

Click! Click! Click!

Across the yard Ono had just stuffed his pouch under the fence and was crouching down to wiggle under when he heard Corq call out his name. "What? Oh, no, let me guess: **now** they want our help? Well, tell them they'd better have something good in trade for it, because it is no longer free!" he said as he stood up and crossed his arms. He was quite offended by the trio's cold shoulder, for he had been excited at the idea of having new neighbors before they had so disrespectfully refused to speak with him.

In the shadows at the corner of the lawn, Corq turned to Ono and discreetly shielded his mouth away from the three with the back of his hand. "I think you need to come see this! There's something not right about these strangers!" he said, sounding disturbed.

Grumbling, Ono waddled back to his friend's side and

glared at the three rude mutes.

"Listen to this," Corq said, then tapped his wand to the
dark figure's chest again. ⌐

Click!

Ono's glare lightened into a perplexed frown when he heard
this, so he pulled his wand as well and tapped it to the
forehead of the figure on the right.

Click! came the exact same noise as the one in the middle.

"Why that's... huh," he wondered and curiously pricked up
his ears.

After a moment of puzzling on the strangers, Corq reached
out and grasped the shoulders of the one standing in the
middle. Then, without much effort, he managed to turn the
dark figure so that it faced away from the shadows. When the
weak glow of the streetlight out front brought the stranger's features into view, Ono gasped and Corq pulled his arms
away in surprise.

The impolite stranger, it appeared, was a lawn gnome.

Now to our kind, such an ornament is usually nothing to
get all worked up over, for they simply add a quaint touch
to the flowers and rose bushes in many a garden, and serve
no other practical purpose- although one's imagination could
tend to become tickled when caught wondering just how the
so-called "myth" of the gnome race got started in the first
place. But the two knew not of our ornaments and fabled
tales about their kind, and were dumbfounded as to what to

make of the statue.

"Oh my..." Ono whispered to himself, then shuffled past Corq to get a better look at the curious thing.

The lawn gnome, to each of them anyway, appeared both ridiculous and awkward. The thing's face was jolly and rosy-cheeked and plump, with arched, bushy eyebrows and a long white flowing beard. Its ears were round and odd though, like a human's, and its robe was bright blue with an orange sash and a gold buckle. On its head was a pointed cap the same color as its robe, and on its feet were what appeared to be large, cumbersome leather boots. A toothy grin was stretched across its face, and it had its hand stretched forward palm-up as if expecting something to be placed in it.

It was completely quiet for several minutes as the two puzzled on the strange ornament, until finally Corq snorted out a laugh and shook his head. "Are you seeing what I'm seeing Ono? Oh, this cannot be right at all. Would you look at that robe?" he said, gesturing with his wand. "How would anyone ever be able to hide wearing such a foolish thing? Or hear anything out of those tiny ears of his? Oh! And those things on his feet! I'd wager a good sum that you'd hear him crunching along through the leaves far before he arrived. Ha! What are these Ono?" he asked, sounding curiously amused.

Not knowing what to say, Ono could only shake his head in

bewilderment and move on to the figure on the left. He grasped it by the shoulders and turned it into the light, finding yet another lawn gnome as preposterous as the first. This one wore a red robe and cap, had the same gold buckle and leather boots, but was leaning on a walking stick with his hand on his belly. A pleasant smile was pulling at the corners of his flowing beard, and his glazed eyes shined happily in the dim light.

To the right, Corq turned the last lawn gnome into the light and snorted out another laugh. It was wearing a yellow robe and cap with a red sash, and was holding in its hand a wicker basket. It was bent over at the waist, seemingly caught frozen in the middle of reaching for something on the ground with an affable grin on its porcelain face.

Ono reached out and rapped his knuckles against the forehead of the lawn gnome before him, receiving a dull clunk in response. "Corq, I.. I think this one is hollow. Can you imagine? Try yours and see what it does," Ono said, then took off his cap and scratched his head in bafflement.

Corq set his pouch down on the grass, then reached out and knocked on its forehead, receiving the same hollow clunk. He struck it quite hard though, and the ornament rocked backwards, teetered precariously, then toppled over into the grass where it landed with its grasping hand held up in the air.

Corq laughed and pointed at the silly thing. "Ha! Look

Ono! He needs a hand getting up again! You should-" he began
to say.

But then the motion detector mounted on the back of the
house suddenly flashed on, beaming its numinous glare down
on them like the accusing sunlight from an angry heaven.
Terrified, Corq and Ono froze as still as the ornaments beside them, their round eyes like those of a deer's while in
the headlights of an approaching vehicle.

A moment later the thumping of heavy feet could be heard
from inside the home as someone ran towards the back door.

CHAPTER SEVENTY NINE

Joey had awoken sometime earlier that night with a rumbling stomach, so he had tiptoed downstairs, crept into the kitchen, and quietly opened the refrigerator door to sneak a snack or two. His parents didn't allow that kind of business between meals, so he was especially careful not to rattle the condiment bottles together as he reached to the back and picked up the quarter-eaten cherry pie. The tin crinkled when he lifted it out, so he grimaced behind his headset as he quietly shut the refrigerator, shuffled to the counter, and gently set it down beside the sink. Then he slowly __ opened the silverware drawer, plucked out a fork, and slid it shut again.

With a sneaky grin that gleamed in the dark kitchen, Joey stabbed the fork a half-inch in from the cut in the crust and lifted a small bite of the cherry pie to his mouth. When he tried to eat it though, the metal clips connecting his braces to the headset kept his jaw from opening.

"Dang id," he mumbled, then peeled back his lips and fiddled with the clips until the one connected to his bottom braces clicked off. After it had, he began chipping away at the edges of the pie, carefully working his way around the v cut out of it. He did this, of course, so that the section missing would not appear any larger to anyone who checked it before putting it away.

Savoring the sweet cherries and crunchy crust of the last

bite, Joey licked the fork clean, polished it to a shine on
the hip of his Batman underwear, then opened the drawer and
placed it right back where he had got it. It was when he was
reaching for the pie to put it back in the refrigerator that
the window above the sink suddenly lit up, freezing him in
the guilty act for a moment until he remembered the new motion sensors his dad had put up the week before.

He had put one up on each corner of the house to keep the
raccoons, or the cats, or whatever bothersome little things
kept getting into the trashcans, away from the house. Joey
had been secretly suspecting that Special was to blame for
the trashcan break-ins, for he could get out at any time
through the doggy door to work his late-night mischief, but
of course mentioned nothing of it.

Hoping to catch him in the act, Joey hopped up on the
countertop, pulled the curtains aside, and squinted out at
the brick walkway that ran alongside the home. The motion
detector's glow was coming from the right, so Joey scooted
his bottom down the counter and leaned over to get a better
look at the back yard. He saw where the fence bent to en-
close the lawn and where the two rows of hedges met that
bordered it, but the slight view from the window only showed
him the very corner of the back yard.

Joey frowned suspiciously for a moment as he peered out
into the night, but after not seeing much of anything he
shrugged, figuring it must have been the wind. He began to

carefully ease himself down off the counter so his feet wouldn't thump on the tile, but stopped when a small movement suddenly caught his eye. Intrigued, he leaned back again and glanced out the window and down the side of the house.

At the very corner of the home there came a queer shifting of shadows on the lawn. Whatever was making them was small, and just out of view though, the motion detector's glow casting its shape down on the obscuring lawn from around the corner. But something was, most definitely, out there.

Suddenly very excited to catch the dog gnawing on a piece of trash, Joey grinned and hopped down off the counter. They'll be so mad at him for this! Oh man, mom'll spank him and rub his nose in it and not let him outside anymore! Ha! he thought as he ran down the dark hallway. His bare feet thumped on the carpet as he went, but he wasn't too worried about the noise, for if his parents' sleep were disturbed by it then they would wake to discover that he had found the offender. And the very same one that spilled the paint and ate the M&M'S! This'll be great! I'm coming for you, you stupid mutt! he thought as he came to the back door. He fumbled the lock with eager fingers, then turned the latch and wrenched open the door and hurried out onto the porch.

Outside the night was cool and quiet and still. At first glance the back yard appeared entirely empty but for the flower pots and bird baths sprinkled about. More than a few

lawn ornaments grinned from the hedges, and the motion detector on the corner of the house to the left cast down just
as many shadows into the nooks and crannies as it did shine
light on.

Plenty of places for a guilty little terrier to hide.

Narrowing his eyes into suspicious slits, Joey snuck
quietly to the top of the steps, his bare feet creaking
softly over the boards. "Spethel... Where are you boy? Come
out, come out, wherever you are..." he whispered as he stood
there studying the shadows for a time.

A breeze hissed across the dark mountain looming just beyond the back fence, and the tall pine trees all whispered
and groaned and swayed together in ghostly unison. Somewhere
out in the night an owl's hoot came from the shadows, and
the neighbor's windchime tinkled eerily. Then the breeze
died out, and all was quiet again.

Suddenly feeling very wary, Joey picked up his father's
old putter leaning beside the stairs and held it in both
hands across his chest. "Spethel? Is that you out here boy?"
he whispered hopefully, his voice nearly a squeak. He had
never been fond of the dark, and a cramp in his belly urged
him to go back inside.

Again, nothing moved.

Gulping nervously, Joey eased down the three stairs and
stepped out onto the lawn, the grass cool and crisp beneath
his feet. He crouched down and checked beneath the porch,

but could see nothing in the shadows past the lattice work. Then he stood back up and ran his gaze along the hedges to the left. It was then that he noticed one of his mother's lawn gnomes had been tipped over.

Huffel, Duffel, and Dori, she had named each of them after she had painted them and placed them just-so in the grass. Huffel and Duffel still stood to the left of their fallen friend, but something seemed strangely amiss about them as well, Joey puzzled with a frown as he fidgeted with the golf club. It took him a moment, but he finally remembered just what it was: Huffel and Duffel were turned in the wrong direction. His mother had faced them towards the gate so they would appear to be greeting any guests coming down the walkway.

Now though, they were faced in towards the lawn, their gleaming, porcelain little eyes fixed directly on him. Both had cheesy grins on their faces that seemed quite unnerving this time of night.

Joey shivered uncomfortably under their gaze, then let out a nervous laugh and glanced around. "Okay Spethel! This is nod funny! Come oud here boy!" he called.

A second later he heard the tinkling of the dog's bell, and a flood of relief washed over him. I knew it! I knew he was out here! Thank goodness it wasn't a monster! he thought as he looked around the yard, expecting to see the terrier emerge from the shadows nearby with its head hung in guilt.

But oddly enough, Special poked his head out from the doggy door and curiously perked up its ears at him.

"Spethel? But I thod I thaw you..?" Joey trailed off, twisting his face in confusion. He had seen something moving around back here, but he was sure there was no way Special could have made it back inside before he came running down the hallway in the other direction.

Looking just as confounded, Special cocked his head to the side and blinked. Then the little terrier seemed to pick up something odd in the air, and he glanced over at the side of the yard towards the lawn gnomes and began to let out a long shrill growl, his snaggled teeth gleaming yellow.

Joey was quite disturbed by the dog's behavior, and was about to tell it to hush up when the motion detector's one minute timer suddenly ended, cutting out the lights and filling the back yard once again with darkness. When it did, Special let out a yelp of surprise and disappeared inside. Alarmed, Joey began flailing the putter in the air and back peddling across the lawn to get the lights back on.

Come on! Turn on you stupid thing! Please turn on! he thought as he whined in fright, sensing that something was very wrong in the darkness around him.

CHAPTER EIGHTY

At the last moment before the back door had been thrown o-
pen, Corq and Ono had darted behind the two lawn gnomes to
hide as the human had come hurrying out onto the porch. Terrified, and knowing they couldn't risk making a break for
it, they could only grasp the ornaments and slowly twist
them in the grass to stay hidden behind them as the human
came down off the stairs. The lawn gnomes were bulky and
wide, so Ono had no trouble at all keeping himself tucked a-
way in the shadow behind his. But poor Corq was crouched and
bent and squeezed into his meager hiding spot, and his ears
trembled and twitched with fright.

"What do we do now?" he turned and mouthed to Ono as the
human snuck across the lawn and crouched down to look beneath the porch, no more than ten yards away. His eyes
seemed about to bulge out of their sockets, and a ring of
brow sweat was beginning to darken his cap.

Having been in this predicament before, and far more pre-
carious ones, Ono was much more calm than his friend. He
kept one eye peeked around the ornament as he bit his tongue
in concentration, and he slowly twisted the lawn gnome to
face the human as it stood back up and glanced around. When
it wasn't looking in their direction, Ono pulled out his
wand, and, not knowing what else to do to reassure his
friend, gave Corq a quick thumbs-up.

Corq gawked at him as if he were insane.

Then the human called something out, and both of them
flinched and ducked back down behind the lawn gnomes. It was
quiet for a moment, until the familiar tinkling of the terrier's bell came to Ono's ears.

Oh no! Snakes! Not that wretched, ugly creature again! And
just when I thought things could not possibly get any worse!
Ono thought as he tightened the grip on his wand and
squeezed his eyes shut with a grimace. He heard the human
mumble something, and whatever it was seemed to anger the
animal, for it began to growl and snarl.

The situation was getting more treacherous by the very
second, and Ono knew he would have to do something soon to
save both himself and his friend, who at the moment seemed
nearly paralyzed with terror. Come on Ono! Think you fool!
Think! he thought, his eyes darting around the yard for
some escape as the terrier's snarls continued.

The human was no more than five yards away now, and
seemed to be looking curiously in their direction for the
source of the dog's irritation. There was some strange bar
covering its mouth, and it glinted frightfully in the light
like a wicked smile filled with gleaming teeth.

Then, as if in answer to a desperate prayer, everything
suddenly went dark again. Seeing a chance at escape, Ono
grabbed Corq by the shoulder. "Come on!" he whispered as the
dog yelped and the human squawked and began to flail its
club in the air. Grabbing their pouches, the two gnomes

shoved away from the ornaments and went scurrying across the lawn and dove beneath the fence just as the lights flashed back on.

CHAPTER EIGHTY ONE

The first thing Joey noticed when the lights came back on was the doggy door. Special's face had vanished from it, and the flap swung emptily back and forth.

"Woosy dog," Joey sighed and lowered his arms. He took a deep breath, and was just beginning to calm down again when he glanced back over at the side of the yard. What he saw made him gasp in absolute horror and fumble the putter in his hands.

When Corq and Ono had darted off the moment before, they had each pushed away from the ornaments to speed their escape, which had set the two lawn gnomes to rocking and tipping from side to side in the grass. Joey had no way of knowing this though, and gaped in terror as the wickedly-smiling ornaments seemed to walk in place like wind-up toys, teetering from foot to foot. Huffel had his little hand stretched forward in evil expectancy as if demanding from him a gruesome token, and Duffel seemed to stab menacingly at the grass with his walking stick as he rocked from side to side. Their beady eyes gleamed in the light, and the darkness of the hedges behind them made their faces dramatically vivid, their frozen smiles taunting and terrible with silent, mocking laughter.

Suddenly, the horror movies Joey's mom had forbidden him to watch came back to him in a flood of scenes like punishment for having gone behind her back to watch them anyway.

He saw the possessed Chucky doll striding down a hallway, the butcher knife held raised in his plastic fist dripping red as he sneered in murderous delight; he recalled the tiny dolls in the Puppet Master scurrying around in the shadows, snickering from the darkness as they closed in on yet another doomed victim with gleaming little blades; he saw the action figures from the movie Toy Soldiers coming to life as the family slept, the crazed Barbie dolls crawling and swarming over the screaming young lady as they bound her to the floor; and, for some reason the most disturbing of all, Joey saw Woody from Toy Story as his head slowly spun backwards, coming to life in grotesque animation in the hands of a trembling, petrified boy.

And all of a sudden, the missing M&M'S, the spilled paint, the rummaged trash, it all made perfect sense- it hadn't been the dog at all, but was instead the mischievous little lawn gnomes standing before him. They came to life at night to cause trouble, then hurried back to their places where they were frozen again with the sun's rays.

Then another thought came to Joey, this one even more frightening than all the others: they had been coming for him when the motion detector had switched off. Luckily, he had managed to turn it back on, stopping them in their tracks before they could get too close.

He had less than one minute before the lights cut out again.

Realizing he had to destroy them quickly, Joey raised the putter high above his head, his knees knocking together in terror and his heart hammering in his chest.

As if daring him to do it, the lawn gnomes only stood there grinning up at him.

"Diiiee!" Joey cried and swung the putter down in an arch, intent on smashing it through their pointed little caps.

"**Joey!** What the hell do you think you're doing?!" his mother suddenly screamed at him.

Surprised, Joey flinched and glanced over at the back door where she stood. The blow missed the lawn gnomes, and the putter thudded harmlessly in the grass at Huffel's feet.

Aghast at finding her half-naked son swinging a golf club at her lawn ornaments in the middle of the night, Joey's mom turned on the light over the back door and hurried out onto the porch. "Get over here **now!** Are you crazy? Put that down!" she yelled. She was in her pink bathrobe and slippers and her hair was in wild disarray.

Joey gawked at her for a moment, trying to think of some reasonable way to tell her that the lawn gnomes were coming to life at night to cause mischief. Nothing at all came to mind, so he pointed a finger down at them and let it all out at once. "Mom! You **have** to believe me! These lawn gnomes are alive! They come to life when it's darg, and they sthole the M&M'S and spilled your paind! I thwear! I tole you it wasn't me!" he shrilled.

Their exchange of words woke several yapping dogs in the
subdivision, and the second story window of the house next
door came alight as the silhouetted neighbors curiously parted the curtains to see what all the commotion was about.

The redness started at the base of his mom's neck where
the veins began to bulge and strain, then gradually worked
its way up to her face like crimson liquid filling a bottle.
Her nostrils flared angrily, and her lips sinched tightly
around her teeth.

"Joey, get... your butt... over here... **Now!**" she hissed.

Joey gulped nervously, then glanced back down at the lawn
gnomes. There was only one way. He would have to prove it.

"Aaahh!" he cried as he lifted the putter over his head
and brought it down with all the strength he could muster.
The putter whooshed down through the air, then struck the
ornament with a splitting Crack! making his mother scream
and cover her mouth in surprise.

To his dismay though, the lawn gnome did not crumble into
a pile of ashes, puff away in a cloud of smoke, nor release
a shrieking bat into the night as he had expected it to.
Instead, smiling Huffel shattered into a hundred pieces,
sending shards and chunks of porcelain exploding across the
lawn.

Then everything went quiet.

Joey stood there in his underwear, blinking in disbelief
as his wide eyes slid over all the pieces. A few of them he

could still tell what they use to be; an ear; half an eye; a gold buckle; what looked to be an elbow. Others had landed painted-side down, showing the white porcelain of Huffel's hollow insides.

Standing on the porch, Joey's mom let out a shocked gasp of breath, then came down the steps at him like a charging bull. "I've had it with you! I've just had it!" she squawked and flailed her arms as she stomped across the lawn. "You're going to military school! First thing in the morning I'm checking you in!"

Horrified, Joey dropped the putter and tried to back away, his face pale and his mouth forming silent words of frantic apology.

"Don't even try it! Don't even! Now come here!" his mom shrieked, then grabbed him by the bars of his headset and drug him by the braces across the yard.

Whimpering and lisping indiscernibly, Joey was pulled head first into the house, his cries cut short by the BANG! of the slamming back door.

CHAPTER EIGHTY TWO

"My word Ono! Did you see how close that human was to us? Ha! And we still waltzed away unnoticed! What dim-witted fools they all must be! To think I've been terrified of them all this time! I've seen coyotes with more cunning!" Corq exclaimed as they made their way back up the mountain some time later.

Ono giggled and agreed, for he was relieved that his friend still wanted to stay after such a scare. "Oh, I don't know Corq," he said as they waddled up through the dark underbrush. "You looked about to wet your robe when that human came out of its dwelling," he teased.

"Right," Corq snorted and made a face. "I'll have you know that I could have easily cast a vicious spell on that dull human at any moment. But I didn't, mind you, because I knew that such a thing wouldn't be necessary to get away," he said and lifted his chin.

"Of course, yes, a spell wasn't at all necessary," Ono nodded in agreement. "Especially when I was there to rescue you..." he trailed off and glanced into the underbrush with his eyebrows raised.

"Bah! Hear you tell it!" Corq scoffed playfully as they rustled and ducked through the tangled branches of a bush. "How I saw it was that you ran away first, and I, being as good a friend as I am, followed after you to protect your rear."

Each laughing at the other's conceit, they emerged out from the other side of the bush and crested the top of Boul-

der Mountain. They climbed over a fallen log and pushed
through a wall of ferns, and were met on the other side by
an impatient looking Igit. She had her arms crossed and her
eyes narrowed at Corq, and her foot was tapping expectantly
in the dirt.

"And just where have you been? Hmm? I've had snacks ready
and waiting for when you came back to unload you know, but
you never did! I've been in a tizzy for hours!" she
squawked, then pointed at the pouch hanging from his shoulder. "Is that all? It took you nearly the whole night to
gather that? While I was standing here worrying over you?"
she asked, sounding incredulous.

Corq stammered and fidgeted with the strap of the pouch.
"Well, you don't understand dear. You see, we were, ugh," he
fumbled along and glanced pleadingly over at Ono.

"Attacked by a human," Ono offered, keeping his gaze far
away from Igit's, for he wanted nothing at all to do with
their spat.

"Yes! Attacked by a giant human! And narrowly escaped with
our lives I might add. You should have seen it! I had my
wand at the ready, and I was just about to-"

"Oh hush it! I'm much too tired to stand here listening
to your prattle," she squawked, then grabbed him by the
sleeve and pulled him off into the underbrush.

Most amused, Ono raised his hand in the air and wiggled
his fingers. "See you tomorrow Corq! And don't forget to

tell her about our plan!" he called out as his wilted friend reluctantly followed his mate back to their burrow.

Once the two had gone rustling and fussing through the ferns, Ono snickered and shook his head, for it was quite a sight to see little Igit dragging tall Corq along like an unruly child. It was a sight he had long missed and was glad to see again. Smiling to himself, Ono took a deep breath through his nostrils and began waddling down the mountain side, whistling happily.

The golden crescent of morning time was just beginning to peek over the mountains, and everything in the forest seemed as it should. As the darkness faded the dew on the leaves glinted and sparkled, and the creatures and critters crawled from their crannies to start their day. An eagle soared among the puffs of clouds above, and as Ono made his way down to the creek he kept a cautious eye trained up at it until the bird turned into the wind and glided off into the distance.

When he arrived at the creek a short time later, Ono sat his things down among the mossy stones, took off his cap, and leaned down to the water's surface. He slurped up his fill and scrubbed his face and hair, then stuck his little finger in his ear and worked it around a bit. Then he pulled it back out and squinted at the yellow glob of wax on his fingertip before shrugging and wiping it on a fern leaf. He cleaned his other ear and washed his hands, then pulled on his cap and picked up his pouch.

Before he turned to leave though, a queer feeling suddenly came upon him that made his whistling cut short and his ears prick up. It wasn't an ominous or frightening sensation, but was rather one that stirred something strange in his belly that tingled and bubbled. Uncertain, Ono frowned and pressed a hand to his stomach, wondering for a moment if he only needed to use the bush. It didn't seem to him that he did, at the moment anyway, so he stood there for a long while puzzling over what it could be. He glanced up into the canopy of branches, but saw nothing more but a robin perched patiently above. A gray squirrel scampered down an oak tree up the mountain, and across the creek a small green frog plopped into the water and went kicking off into the ripples. Besides the morning breeze that hissed through the trees, everything else was quiet.

"Hmm," Ono wondered and nibbled his lip. Something certainly seemed amiss in some vague way, but whatever it was didn't feel in the least bit menacing, so Ono flipped a hand in the air and decided to ignore it.

Resuming his cheerful whistling once again, he hopped down off the mossy stone and began waddling back up the mountain towards his burrow. On his way through the underbrush he couldn't help but think of the plan he and Corq had thought up, for the very idea of it put a crooked grin on his face.

Oh is it genius! There's no way they won't follow us back,

what with all our treasures and goods in tow. Even Ezquit
and Nez will be green with envy! Ha! he thought to himself
and shivered with excitement. But I wonder what I should
take? Perhaps that clicking thing on the wall that lights
up? Or those beautiful trinkets I snatched from the two humans? Or maybe even that colorful ball on the shelf? Oh,
there's just so much to choose from!

It was a very good thing, to have hope instead of apprehension for the future once more.

Ono went rustling through a bed of ferns, startling up a
few brown quail as he went, before arriving back at the old
gnarled pine tree. He was deep in thought about many things
as he pushed through the bushed; whether or not to act non-
chalant about his riches when he arrived in the new land,
and if the other gnomes would think there were much more to
be had if he did so; what robe and cap to wear when he arrived so that he would be looking his very best for Bej; and
especially how to explain the humans' behavior in a way that
wasn't bone-chilling and discomforting like all the tales
told before.

But as he emerged from the brush and stopped before the
slab of bark, every thought he had in his mind suddenly became very unimportant, crumbling to tiny pieces and blowing
out of his mind like dust on the breeze. His breath caught
in his throat, and his heart seemed to stop beating in his
chest.

On the ground beside the entrance to his burrow, Bej laid curled and asleep. Her head was resting on a small pouch filled with what looked to be a single change of clothes and a few bits of food, and was the only luggage she had with her. She wore a dark brown dress that was stained and blotched, and her feet and toes were dirty with travel. Her hands were clasped to her chest, and her dark hair was tied back in a messy tail that had bits of leaves and pine needles stuck in it. Her delicate face was placid and exhausted as she slept, and a streak of dirt was smudged along her cheek.

Seeing her, Ono didn't jump up and down and squeal with joy like he had done at Corq and Igit's arrival, nor did he clap his hands and dance a jig. His eyes didn't spring open and bug out with surprise, and he didn't rush over to her and wake her with a barrage of kisses and hugs.

Shocked expressionless, he just stood there for a time and watched her as she slept, not thinking of how or why she had returned, but only taking in her beauty as the sight of her warmed his heart. She had obviously made the long journey back all alone, and he didn't want to disturb her rest with all the things he wanted to ask and say to her.

With trembling ears and tears welling up in his eyes, Ono set his pouch on the ground and quietly moved aside the slab of bark. Then he crouched down beside her, slowly worked his hands under her limp body, and gently lifted her in his arms. Bej stirred and mumbled softly, then rested her head on his shoulder and began to breathe heavily once more.

Ono kissed her forehead and smiled, his chin aquiver beneath his beard. Then, as tears of happiness rolled down his face, he carried her inside.

A SHORT TIME LATER...

"Here we are!" Ono said as he shook open the scrap of red flannel and laid it on the forest floor.

"Excellent! I like this spot Ono!" Bej said and smiled down at him as he smoothed out the wrinkles. She had her hair braided and tied with flower stems into two neat tails that were tucked behind her ears, and her face was clean and beautiful and dotted with dimples. She wore a light green dress that Igit had sewn for her from the fabric of a pillow case, and it fit her pretty and proper. In her hands was a basket filled with blueberries, picked from the forest, and several small strawberries, discreetly plucked from a human's garden the night before.

The two were at the top of Mud Hill in a tiny clearing nestled amongst several mossy boulders that cupped them from view of the forest behind them. The mountain fell away before them though, and through the trees the full view of the subdivision could be seen. The sun was just beginning to set behind the brilliant orange and reds of the clouds in the distance, and the humans below were going about their last chores of the day. The evening was both warm and mellow, the faint aroma of barbecue smoke drifting pleasantly on the breeze.

"It's all set. Here, let me take that for you," Ono said, then lifted the basket from her hands and motioned for her to sit with a sweep of his hand. He had a smile on his face that stretched from nearly ear to ear, and his beard was carefully combed. He wore a handsome robe and cap made from a brown pair of corduroy pants, and his black shoelace sash was tied in a neat knot.

"Why thank you Ono," Bej giggled with a curtsy and sat down on the blanket.

Ono eagerly sat down beside her and rubbed his hands together. "I think we've come just in time! Oh! I can't wait for you to see it happen, you'll be amazed!" he said as he plucked two blueberries from the basket and handed her one.

Bej took it and frowned down at the subdivision. "What exactly is supposed to happen Ono? Would you just tell me already? And how can it get any more peculiar than that?" She puzzled and took a bite from her berry.

"Aha! You'll have to be patient and see it for yourself my dear. But trust me, it'll be more than worth it once it happens," Ono said and gave her a wink.

Bej narrowed her green eyes at him, and they shined like slits of jade in the twilight. "It had better be. You know how I just hate waiting," she said and playfully bumped him with her elbow.

"Oh, that I do!" Ono laughed in agreement and nearly toppled over.

Since she had returned Bej had not let him forget for a moment what a frightening experience it had been making the trip back all alone. She had explained that when Corq and

Igit had set out, she was simply too terrified at the idea of finding him dead, or not finding him anywhere at all, to go along. So like everyone else she had opted to stay behind and wait for the news, which everyone thought was surely to be dire.

But when Corq and Igit had failed to return promptly with word, Bej had become agitated and impatient. Desperate, she had pleaded with several other gnomes to make the journey with her to find out what had happened, but was only met with scoffs and gasps of disbelief. "Fine then! I shall go by myself!" she had squawked and shook her fists before stomping away in a stink.

Leaving everything else behind, she had only taken what she could carry and set out all alone. On the way, she explained that the hooting of owls and the hungry cry of wolves seemed to come from all directions in the unfamiliar forests, as did the strange rustling of bushes and the sinister snapping of sticks. And so she had hurried along as quickly as she could for three days straight with hardly any sleep at all, only to finally arrive at his burrow and find him gone. Exhausted and devastated, she had collapsed where she stood, unable to go on any longer.

"So what shall we do until this show of yours happens?" Bej asked suddenly and cocked a flirty eyebrow at him.

Caught off guard by the question, Ono had been in the middle of chewing a bite from his berry when he began to choke and sputter.

"Oh Ono! Are you alright?" Bej worried and patted his
back.

"Yes... quite, quite fine... thank you," he managed between hacks and coughs. Then he cleared his throat and wiped
the berry juice from his whiskers on the back of his hand
and smiled. His teeth had all been stained blue.

Unable to help herself, Bej pointed at him and laughed.
"Your teeth Ono! They're all blue! You look ridiculous!"
she giggled behind her tiny hands.

Ono frowned and crossed his eyes as if to try and see his
own teeth, then glared at her and cocked his head. "Is that
so? Well then let's see your and compare!" he said, snatching at her hands and pulling them from her face. Bej stubbornly sucked her lips shut and tried to hide them, but when
Ono poked her in the belly she burst out with shrill laughter, revealing her own set of brightly stained teeth. "Aha!
You've a lot of nerve to tease me, you blue-mouth!"

With matching smiles they laughed and joked for a time,
each as happy as ever to once again have the other sitting
beside them. Then the faint barking of a dog sounded in the
distance, and Bej's ears perked up in alarm.

"What was that Ono?" She asked and glanced around.

Ono batted a hand in the air. "Don't worry, it's down
there with the humans," he said and pointed down the mountain at the neighborhood.

In the back yard of a home below, the same young man with the long sideburns was playing with his big black dog. He threw a tennis ball for it, and the dog went sprinting across the lawn in pursuit. "Now bring it back Buddy! Bring it here!" the young man said and slapped his thighs as the dog picked up the ball and pranced around with it held in its mouth like a prize.

Bej seemed confused. "Is that... is that a coyote that human is playing with?" she puzzled.

Ono shrugged. "Some animal of the sort I suppose," he said, then pointed through the trees to the far side of the subdivision to the left. "Look over there! Quickly!" he whispered.

Bej followed the direction of his finger and squinted into the distance. "What...?" she asked, not noticing anything at first. Then her eyes sprang open in surprise. "Oh my! What are they doing?!" she cried.

At the edge of the forest where the fence bordered the neighborhood, a small herd of deer was gathered. Just on the other side of the fence a couple had their two small children up on their shoulders so they could see over at the deer. The children were giggling and pointing as their parents tossed over carrots and apples, and the skittish deer didn't seem to mind them at all as they crunched on the tasty morsels just feet away.

"Ha ha! My word Ono, that's lovely! Who would have

thought, after all those tales? Is this the show you wanted

me to see?" she asked, keeping her eyes on the strange hu-

mans as they fed the deer.

"No, but that's coming soon. It's even better!" he said

and leaned back on his elbows.

Bej continued to watch the humans for some time with a

look of bewildered interest on her face, her gleaming eyes

sliding this way and that as she watched them finish up for

the day. There was an old man sitting in a rocking chair on

his porch tossing out handfuls of seeds to a group of birds

that pecked and jostled in the grass; a father and a son

hosing off their dirt bikes and bragging to one another be-

fore rolling them into the garage; a young blonde woman

tapping out a can of food into her cat's dish on the back

step; a mother in a living room window combing her daugh-

ter's hair as they watched tv; and a large family laughing

as they cleaned up the scattered mess of a water fight from

earlier in the day.

Ono was used to the humans by now, and he laid there nib-

bling on his berry and watching Bej's face while she took

it all in.

"They're really not so bad, are they Ono? The humans I

mean," she turned and asked after a long while of silence.

It was getting dark, and as the stars began to sparkle above

the humans in the neighborhood below began to retire to

their dwellings. The nighttime insects had begun to chirp

and click, and the trees creaked in the breeze.

Ono smiled to himself, remembering all the things he had
gone through because of their kind. "No, I suppose not. Different, of course, but not entirely bad," he said. "But for
the moment I've had my fill of them, and quite the opposite
of you, so come here!" he said and grabbed her hand and
pulled her back.

"Ono! Ha!" Bej laughed and laid down beside him. "You act
as though you've missed me some!"

"Oh, I suppose you could say that," he said and stole a
kiss from her cheek.

Bej blushed and batted her eyes. "You! Why, I never!" she
giggled and tickled his ear.

"Is that so? Then why exactly did you carve my name in
the wall of your burrow?" he teased.

Bej gasped and playfully slapped at his chest. "How did
you know that? Ono! Did you go in there after I left? Oh, it
was a mess how I left it!" she shrilled.

Ono rolled his eyes and looked away. "I do confess that I
was a bit lonely," he sighed.

Giggling, Bej pinched his chin hairs and turned his face
back to hers. "I suppose I can forgive you for trespassing,
since I missed you as well," she said and kissed him on the
lips. Ono smiled and put his arm around her, and was leaning
in to give her a kiss of his own when he was suddenly interrupted.

"Here he is! I found him everyone! Over here!" Sked's voice shrilled, making both Ono and Bej groan.

The tender moment lost, Ono sat up and pushed his cap back on his head. "Yes? What is it?" he asked, irritated with the little youngster.

Sked's head was poked up over the top of a boulder on the right, his floppy ears and unruly hair making an unmistakable silhouette against the dark purple sky. Then an exact double popped up right beside him. "Hi Ono! We've all been looking for you! Were you hiding?" Kei asked before noticing Bej sitting beside him. "Ha! Hello there Bej! What are you two doing all the way up here?" he puzzled, sounding suspicious.

Bej stammered for a reasonable explanation and Ono slapped his forehead. Snakes to these whelps! Everything was going perfect before they came! Perfect! he thought. He was about to tell them to mind their own business when suddenly a third silhouette popped up beside them, this one wearing a large-brimmed cap.

"There you are Ono! Why, we've been looking everywhere for you!" Ezquit said. "Corq and I and a few others are leading a sally down into the humans' land, and we were wondering if you would like to..." he trailed off and perked up his ears. "Oh, hello Bej... How rude of me. I didn't see you there."

"Yes, hello Ezquit. A fine night, is it not?" she asked.

"Yes... A fine night indeed. Ugh, very well," he said,

sounding happily amused. Then he cleared his throat and
turned to the youngsters. "Come along you two! Ono won't be
joining us tonight." ·

"Ohhh! But why?!" Sced and Kei whined in unison.

"Because I said so! Now get moving!" Ezquit instructed.

The three silhouettes vanished from the boulder top, and
the sound of their feet pittering over the fallen leaves
disappeared into the forest.

After they were gone Bej and Ono glanced over at one another and began to giggle in embarrassment. "Well, that's
it I suppose! Imagine all the gossip that'll be heard in
the morning!" Bej laughed and put her face in her hands.

Ono put his arm around her shoulders and gave her a
squeeze. He was about to say that at least everyone had
come back when the first of the streetlights suddenly
flicked on. "Bej! This is it! Look!" he said and pointed out
at the subdivision.

The dots of yellow light blinked on slowly at first, illu-
minating patches of street and sidewalk with their magical
glow. Then as the sun's last rays died from the horizon all
the others began to flick on faster and faster, like corn
kernels popping to life on a hot stove.

"Oh my Ono! Ha ha! It's amazing!" Bej cried and clapped
her hands as they blinked on. After all the streetlights
had come alight, the neighborhood below looked to Bej as if
giant fireflies were hovering just above it, glowing and

shining like fallen stars from the heavens.

"That's beautiful! It's magical, isn't it?" she turned and asked him, the streetlights' glow putting sparkling dots in her eyes.

Ono furrowed his brow and seemed to ponder her question. "It could very well be magic," he said and smiled bashfully, "but the only beauty I see anywhere near is you, me dear."

Flattered beyond words, Bej put her hand in his and scooted closer to him. Then he turned and kissed her, and she kissed him back as they laid down beside one another on the blanket, giggling and cuddling.

And so it is here, my friend, that we shall politely cover our eyes, quietly back away through the ferns, and end this tale by giving these two some privacy.